8/97

ZERO
PHILADELPHIA

ZERO

PHILADELPHIA

A Novel

JAMES DOUGLAS

Translated by Peter Edler

MARLOWE & COMPANY • NEW YORK

Published by
Marlowe & Company
632 Broadway, Seventh Floor
New York, NY 10012

Copyright © 1997 by James Douglas
A translation of Brennpunkt Philadelphia, copyright © 1994 by Verlag Ullstein
GmbH, Frankfurt/Main; Berlin.

Library of Congress Catalog Card Number 97-71755

Manufactured in the United States of America

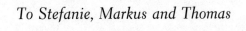

To Stefanie, Markus and Thomas

ZERO
PHILADELPHIA

Oppressive heat hung over the narrow air-strip near Puerto Quepos, a sleepy little town embedded in lush tropic greenery on Costa Rica's Pacific side. The supposedly perspiration-proof marvel of his Van Heusen shirt had dutifully absorbed as much as it could of Ken Custer's sweat. Now it clung like a drowning sponge to his back and chest. He stood by the Panama-registered Cessna, shouting encouragement and curses at the laborers of CR Global Exports, trying to hurry them up.

As usual, transshipment was the toughest, most dangerous part of the operation. The crates stood right out in the open, as if on a platter for anybody to grab. CR Global's personnel were armed to the teeth, but the Indios had left their automatics stacked on the side of the runway. A couple of the workers even unhitched the heavy revolvers that got in the way as they worked. Ken shook his head. There wouldn't be much these kids could do against the trigger-happy local militia. The only thing that protected them was speed: touchdown, transfer, takeoff—let's get the hell out of here!

Custer cocked his head, squinting at the ominously brilliant sky, straining his ears to detect the distant wokka-wokka-wokka of po-lice choppers. Cupping his hands around his mouth, he shouted each word thunderously through the makeshift megaphone, *"¡Adelante, compadres!* Get the lead out!"

Silence redescended, broken only by the breathing of the men, sweat glistening on their necks and faces as they lugged crates to the three Toyota 4WDs positioned at the edge of the strip. From behind slitted lids, Ken scanned the godforsaken runway that was fighting a losing battle with the weeds. At the far end it cut an ugly gash into the lush rain-forest greenery. Nothing was stirring. But even if something happened, their goose was cooked! Ken mopped his forehead with the back of one hand, watching the Colombian pilot who squatted under the Cessna's right wing, inspecting the landing gear.

The man glanced impatiently at his watch. "Ten minutes max, Boss, then we'd better be out of here. Those Costa Ricans control their airspace like vampire bats. If we're out of luck they already know we're here."

Checking the slip of paper he held in his hand, Custer nodded. "Don't sweat it, Gomez, we'll make it. You just get us ready for takeoff."

Most of the crates were already loaded onto the Toyotas. Those Indio kids sling crates almost as well as guns, Ken thought. No wonder, this means big bucks for them—and they've got healthy survival instincts, bless 'em!

"Mucho caliente, muchos dólares, niños," he shouted at them. A couple bared their teeth in grins that could easily turn into snarls.

A lanky, pale-skinned dude wearing a drooping, sweat-stained Stetson and a faded denim shirt supervised the weighing of the merchandise. Leaning motionless against the hood of one of the Toyotas, he was a picture of indolence in action. Two helpers placed one crate on an electronic scale and called out the weight. As far as Custer was concerned, they were wasting precious time. On the other hand, he thought, in the mutual-faith-and-trust department this business wasn't exactly blessed by Mother Teresa!

Stetson jotted down the weight of the final crate, then gave Custer a nonchalant, slow-motion wave of the hand, even though Custer was already practically by his side. Years in the field, plus a healthy touch of the professional paranoia that had saved his life on a number of occasions, told him that Stetson was stalling.

"Let's get it over with," Ken growled. "600 kilos gross, tare marked 100 kilos. It'll be weighed at unpacking."

Unfazed, Stetson was still leaning casually against the hood of the 4WD. Behind Custer's back, the Cessna came alive, its eager start-up whine shifting to a steady hum. "Check," said Ken, "sign this!"

He handed the cowboy a regular bill of lading. The Stetson-hatted president and CEO of CR Global Exports scrawled his name, acknowledging receipt of half a ton of cocaine.

Snorting like a surfacing whale, Custer shouted, "Now let's get the hell out of—"

His joyful exclamation was cut short by the sight of the big handgun Stetson held pointed at him. Custer froze.

"What's this? Are you nuts?"

"Easy, hombre, easy does it! Just turn around now, nice and easy!" If the Cheshire Cat had been made by Frankenstein and wore a Stetson, it might have grinned like this. The gun's muzzle cut into Custer's chest.

"I said turn around!"

Feeling curiously detached from his predicament, Custer stared at the weapon. He gave a nod of professional appreciation, heard his own hoarse voice say, "Now where would a bum like you get hold of a nine-millimeter Glock 17 Police Special like this one?"

As he spoke, something stirred at the periphery of his vision: a man crouching low, moving stealthily around behind the vehicle. A bit of acting was called for. Custer's shoulders sagged, as if in acceptance of his fate, but his gaze held Stetson's, whose chin was up, tongue nervously wetting his lips.

"You know you'll regret this, Copface," Custer said, his voice sounding flat as he moved his shoulders, moving to turn away. Stetson angled a long step forward to cut Custer off. The heavy automatic floated upward to the height of Custer's eyes. For a moment, the scene was frozen in the fallow light of the limbo that precedes swift bursts of violence.

Then two unlikely objects met. A greasy jack came down on the sweat-stained Stetson, causing two indelible imprints—one on the mind of Kenneth William Custer. Brutal as this impression was, Ken couldn't help admiring the two-fisted, pro-circuit grip his savior employed to smash the makeshift weapon down on Stetson's skull. The man glowered at his victim like some ill-tempered blond McEnroe. The Stetson's vapid grin blew away, his eyes bulged as the light went out of them, and his teeth made a horrible crunching noise, cutting off the tip of his tongue. Blood spurted and Stetson went down like ripe red timber, in a mist of blood, crashing flat on his face into the dust at Custer's feet.

"Let's go!" The blond avenger grabbed Custer's arm, pulling him away from the entrancingly macabre sight. Fueled by adrenaline, he swung his jack wildly, as if warding off a whole army of invisible attackers, even though the Indios seemed rooted to the spot. As they ran to the plane, Ken caught a glimpse of at least one set of teeth flashing in a dark-hued face. Even before his chance encounter with the greasy tool, Stetson hadn't exactly looked like the kind of guy for whom the locals would celebrate extra Masses.

Custer and his rescuer lunged through the wide-open cabin door an instant before the plane leapt forward at full throttle.

"¡Madre de Dios!" Gomez pointed down the weedy stretch of jungle dirt that passed for an airstrip. At the far end, where the wannabe tarmac cut into the jungle, a huge cloud of yellowish dust trailed behind three black vehicles heading straight toward them like giant killer ants on a rampage. The three lead Humvees, which Custer—with an oldtimer's deliberate stubbornness—wrongly identified as Jeeps, were followed by three more. All six vehicles now fanned out in a V-formation. Ken found the view impressive.

"Look at those cops!" he shouted, checking the pilot, whose right hand clutched the manual throttle. They had started about halfway down the runway and needed every inch for takeoff as they blasted, still earthbound, toward the wall of jungle at the far end. Trembling lightly from the effort, the craft finally lifted off, skimming the treetops, banking away, giving Custer a panoramic view of the action below. Tracer ammo from a machine gun mounted on the lead vehicle raked the area around the convoy of Toyotas. Custer didn't waste energy trying to suppress a smile: the cops were deliberately firing above the heads of Stetson's crew! The gang of Indios made a fine sight, flat on the ground, seeking cover behind the cars.

And Mr. Stetson himself lay just as they'd left him. Custer exploded an exhalation; he felt as if he hadn't breathed since the moment he looked down the barrel of that ugly Glock 17. Well, old Stetson just might get lucky and wake up with nothing more than a gash in the head and a serious concussion. Or he might not. Custer felt much too comfortable in the copilot seat to pretend he gave a damn.

"Phew, that was close!" He put on a headset and switched on

the mike. "Great getaway, Gomez, my compliments!" Jerking a thumb up and down over his left shoulder, he added, "Fifty million down the drain!"

Gomez shrugged but made no reply. His jaw with its three-day stubble of beard stood out sharply as he concentrated on the business at hand, which was getting the Cessna back to base. Custer turned his head to fix his benevolent gaze on the man who had presumably just saved his life.

"Who are you and where in hell did you come from? I really owe you one, don't I? Don't think I ever got this close before!"

The tanned face behind Custer exhibited a charming set of large, even teeth. "I'm John Rutherford. That unfortunate gentleman back there was about to turn you into an SIB statistic . . ."

"SIB?"

"Shot-in-back. I guess I've seen too many bad movies to let that happen." Rutherford moved his shoulders apologetically. Both men laughed, releasing more tension.

Rutherford, Rutherford . . . the name connected to something in Custer's memory. "You wouldn't happen to be old Bill Rutherford's son, would you?"

"As a matter of fact, I am. Doing a piece on the drug syndicates for the *New York Times*."

"Well, I'll be damned!" Custer pivoted still further in his seat. "John-o, isn't that right? I remember you."

Startled, Rutherford leaned forward. Custer reached around his seat and held a palm to about three feet above the plane's floor. "You were about yea high and cute as a button! I worked for your daddy. He taught me all I know about movie-making—most of which I've forgotten. What a director! And teacher! Then . . . well, let's just say we lost touch."

Rutherford stared saucer-eyed at the rugged-looking character, trying to dredge up a face from infant memories.

"So, tell me, how is the great William H. Rutherford?" Ken asked. "I hope he's okay."

The former John-o sounded worried. "He's just had major surgery. When I talked to him a couple of days ago he told me he had at least three of his nine lives left, but they were pumping him so full of liquids he was in danger of peeing them all away."

Custer tried to smile but couldn't bring himself to say anything. Sounded like cancer. He suppressed a sigh. He remembered Bill Rutherford as a confirmed workaholic with a temper like a leaky faucet. Even fifteen years ago the old goat had been lucky to still count himself among the living!

"The killer with the fedora back there called you Custer. Are you Ken Custer? The man who saved Qaddafi?"

Custer nodded, frowning. Rutherford's questions made him uncomfortable. "We'll let sleeping dogs lie, John. I need publicity the way I need a hole in the head. Or back!"

Rutherford touched the older man's shoulder reassuringly. "No problem, sir, your past is safe with me. In fact, I wish I could have been there. I don't remember you from when I was little but dad talked a lot about you, especially after the Qaddafi raid. You can trust me." Rutherford pointed his chin at the pilot. "Apropos trust: what about him?"

Custer gave a quick thumbs-up sign. Rutherford nodded and unbuckled the bulky, maroon-colored camera case he was wearing; he zipped it open and began to rummage through it. "I think I'm gonna hang around these parts a bit longer, then mosey on down into Colombia," he casually informed Custer. "I hope we'll run into each other again, Ken. You don't mind if I call you Ken, sir?"

"Oh yes I do, John-o," Custer grinned, "I find that really insulting. You can save my life anytime, just don't ever call me by my first name!"

Rutherford emitted a horsey guffaw of a laugh.

Gomez was holding the Cessna steady on a southerly course toward the coast. He concentrated fully on flying and checking the instruments. The muffled hum of the engine made a nice counterpoint to the pensive silence that now reigned in the cabin. After a while Gomez said, "In about twenty minutes we'll turn east along nine degrees latitude. From there it's about three hundred miles to Panama City."

Ken nodded agreement.

"Suits me perfectly," said Rutherford.

"How long're you staying in Panama?" Custer inquired.

"Not too long. I'm going down to Medellín. And you?"

Custer leaned back in his seat and closed his eyes. "I'm flying back to New York tonight."

The hum of the engines calmed down his agitated mind. Still, he cursed his own recklessness. This was a really stupid thing! If it hadn't been for the Rutherford kid, he himself would still be there, face down in the dust, like Mr. Stetson. As head strategist for the Mexi-Colombian Super Drug Syndicate—the Super Cartel—he should know better than to follow each childish impulse to adventure. I'm supposed to be the guy who pulls the strings behind the scenes of a multinational group, he thought, not some dog soldier digging dirt on the ground, getting my lungs aired out with a couple of nine-millimeter slugs.

Not that the cocaine was necessarily lost. Inside the Costa Rican police, the cartel had a man who would quickly find out if Stetson had tried to cop the shipment for himself. In a few days most of the powder should be back in the cartel's hands, all according to the magic formula known as *Plomo o Plata:* Take the money or the bullet.

That was the law. Simple and effective.

His eyes closed, his face relaxed, Custer seemed fast asleep as Gomez took the Cessna into a long, slow bank, pointing its nose toward Panama City. Half a million dollars to the charity foundation of the Guardia Civil would do the trick. Custer figured some ninety percent of the cocaine would be returned, with ten percent retained by the police as a finder's fee; it was the polite thing to do, the honorable thing, even. And fifty kilos was still a fine haul to be showed off to the media. Make the gringos happy. Another smashing victory in the relentless battle against drugs, or something like that. As for Stetson, if Rutherford's two-fisted assault with a deadly weapon hadn't done the job, a kill team from the Super Cartel would be more than happy to dispatch a load of *plomo* from an AK-47 to do the rest.

As he drifted into sleep, Custer's mind moved into a no-man's-land of thought where everything and nothing made sense. John-o Rutherford, for example. The kid had shown tremendous courage and resolve. He was obviously working some inside track; how else could he have known about this delivery? And he'd seemed sincere in his admiration of the little-known Qaddafi exploit. But how come he acted so casual about continuing on down to Medellín? Shouldn't his investigative instincts have been stirred by encountering me? Custer wondered. Why doesn't Rutherford seem interested in attaching himself to me, someone who knows his father and has just delivered half a ton of cocaine?

His eyes still closed, Custer turned his face slightly to the left, tucked in his chin and prepared to cross over into some serious shut-eye. But something pulled him back—a bit of turbulence? A vague premonition? He lazily pushed himself up, twisted his shoulders to look at young Rutherford. "Why Medellín, of all places,

John? What could you possibly want in that godforsaken hellhole? Just stay away from there, kid. Pedro Ruiz is a nasty customer, to say nothing of the Cali gang. I'm serious, John, stay in Panama. I'll give you all the information you want."

"Well, I've got a job to do. Gotta pay the rent, you know," Rutherford replied with casual, charming, confidence. "I'll be all right, sir. We made it through today, didn't we?"

With a resigned shrug, Custer slid back down into a semi-fetal sleeping crouch. The kid was right, of course. Gotta pay the rent!

New York City, Saturday, June 30

Once again Ken experienced that endless fall into the unfathomable abyss, his body drifting in slow motion down into the black maelstrom. The bottomless hole, the pulsing spray from the rapids, would pull him down, swallow him up.

Gently, the deadly waters drew him in. Curiously, there was no pain, just a surge of honey-sweet sensations through his body, as a rushing whirl of velvet blue enveloped and carried him past dark green grottoes to deposit him on a gleaming bright sandbank, where it left him to die. He felt neither wetness, nor cold, nor fear. His father's benign countenance, his mom's loving smile dissolved into the grotesquely contorted face of the enemy with whom he'd been wrestling high above the whirlpool. Then everything around him began to spin.

Happy memories, the feeling of gentle contentment, dissolved. The light faded; it grew dark and cold. No, not this! He fought against it, tried to swim, break through to the surface, but his body refused. He wanted to scream, but his voice was gone. With the utmost exertion he managed to move his hands a couple of inches, no more. His last, desperate awareness was of darkness closing in on him, the light being extinguished, and a cold, relentless pain lancing his heart.

"Rise 'n shine, my boy, time to get up, we still need you." The voice that called to him was pleasant, energetic, insistent. Coughing, gasping for air, Ken glimpsed a face, strands of blond hair framing an expression of concern. "Wake up, kid, come on, you can do it!"

Soaked in sweat, Custer bolted upright. The automatic alarm had switched on the radio. A woman's voice was reading the news. Fighting to keep his eyes open, he made out the digits 17:02 on the clock. He jumped out of bed and yanked up the venetian blinds. Another three hours of sleep ruined by that damn nightmare!

Custer squinted into the bright glare reflected by the abysmally neutral facade of the house across the street. Nightmares regular as Monday going back twenty years. He'd been declared missing, dead, just another foolish would-be mountaineer taken by the river. No one yet had plunged into those swift, icy currents and lived to tell the story. No one, that is, except me, he reflected grimly. A miracle, yes, but at what price! A nightmare that ripped into the flesh of his sleep, unpredictably, with devastating suddenness and ferocity: a wild beast clawing into him as if . . . as if?

He shook his head. As if—to wake him, warn him, yeah, maybe that was it. Mortal danger, sensing its own kind, digging deep into him to release . . . itself!

"Yeah, right," he sighed. Yawning outrageously he shuffled into the kitchen, pushed the button on the espresso maker, missing it by a mile. Slowly, steadying his right hand with his left, he succeeded on the second try. Nightmares schmightmares, to hell with premonitions, this time he'd pay no attention to . . .

The speaker phone bleeped. It sounded reassuringly high-tech. Custer activated the voice trigger by uttering a gravelly "Yes."

"Señor Custer? We have an urgent message for you."

The familiar voice was that of a woman, sounding cool and businesslike, instructing him to fly to Zurich. He was to take the Gulfstream IV from Newark that evening, and contact the boss as soon as he stepped aboard.

Europe! Custer received the news calmly; he'd been expecting the assignment. A change of scenery might be exactly what the doctor ordered. Like this coffee: each time he took the first sip of the strong, delicious brew, he congratulated himself on having allowed the owner of the espresso joint at the corner—a formerly dashing, now paunchy and balding neighborhood playboy named Giovanni—to palm off on him the broken-down espresso machine, for the outrageous sum of one hundred U.S. dollars in cash. He took another sip, then carried the cup into the bathroom and set it down in front of the mirror.

Facing himself, he saw a man in his early forties, tall but no longer quite as tall as he had seemed at twenty. Since then the average height of men in the U.S. had gone up another quarter of an inch! All right, so relatively speaking I'm shrinking, he thought, ruefully massaging his chin. Still, I'm not an ugly man. He flashed the Custer smile at his mirror image. He had broad shoulders, his face was symmetrical and open, and even Kirk Douglas would not have rejected his chin, although compared to the actor's it was only modestly clefted.

Ken shot a searching glance at himself, looking out of gray eyes known to produce bolts of laser sharpness on occasion. Satisfied that he still had what Giovanni down on the corner called "the old zappola," he brushed back his dark blond hair, actually touching the frown on his forehead. Who was it that had pushed him down that stupendous rockface in Switzerland all those years ago? Who was the bastard?

Scarlett, his mother, was the only one who might know. And she wasn't talking. "Time will tell, Kenny," was all she'd ever say on the subject.

He stepped into a pair of dark-blue trousers, slipped on a mauve shirt with short sleeves. He threw his blue-and-yellow striped bathrobe and a rather aggressively floral-patterned tie on the bed, next to other stuff to be packed. He opened the top drawer in his desk and took out his passport, the multi-fold of credit cards, and his wallet. From a shelf by the piano he picked a volume of Emily Dickinson poems, carefully placed it in the attaché case. Relaxed and methodical, he worked on until he had packed the final items: the notebook computer with his personal data base, the micro-recorder, and the cellular phone. Finishing in good time, he rang Susan on the other side of the park. She picked up, out of breath, on the third ring.

"Helloooh," he said, "am I interrupting something?"

"I was in the shower!"

"They say cleanliness is next to godliness. Or something. Suss, I feel like catching up on some shopping and maybe work out a little on the Eiger, the north wall, so I'm hopping over to Switzerland. I'll call you from Zurich in the morning, okay?"

"Well, bully for you. I'm so thrilled. Have fun," she cooed sweetly, giving him the finger as she hung up. Why did these men of action always seem to be barking out instructions? *Catching up on some shopping,* what was that supposed to mean? *Working out on the Eiger? The north wall?!*

Cursing, dripping, laughing at herself, Susan bounded back into the bathroom. She'd learned a long time ago not to pry. That was the price she paid for getting some of the prime action this particular action guy had to offer.

By the time Susan settled down to an evening of chatting on the phone and noting down product numbers while watching sellavision, Custer was moving through the stateroom aboard the Gulfstream. He was unimpressed by the familiar soft lighting and elegantly understated decor that included natural-oak wall panels and powder-blue Chinese carpeting. After carelessly depositing his gear on the king-size bed he went back into the salon. Time to make that call!

As always, Custer found conversing with Don Cali a mixed blessing, a little like trying to talk with an intelligent cement mixer. In a calm, stentorian voice, the boss of the Super Cartel instructed him to implement the initial active phase of the operation they both knew down to the smallest detail. They fixed two time slots for video conferences to allow for possible course corrections.

As Cali rang off with a simple *"¡Hasta la vista!,"* the steward served Custer his requested meal: a pastrami sandwich on rye, a Scotch, and a glass of milk. The latter constituted Ken's personal recipe for fighting jet lag, from which he suffered more than most. Even relatively short travel across time zones made his body clock run slower or faster, which he tried to counter by storing up on sleep. A pair of dark glasses to combat daylight for when his body was fighting to catch up, and a reflector mask with tiny, battery-powered light bulbs, which he used to simulate daylight, completed his anti-jetlag kit.

It had been stupid of him to test the Gulfstream's kitchen by ordering a pastrami sandwich on rye. Instead of the vibrant golden sheen that trembled along the edges of the pastrami served in his favorite Manhattan delicatessen, the meat in this one sagged with a deathly gray pallor. It tasted like *New York Times* newsprint. Reclining on the luxurious bed, chewing tenaciously, sipping Scotch and milk, Ken grumbled against the loneliness of his job. One day soon he'd chuck this sort of life. Time to stop pulling the chestnuts out of other people's fires, doing their dirty work for them, sticking out his neck for theirs!

It wouldn't be half as bad if they could bring themselves to stop talking about freedom, democracy, the just cause—it was enough to make a fella puke! On the other hand, he reflected, who'm I kidding? Here I am, jetting this way and that, living the life of Riley, complaining about a pastrami sandwich?

Susan in the shower flashed through his mind. Why, instead of a pastrami sandwich he could have ordered a woman! This produced a grin which he couldn't hold on to. Blame it on Vietnam, then. Yes, that's what threw him off course.

A couple or three terms of law at Harvard had convinced him he should try his luck in movies. And he'd been well into a career as a producer, first under Bill Rutherford's tutelage, then on his own. But just when his breakthrough *Gasp for Life* started breaking all records at the box office (well, he recalled with a smile, at least some records, at some box offices), along came 'Nam. And instead of allowing him to conquer tinseltown, they shipped him to Saigon. So much for *Sturm und Drang!*

He'd been lucky, made it into Intelligence, then the Agency, where they told him looking like a glamor boy didn't exactly make for a promising future as an undercover agent. Years later (he was still their glamor boy) they picked him for that assignment in Libya. Put him on a special Air Force transport, very much like the Gulfstream, only not quite as ritzy—for, despite its comfortably refitted interior, the thing had reeked of petroleum jelly. It had reminded him of *Gasp for Life*, a real stinker!

Come to think of it, maybe this here was what he was born to do, starting with that nasty little thing in Libya where he'd finally made his bones—by saving someone else's.

Over the Atlantic, Sunday, July 1

Ken's stomach decided to tough out the *New-York-Times*-newsprint-flavored pastrami. His senses pleasantly lulled by the whiskey and the milk, Ken felt as if he were back in the projection room, watching the rushes. No, not the rushes—the final cut of his past, the reel labeled *Libya*. Watching it as if it had happened yesterday, even though it was many years ago: a fateful night like any other, or so it had seemed. . . .

In the spring of 1986, when Ken Custer was getting ready for the assignment in Libya, relations between that country and the U.S. were strained to the breaking point. Terrorists thought to be in Qaddafi's pay were harvesting a bloody toll of American lives each week. A public sense of helplessness and frustration, fanned by the media, created a climate that called for action, revenge. Enough was enough; it was high time the U.S. settled accounts with Colonel Muammar al Qaddafi!

The White House responded to the opinion polls by blaming the Libyan strongboy for much of the evil under the sun, including most if not all of the 938 victims of terror actions during the preceding year. At last, the upstart Colonel was to be taught a lesson.

"He's a mad dog and we'll stop him," the president was reported to have said.

Precisely what was meant by "stopping the mad dog," Ken learned en route to Libya. Comfortably reclining in a sky-blue swivel armchair on board the C 208 that had just left Andrews Air Force Base, he opened the yellow, double-sealed envelope, extracted his orders, and studied the areas marked on sections of a detailed map of Tripoli. "Piece of pie!" he mumbled to himself as the jet roared into the night, banking away from the wavering sea of lights that was Atlantic City.

Custer went carefully through the instructions, committing targets, coordinates, optional countermoves and other vital information to memory. The plane headed for Nova Scotia, to begin the crossing from Halifax, then on toward Shannon, Ireland. Custer sipped his Saratoga mineral water with lemon slice from a large cut-glass tumbler. He examined the red, cordless telephone recessed into the armrest, then glanced at the five bright yellow, numbered phone sets mounted on the forward cabin wall. Beneath them he noted a keyboard console with earphones and miniature monitoring devices for decoders, encryptors, scramblers and other technological paraphernalia whose purpose he could only vaguely guess at. The entire aircraft was crammed with transmission equipment and electronic gadgetry. Custer couldn't help wondering why he, of all people, was being given the VIP top-priority treatment aboard this airborne command post.

Not much later, the red unit in his armrest began to emit discreetly insistent ululations, while the navigator's voice on the intercom informed him there was a call from the White House ". . . for you, Colonel Custer."

Custer picked up and immediately recognized the sonorously jovial voice of the man they called The Great Communicator.

"I was just wondering, Colonel, are they treating you decent up there? Is the chow up to par?"

"Yes, sir, Mr. President, no complaints," Custer grinned, yielding instantly to the man's relaxed charm.

"Now, Colonel, we're entrusting you with important, uh, business, and I'm counting on you. Matter of fact, I've got a little wager going on you, so you'd better not let me down. I'm going to put Jeff on now. He'll brief you further on some of the details we don't want to put on paper. Jeff is a special Air Force staffer attached to this, uh, operation. He reports directly to me. Jeff's a real nice guy and you'll find him most cooperative. . . ."

There was an extended pause, due, Custer thought, to faulty transmission. It turned out to have been a deliberate moment of silence contrived to introduce a dramatic followup, ". . . on the other hand, I want you to do, uh, exactly as he says, do you read me?"

"Loud and clear, Mr. President, thank you."

Jeff came on and Custer listened, punctuating attentive silence with an occasional "Yes, sir" or "Roger, sir." After a minute or so he hung up with a final "Thank you, sir."

So they were going after Qaddafi! Jeff's key words kept revolving through Custer's mind: *He's our target, Colonel, we must not miss. It is essential we know his precise whereabouts at H-hour.*

Upon his arrival in London, Custer was given a new identity as Kenneth W. Carter, engineer and oil specialist. The alias allowed him to move freely at ministries and government agencies in Libya: the Libyans welcomed British specialists, whose know-how was essential in all phases of oil extraction and processing. It took Custer less than a week to obtain copies of the original engineering plans for Bab al Azizia, the military complex and headquarters where Qaddafi spent most of his time.

Custer found life in Libya surprisingly laid-back. The lesson Qaddafi's Air Force had been taught by the U.S. Sixth Fleet in the Gulf of Sirte appeared not to have affected the Libyans' evident self-confidence and joie de vivre. Custer couldn't help but admire these people who had become the target of all the anger, hate, and contempt heaped on them by the Western world. Well, not the entire West—Britain and Switzerland were exceptions. British specialists kept Libyan oil production going, and Swiss companies provided aircraft, spare parts, machinery, and equipment.

As luck would have it, the man in charge of Qaddafi's nonmilitary logistics was Theo von Alp, whom Custer had met some years back in Angola. The forty-year-old Swiss soldier of fortune brought in spare parts and purchased new equipment to meet all of Libya's civil aviation requirements.

The years in Angola had perfected von Alp's rum-running skills to where he seemed to have no trouble finding holes in the embargo imposed on Libya by the U.S. Rumors circulating inside the colony of foreigners who frequented the coffee houses of Tripoli had it that his position as supply chief for Libya's civilian air fleet was no more than a cover for a much more important pastime: keeping Libyan military aircraft and equipment in fighting trim.

Custer didn't have to move beyond the confines of the cafeteria in the Hotel Miramar, where he was staying, to learn that this was true: After Colonel Qaddafi had found it expedient to send his Soviet military advisors packing, von Alp was picked for the Herculean job of cleaning up the mess left behind by the Soviets. It took him the better part of two years to put the near-defunct fleet of MIGs, MI attack choppers, and transports back in reasonable operating shape. A colorful character, relatively unconcerned with the demands of discretion imposed on him by Qaddafi, von Alp spent much of his time cultivating top echelon officials at tea and coffee siestas during the long, hot afternoons.

Custer had run into him on his third evening at the Miramar. They'd had a few drinks, refreshed old memories and parted with assurances of meeting soon again. That very night von Alp warned Custer of an impending dragnet operation, to be conducted by the militia, with the purpose of hauling in all English-speaking foreigners. Appropriately appreciative, Custer had taken a long, scenic taxi ride through the countryside, telling himself this didn't look good at all. He had absolutely no plans for ending his days in some scorpion- and homophile-infested Libyan dungeon. That would have been too high a price to pay for giving up Hollywood in favor of the CIA!

Moreover, Custer was beginning to think that the planned operation against Qaddafi was much more than a diversion for something else he hadn't figured out yet. What about President Ford's Executive Order No. 12333, forbidding the U.S. to plan, carry out, or otherwise participate in the assassination of dictators whom it happened to look upon with disfavor? And what was a surgical air strike targeted to take out Qaddafi's headquarters, other than a kill operation with a fancy name?

Custer spent a couple of hours, nursing first one, then another Turkish coffee, pondering the implications of these volatile prospects. What if the Great Communicator wasn't giving him the whole story? What if they'd decided to carpet-bomb Tripoli? He might end up a sitting duck, or rather a dead one, in the rubble of the Miramar. In his wartime experience, most of the guys they called paranoid were still alive, whereas . . .

He tilted the coffee cup high, let a final drop run into his mouth. Yes, indeed: his best policy under the circumstance would be to keep looking out for Number One.

Just ahead, the People's Palace lay brilliantly illuminated as von Alp bullied his ancient, dark-green Landrover into Annasr Street. As the vehicle bounced over a wide crack in the road, Custer barely managed to avoid serious rectal injury by twisting his butt away from a spring which jutted menacingly through what was left of the front seat upholstery. Ken lit a cigarette. Masses of people were strolling along the nocturnal sidewalks; shops and storefronts were brilliantly illuminated. Custer jerked his chin at the peaceful scene.

"Look at all those people, and all those lights! As if they've never heard of Beirut. The whole town's lit up like a Christmas tree!"

Von Alp shot him a quick, eloquent glance. "So that's it," he bellowed, "I might have known when I first laid eyes on you at the Miramar, Mr. Carter! Out with it, let's hear it—what sort of yankee doodle dandy are you working on this time?"

Custer allowed a pointed silence to build up, then he said, "Look, Theo, you're the doctor here. You tell me. How strong is Qaddafi? Do the people support him? I don't see anybody suffering here. Business seems to be booming, anybody can see that." He gestured at the lively street scene, the busy shops, people crowding the displays.

"Right, this is a good street for business," said von Alp, "and the people love their Colonel. They're certainly not doing badly—a hell of a lot better than the Tunisians or Algerians anyway, thanks to the oil. To his credit, he surrounds himself with experts, he's open to advice, his economists have studied at the Sorbonne, Geneva, Oxford, Yale. They're no dummies, these Libyans. But all the world ever hears about is big bad Qaddafi and his terrorists."

"Well, of course, what do you expect?" Custer replied. "He supports terrorism. He gives shelter to infamous killers like Abu Nidal, who maintains a comfortable hideaway in this very town—correct me if I'm wrong. Maybe we can drive by Nidal's place and wave. I'm sure he won't mind. The Libyan authorities don't give a damn how many international warrants for his arrest they get. Hell, they probably send him copies to keep him up to date."

Flicking the ash off his cigarette, Ken continued, "Besides, everybody knows about the boot camps maintained by any number of so-called liberation organizations south of Benghazi, or even right here in Tripoli, not far from the airport. What about those?"

"Well, what about them?" Von Alp took a left into a side street narrow enough to pass for an alley. Custer glanced up at an ancient, delapidated street sign: As-Sarim Street.

"Propaganda, suspicions, insinuations," von Alp rasped, "not a shred of real evidence. The Reagan administration needs a hate object, that's all, and Qaddafi suits the bill. As a fall guy he's so perfect that if he didn't already exist, they would have had to invent him."

When Custer said nothing, von Alp lowered his voice. "Name one, just one, Western power that doesn't maintain training camps. There's the Special Air Services in case you've forgotten. The French train their Action Service somewhere in the foothills of the Pyrenees and God knows where else. And do I have to mention the United States Army's Special Forces with their basic and specialized military skills, such as training and controlling indigenous forces in guerilla warfare and counter-insurgency operations?"

He waved a hand at a long, high wall. "Here we are, Mr. Carter."

Driving slowly along the wall, they passed the gate, guarded by heavily armed MPs, their hands resting close to the triggers of their Kalashnikovs. In a shady space inside, to the right, Custer glimpsed a Soviet BMD tank armed with a 20-mm gun.

He smiled. "So this is where your son of the desert hangs out!" It was only half a question, and a rhetorical one at that, since he was already familiar with the Bab al Azizia complex and its function, at least on paper.

"I'm in there quite a bit," von Alp confided, shrugging. "The Colonel has a simple lifestyle, sleeps in a nomad's tent. From what I've seen, he's a nature boy, a romantic. And a patriot, of course. Operations, communications and control facilities are in a new addition in the back of the compound, built into the old fortification wall. All state-of-the-art equipment, like in the White House war room."

"Would you say he's in there right now?"

"He is. I saw him a couple of hours ago when I was here to go over a spare parts checklist with the commander of the Air Force. He was walking over to his private quarters. We waved at each other. Shit, Custer, stop pussyfooting around!"

Clearly irritated, von Alp stepped on the brake. Custer's head shot forward but he managed to avoid hitting the windshield.

Von Alp's next words sounded positively menacing. "I want to know right now what you're up to! No more sightseeing until you tell me what's going on. I don't want some damn Yankee laser designator pointing at me some night while I'm in bed dreaming of a better tomorrow. Or get a laser-guided rocket up my ass when the shit hits the fan in my neighborhood!"

"EDC," Custer mumbled absently, watching the lively action along the wall. At a safe distance from the sentries, kids were rolling around in the dust under the lights on the wall, firing at each other with imaginary guns. Men stood around in small groups, talking and gesticulating. Hard rock music from a roadside bar reverberated from the sandstone ashlars of the ancient fortress restructured to serve as Qaddafi's headquarters.

"Damn all this commotion! Is it always this busy around here? I thought this was supposed to be 'El Dorado Canyon,'" Custer said slowly, his voice close to a whisper. "That's the code name for the air strike we're planning. The target is—" he waved casually at the compound across the road, "—this place. The Pentagon is planning to execute your friendly neighborhood dictator with laser-guided weapons. An assassination attempt at the operational level, if you like!"

Von Alp stared straight ahead, his right incisor busy trying to dig a hole into his lower lip. Half a minute passed before he recaptured his voice.

"And when is all this supposed to happen?"

"You know that's extremely privileged information, Theo. So I have to ask you what's in it for me."

Now that he was over the first shock, von Alp was eager to show off his own topspin. "I could have you arrested."

"Sure." Custer's voice was level, cool.

"All right, name your price."

"I want out. That means safe conduct, a smooth exit, VIP treatment, including a first-class ticket to Zurich. Plus a hundred thousand dollars."

"That's not exactly fly shit, Ken."

Custer bared his teeth in a theatrical snarl. "Are you kidding? I'm being really modest here, Theo, think about it. Not only am I giving away the entire operation, for Pete's sake, but Qaddafi lives and we avoid destabilizing Libya. Plus you'll keep that cushy job of yours as long as you like. The Colonel will be eternally grateful to you. Why, I'm making you a hero of the Libyan people. So don't give me that fly-shit crap!"

At last they were down to brass tacks again, the way it used to be in Angola. A smile of nostalgic bliss bloomed on von Alp's leathery features. His eyes shone in anticipation of a major caper, with himself as the kingpin, the kind of action he'd been missing lately. Ken was right, of course, his job was cushy. A little too cushy for his taste, even. This thing here, on the other hand . . .

Von Alp couldn't help himself. His big, meaty left fist crossed over his chest, drove into Custer's shoulder.

"Action!" he roared.

The blow hurt like hell. Massaging his shoulder, Custer wished Theo was just a little more of a wimp.

"You've got yourself a deal," von Alp was saying, "safe conduct to Zurich, first-class ticket. Tonight, if you like."

"What if all the flights are fully booked?" Ken's somewhat facetious question was rewarded with a doleful look from his old buddy.

"We'll shoot a passenger."

Their laughter did much to dissolve the pain in Custer's shoulder. He was still catching his breath when von Alp asked, "So when will they actually strike?"

"During the night, probably around one in the morning," Custer said calmly. He was fully aware that, to put it charitably, he had just resigned from the CIA.

Von Alp checked his Rolex: 2251 hours. He kicked the Landrover to life and backed straight into a gang of kids who scurried, screaming, in all directions. Clutching brutally, he jammed into first and the car leapt forward. They were tearing down the road along the wall in the direction from which they'd come, and had almost reached the gate when Custer barked, "Easy, Theo! Two palefaces in a hurry doesn't look too good."

Dispensing tourist smiles all around, they trundled past the gate at an unobtrusive speed.

Just about at this time, a detachment of a dozen or so airborne F-111 fighter bombers was on course, bound for the western Mediterranean. The group was made up of planes from three British air bases—Lakenheath, Mildenhall and Upper Heyford, all located in the mid-England region. They had rendezvoused north of London and now kept a steady southwesterly course over the Atlantic to avoid violating French and Spanish airspace.

In Washington, D.C., at 1650 hours EST, an extended briefing session began for the President of the United States. It took place in the operations center known as the War Room, located in the subbasement of the White House. The Great Communicator appeared to be in excellent spirits, as he sat listening, leaning forward in a dynamic pose reminiscent of the athletic Knute Rockne character he had once portrayed on the silver screen.

As the five lead F-111s were screaming down the home stretch toward the target area at 2 A.M. that April 14, a brilliantly illuminated Tripoli seemed to be welcoming them. They discharged their laser-guided rockets and veered away to head back toward Upper Heyford. The entire show lasted 11.5 minutes precisely. One of the planes pulled up a moment too late and was caught by a burst of AAA fire. In order to reduce their weight, Captain Critelli dropped the bomb load, then tried to ditch the plane. Just above the surface, the aircraft exploded in a great, blinding flash of a fireball, an event celebrated wildly by the Libyan anti-aircraft artillery team. They had good reason to jump for joy: downing an F-111 with a 20-mm Oerlikon cannon was a feat rather unheard of in the annals of modern computerized warfare. The U.S. electronic countermeasures had neutralized the Libyans' Soviet SAM-3 anti aircraft artillery guidance systems, but no matter—the good old radarless, manually operated Oerlikon had done the job!

The following afternoon, Custer boarded Swissair SR 229 for a nonstop flight to Zurich. It felt good to be on a Swiss plane. That morning, crowds of Libyans had vented their seething anger on foreign property and businesses, trashing travel agencies, airlines, embassies and consulates. Behind closed eyes, Custer relived those turbulent, dangerous hours, with the Miramar guarded by grimfaced militiamen who looked ready at any moment to turn away from the mob and wipe out the people they were supposed to protect.

The Swiss Embassy, Swiss property and businesses, anything with a Swiss emblem or a Swiss flag waving over it, escaped unharmed. Maybe, Custer mused, the Libyans have trouble telling the Swiss Cross from the Red Cross, who knows? A red cross in a field of white, a white cross in a field of red—maybe they're mistaking Switzerland for some sort of super medical or charitable organization!

Appreciating the notion, Ken chuckled to himself. The Swiss papers called Qaddafi everything from "a wily fox" to a "mangy desert rat." The fact was that the Colonel had survived. Safe outside the target perimeters, he had spent the night in the desert, under the stars. While U.S. bombs devastated his home, Colonel Qaddafi prayed to Allah to protect and deliver his people. His daughter had been killed in the raid; she was certain to be enshrined as a martyr of the Libyan people.

Aboard the Gulfstream IV, back in the here and now, Custer heaved a deep, not entirely untroubled sigh. All that was far in the past—let bygones be bygones! Try as he might, however, he couldn't get rid of a nagging *déjà vu* feeling that, in some strange way, history was repeating itself.

Juan Antonio Gabriel Cali de Cali climbed out of the helicopter and stepped onto hallowed ground. Following Don Cali's instructions, the pilot had landed in a spot commanding a mountain valley that rose gradually from the south to a ridge, then opened toward the northeast on an immense plain of coca plants whose distant reaches were lost in misty blue pallor. The southern portion of the valley was dominated by monumental edifices of stone, spaced some two hundred yards apart, reaching to the sky out of the lush green of the valley floor. Near the ridge, four such buildings, fashioned from great blood-red boulders, formed a triangular configuration that pointed toward the coca plain. The chopper had set down precisely in the center of that triangle.

There were about two dozen of these ancient-looking edifices, all designed along identical architectural lines: huge boulders, each some fifty feet high, forming stupendously tall walls that rose ominously into the sky, topped by a cantilevered roof of enormous stone slabs. Each of these fortresslike bulwarks of red rock was approximately the size of a hundred-foot-long apartment building some four stories high.

In spite of the buildings' great size, it was difficult to make them out from the air. A luxuriant growth of lichen, moss, and bushes covered the rock, providing plenty of natural camouflage. A few months ago, when the pilot had first flown the druglord to this place, coming in at an altitude of about a hundred feet, he'd counted some twenty-five of the monumental edifices. Staring at the ancient cult complex, he was filled with reverence, and with awe, and an eerie foreboding.

"Ground markers," Cali's voice had soberly informed him on that occasion, as if the drug boss had read his thoughts. According to Señor Cali de Cali, the antedeluvian monuments were put here by the Archangel Gabriel himself, for the purpose of showing Don Gabriel, the chosen *Líder*, the truly illuminated path, a path that would lead first to the great plain, then on to the Isthmus, and then beyond, into the soft underbelly of North America.

Cali had gestured effusively in the round, indicating the great, cultivated high plateau where coca plants grew in endless rows, proudly proclaiming this the greatest coca plantation in the world. All the while, as if in constant reaffirmation of the sacred bond that existed between himself and the holy plant from which all his power and wealth derived, he had been chewing on a single coca leaf, Indio-fashion.

"Death to all infidels, and welcome, Don Gabriel, to the seat of wisdom and fertility!" The booming voice of a robed, silver-haired old man reverberated in the silence that had recaptured the valley after the rotor blades slowed to a halt. A diminishing echo answered from the ancient walls: "Death—death—death . . . infidels—infidels—infidels."

Don Cali walked toward the ancient figure that seemed to have magically emerged from the rock. "Praised be the Archangel, death and destruction to the gringos! Hail, Venerable Prophet," Cali said, returning the old man's welcome as they embraced.

"What brings you here, my son?"

"The day of reckoning is near, Wise One. I'm here to acquaint you with the details of my plan. And, of course, the blessings of the Archangel are needed, for myself and for our enterprise."

The great stone building from which the old man had emerged housed an ancient temple. The two men, arm in arm, now headed there.

As the pilot strolled back to his craft, a din of agitated voices could be heard in the distance. The sun, beating down on the open space at the entrance to the temple, transformed the clear mountain air into a shimmering curtain of light which the old priest now parted, spreading his arms in a solemn gesture that encompassed the great avenue of monuments before him.

"This is the source of power, my son. Here you will find the strength. Yes, infinite power . . . and riches beyond compare!" Lowering his voice to a whisper, the old man added conspiratorially, "Of course, the Archangel demands a sacrifice. He has waited long—too long!"

Inwardly, Don Gabriel recoiled. "A sacrifice?"

"Yes. Come now, let us go inside."

The voices were becoming more distinct, the pilot noted; a quarrel seemed to be in progress. The plantation facilities were close by, and the foremen were obligated to report anything out of the ordinary to headquarters, which were located in the triangle.

The Super Cartel had long been operating in the shadow of its principal competitor and opponent in Medellín. Much too long, in Don Cali's opinion. However, a new era was dawning; harvest time was near, years of preparation coming to fruition.

A comprehensive, patiently built-up network of contacts in the key centers of the West would soon make Don Cali de Cali the single emperor of all drug cartels. This prospect stirred the Don's very soul. Trembling, the world would ask who this powerful drug-lord might be, the man who wielded the flaming sword of the Archangel. Then, oh, then—Don Cali stuffed an extra coca leaf in his mouth and continued masticating in excitement—then that soft-bellied gringo in the White House would smile and slobber and bully and beg. And finally he would be on his knees, to do exactly as her—

Powerful low vibrations from a gong tore Cali from his sweet dreams of glory. He stood in awe before the giant sacred image that rose directly in front of him. Nearly petrified with fear, he stared at the great statue with its threatening arms raised to deliver the killing blow. Yes, this was Gabriel, the merciless avenger, wielding the sword of the apocalypse. How many times had Cali stood rooted to the floor before the wrathful deity—a hundred times? A thousand? And yet he had been chosen, only he, Cali de Cali, to receive its blessing, and to appoint its executioner.

The two huge figures were hewn from marble. The shaggy goat was black, its marble hair matted in greasy braids; a mighty, single horn thick as a man's thigh rose from the space between its eyes.

Above the sacrifice, brilliantly white and veined with gold, towered the archangel, his sword descending mercilessly on goat head and horn.

At a gesture from the ancient one, Don Cali fell prostrate, his face touching the marble slab at the feet of the images. Now the priest intoned in a sonorous voice:

"O mortal, sprung from mortal flesh, witness now what is approaching at the end of time! The power of the North is the great horn between the eyes of the goat. The end of that great empire is at hand, the measure of its evil deeds is full. Its cunning emperors, called presidents, stand at the pinnacle of power. Villainy and deception are the lies that allow them to succeed. In arrogant delusion they and their people make bold to rise up against the Great Avenger, the Archangel, who has chosen you, my son, to wield his sword. His sacred message is: Prepare for war! Rise up now and unveil your plans to me!"

Cali slid backwards on the slab, then pushed himself up and turned slowly to face the priest.

"Yes, Venerable One, I am about to pronounce the ultimate judgment. We have nuclear devices."

The servant of the temple raised one brow. "You have a bomb?"

"Not one, Padre, several. Custer, my brilliant chief of operations, is on his way to Europe. He will return with state-of-the-art technology, nuclear minipacks, devices of enormous explosive power equaling thousands of tons of TNT."

"I understand. Continue!"

"The first device will be detonated three days from now, on the 4th, their Independence Day. We will wipe out the historic center of Philadelphia."

The old man's hands came up, palms outward, as if warding off some unseen danger. Cali nodded, his voice calm and reassuring.

"Custer may be brilliant, but he's still a gringo. He would never go along with destroying Philadelphia. You know these Americans, they may be rapists, arsonists, murderers, but threaten their country and the most callous among them will touch hand to heart and salute the Stars and Stripes. So, you can rest easy, Padre, I would never trust a man like Custer all the way."

The priest thoughtfully fondled his beard. "But didn't you just tell me Custer is the one who is getting the bombs? How then can you keep him out of your planning for Philadelphia?"

"*Bien*, Padre, it is very simple. I am conducting separate operations. Custer is under orders to obtain the latest nuclear devices of the carry-on type. These are minipacks the size of a regular suitcase, though somewhat heavier. All Custer knows is that we're building up an arsenal. He is a very practical man, and to him, that is a practical thing to do. So the fact that he is getting some pocket-size Atomic weapons for us is kept entirely separate from the Independence Day operation. One has nothing to do with the other. Nothing at all."

"So?" The ancient one's eloquent silver brows projected a touch of puzzlement.

"Our Philadelphia operation is in the hands of an Iraqi who calls himself Hazmoudi. Hazmoudi will not be using one of the carry-on bombs, but rather a different type of nuclear device. Trigger and charge will be concealed in the base of a Swiss clock by Clissot, an outdoor model called the Rock'O'Clock. This is a large, almost man-sized clock encased in granite. It has four dials. These stupid clocks have become extremely popular with city administrations around the world, which suits us fine. So, on the 4th of July, Switzerland will present the City of Philadelphia with another one of their famous Rock'O'Clocks, how original! In good time before the presentation ceremony, the gift clock will be exchanged with an identical one that has been fitted with the nuclear charge. As for Custer, he has no idea this is happening. I am keeping these two operations totally separate. How do the Americanos say: Once a gringo, always a gringo?"

Cali stopped chewing for a moment, allowing the tanned, leathery skin of his skeletal face to relax in a self-congratulatory grin.

"Are you sure you've thought of everything, my son?"

"*Absolutamente*, Padre. Hazmoudi is already in place in Switzerland. He will strike tomorrow. We will have our very own nuclear Rock'O'Clock in plenty of time to fly it to Philadelphia and exchange it for the harmless one."

The old man smiled. "I admire your planning skills, but exploding a nuclear bomb in Philadelphia is likely to give us serious problems. The gringos will certainly try to retaliate."

Cali moved his shoulders to indicate unconcern. "Of course they'll be shocked. After all, the historic core of the city will cease to exist. But their rage will turn on the Muslims rather than on us."

"Why the Muslims?"

"Because Hazmoudi is our Oswald; we're using him as a patsy.

He also happens to be an Iraqi national. He'll live just long enough for the world to make the connection. I'm certain the Americans will then shower Iraq with Tomahawk missiles. That is my concept."

"Ingenious, Don Cali."

"This blow will drive the U.S. deeper into desperation. For the gringos, who do everything to excess, cocaine has been the drug of choice for decades. After Wednesday it will be the drug of necessity. There will be an unprecedented boom. I'm thinking about detonating one of Custer's carry-on bombs on the high seas, just to show that we too have nuclear clout. Isn't free enterprise the soul of capitalism? So we can't have a nuclear monopoly controlled by General Motors, can we now? Which gives me an idea, Padre, maybe we can print 'Body by Cali' on each of our nuclear suitcases . . ."

The drug lord's high-pitched laughter seemed in eerie harmony with the group of weirdly sculpted images forming the great sepulchre where they stood.

". . . or, even better, we actually show our bombs to the Americans. After they've wiped out Baghdad, of course. The shock of Philadelphia will still be fresh in the marrow of their bones, so they will listen very attentively to whatever it is we have to say to them."

The priest's eyes seemed to be gazing inward behind contracted lids in an impassive face. "And how will you show them our terrible sword, my son?"

"Through video, Padre, on TV. We'll show them our bombs live, on screens in the White House and in the Pentagon, for select viewing only." Cali's eyes sparkled; his jaws chomped furiously on what remained of the double ration of coca. "That way we won't have to bother setting off bombs ourselves!"

"Your plan appears sound, my son."

In response to the praise, Cali gestured with feigned humbleness. "The awesome sight of a mushroom cloud above Philadelphia will shake the world to its foundations, Padre. Then we, the coca growers, will be the ones to dictate terms—to Bogotá, to the Americans, to the world! We will seize power in Colombia, use our air force and our navy to transport our merchandise. Yes, Padre, at last Colombia will be ours!"

"And the Americans?"

"The U.S. Government will do as we tell them to do. We will hold America hostage with our bombs, each one of which is more powerful than the Hiroshima bomb. We'll be able to produce as much cocaine as we like and nobody will dare attack our fields, or our factories, or our distribution centers. Production will increase enormously. There'll be an unprecedented boom in exports to the north. No more hunting down our ships and planes and couriers, Padre, all that will be a thing of the past. And their drug agencies will have to stand idly by with their hands tied because, if they don't, another little suitcase will produce another little mushroom cloud in some other densely populated area in the poor little U.S. of A."

Cali paused to look up at the gleaming deity and its dismal, one-horned victim. As if seized by an involuntary reflex, he leaned back from the waist, spreading his arms, booming out his message of doom.

"Not only cocaine! Our laboratories will create new drugs that turn gringo brains to jelly! We will flood them with our merchandise and they will love it and scream for more. They will be begging for the poison that kills them. And we will harvest as we've never harvested before. We will take everything: their children, their women, their games and entertainments, their businesses, everything!"

The ancient idol worshipper laid a paternal arm around Don Cali's shoulder. "Truly, an inspired project!"

At this moment, angry voices burst into confused cacophony just outside the temple door. Cali shook his head, as if waking from deep sleep, a frown furrowing his forehead. "Come, Padre, let's see what's going on out there!"

On the landing pad outside, the pilot cautiously lifted a corner of the camouflage netting draped over the helicopter. "Damn those peons!" he cursed, having been roused from a well-deserved nap by the babble of voices. What he saw made him pull the netting back in place and peek out through the mesh of the dark-green fabric.

It was not a pretty sight: guards were dragging a man who clearly did not belong here to the temple door. They were screaming at him, kicking him, prodding him with the butts of their AK-47s. The sturdy-looking young man with the mop of blond hair shielded himself as best he could, which was not very well. One of the guards was making a dumb show of dragging an expensive-looking maroon camera case through the dust, pantomiming an effeminate dog owner having trouble with a mean-tempered lap dog. Don

Cali's shout made the guard, who was outrageously swiveling his hips, freeze.

"*¡Deja de hacerte el tonto!*" The cutting tone of Cali's voice stopped the entire group, including the blond foreigner, dead in their tracks. The leader of the guards stepped forward, proffered a brisk military salute which Cali didn't acknowledge, and reported something the pilot could not quite understand. To the chopper pilot the prisoner looked like a fellow American, maybe a photographer or TV reporter. The man now stepped away from the group and walked toward Cali.

The guard sergeant saluted again and signaled to his men. They responded by forming two sloppy-looking files and shuffling off toward the coca fields, while the priest motioned to the prisoner to follow him and Cali into the temple. The square around the helicopter pad now lay deserted, encouraging the pilot to venture out of hiding and look around. Not a soul was in sight.

The northwest side of the triangle housed Don Cali's quarters, ancient walls encasing an elegantly-shaped steel shell which in turn contained several luxuriously appointed suites of rooms. Separated from Don Cali's living space by an olympic-size swimming pool and a tennis court under a camouflage roof were a number of visitors' bungalows. Daylight fell through glassed-over spaces between the roof slabs, and countless small halogen lamps, positioned strategically, illuminated Don Cali's residential interiors at night. He was not a man to scoff at creature comforts and high-tech conveniences, which included a command center stuffed with sophisticated communications technology, located inside the opposite walls on the northeast side of the triangle. Above communications were the barracks, where guard personnel, technicians and communications specialists were stationed, while conference and office space occupied the rear portion of the building.

Cali allowed no visible construction to mar the surface of this, his Tierra Sagrada. All service facilities were housed two stories underground. Apart from the helicopter, virtually invisible from the air under its camouflage netting, no objects of recent manufacture were to be seen. Great boulders, ground markings, road signs; that was all there was.

"Road signs, yeah, but to where?" The chopper pilot ground his teeth, making heavy strands of jaw muscles stand out in his narrow face. The North Carolina native had all reason to proceed with the utmost caution. Life expectancy for rogue gringo pilots in the service of drug bosses wasn't exactly breaking any Guinness records these days, and all he had for life insurance were his skills as a flyboy. Not too many locals knew how to handle heavy-duty rotary wings, or speedy little jets, or bulky vintage transports for that matter.

He'd heard of pilots buried farther north, beyond the great coca field, near a power plant. In order to rapidly and economically build up a transport fleet, drug chiefs regularly rented small planes in Brazil and hired Brazilian pilots to fly them up to the Tierra Sagrada. They then killed the pilots and kept the planes. Step lightly, Jeremy Kline, the pilot mumbled to himself as he approached the portals through which the group had disappeared, or you'll never see Charleston again!

Inside the temple, a ritual was in progress. Kline eased himself into a dark, tight space between two massive protrusions of stone. He blinked once, twice, to make sure he wasn't dreaming. His blond compatriot stood tied to a stake fashioned from a tree trunk stripped of bark and painted white. The man was gagged and naked to the waist. Some twenty white-robed figures formed a semicircle around him, their backs turned to Kline, while Don Cali squatted Indio-fashion a few paces to the left of the group. In obeisance to an incantatory command from the old priest, the idolators now fell to their knees, raising their arms above their heads.

Kline looked upwards and beheld the object of their worship: a marble angel wielding a sword above a monstrous, one-horned goat. The priest slowly strode forward and, turning toward the worshippers, positioned himself near the man writhing at the stake. In his hands, the silver-haired ancient held a golden bowl which he now raised to chest level. A gong began to sound with a steady, gradually intensifying beat. Soon, the vibrations from the instrument filled the vast, gloomy interior, reverberating deafeningly from the walls as the unseen percussionist labored ever more frantically.

One of the worshippers, a man of powerful physique and proud carriage, now rose and walked to the stake, his head held high. Kline blinked again as a dull flash of metal from a blade in the man's right hand struck his eyes. The pilot felt goose bumps rise up on his arms and sweat break out around the back of his neck.

Even though he saw no one near him, an eerie whisper reaching Kline's ears identified the executioner:

"It's Filiberto, Don Cali's son!"

This was like a bad movie or a bad dream! No, it was like a hideous nightmare in a horror movie. Steady now, Jerry-boy! the pilot told himself, you've seen worse than this. Besides, this ain't really happening. Things like this just don't happen no more except in movies or nightmares. So wake up, boy, you're having a nightmare. Or else you've fallen asleep in a picture show!

The knife flashed again, bright as lightning this time. It slashed into the captive's chest, hacking away at his flesh, again and again and again: slashing, slicing, hacking. Eyes wide open, Kline stared in chilled horror as the crazy, clumsy executioner finally managed to cut open the sacrificial victim's chest and thrust one hand into it, reaching for the heart. That resilient, still pulsating organ put up a bloody fight. The killer hadn't expected this. For an instant, stunned, he hesitated. Then, in one madly exuberant arc, he cut the veins and filaments and tissue that so tenaciously bound heart to body and threw the mutilated organ into the golden bowl. A hoarse, ecstatic roar rose up from the robed idolators, so powerful it momentarily drowned out even the terrible beat of the gong.

Bent low on shaky legs, Kline scurried out into the light. He managed, just barely, to reach the camouflage tarp and slip under it. On his knees, his head spinning, he vomited until there was nothing left to chuck up.

While the hapless pilot was trying to literally puke his guts out, the mighty drug lord, Don Cali de Cali, headed for his air-conditioned residence to pour himself a sturdy tumbler of Cutty Sark.

¡Maldición! he thought, I must be getting old, look at my hands shaking! He downed the whiskey voluptuously, in two huge gulps, then reached for a jar filled with coca leaves, unscrewed the lid and selected three. Don Cali needed the boost to his courage.

When his hands had finally steadied, he picked up a phone and punched in a number in New York. At that very moment in the city of Medellín, the dreaded Fourth Brigade waited, poised for the attack on Don Cali's arch rival and main competitor. A special-forces assault unit now faced the druglord's heavily fortified hide-out. At a signal, the demolition team fired an armor-piercing, shoulder-launched rocket at the re-enforced steel door. As the shell impacted, fiercely shouting men in black coveralls jumped up and ran at the gaping hole, their AK-47s blasting as they leaped through the smoke into the interior. The forty-four-year-old boss of the Medellín Cartel died instantly in a hail of bullets.

So perfectly timed was the operation that Don Cali had barely settled down by the swimming pool to watch his son splash about in apparently carefree abandon, when the cellular phone emitted a series of melodious electronic warbles. Cali picked up and answered, "Sí, *Operación Angel.*"

He listened intently to the scratchy voice of the special forces commander reporting on the success of the assault and confirming the death of Pedro Ruiz. After uttering a few sparse words of praise and accepting the commander's profuse thanks for the tip, Cali put down the phone and nodded at Filiberto, who was half in and half out of the water, supporting himself with both arms on the tiled edge of the pool.

"Ruiz the Rat is no more," Cali said, his voice vibrating with satisfaction.

"Good," Filiberto replied, shaking his mop of black curly hair so that a cascade of drops flew in all directions. Cali noticed a pink discoloration of the water around his son's body. This caused him to frown.

"Did you take a shower before you went into the pool?"

"Of course."

"You pig," Cali said, half in jest, but Filiberto had already slid back into the water and was splashing his way toward the opposite side. His father's thoughts turned back to *Operación Angel.*

Don Cali was acting in accordance with the terrible dictum of *three eyes for one eye—three teeth for one tooth,* to smash his rivals in Medellín. All he had had to do was tip off his man inside the Fourth Brigade, then watch the police do the dirty work. In recent months, thanks to Cali, the Medellín PD had mounted a series of uncommonly successful raids on drug operators. Consequently the generous, charismatic Cali was well liked by the department's insiders. They were aware that what he was really doing was trying to unify the Colombian drug trade by eliminating competition and creating a classic monopoly. Don Cali had never really made any bones about his ambition to enthrone himself as the world's leading drug czar.

Nor was there any mistaking his ultimate goal of seizing all power and installing himself in the presidential palace in Bogotá. The insiders smiled. Don Cali was not the first to try, and he wouldn't be the last. There was an old saying which many felt was as valid today as when it had been coined a hundred years ago: In Colombia, it is impossible not to get rich or not to get killed.

Zurich, Sunday, July 1

Accompanied by a high-pitched whine from its power plants, the white Gulf-stream IV arriving from Newark, New Jersey, rolled toward the General Aviation gate at Zurich-Kloten and came to a stop in the designated parking area. A mere ten minutes later Ken Custer was leaning on the counter at Avis. He showed his British driver's license, had his plastic checked and imprinted, and signed the contract. Then he signed again for no-fault insurance coverage.

A little later, approximately the same time that Custer turned the sleek, white Lancia onto N-1 and headed for Bern, an airport-police car stopped in front of the General Aviation building. An officer of the Canton Police, carrying a sheaf of papers in his hand, got out and walked into the building. He waved the forms at the man who had processed Custer.

"Seems they finally remembered you, too," he grinned, wiggling his brows significantly.

The stocky passport officer slowly leafed through the APB tags and did a double take. There was the face of the smoothie he had waved through only fifteen minutes ago! So his name was Kenneth

W. Custer, alias >Keycop<. Looked like a big fish, too. Damn oh damn oh damn!

He yanked the receiver from its cradle and punched in a three-digit number. His fingers nervously drummed on the desk as he waited for someone to pick up, all the while watching his colleague on the police force amble lazily back to the squad car.

After thirty minutes at a steady seventy-five miles per hour, Custer pulled the Lancia into a roadside rest area. He found a pay phone and made a collect call to a round-the-clock number in New York, only to hear Susan tell him not to initiate further contacts until instructed otherwise.

"During the current One Alert phase," she said slowly and calmly, enunciating each word clearly, "Cosmo wants you to lie low. New instructions will follow."

Brief and to the point, Custer thought grimly, massaging his chin. Neat and tidy, too! So now my mug's gracing the Wanted bulletins of America and Europe, how thrilling! One Alert meant it was open season for taking potshots at Ken Custer. And as Ken knew from experience, whoever the CIA wished to take down, they usually took down.

Custer shrugged: he'd been expecting this. Keeping the rearview mirrors in his peripheral vision, he threaded his way back into now-heavier traffic. He turned on the car's radio and pressed the search key on the FM band. The digital display pulsed 107.5 and the tune was Stevie Ray Vaughan's *Double Trouble*. Custer grimaced rue-fully, humming along. Stevie Ray didn't know the half of it! Man oh man, the trouble this boy's in!

He might have been traveling for an hour, when he passed a large green road sign announcing the City of Bern. Taken by sur-prise, Custer got hold of the map on the passenger seat. He flicked it open with one hand, never taking his eyes off the road. Had he really driven eighty miles so deep in thought that he never noticed? Well, there was plenty to think about. That he was on the CIA Wanted list could only mean that a warrant for his arrest had already been issued to all national police agencies in Europe, cour-tesy of Interpol. To say nothing of the local feds, known for their thoroughness, who'd probably already distributed his mug shot into the farthest nooks and crannies of Switzerland.

He caught himself routinely checking the rearview mirror for rotating blue lights, or inconspicuously dark Volvos inconspicuously tailing him at a discreet distance. There weren't any. He glanced at the map, looking for an exit to the west of the capital, just as he crested a rise and saw that he was approaching precisely such a turnoff.

Damn Langley! A real nuisance that they had to start chasing him right now. He didn't have time for their silly games! On the other hand, he couldn't remember the last time he'd done anything he enjoyed except under trying circumstances.

Also, there was Theo. Hunching his shoulders closer to the wheel, Custer recalled some of the many occasions when von Alp had bailed him out of a rough spot. Now there was a man you could count on! As he drove around the city along the western periphery, he decided to phone his old friend. He could just see him, with those twinkly little eyes and that mischievous grin, happily mapping out one more plan of action.

Preparing to turn off N-1, he moved the Lancia into the slow lane. A few kilometers after leaving the freeway he turned into a back road that led down to a shabby little motel by a dammed-up stretch of the river. On a narrow bridge he passed a big, black Mercedes going the opposite way. He caught a glimpse of a face inside—pale, vaguely familiar—some big shot, no doubt, being driven around the countryside by his chauffeur.

He pulled into the delapidated motel court, got out, and walked up three steps into the office. A fat, sullen-looking woman who acted as if she owned the place, and probably did, took his money and unceremoniously showed him the way to Number Eleven.

"We got a nice view here," she rasped in a commendable attempt at polite conversation, waving her fat arms at the lake and the distant Alps. Custer was too exhausted to be disturbed by the curtains of upper-arm cellulite that framed the view.

Once in the gloomy room, with its threadbare, rust-red carpet, Custer threw down his bags. They came to rest against a much-scuffed floor strip under faded beige wallpaper. He flopped down on the bed and lay there, practically dead to the world. After a while he sat up, balancing on the edge of the bed. He lifted the receiver off the ancient dust-gray phone on the night table, and dialed von Alp's number.

Halfway through, he hesitated, then hung up. How could he be so stupid! This might be a terminal case of a motel, but they probably still kept an itemized record of all outgoing calls. Better to call from a booth somewhere! He got up, pulled the curtains tight, threw himself back down on the hang-belly bed. Fully dressed as he was, he instantly plummeted into the leaden sleep imposed on him by a vicious jet lag.

The face Custer had glimpsed on the bridge near the motel was that of Switzerland's prime minister, Peter Kern. Moments after they passed each other, Kern reached for the car phone to call the chief secretary of his department at his home, and relay the alarming observations he had made less than an hour ago at some underground research facilities in the little town of Nucleanne, west of Bern.

Kern listened to the secretary's phone as it rang endlessly. The man was a nature freak, just then probably pumping up a steep alpine grade on his mountain bike: jaw jutting, lips compressed, doggedly pursuing some stringent ideal of physical well-being.

Pensively massaging his chin, Kern put the handset back in its clip. This might just be a blessing in disguise. Maybe it was better to hold on to this bit of news a while longer, which was more in keeping with his unhurried way of handling business anyway. Indeed, in his experience, haste usually did make waste. Let's take a close look at Schlammer's licensing contracts first, he told himself, then . . . well, then, Stephanie!

If his suspicions turned out to be right, he'd tell her everything— well, not quite everything, just enough to whet her appetite. Just enough for her to be able to go after this fine fellow, Adam Schlammer, Esq., the arrogant wimp! Kern chuckled softly to himself: Probably changed his name from Slime! Yes, Adam Slime, Esq. would be nothing short of perfect.

Later, tonight, he'd give Stephanie the scoop. The way he figured it, she wouldn't be Stephanie Kramer if she didn't rise to the bait. A nice little indiscretion, straight from the horse's mouth, or at least the horse's manger—the office of the prime minister—just the thing to stir up public opinion. After all, his fellow countrymen and -women had a perfect right to know what sinister plans were being hatched deep in the secret recesses of their beloved picture-postcard mountains.

Not that he had the foggiest notion what such sinister plans might be. But then, that wasn't really his department, was it? He was not the investigative reporter, she was! No one was better suited for this thing than this brightly burning, beautiful, and ambitious woman whose incisive stories not only captured the imagination of a broad readership, but also commanded the respect of the intelligentsia.

Relieved to have arrived at a viable solution, the prime minister glanced at his watch. He had only moments to enjoy his newfound peace of mind before the car phone buzzed discreetly. Kern picked it up. It was the departmental secretary on duty, reporting on an incident involving nuclear contraband on the Italian side of the Simplon Tunnel. An Italian border guard had been shot, allegedly by Swiss customs personnel. Italy was demanding an immediate and exhaustive explanation from the Swiss government.

Shocked out of the pleasant illusion of being in control of things, Kern shouted into the phone, "What kind of cockamamie goatshit is this? Why don't they clean up in their own pigsty first! I'll get to it when I get to it, okay?"

He jammed the phone set back into the clip, badly pinching his right index finger. Managing to suppress a savage howl, he popped the finger into his mouth and started sucking on it, his anger diffused by very real, very focused pain. Suddenly, the great statesman had to laugh: A man had just been shot to death in something that had all the makings of a really nasty border incident, with Italy at that, and here he was, unable to think of anything but his stupid finger! How wonderful, he thought. That, my dear Stephanie, is the difference between affairs of state and affairs of the flesh.

Late that afternoon, the young clerk behind the Avis Rent-a-Car counter at Zurich-Kloten took his time examining the photograph held out to him by two plainclothesmen from the Canton Police. He had recognized the face immediately: the American with the friendly eyes and the good-humored smile. The man had shown him a British driver's license, then casually signed for a whole week. A cool kind of dude. Seemed to be in the habit of tipping generously. Regrettably, the clerk had had to turn down the American's offer of two large bills in Switzerland's finest paper. Regulations! He suppressed a decidedly uncool sigh.

From under identically raised eyebrows, the plainclothes heavies were watching him attentively.

"How about it now, sir," asked the taller of the two. "Do you recognize this man?"

The Avis-jockey was in no mood to hand over a friendly, generous client like Custer, at least not without a fight. Shrugging his shoulders, he took another look at the picture.

"Can you tell me what this is all about?" he asked innocently.

The two cops exchanged meaningful glances. The shorter one said, "U.S. authorities, FBI. A big fish. All right, now, have you seen him or haven't you?"

"Well, actually, yes, the more I look at this picture, the more I believe I have seen him," the clerk drawled. First things first, no use getting on the bad side of the authorities. He pulled out Custer's rental contract and showed it to the cops, telling them, rather unnecessarily, that this had to be their man.

Only minutes later, the Avis Lancia's license number ZH V 7619 flashed onto the screens in all police stations and all computer-equipped patrol cars in Switzerland. All other police cars were alerted via radio.

The retired warrior known as the Old Man was leafing through a yachting magazine when there was a knock on the door and his favorite reporter walked in. Each time he saw her, an infinitesimal hesitation occurred in his mind: Should he think of her as newswoman, newsperson, reportress, reporter, sweetheart—for, indeed, he was a little sweet on her—or just plain Stephanie?

He usually had no trouble clearing this mental hurdle and settling for pleasantly embarrassing ambiguity as they touched cheeks—left, right, left; his grizzled against her smooth one. Every time they did this it occurred to him that she must have shed the very last of her baby down just before stepping into his office. This usually made him sigh.

Today Stephanie Kramer wore her dark blonde hair combed demurely upward to form a thick nest that said I'm-all-business on the crown of her head, imparting an air of sober maturity to her achingly girlish features. The ensemble she wore, skirt, blouse, and jacket, made her look like a successful assistant DA about to cross-examine a defense witness. But the Old Man adroitly welcomed her, gesturing for her to sit down in one of three old-fashioned, comfortable armchairs that surrounded a small, low table.

"Have you ever considered changing your name to Aurora, my dear?" he asked.

"Certainly not, why?" she replied as she was being swallowed up by one of the bulky, overstuffed chairs.

"Because I could then pretend you had dawned on me twenty years ago," he smiled. "And what would the lady prefer: coffee, tea, Scotch?"

"Just plain water, please."

The Old Man opened a bottle of mineral water, poured some in a glass, placed bottle and glass in front of Stephanie, then returned to his desk and sat down.

Since the room's only window was located behind the desk, he had the position of power: Stephanie would see his face enigmatically shaded, with bright contours, while she herself looked into bright daylight that accentuated the slightest shift in facial mood. She turned her head to look up at the gallery of framed photographs on the wall, dominated by a military portrait of the Old Man in his youth. It depicted the young, dashing Arik posing as the immortal warrior, waving from the open cockpit of a jet fighter.

Following the Six-Day War, Arik had lingered on in the air force for a couple of years, before embarking on a new career as materiel procurement agent for the Israeli government. Later, he moved to Zurich, a city conveniently located for building up a flourishing business in spare parts for aircraft—as well as a lucrative trade in intelligence, or so the rumors went.

Much later, he had met Stephanie in Tel Aviv, at Ben Gurion Airport, where he used his clout to get her a seat in the first-class section of a fully booked flight to Zurich. Not surprisingly, he had turned up in the adjoining seat to regale her with stories of his great passion, flying. Again not surprisingly, she had found him immensely attractive. He exuded a fighter pilot's reckless optimism, generating kinetic energy so the air around him seemed to crackle. Just the kind of gentleman by whom she wouldn't mind being carried off to a desert island. Or why not a desert hotel?

Instead, he had taken her to elegant restaurants in Zurich. She had admired his talent for improvisation, which he charmingly combined with casually urbane eloquence in several languages.

Having majored in physics, Stephanie profited from Arik's broadly based technological know-how.

Indeed, the Old Man's favorite techno-hobby, modern weapons technology, was what brought her to Zurich on this sparkling summer's day. She needed answers to a number of disturbing questions, and she didn't feel like beating around the bush.

"What makes you think that components for nuclear weapons and other ghastly stuff are being manufactured in beautiful Switzerland?" she asked after a preliminary sip of mineral water.

The old warrior wagged a playful finger at her. "If this is an interview, I ask that you deactivate your voice-controlled pocket recorder, okay?"

"If only I could remember the proper tone of voice," she smiled.

More than pleased to unleash some of his formidable knowledge on a captive audience, Arik was already three steps into a lecture on the virtues of Switzerland: the punctuality of its trains, the high-precision technology of its watches, the world-renowned genius of its scientists and the skill of its inventors, not to mention the outstanding quality and reliability of its industrial products.

"Yours is a nation of tinkerers and inventors," he bragged recklessly. "There aren't any great mineral treasures in this rocky soil, so ideas sprout all the more luxuriantly. The Swiss use their imagination to transform raw materials from all over the world into sparkling new export products. Can you think of a more industrious nation of comparable size in the world, except maybe Taiwan?"

Stephanie answered with a conspicuous, if charming yawn, hoping he would take the hint. It only spurred him on to greater exertions. Space exploration! As far as Stephanie could see, this was an area of endeavor not easily associable with Switzerland. Arik waved aside any such notions, if unspoken. Swiss industry produced vital components of superior quality for space technology, he lectured, chatting amiably about solar panels on the moon, telescopes, astronauts, and rocket guidance systems. Then, so abruptly it made her gulp, he plunged back to earth.

"You see, Stephanie, most people abroad have a distorted picture of your country. They see picturesque alpine meadows surrounded by snow-covered mountain peaks incandescent with the blush of dawn, where quaintly colorful, well-fed cows graze, eager to produce milk for those famous Swiss cheeses and chocolates.

And they imagine vast mountain caverns full of native craftsmen with bent backs poking about in Swiss clockworks before a background of impregnable bank vaults filled to bursting with gold. They never imagine Switzerland as a superbly industrialized nation."

If the Old Man had intended this final remark to conclude his dissertation, he hadn't counted on Stephanie Kramer's ability to get caught up in his enthusiasm.

"I totally agree," she said. "Just look at our chemical industry, our pharmaceutical concerns, our pioneering work in genetic technology such as gene-splicing and cloning. Our banks and insurance companies have cornered a substantial portion of the world market, making the Swiss Franc one of the world's most stable currencies, if not *the* most stable."

Barely stopping to catch her breath, she told him that he was absolutely right about Switzerland's Nobel-Prize density, the nation having produced the largest number of winners per capita in the world. In nuclear medicine and in physics, and in many other areas of science and technology, Switzerland was at the cutting edge of progress.

Once she got going, the reporter laid it on so thick that the Old Man had to cut her off with a gesture and a gruff, unintelligible exclamation. As he saw it, he himself had already exhausted the subject.

In a calculated gesture of submission, Stephanie raised her glass and drank some more water. It gave her time to take stock of the situation.

Deciding to do something about the blinding light, she got up, went to the window and adjusted the venetian blinds. Having thus restored at least some of the balance of power, she pivoted and caught the Old Man looking at her with the kind of open-focus, wrap-around glance that told her she had him in the palm of her hand. There weren't many secrets he could keep from her.

She noted that he didn't blink. Good old Arik, he didn't know the meaning of the word fear—or embarrassment!

"Switzerland is a perfect place to hide a nuclear weapons plant," he said, then paused. Stephanie remained posed discreetly by the window. He continued, "Conditions for such a venture are ideal—a high-tech industry, a number of nuclear power plants, and a secretive, conspiratorial climate."

"Aren't you exaggerating a little?" she baited him. "How would we be more conspiratorial than other nations?"

Shrugging, the Old Man reminded her of the scandal that had erupted over the disclosure that Switzerland had been maintaining what amounted to a secret army, something no one would have thought possible. If a secret underground militia of such size could be built up without attracting public attention, why shouldn't clandestine manufacturing of nuclear weapons be possible?

"Come on," she teased, "this secret society was under army control, after all, while a nuclear weapons plant would constitute a criminal conspiracy and probably even be considered high treason."

"Treason is exactly what it is, my sweet. And the conspirators have sufficient power to blackmail the duly elected government. They might even be able to force it to resign."

Now that her dear old fish had swallowed the bait, Stephanie was in no hurry. Absently parting the slats of the venetian blinds, she peered out into the waning afternoon, pretending to be admiring the way the buttery sunshine transformed a chestnut tree outside into a fountain of emerald gold.

"Tell me, Richie," she said, using a code name of his she had stumbled upon some years ago, "how are your old buddies in the Mossad? Not too old for an occasional round of golf on the Costa del Sol, I hope."

"Flattery will get you everywhere," he grinned, "but please keep your sweet little paws out of the spy business. That's the department of dirty tricks and you don't want to be caught in there. Stick to your own rules and do what you do best. You're a top-notch investigative journalist and you've got plenty of what they call hunchability. And there's a man who might be able to shed some light on all of this, a man codenamed >Keycop< . . . but for right now, how about dinner at the Kronenhalle?"

So that's what this is all about, she thought as the Old Man leaned forward, fixing her in what no doubt he thought was the devastatingly steady gaze of his immortal warrior days. Tit for tat.

"This is terrible," she said, producing an apologetic pout that emphasized the sinuous curve of her lips, "but I really have to get back to Bern. There's a pile of work on my desk. But who's this >Keycop<, one of your secret agents?"

Instead of answering, Arik saw her to the elevator.

Later, in an air-conditioned compartment on the Zurich–Bern

intercity express, Stephanie took stock of her situation. Arik had been cooperative as usual; sooner than he expected she'd show up on his estate and get some of that sensational information on videotape. Outside, an especially picturesque portion of what Switzerland's rebellious youngsters liked to refer to as the "green hell" flashed by the train's windows. Picture-postcard farms with picture-postcard cows, in a picture-postcard scenery—precisely as Arik had described it. Even she had trouble believing that a sinister nuclear plot was being hatched beneath this idyllic surface.

She leaned back in the comfortably upholstered seat and half-closed her eyes, enjoying the high-speed vibration and the gently rocking motion of the train. Unhurried, pleasantly, her thoughts turned to Peter Kern. She was meeting him for dinner that evening, and she wondered what he would think of the Old Man's outrageous theory. On the other hand, who knows, she thought, maybe I'm on to something here.

The train thundered into a plain. Steam clouds rose from the refrigeration silo of a nuclear plant, silhouetted against limestone cliffs of dazzling white. Stephanie gazed abstractedly at the point where the clouds turned to wisps of steam and dissolved into thin air. A drowsy sort of gaiety bubbled up in her: the man she would have dinner with was nothing like his position would lead one to imagine. Having served as energy resources minister, this year he was president of the Swiss Confederation—job titles that conjured up an image of sober responsibility. In fact, he could be a lot of fun. She was looking forward to a wonderful evening—laughter and interesting conversation in a setting of elegant, beautiful people, or at least people who commanded so much wealth and power that it would have been foolish not to think of them as beautiful.

Considering all these prospects, and given the fact that, as usual, the train arrived precisely on time at Bern's Central Station, Stephanie had every reason to step lightly onto the platform and move swiftly toward the exit. She felt perfectly in harmony with herself and with the immediate future. She would make a couple of phone calls, then get ready for the evening. Everything was fine. She'd have a great time.

She walked toward the line of taxis outside the station. Yes, it was the beginning of a wonderful evening. Or it was until it occurred to her, with a sickening sag of the heart, that she was protesting too much.

Bern, Sunday, July 1

About midnight, two cops in a traffic patrol car pulled up in front of the Lakeview Motel. Having just finished a difficult eight-hour shift, the two men were dead tired. The co-driver, a mustachioed constable, slowly climbed out of the red-and-white Volvo and waddled wearily over to the soft drink dispenser in the tiny motel lobby. As he fed coins to the machine and waited for the cans of Coke to hit the dispenser, the frowsy-looking matron who earlier had received Custer came shuffling up to him and handed him a bunch of registration cards. Too tired to be surprised, he accepted them. Strictly speaking, this had nothing to do with him: someone from headquarters in the city would be by to pick them up in the morning. Still . . . might as well take a look at it.

Suddenly, he was all eyes. What have we here! ZH V 7619—wasn't that the number they had . . . ?

The sluggishness the two patrol officers felt was gone in a flash. They were ready for action. Keeping close to the side of the motel, they moved cautiously to the right, in the direction of Room Eleven, working the actions on their SIG Sauer service automatics.

Ducking low, communicating in whispers and gestures, they sidled along a wall, then sprinted toward the door, weapons at the ready.

As he pressed his head and back against flaking paint, the constable shook off a brief mental vision of two dewy-moist cans of ice-cold Coke slowly warming in the hotel lobby. This was serious business! His handgun lay steady at eye level, his equally steady gaze just fixed on the door.

The second patrol officer, a burly fellow, took three steps back, then charged with a kangaroolike leap. A no-nonsense kick with his right boot smashed the flimsy plywood door open. Splinters went flying, a black hole yawned before them.

Pivoting, the constable stormed through the door, shouting, "Police! Don't move! Hands above your heads!" His door-kicking partner followed close behind, providing cover, fumbling for the light switch.

In the dismal glare of a single light bulb encased within a threadbare Chinese paper lampshade, their faces looked pale and pained. Number Eleven appeared to be utterly unoccupied. As for the white Lancia, there was no trace of it in the parking lot or anywhere else on the motel premises.

At exactly the same time as the two cops trotted in disappointment back to their car, Custer was not far away. He sat in the dining room of the Crown Inn, watching the inkeeper's wife deposit a dish of veal cutlets on his table. He poked cautiously at a potato, eyeing it suspiciously. Maybe the local gendarmes were already looking for him? It was enough to ruin one's appetite! Maybe they were already checking hotels, motels . . . though not likely.

He sawed a cutlet in two, impaled it, American-style, on his fork and lifted it to his mouth, all the while keeping his eyes on the entrance. As he chewed on the veal, he saw himself about half an hour ago, back at the motel . . .

. . . dreaming, plunging headlong into a black abyss, crossing his hands in front of his face to protect it, then bolting up in bed, drenched in sweat. Which bed, where—Bogotá, New York? Fumbling for the light switch he knocked the clock radio off the table; it clattered to the floor. Fluorescent green digits swam in the dark, slowly came into focus: SUNDAY 23:30. His head hurt as if he'd actually hit bottom in that nightmare ravine! All hope of sleep was gone, and the realization that he was in Switzerland hit him. He jumped up, still confused, cursing the damn clock. It seemed at most an hour ago he'd dropped off, but now it was dark outside, going on midnight.

It had taken him only a few minutes to pack. Years of practice! He'd slipped into his loafers, cautiously opened the door, and moved silently out to the Lancia. As he eased the car out of the parking area, he noticed a red-and-white patrol car parked at the canopied entrance to the motel office. Rolling by it, he caught a fleeting glimpse of the cop in the passenger seat in front, watching his colleague walk up the three stairs to the door marked Reception and reaching for the handle on the big glass door. The driver's door stood wide open.

Any moment, Custer had expected the man at the top of the stairs to turn, eyes to peer after him, scanning his license plate. It didn't happen. They took no notice of the Lancia. A bit down the road, he had jumped on the gas, hightailing it out of there. . . .

Suddenly ravenously hungry, Custer attacked what remained of the veal, then turned his attention to the small mountain of golden-brown roast potatoes, a specialty of the house. The meal was complemented by a side order of garden-fresh spinach, served in a separate dish with a generous, encouraging smile by the mistress of the house. Custer looked from the bosomy woman to the spinach, then back up to the bosomy woman who, unabashed, kept smiling down on him.

"*Enjoy*," she finally told him, in the broad, soft dialect of the region. Deep down in his gut he knew exactly what she meant, but translated automatically: Enjoy your meal. He smiled sheepishly back up at her. Enjoy what? The spinach? She'd been smiling down. On him, not necessarily the spinach. As she turned back toward the kitchen, he stealthily glanced down along his trousers. Such things were known to happen, after all! But he saw nothing extraordinary. He grinned, shaking his head. Everything looked perfectly natural. Maybe that's why she had smiled!

When he left the inn a little later, a plump, full moon had just cleared the distant mountains, its silvery glare dusting the gradually ascending road. Just before reaching the little town where von Alp lived, he slowed down to cross a plunging, darkly romantic ravine.

Moonlight glittered below on the dark, swift waters, broken up by the bridge railing struts. Somber fragments of his recurring nightmare moved past him like film frames, taking him back to his beginnings: the souls of his ancestors were calling to him. He sensed—and ached from the feeling—the very roots of his innermost being.

Long after midnight, Custer left the road to Guggisberg and turned into a gravel-topped parking area. He cut the engine, activated the dashboard lights and studied his map. Nucleanne was approximately eighty kilometers farther west. Tomorrow, it would take an hour or so to get there. He opened the glove compartment, took out his Walther PPK and carefully slid it into its customary spot, between trousers and belt. Then he got out and walked toward an old, two-story mansion. Three huge linden trees, from which von Alp's home derived the name "Lindenegg," stood menacingly silhouetted in black against a star-studded sky.

Lindenegg, von Alp's chalet, stood apart from the village, on ground rising above it. The site commanded a panoramic view down across the slanting terrain, all the way to the castle, whose silhouette dominated the southern portion of the area. The castle housed the municipal court and the police station.

There were a number of excellent reasons why von Alp had chosen this particular location for his base of operations. At an elevation of some eight hundred meters above sea level, this region of gently rolling hills bordered to the south on the impregnable natural bastion of the Lower Alps. With the town's location creating optimum conditions for radio transmission, Radio Switzerland International for several decades had maintained a shortwave station. During the eighties, it was expanded to include satellite functions.

To the north, the east, and the west, deep gorges converged to form another natural barrier. Anyone wishing to get into this valley by land had to cross one of three principal bridges. The surrounding countryside of fields and meadows lay open to view day and night. Chalet Lindenegg thus provided the old soldier of fortune with all the advantages of a commanding position on high ground.

Custer opened the front door and cautiously advanced into the hall, where he saw light coming from the kitchen. A female voice called to him, "Welcome to Lindenegg, Mr. Custer, we've been expecting you. If our infrared cameras hadn't identified you, you wouldn't have got very far."

Relaxing, Custer let out his breath. Seated on a swivel chair in front of a battery of screens, a smiling young woman in black corduroy pants and a blousy, olive-green shirt waved at him. She bounced up, touching her right hand to a black baseball cap that didn't do much to restrain a profusion of red hair.

"Hi, I'm Claudia. Theo should be here any moment."

They shook hands. Looking into hazel eyes that seemed to sparkle with alertness, Custer said, "Pleased to meet you. I hope I'm not intruding. Say, that's nice equipment you've got here."

"Oh, sure," she smiled pleasantly, "feel free to take a look. This here's our surface monitor, infrared, 360-degree radial coverage. With a light-enhancement factor of 40,000, which is double the normal for military applications. Over here, these green screens? They report from movement sensors. Huh, look, we've got some action in Sector A!"

Moving energetically, she activated one of the cameras. "There he is. Carlos!"

"And who might Carlos be?" All Custer saw was a smudgy shadow moving across the screen.

"Carlos is a fox. See that long, shaggy tail? He turns up almost every night, as if to tease us, then vanishes. That's Carlos for you!"

Custer scanned the sixteen monitors arranged in a tightly linked block of four tiers, each with four screens, creating the impression of a single, large, checkerboard screen. The top edge, left to right, was numbered 1 through 4, while the left rim, top to bottom, read A through D. New York Stock Exchange prices appeared bottom right, on the D-4 screen.

As Ken set down his bag, a bright orange message—CAPO—started blinking on the A-2 monitor. He tapped a finger against the screen.

"What's CAPO?"

"That's one of Theo's little jokes," Claudia said. "Watch!" Her fingers playfully tapped the keyboard. The CAPO legend winked off and the electronic void on C-2 began to fill with distinct, greenish contours. An overhead perspective of the area around the chalet emerged. Roof-mounted cameras, Custer figured. On the screen, a slow zoom showed a gate opening slowly to admit a minivan.

"That's Theo, all right," she confirmed, handing Custer a microphone. "Say hello to him." The outdoor microphones faithfully reported the crunch of tires on gravel.

Holding the mike, Custer struck a drill-sergeant pose and barked, "Fall in for reveille in two minutes, Captain!"

"You bet your life, Colonel," von Alp's hoarse baritone boomed back.

Moments later they were embracing, pounding each other's backs.

"You're looking great, Ken, what's your secret?"

"My secret?" Custer darted a quick glance in Claudia's direction. "When I'm looking at the ageless Casanova himself? Ageless and incorrigible, I should say!"

Von Alp slowly twisted his sunburnt features, topped by curly, closely-cropped, grayish blond hair, into an appreciative grimace. Custer had no difficulty linking the flattered, lopsided grin with his old buddy's favorite motto: *Life's too short not to scratch when it itches.* Especially when the scratcher looked like Claudia.

Aloud, he asked, "Everything okay?"

Von Alp wagged his head. "Somebody followed you."

Custer frowned, but von Alp gave a thumbs-up sign. "We grabbed the fellow." He produced a pistol and laid it on the table. "This is his, an American make. And here's his badge."

Custer briefly glanced at the badge. The name James Murphy was stenciled next to a silver eagle with the National Security Agency insignia. He gave an amused shake of the head. "Old Jim Murphy, huh?"

"You know him?"

"No."

Claudia and von Alp chuckled at Custer's poker face.

"So, what did you do with him?"

"Turned him over to the cops," von Alp grinned. "Gave him a chance to sleep it off."

"Sleep what off, Theo? What the fuck did you do with him?"

"Oh, not much. Engineered a minor drunk-driving accident, that's all. Cost me half a bottle of Chivas, too. His car looks a bit worse for wear, though, especially front right. Just a little something to remember me by, you know."

Smiling, Custer said, "Wouldn't it have been better to bring him here?"

Von Alp shook his head. "Operatives like Murphy are usually wired, often subcutaneously." He playfully jabbed an elbow into Claudia's side. "That's secret service lingo for under the skin, darling."

"Very cute," she fired back. "Very sub cute!"

"Anyhow, I didn't want to risk having him pinpoint our location. Also, I don't think we should burden our organization with prisoners. It ties us up, and we've got other priorities. Will we need a satellite link tonight?"

"Not before Tuesday," Custer said, "for a video conference."

"I'll take your bag upstairs and turn back the sheets," Claudia smiled, neatly sidestepping Custer's mock preemptive move.

"Look, I can take care . . ."

"Colonel Custer," she laughed, "are you patronizing me?"

Custer raised his hands in a half helpless, half apologetic gesture.

"In this house we all have equal rank," she called cheerfully, bounding up the stairs.

"Scotch or white wine, Ken?"

"Scotch, please."

They carried their drinks to the spacious living room and slumped into a couple of huge armchairs. Velvety summer night air streaming in through half-open terrace doors carried the chirp-chirp-chirp of crickets.

Custer's memory winged back to the carefree days of his childhood. Days without aim, carefree as crickets chirping in the night. And with it came this painful inability to recall precisely when, where, he'd been that happy! One day the gap would close, he knew. Memory would cover the final stretch of lost ground and take him to his very own Sesame mountain where his childhood treasures were locked up.

"Open Sesame!" he mumbled, gulping down a big mouthful of Scotch.

"Is that the new code?"

"What? Oh, no, it's nothing. I was just . . . just . . ."

Sensing his friend's mood, von Alp gestured efficiently. "So, are we sending tomorrow?"

"I don't think so. Let's lie low for a while. You can be pretty sure the NSA has a relay station somewhere in the area, so they may already be trying to lock in on your beam. Our friend Murphy got much too close for comfort. I say let's take another good look at our situation in the morning, okay? I mean later today."

Von Alp flipped back the cover of a cigar box and held it out to Custer. "Cigar?" Custer took one and lit it.

"All right, let's have it then," von Alp urged. "What's this all about?"

Custer was puffing mightily on his cigar, exhaling a huge burst of smoke, coughing a little, holding the dark-brown stogie to his nose, sniffing on it. Grimacing.

Frowning dangerously, von Alp said, "Genuine Havana!"

"My sentiments exactly," Custer replied, puffing and coughing. "Look, Theo, to make a long story short, will you go with me to Nucleanne?"

"Nucleanne? The old reactor?"

Custer's brows went up. "Did you say reactor?"

"Yes. They've turned it into a big underground storage depot for nuclear waste materials. It's supposed to be the only one of its kind in Europe. Run by the Schlammer Group."

Custer had no intention of interrupting the narrative flow.

"Getting rid of radioactive wastes is a hot issue," von Alp went on, "though that doesn't seem to bother Schlammer. From what I hear, he's turned that nuclear dump of his into a veritable gold mine."

With a devil-may-care flick of the wrist, Custer tossed back the remainder of his Scotch, sucked happily on his cigar. "That's really interesting," he said, "because I happen to have an appointment with Schlammer tomorrow."

Von Alp took the cigar out of his mouth, and the mouth remained open. "No, really?"

"Yes indeed, pal! Here we are, getting into business, and I don't even know the guy. Maybe you can help me. In fact, I know you can. Didn't you once tell me you had data bases on everything from Sidewinder missiles to frogs' ears?"

There followed the practiced pause, a wistful interlude whose length they had worked out in countless Scotch and Bourbon sessions.

"Do frogs have ears?" von Alp finally asked.

"Company frogs do," Custer replied happily, in a blatant allusion to the CIA. Their funny wires crossed, an explosion of laughter rocked both of them.

With a death-defying gulp Custer downed the last of his whiskey.

"Seriously, though, Theo," he rasped, pulling valiantly on his cigar, "I need everything you have on Schlammer. Everything, back to his diaper rash."

"I understand—know your enemy," von Alp laughed. "Well, you already know he's a big-time operator, the power broker type. The sort of fellow you wouldn't want to meet in a dark alley or on the trading floor of a stock exchange. Or in a karate dojo, for that matter. Entirely self-made, which I find nothing wrong with. But no problem, I'll brief you in the morning. Now do your body a favor and go to bed."

Custer climbed the stairs, found his room, went in, and closed the door. He unzipped his bag, took out his reflector visor, put it on and switched on the tiny bulbs. He got the usual chuckle out of catching a brief glance of himself in a mirror, looking like a certified nut. Again, he'd fallen into the jet-lag hole. His incorruptibly healthy body chronometer signaled a dynamic Manhattan at dinnertime: sleep was out of the question.

He unpacked his laptop computer, tilted up the screen, switched it on, and sat down to write. Now and then he paused to look out through the large window, up into the night sky. Untouchably dependable stars blinked down on him from the big galactic screen. His hands were on the keyboard. Hitting the Caps Lock key, he tapped out *THE TURNING POINT*. Then used the cursor to mark it. Then touched the space bar as his jet-lag enriched insight dissolved into the virtual void.

 One of the tiny bulbs in Custer's jet-lag visor flickered, then winked off. He paid no attention to it. As he tapped out another line on the computer screen, a second bulb failed with a soft, implosive fizzle. Irritated, he took off his homemade headgear. The two bulbs were still warm to the touch as he pulled them out of their sockets, got up, and started rummaging through his bag for spares.

There was a knock on the door and von Alp entered.

"Good, you're up," he said. "We should get going in about an hour."

Custer had replaced the two burnt-out bulbs and put the visor back on. Staring, von Alp theatrically clutched his chest. "My my my," he went, "I believe I'd know you anywhere!"

Custer shrugged. "I'm patenting this thing to fight jet lag. On second thought, I think I'll patent it as a health and beauty aid for shell-shocked former CIA agents, how about that?" He wrenched it off his head, clicked off the battery switch, and threw it on the bed.

Von Alp grabbed him by the scruff of his neck and started pulling him out through the door.

"Playtime's over, kid. Come on, I wanna show you something."

As von Alp sat down in front of the sixteen-module monitor panel in the darkened control room, a bulky, hairy shape dashed across one of the screens.

"Ghostbusters!" Custer crowed.

"Nothing ghostly about them, they're wild boars. We train them ourselves. They're better than any Dobie, Shepherd, or Rottweiler you care to mention. A direct hit from one of those will send any intruder flying all the way back to Bern."

"Very humane!"

Von Alp grinned proudly. "You said it—humane and no pain. Like this decoder here. Right now I'm accessing ISIS, the central police register, all classified info: search ID 'Schlammer Adam.' See, now it's asking for the search code."

Von Alp lifted the cover of a pocketbook-size red box with a small digital keyboard at the top and tapped out a series of numbers. For long moments nothing happened on the screen. Then, suddenly, it seemed as if someone had emptied a bucket of paint over it. Long fluid electronic filaments slid and dripped from top to bottom. This was followed by a chaotic turbulence of indecipherable hieroglyphics, digits, and letters. Custer could not tear his eyes off the whirling, hypnotic spectacle.

Gradually, a certain order began to insinuate itself into the wild electronic dance. Out of the whirling digits a pattern emerged, forming the words: RESTRICTED DATA, ENTER NAME.

"That's the VIP pool," von Alp explained. "Let's see now, who shall we . . . well, let's start at the top, Prime Minister Kern."

He entered the name Kern. In a matter of seconds a neatly columned brief appeared. Von Alp quickly scanned the information, rolled down to the next page, whistling softly to himself.

"Will you take a look at that! MARITAL STATUS WIDOWER. MAINTAINS INTIMATE RELATIONS WITH KRAMER STEPHANIE, FREE-LANCE JOURNALIST, CURRENTLY AFFILIATED WITH THE BERNER TAGESBLATT, A LIBERAL DAILY."

Von Alp looked up at Custer, gave him a quick wink, then turned his attention back to the screen.

"Close your eyes, Ken, this is hot stuff. Look, I don't believe it: PSYCHOSEXUAL PROFILE DOMINANT-SUBMISSIVE WITH DISTINCT SADOMASOCHISTIC . . . They must be kidding!"

With a snort of mock disgust, he continued to roll the text, abruptly stopped again. Reading from the screen, he said,

"PERIMETERS OF INSTABILITY AND HOMICIDAL PO-
TENTIAL INCLUDE NUCLEAR LOBBY, ENVIRONMENTAL
ACTIVISTS, ISLAMIC FUNDAMENTALISTS, MILITANT
FEMINISTS. Feminists? Isn't that a little off the carpet?"

He exited the Kern file, entered the legend SCHLAMMER
ADAM in the dialogue column and activated the print function.
Impressed, Custer patted the red box that had sliced through all
access barriers like a knife through butter. Von Alp made a face
that didn't fool Custer: his old buddy was clearly flattered.

"It works on the Mario Principle," von Alp intoned. Seeing Custer's puzzled frown, he continued, "That's Super Mario Brothers,
the Nintendo computer game. A little mustachioed fellow fights
his way through all kinds of dangers and turbulences, like dodging
falling comets, blasting ambushers, leaping over tiger pits, that sort
of thing."

Custer sneaked a longing glance at the couch in the big room,
but von Alp was not to be deterred in his lecture.

Whether or not Mario finally reached his destination depended
on how many mistakes he made; too many, and he had to go back
to Square One. If he fought well, he'd reach home, paradise,
heaven, nirvana, you name it. By contrast, the little red box always
fought perfectly—in nanoseconds it flashed through all the possible combinations of digits to find the code word.

"That's how encryptors and decoders work nowadays," von Alp
finished.

Custer squinted at him. "You're wasting your time," he said,
"it's all gibberish to me. Tell it to the ten-year-olds they're training
at Rand and in the Pentagon, they'll understand. What I need is
the horizontal. Wake me if I doze off."

"Wake you up? What's wrong with that Las Vegas hairdryer of
yours?"

Smiling faintly, Custer had just enough strength to fold the perforated printout sheets labeled *Schlammer* into a neat sheaf. He
tossed it carelessly on the glass top of the low, rectangular table by
the couch, then folded his weary body into the welcoming cush-
ions. Why do I live like this, he asked himself. Why am I doing
this to myself? How did I ever get into this? Good questions that
would serve to keep him awake.

He'd been working for the Super Cartel ever since U.S. troops went
into Panama in 1989. One hazardous assignment after another. In

the dope trade, one little slip-up often spelled death. Yes, these days he found himself acting like a demigod. Talk about a false sense of security! In my case, he reflected ruefully, it's more like an authentic sense of being immortal.

Custer burrowed more deeply into the couch. Locking his hands behind his head, he closed his eyes: Yes, how had he got himself into this mess anyway, how did it all start?

He had established himself with the Super Cartel by developing a system for laundering money—assisted by his legendary good fortune, of course. To say nothing of his chutzpah. Why not go straight to the horse's mouth, into Bankland, he'd asked himself.

Swiss banks ran as perfectly—and predictably—as Swiss watches. He'd taken a couple of weeks to steep himself in relevant literature, reports, regulations and eyes-only data provided by discreet, well-informed friends from his Washington network. On his first trip to Switzerland, his strategy was simple: beat them at their own game. Establish your base of operations where they least expect it—inside a Swiss bank.

When he first broached this idea to the inner circle around Don Cali de Cali, most of them had shaken their heads at the crazy gringo. Most, but, notably, not Don Cali himself.

Even now, as he ran those scenes across his memory screen, Custer had to chuckle at the way Cali laid a fatherly hand on his shoulder when they left the conference room. You had to hand it to the leathery old vulture, he made no bones about how corrupt he was. However, Don Cali went far beyond mere primitive candor; he actually loved corruption. He was the kind of man who, given the choice of manipulating an innocent man into doing something illegal, or bribing him to do it, would rather bribe him. On top of that, Cali had an old axe to grind.

Some years ago, that fancy organization, the Swiss Banking Union, had refused to accept Don Juan Antonio Gabriel Cali de Cali as a client. None other than the chairman of the board personally had indicated that respect for the bank's hallowed traditions imposed the necessity for circumspection when considering entering into business relations with private parties whose résumés did not include at least a modicum of orderly professional history.

Fancy gringo talk, Cali had thought. He'd show the bastard!

Two months later, Don Cali registered a company called "The Institute" in Vaduz, Liechtenstein, only a stone's throw from SBU head offices in Switzerland. Not long after that, the sum of U.S.-

$20 million was transferred to The Institute's newly opened account with the Swiss Banking Union. And not long after that, the manager of The Institute, a blue-chip attorney based in Vaduz, Liechtenstein, received an invitation to lunch from the very same chairman of the board who had tried to smear Don Cali de Cali's honor with a lot of fancy gringo double-talk.

The chairman had expressed his appreciation of and gratitude for The Institute's interest in the Swiss Banking Union and assured the attorney of the bank's unfailing cooperation, now and in the future. As the luncheon progressed, the chairman discreetly expressed the hope that The Institute would recommend the SBU's services to some of its own clients, preferrably the major ones. Such efforts, he assured the attorney, would be appropriately rewarded with—at this point he lifted his fork, on which a small potato was delicately impaled—"a nice, plump referral fee." When it suited him, the chairman of the board of the Swiss Banking Union could speak quite earthily to the point.

Don Cali, who loved to tell this story in the company of friends and trusted associates, was clearly delighted by Custer's idea. As luck would have it, preparations had unwittingly been started some years before. Early in 1987, as de facto head of Panama's secret service, G-2, Custer had founded the Commerce & Trade Bank of Panama.

The CTBP was the result of a name change of an old, well-established Panamanian bank, the Garcia y Garcia Trading Bank of Panama. Principal shareholder of the newly evolved Commerce & Trade Bank was the Panamanian Chamber of Commerce, a semi-public institution, which defined the bank's purpose as the "advancement, support, and promotion of trade, commerce, and prosperity in Central America."

Next, Custer had the bank's investment reserves increased to U.S.-$100 million. Practically overnight, the CTBP was propelled upward into the exclusive circle of the twenty international banks with the highest ratio of self-financing. In the cartel's push to enter the great monetary arena of Switzerland, this move turned out to have been decisive, allowing as it were the establishment in Geneva of the CTBP Commerce & Trade Bank (Switzerland) Ltd.

The smooth implementation of Custer's concept was aided by the political climate at that time. Switzerland's foreign policy was in transition, with international cooperation being viewed as a top priority. Projects involving exports to Third World countries were strongly encouraged. The focus of Custer's CTBP-CTBS on promoting commerce and trade in the Central-American region happened to be right on target.

For Custer, this unexpected development came as a bonus. His original planning had relied mainly on the customary reciprocity in international business relations. With Swiss banks maintaining business offices in Panama, the government in Bern felt obliged to allow the establishment of a Panamanian bank in Switzerland.

The rest was largely a matter of paperwork. Custer still had a vivid picture of his meeting with the Swiss attorney, a relaxed and confident operator in his late thirties, looking cool and dapper as he detailed the requirements for establishing a bank in Switzerland. They sat at an antique round table with magnificently crafted marquetry, in the attorney's elegant office suite in Zurich's lakeshore district.

"What you need, Mr. Custer, is money and the right names." Apparently twenty million dollars start-up capital was sufficient; Dr. Grossenbacher seemed neither particularly impressed nor disappointed by this sum. So Custer figured the missing ingredient had to be the right names.

The attorney's gray-blue eyes held a mildly amused expression as he lectured Custer on the management policies of Swiss banks. "Faultless, expert management is, of course, the basic requirement, Mr. Custer. Individuals of unimpeachable character and expertise, with an impeccable business record, are a must. That's what is meant by the right names."

Custer's left hand went to his chin and rested there. "And where do I look for this type of highly qualified integrity?"

"That is something I can help you with," Grossenbacher said, apparently assuming that the investors who sponsored Custer would not measure up to the standards he had outlined. Even though Custer had been in a high-stakes poker game or two during his turbulent career, the attorney's casual condescension came as a mild shock to him. Feigning equanimity, he managed to ask what else might be required.

The attorney hesitated for a moment, then looked unabashedly at Custer. "Firstly, of course, the money." He jotted down an account number on a notepad, tore off the sheet and handed it to Custer.

"And second?" Custer asked, resisting the temptation to ape Grossenbacher's excessively precise grammar.

The attorney squared his shoulders and laid his final card on the table.

"Well, frankly, sir, how do I know that the establishment of this bank will be—how shall I put it—a matter above reproach? You do understand, I'm sure. At this point all I know about the background of this venture, and of your backers, is what you yourself have told me. Before we proceed, I must have some sort of impartial, independent, authoritative substantiation. What would you suggest?"

Well prepared for such an eventuality, Custer had suggested they meet again the following afternoon, in the vault of Daumier Reich & Cie, a good-as-gold private bank in Zurich. The safe-deposit box Custer opened on that occasion contained a single item, an envelope, which he handed the attorney. Grossenbacher tore off a corner, inserted the middle finger of his right hand and ripped the envelope open. Marveling at the primitive explosivity of this action, Custer watched the attorney's pupils contract as he absorbed the information on the paper he had extracted.

In his dealings with key players in the international money market, Dr. Grossenbacher had perused many letters of recommendation. He now had to admit to himself that this one was in a class of its own. In fact, it was unique. Which also made it slightly suspect. He slowly, carefully folded the paper back into its original oblong shape, looking earnestly at Custer.

"Can you authenticate this letter, sir?"

Ken took the folded-up sheet from the attorney, unfolded it, tapped a fingertip against the bottom edge. "This number is all you need."

The attorney uncapped a golden-nibbed fountain pen and entered the number in his black-and-gold embossed notebook. Then he read it aloud to Custer: "SM 3112-42."

"That's correct." Custer pointed at the letterhead. "Call them and ask for Verification, okay?"

Grossenbacher nodded.

Custer said, "When they answer, you give them everything in front of the dash."

"The dash?"

"Okay, the hyphen," Custer said, grinning obsequiously. "You read everything in front of the hyphen. If this document is genuine, Verification will then give you the numbers 4 and 2. If it isn't, they will hang up on you."

Grossenbacher's thin smile widened a millimeter or two, indicating approval. "Delighted, Mr. Custer. This will be entirely to my satisfaction."

They shook hands, and Custer closed and locked the safety-deposit box. Back in the street, a monstrous streetcar thundered past them. In its passing shadow, Custer pushed the attorney against a wall. Holding him off balance with one hand, he placed a heavy fist against Grossenbacher's chest, exerting painful pressure on the clavicle joint.

"Now get this and get it straight, Grossenbacher! You're my attorney. Everything that just happened down there in the vault stays down there. If you as much as breathe a word of this to anyone, you're through. I repeat—through."

Grossenbacher surprised Custer by gently seizing his wrist and lifting the fist off his chest, handling him the way a big kid might handle a little kid.

"Mr. Custer, sir," he said softly, but with a special, cutting emphasis, "we are in Switzerland, not in the Bronx. If you'll allow me, I assure you I will handle our business entirely to your satisfaction. However, you must understand that this little scene will cost you extra."

Caught mentally off guard by the attorney's quick barb, Custer stared at him for a split second. Then both men broke into laughter, defusing the situation. To his surprise, Grossenbacher found himself amused by this oafy, straightforward American.

At the height of the grand ball celebrating the opening of the CTBP Commerce & Trade Bank (Switzerland) Ltd. in Geneva, an affair attended by numerous Swiss and Latin American dignitaries, Dr. Grossenbacher received a telephone call from Ken Custer in Toronto.

The attorney had just stepped down from the rostrum after delivering an address in which he assured the assembled guests, in flawless French and Spanish, that the newly opened bank would do its utmost to continue the great tradition of friendly relations between Switzerland and Central America. Naturally, it would not have been discreet of him to mention how carefully he had picked key members of the bank's executive management, and how successful he had been, especially when he managed to persuade Fritz Wartenweil to join as chairman of the board. No one in Swiss and international banking circles could doubt that a person of Wartenweil's impeccable history and reputation guaranteed irreproachable business operations.

Custer kept the call short.

"You may proceed to the next phase we agreed on, Dr. Grossenbacher, establishing an investment bank in Zurich. The funds for that venture have been allocated and transmitted." In a thoughtful concession to the spirit of big money and good manners the attorney so smoothly embodied, he added, "I trust you'll continue to enjoy what I'm sure has already been a very pleasant evening. Good night."

Custer's strategy relied on a simple principle, best expressed by the word "credibility." The CTBP Commerce & Trade Bank (Switzerland) Ltd. started operations with a series of investments in attractive export ventures. Front corporations in Panama, Costa Rica, Mexico, and Venezuela purchased a wide range of Swiss products, including textile machinery, pharmaceuticals, PC-7 aircraft, food products, Eternit fiberboard, fertilizer, agricultural machinery and equipment, a shipload of SIG machine guns, as well as portable transceivers made by Schlammer Holdings.

CTBP in Panama City opened letters of credit for its Swiss business associates, which amounted to a cash-on-delivery arrangement. Not surprising, then, that Switzerland's export community went after these exciting opportunities with a vengeance. The CTBP-CTBS was literally deluged with business offers and proposals.

The crowning jewel of Ken Custer's credibility strategy, however, was the founding of CAARS, the Central American Air Rescue Service. Modeled on successful European air-rescue services, CAARS specialized in human emergency situations in the mountains and at sea. The flagship of the CAARS fleet, a vintage nine-passenger, three-engine Falcon 50 painted a dazzling white, made monthly trips to Geneva, where CAARS had cultivated contacts with the International Committee of the Red Cross, ICRC.

The comfortably appointed intercontinental jet carried coffee and precious stones to Switzerland, returning with medical supplies and containers full of donated clothing, blankets, and shoes. In the space of a few short months, this humanitarian shuttle traffic became an accepted workaday routine at Geneva Airport. Nobody bothered to pay any attention to what was being loaded, or unloaded for that matter. A number of small, gray, suitcase-shaped containers were transferred into limousines and taken into the city.

These containers were tightly packed with twenty- and one hundred-dollar bills, soon carefully hand-sorted, bundled and banderoled in the vaults of the CTBP Commerce & Trade Bank (Switzerland) Ltd. The paper band around each bundle of bills bore the legend VERIFIED: CTBP COMMERCE & TRADE BANK (SWITZERLAND) LTD.

Beginning in mid-1989, hundreds of millions of drug-cartel dollars flowed through this channel into Switzerland. The system worked so smoothly that Custer was obliged to restrain the enthusiasm of his Colombian associates, reminding them that, historically, many an excellent system had been wrecked by abuse. Don Cali subsequently succeeded in convincing his partners to put Custer in charge of all money-laundering operations in Switzerland.

The day Ken Custer's appointment as head honcho for the Swiss operation was confirmed, Cali made a little speech to the inner circle of his associates. "As you know, Operation 'Go Swiss' has been a blessed success for all of us. The man we have to thank for this is our brilliant financial strategist, Ken Custer."

Cali raised his hands to restrain the enthusiastic drumming of flat palms on the conference table—a traditional South American expression of approval.

"Some of you probably think of Señor Custer as a gringo, but I tell you from the bottom of my heart, this man is one of us!"

It was a momentous and unprecedented statement coming from Don Cali de Cali, who was known to be as unsentimental as they come. It installed Custer firmly as one of the half dozen top men in the Super Cartel, a position he had just begun to enjoy when the turbulence struck. . . .

"All systems go, we're leaving in twenty minutes," von Alp called into the front room. Custer pushed himself up, trying to shake off these pictures from the past. Von Alp stood in the large open space between the sliding doors, his arms aggressively akimbo.

"We're talking hot merchandise, Ken, aren't we?"

Custer squinted at his friend. His eyeballs felt hot, tired, and swollen to the size of golf balls. Von Alp stared back at him with his best soldier-of-fortune stone face.

"All right, Theo, you want me to spill it?"

"Do!"

"Well, you already know it's Schlammer. What you don't know is that one of Adam Schlammer's outfits, Schlammer Engineering, is in possession of two miniature nuclear devices which Schlammer is selling to my boss. I'm here to pick them up. That's our job. Voilà, my boy!"

Flabbergasted, von Alp heard himself exclaim, "Shit, it's Libya all over again!"

And Zaire, and Angola, and Kuwait, all wrapped in one, if what Ken was saying was true. Mini nukes? Shit! He let himself fall into an armchair, blowing out air like a trumpeting walrus. He began to massage his neck as if trying to move blood clots out of his carotid artery. Then he abruptly leaned forward.

"When you say boss, you mean Cali? The cocaine mafia, drugs? And nukes? If this is your idea of a joke, Ken, lemme tell you that I—"

Custer threw up his arms. "Whoa there, hold your horses, kid! A few years ago you couldn't have imagined Hussein would put the torch to seven hundred and forty oil wells, could you? It didn't make sense, it was irrational. Which is precisely my point—you can't rationalize the irrational. That's why it always catches us off guard. Let's get real about this: In Latin America, the name Cali de Cali is synonymous with power. The Super Cartel is a state unto itself. So, why shouldn't he want the type of weapons other nations have, like North Korea, Algeria, Brazil, Iran? It doesn't necessarily mean he wants to use these—you might as well get used to the latest buzzword—these carry-on nukes. That's the term, nuclear hand luggage . . ."

Von Alp grimly pumped his head up and down.

"Fine, all right, tell me just one thing. Why wouldn't he use your precious . . . carry-on nukes. Will you tell me that?"

"I'll tell you," Custer answered, wide awake now, his brain working with the precision of a Clissot atomic clock. "Because Don Cali de Cali is a megalomaniacal braggart and bully, a pathologically dysfunctional child. He wants to be the biggest kid on the block, playing with the biggest and flashiest toys money can buy or make. Others of his type are happy if they can play with Ferraris or race horses. Or with yachts, or dune buggies or, heaven be praised, with women! But Cali happens to be a weapons freak. He's Billy the Kid, a crazy with the biggest, newest, flashiest six-shooter you ever saw. He wants to blow a great big hole through that big ugly gringo head of yours. And mine. And Claudia's. And everybody else's. By the way, where is Claudia?"

"Fixing breakfast in the kitchen."

"Why aren't you fixing breakfast in the kitchen?"

"Because she likes to fix breakfast and I don't. Don't try to change the subject. You still haven't told me the real reason why Cali is trying to crash the nuclear party."

"Okay, I'll give it to you in one word: extortion. He wants to blackmail the Americans. Or maybe he just wants to have something up his sleeve to protect his little kingdom of heaven in case the Pentagon gets the idea they can send the marines into Colombia to wipe out the drug mafia like they did in Panama. Surely you haven't forgotten Panama 1989, old pineapple Noriega? So, you see, holding a couple of teensy-weensy little nukie-nukies behind his back might just turn out to be a very effective deterrent to Uncle Sam. But . . ."

"But what?"

"He'll never use them."

"And what makes you so sure?"

"It's my understanding the CIA and other agencies will snatch them from him long before he can get into nuclear mischief. Let's say Cali is just a little too clever for his own good. Which translates into he's just a dumb, superstitious, mountain Indio, and that's no reflection on the many wonderful, honest, hard-working, coca-leaf chewing Indios I know. Cali's got the blinders on. He's simply too simpleminded to get away with whatever it is he's planning. The CIA and—"

"Yeah, I can imagine," von Alp gestured impatiently, "we're looking at another El Dorado Canyon, like back there when, in Tripoli, huh, Ken? Are you telling me they're planning another cute little air raid, this time on an Indio named Cali instead of an Arab named Qaddafi?"

At that moment Claudia swooped into view. She was smiling radiantly. A silk scarf of iridescent emerald greens and velvety blacks artfully restrained her profusion of red hair. She was all designer denim, set off by turquoise and silver Navajo jewelry, a picture of country elegance and glowing health.

"Gentlemen, I'm serving breakfast in the kitchen."

Every bone in his body creaking and aching, Custer managed to get up from the couch. He put a hand on von Alp's shoulder, as much for support as to reassure his friend.

"Let's talk more later. First, we'll do the job. Which is what we're getting paid for, and handsomely, to say the least. Other bridges, we'll cross when we come to them."

Fifteen minutes later, stuffed with whole-wheat pancakes smothered in maple syrup, they walked across the terrace to the cars parked in front of the garage. Custer squinted up at the sky.

"Well, this is as good a day as any," he said, reciting their favorite Angolan formula for life and death. Whichever came first.

"As good a day as any, and better than most," von Alp cheerfully chanted back.

In his memory, Peter Kern had a clear picture of his wife. He saw her exactly the way she looked two years ago, when he had come home and found her dead in the pool. Drowned. Her naked body gleamed up at him through the clear, blue, chlorinated water. She lay face up, stretched out on the tiled bottom of the pool. And then . . . those water bugs, in iridescent purple, like mother-of-pearl buttons, swarming at her in perfect attack formation. The water had drained off. The army of bugs fell upon the corpse. In seconds—zap zap zap—nothing remained of her. Only some brownish dust on the tiles, dust that . . . grew, horribly, into the shape of baked mackerels, bulging hideously, bigger and bigger, turning into huge, disgustingly squishy, goggle-eyed brown fishes, thrashing about in the empty pool that brimmed over with them, flopping over the sides. . . .

Kern woke, bathed in sweat. What—where—was he?

"Come, darling," a soft, dark voice beckoned. Whose voice? He tried to focus: Was it Stephanie? A knee was gently thrust into the crack of his butt, a hand reached around his waist, got hold of his thickly erected penis. Fingers lovingly started strumming the foreskin, slowly, expertly, then more passionately.

Moaning voluptuously, Kern shifted sideways, pushing his pelvis up toward those gentle fingers. Now the hand exerted pressure on his turgid staff, drew it down until it touched his belly, then released it as if testing its spring action; pushed it down again, released it as Kern's rod ardently played the game.

Groaning with pleasure, the prime minister rotated his body toward the woman, kissed her on the lips. Ulla-Britt thrust her tongue deep into his mouth. His left hand slid over her small breasts, fingers encircling, tickling, gently twirling the taut nipples, while his right moved lightly as breath over the inside of her thighs, the thumb probing deeper into the trembling crevice of her groin.

"Come, darling, come, I want you inside," she whispered, pushing one leg across his hips, her body blindly searching for his throbbing member.

Kern lay on his back, pulling Ulla-Britt up on top of him. She let out a low, almost reluctant moan, as she straddled him, moving somnambulently in the age-old docking dance. His hands lustily kneaded her superbly firm, perfectly rounded buttocks, pressing her down, guiding her onto his penis. Exhaling noisily as if the air was being forced out of her, she arched her back in order to receive him to his full length.

For a heartbeat—two, three—it seemed as if her breath had stopped. Then a drawn-out, guttural groan escaped her, a booming sound like something giving way deep inside of her. Slowly, rhythmically, she began to slide up and down on his staff, labia clinging tight to it, her finely drawn lips moist, slightly apart, eyes closed.

Watching, fascinated, Kern reveled in the glow of that dear face, transformed in ecstasy, straw-blonde strands of hair falling into it. He loved her uninhibited Swedish spontaneity. Just last night, after she'd finished work at the clinic, she had suddenly appeared in his doorway, made him put down the confounded report he was reading. . . .

They came together. Kern felt as if each cell in his body had released its purest, sweetest essence into his system, all melting into a swell of bliss, a wave that mounted, carrying him forward, up, into exalted oblivion. For long moments, all imperfections were wiped away: the recurrent nightmare, the job, the ominous discovery he had made at Nucleanne, the bodyguard waiting for him outside.

Then the lovers lay, dissolved, spent, their limbs entwined. Until Kern once again sensed the faint ticking of his internal clock. Gently extricating himself from their embrace, he swung his legs over the edge of the bed, sat up and, sighing, pushed himself into the perpendicular.

"*Vart ska du, älskling?*" he heard her murmuring sleepily as he tiptoed into the bathroom. He loved it when she spoke Swedish, even if he understood only the *älskling*. On the other hand he was running late. He stepped quickly into the shower, adjusted the water to medium hot, thinking forward into the day: lots of meetings, lots of . . . a searing flash of pain traveled down his spine, into the groin.

"Damn stress," he muttered, soaping down the strained area with Green Apple Gel, his favorite. At moments like this, Kern cursed his life as a government executive, pronounced damnation upon his career, his ambition. At moments like this, he longed to simply be himself, a man like others, free to do whatever he pleased.

How childish of him! If he was who he was now, could he ever have been "simply himself"? Didn't he vaguely remember feeling like this when he was a boy? Well, no matter, duty was calling. Political frustration rather than sensual satiation would be his lot today, not lust but frust.

He glanced despondently at the Swatch on his wrist: Stephanie would be here any minute. Thank god Ulla-Britt's flashy electrocar was safely tucked away in the garage, so Stephanie wouldn't suspect a thing. On the other hand, an early morning tryst with both Ulla-Britt and Stephanie would be far better exercise than the dull jogging round coming up! Chuckling to himself, Kern considered the implications: a prime minister, an investigative reporter, and a clinical technician who was anything but clinical and far beyond mere technique. Ah, well, maybe that would be a little too much exercise, after all!

Abruptly, his nagging conscience made itself felt. If only he hadn't called off last night's dinner with Stephanie. When she'd called, he was totally immersed in the media circus surrounding the nuclear contraband incident on the Italian border. Discovery of a trafficking operation in radioactive materials had created a more than somewhat embarrassing operation, not simply because a Swiss border guard had opened fire and killed a man, but because it immediately became apparent that corrupt officials for years had covered for the operation. The Italian police quickly arrested several of their own: two secret service agents, a highly placed executive of the Italian treasury police and, last but far from least, the public prosecutor of the City of Como.

Kern was well aware of having been irritable with the charming newswoman the night before. He liked her, a lot. So why had he mauled her like that?

He'd tried to calm her with, "Believe me, it pains me in my soul," and felt himself failing as he said the words.

"Earth to Kern, earth to Kern," she had mocked, "this is me, Stephanie, remember? It's Saturday night and we have a date, yes? We're supposed to meet in Les Vacances, you do recall. The place where the filthy rich and the glitterati, and the filthy rich glitterati, can barely wait to see you so they can stroke your beard and kiss your cute behind? So if that's what hurts you, it's your vanity, not your soul. Which is something I can believe and understand."

"Now I'm really hurt," he had laughed.

Ulla-Britt was great, but Stephanie was a woman after his taste and his heart—tough and pliant, rough and gentle, and mysterious, all in one breath. Ruefully, he had tried to call her later, from the mess of a vicious conference, letting the phone ring a dozen times or more. He might have guessed she'd go out, not even bothering to turn on her answering machine.

Tonight, however, he'd make up for everything. Yes, he told himself as he pulled on his jogging pants, tonight, come what may, sweet Steph will be in my bed!

Stephanie was also suffering the pangs of a guilty conscience, but one of a more social sort, as she wrestled her little Audi through the dense morning traffic. She'd be late! Checking her jade-granite quartz watch one time too many, she narrowly avoided rear-ending the car in front of her.

I should have gone to see him last night, and everything would have run its natural course! she told herself.

As she passed the car she had almost bumped, the driver, a mountain man with a red face and an enormous bushy red beard, gave her what up there in the higher altitudes no doubt was exactly what it meant down here: a lascivious, drooling grin. She couldn't help herself and stuck out her tongue. After all, in Tibet sticking out one's tongue was a popular way of saying hello. Meanwhile, the Audi performed small miracles of circumvention until the entire twin column of cars came to a sudden halt.

"What's going on?" Stephanie asked of a young man on a bicycle who was moving deftly through the narrow spaces between the cars.

Without looking at her he brusquely shouted, "Accident," then did a doubletake. "Ah, would the lady like a ride?"

Stephanie had to laugh loudly at the kid's innocently lecherous grin. Bless those hormones! All her stress was suddenly wiped away.

Why worry anyway, with a little luck she'd get there in time. Up ahead, at an intersection, two cars were being pushed out of traffic and deposited against the curb—wounded warriors suffering from battle fatigue. Traffic began to move again. She turned on the radio. A monotonous androgynous voice reported on a rocket mishap in southern California. Only half-listening, Stephanie had her hands full taking herself through the shards of glass around the disabled cars. She pressed on with a series of skillful and risky maneuvers. To her right, the pale gold of ripening wheat set off broad, red roofs of farm houses. Braking, she pulled up to within inches of the car in front, then accelerated as the gap between them began to widen again. She was starting to feel tough in her green-and-black jumpsuit and white Hermes designer sneakers, all of which Kern jokingly referred to as her jungle combat outfit.

The prime minister was just then securing the laces on his air-cushioned jogging boots, thinking of how he'd make it up to Stephanie. He'd simply let her in on what he discovered the previous afternoon in the west of Switzerland. Lightly bobbing up and down to test the fit of his boots, Kern was thinking what a perfect leak this would be, coming directly from the horse's mouth: his.

He checked his watch. Ten to seven—she was twenty minutes late!

He did a few warm-up exercises, rotating low at the waist, then stretching up on his toes. It still bothered him that, yesterday, he hadn't had the presence of mind to insist upon an explanation for the purpose of the mysterious laboratory he had stumbled onto. Especially since they'd even asked if there was anything else they could do for the prime minister. Those disgustingly obsequious bootlickers! He must have caught them totally by surprise, else why would he have been able to walk right through a dangerous-radiation security area into a lab nobody knew existed?

Kern slipped on a blue Nike top. He went into the kitchen to pour himself an extra glass of orange juice. Even the head of the Swiss Federal Council would have to pass through a number of control points and ID checks before being admitted to a restricted area, so there should have been no way for him to stroll into a radioactive waste materials processing plant!

As he opened the front door in response to the chimes, the clock on the belfry of nearby Saint Georgius church struck seven. Kern stepped outside to welcome Lieutenant Bachmann, a Special Services officer in the Federal Police. Even though Kern had often told him not to, Bachmann saluted briskly.

"Good morning, sir. Perfect jogging weather, I'd say."

"Morning, Lieutenant." Kern inhaled deeply, turning his face into a gentle, warm breeze that blew in from the west. "Let's take the river route."

"Yes, sir. Will we be a threesome this morning, sir?"

"Doesn't look like it. Ms. Kramer was supposed to join us, however . . ."

He cast a hopeful glance up the nearby road, knowing full well that it was virtually impossible to distinguish a car moving toward the house on the far side of all that city-bound traffic. Too late to chat over breakfast. He was in a hurry: that nuclear waste disposal operation needed some serious looking into. He'd be at his desk at eight sharp, and those coffee-break experts in Documentation had better pick up on the first ring!

Kern's adrenaline was starting to pump. He pushed the door shut and motioned to Bachmann to get going. They crossed the circular patch of carefully tended lawn in front of the house, jogging in a loose lope that gave Kern's gangly frame a slightly comic, ostrich-like appearance. At the far edge of the estate grounds they turned into a gravel path lined with fruit trees leading up to and over a rise in the terrain.

Still partially shrouded in morning mists, the silhouette of nearby Bern beckoned with the distinctive outline of its Parliament building, which also housed Kern's suite of offices, conference rooms, and salons. In the far distance beyond the capital the bright glare of morning sunlight highlighted the towering contours of the Bernese Alps. So dramatically, yet so delicately, did light and shadow contrast in this panorama, that it seemed as if a great bastion of snow clouds furrowed by bluish crevasses had descended from the sky and come to rest on earth—all expressly for the glory of the city of Bern.

The wind blowing through the open window didn't do much to relieve Stephanie's frustration. First that stupid conversation with Peter last night, and now this mess on the road! The car in front of her slowly began to move to the right, preparing to exit. Stephanie thumped her horn with her fist, accelerating to pass the slowpoke, and nearly sideswiping him. So men were better drivers than women, were they!

On the outward-bound lanes the road now lay open before her. She gunned the Audi up the grade, cresting the hill dotted with fruit trees, then descended at high speed. The Audi's tires actually squealed as she swung into the narrow approach to Kern's mansion. Beyond the lush greenery in which it nestled sparkled the river. Trees swished past the open window of the speeding car.

A moment later the Audi slid to a crunching stop in the gravel pathway around the circular lawn. Nothing moved in or around the house; the place felt deserted. With a sigh of resignation, Stephanie jumped out, triggered the electronic lock, and started running toward the meadow and the path up the hill, taking the route she knew well from previous jogging outings with the prime minister.

Lieutenant Bachmann, who was in superb shape, got a kick out of jogging alongside the athletic, popular prime minister. They would be running about forty-five minutes, with Bachmann acting as bodyguard as well as running mate. A Glockner 7.65 mm handgun was strapped to his waist, positioned for minimum interference while running. In addition, he carried a high-powered transmitter-receiver unit with a built-in recording function, the entire set disguised as a Sony Walkman. As far as Bachmann was concerned, one couldn't be too careful these days. Since the assassination of the Swedish prime minister in the eighties, anything seemed possible, even in peaceful, neutral Switzerland.

Of course, no one ever seriously expected anything serious to happen. Ministers of state running around in the countryside at seven A.M. constituted, at worst, a health hazard to themselves. They might have a heart attack, or injure themselves in a fall!

The path now swung in a wide arc down toward the river. With gravity on their side, Kern and Bachmann were moving lightly down the incline, enjoying a magnificent view of the swiftly flowing, dark-green waters.

At first, Kern had objected to being assigned a bodyguard. In Switzerland, ministers of state were used to moving about freely wherever and whenever they liked. During the past hundred years no Swiss M.P. had ever been attacked, let alone assassinated. Still, he quickly learned to appreciate the lieutenant as a man who knew when to speak and when to listen—especially the latter.

Bachmann made an ideal sounding board for the prime minister's ideas. On a day like this, facing a conference on nuclear terrorism, one that had been called on extremely short notice under the auspices of the U.S. embassy, Kern really welcomed the lieutenant's company. Regrettably, he thought, stumbling into this suspicious nuclear setup fits right in with the conference theme. Could it be that the Americans know more than our own . . . ? But no, that wasn't possible: this was still Switzerland, after all, the hitherto impregnable fortress, a tradition that, hopefully, held for internal security as well.

Kern felt light and enterprising, on his feet as well as in his mind. Even the thought that the subterranean facilities he had discovered by surprise might be supplying equipment, components, or whatever to nuclear terrorists did little to dampen his sense of physical well-being as they trotted through the idyllic countryside.

"Tell me, Lieutenant," he said, "does the term 'carry-on nukes' mean anything to you?"

Bachmann shook his head.

The path was just wide enough to allow them to run side by side. Now and then their shoulders touched, often when low branches or underbrush along the sides forced them to the middle. As they shifted to a higher speed, the soft, dew-soaked ground under the gravel did much to cushion their pounding stride. Kern was panting now, yet he insisted on lecturing to his subordinate.

"So-called carry-on nukes are miniature nuclear devices that can be carried like hand luggage. This type of miniaturization of nuclear bombs wasn't possible until quite recently, due to advances in microtechnology."

Kern's breath came in short, forceful bursts. Bachmann, who kept silent, was hoping the man entrusted to him would slow down. A heart attack would not look good on the record. But Kern was enjoying listening to the sound of accelerated blood rushing through his veins, which mingled with the low murmur of the fast-flowing river to their left.

"Listen to this, Lieutenant! On impulse, yesterday, I visited one of our strategic underground installations in western Switzerland. Nobody there knew I was coming. I caught them, so to speak, with their pants down. Would you believe it possible that someone there is tinkering with nuclear bombs?"

Bachmann noted with professional detachment that Kern's breathing sounded labored. It reminded the bodyguard of the defective irrigation pump in his vegetable garden, which his wife had been after him to fix. Kern's habit of spicing up a leisurely jog with intensive bursts of speed was not his idea of safety for a top echelon administrator. So Bachmann slowed down a little.

"Frankly, sir," he replied, "I'd say that's a lot of poppycock, just the type of science fiction you might read—well, actually, I really don't know, sir. But if you're concerned . . ."

As he spoke, and without breaking stride, he activated the recording function on the innocent-looking Walkman. This type of information, no matter who conveyed it, could get a man in trouble if he wasn't careful, and Lieutenant Bachmann was certainly a careful man. As they swung away from the river, following the path upward toward the crest of the wooded hillside, Bachmann decided to get the location of Kern's mysterious nuclear facility on tape. And the prime minister replied without the slightest hesitation to the lieutenant's direct question, even though the steepening terrain made them shorten their stride.

Stephanie was literally sprinting after the two men. As she reached a turn in the path, she saw them entering a forested area. She shouted after them but they gave no indication of having heard her. Determined to catch up with them, she cut away from the path, ran across a sloping meadow and arrived at the point where they had entered the forest. She was close on their heels.

Kern attacked the forest hillside. It seemed to him as if he'd heard a voice calling after them, but he was too busy chasing his second wind and concentrating on yesterday's events to bother with anything else.

"Lieutenant Bachmann . . . ," he huffed.

"Yes, sir." Bachmann was unused to Kern calling him both Lieutenant and Bachmann in the same breath: normally it was either Bachmann or Lieutenant. The prime minister was not a man to stand on protocol. In fact, political opponents occasionally stooped to calling him a hippie, to which Kern had once responded by pantomiming a deep drag on an invisible marijuana cigarette.

"I want you to dig into this for me!" Kern's breathing sounded critical; each word was forcefully expelled, the sentences came piecemeal. "Get all the information you can, do whatever you have to do on my full authority, using extreme caution. Report directly to me, no one else. And not a word about this to anyone. That includes this conversation."

Running full tilt now, Stephanie had only one thought—to catch up. Her conscious mind fully focused on this task, releasing unconscious images. Before her inner eye, a darkly shrouded picture emerged. As she ran on, the picture grew more distinct: it was of herself, running, as seen from above. Yet, somehow, the path on which she ran had an ethereal quality, pulsing with a vibrant luminosity. There was the forest, seen from a height, and there was she herself who, in normal vision, would not have been visible under the dense cover of tree foliage. As she ran in the physical world, so did her visionary counterpart in that ethereal realm of which she had had glimpses and indications all her life.

When she'd sprinted away from Kern's mansion, all she thought of was business: Arik's conspiracy theory and what Peter would have to say about it. She was sure he would offer to help her in any way he could. But now, as she saw her ethereal double sprinting along a brilliant path that might be the very path of her life, she felt awe—and consternation. What was she doing, rushing through life like this?

Kern had to fight for every breath as he spoke.

"This is hazardous business. You'll be risking your life. What I saw yesterday spells death. We're dealing with a ruthless organization. A fight in the jungle is what we're in for. And once you start there's . . . no . . . turning . . . back. So. Can I count on you?"

Straining mightily, Kern reached the top of the hillside slightly ahead of his bodyguard, whose efforts to slow him down he had noticed and ignored. A level stretch of sun-dappled path now lay before them. Patches of sunlight falling through the trees warmed their backs. As they jogged along on level ground, Kern's breathing began to recapture a more normal rhythm.

Bachmann was again running at Kern's side. The lieutenant's loyalty to Switzerland and to the man he was protecting could never have been questioned by anyone but himself. The path began to turn sharply to the right. Bachmann's right hand checked the Walkman to make sure it would record his reply to the prime minister.

As the two men leaned into the turn, they saw a darkly swathed figure wearing a brown skiing hood. The man cowered on the path no more than ten meters ahead. From the Walkman to the Glockner 7.65 was a distance Bachmann's hand might have traveled in less than half a second—yet even that was not enough to forestall destiny.

Even as the assassin fired a long burst from a black Uzi, Bachmann flung himself diagonally forward to shield the prime minister. A dozen rounds smashed into them, transforming them from living men instinctively diving for cover into slack bodies flopping on the ground.

The burst of gunfire ahead tore Stephanie's vision apart. She found herself acting as if in a waking dream: her hearing painfully acute, her brain computing the available information at lightning speed. With two, three tremendous leaps she cut to the right into the forest, crouching low as she clambered over the hill. Her mind was clear, detached; her body lithe and strong.

Later, she would reflect that she had been frightened out of her wits. Later, she would find that everything she wore was soaked with sweat and reeked of something she could only define as the stench of mortal fear. Later, much later, she would vomit—again and again. But in this moment, in this instant of action, all she knew was that there were two more shots—first one—just as she cautiously parted some bushes with trembling hands—then another. Then . . .

A savage scream of hopeless terror died behind her tightly compressed lips. The tableau she beheld on the path below etched itself indelibly in her mind. A man with a skiing hood, in bulky, dark coveralls, stood beside two bodies that lay draped on the ground in the loose and casual finality of dead flesh. The man fired again: a single shot from his automatic weapon.

Stephanie watched what happened to Kern. She saw Peter's head jerk, blood and brains splattering in a sickening, soupy splash, as if somebody had emptied a pail of pig slop on the path. Then, turning slightly at the waist, the killer repeated the procedure and tore apart Lieutenant Bachmann's head.

So this is what happens to a great . . . brain, she was thinking, a Brain of Peace! A brain that loved Switzerland. And, me?

Yes. Given time it might have. He, the whole man, would have! She was certain. Yes she was.

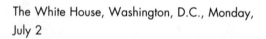

The White House, Washington, D.C., Monday, July 2

Louis XIII had listened to Cardinal Richelieu; Czar Nicholas II was led by Rasputin; Nixon had Kissinger; and the current president of the United States confided in Jack Weisborn. Some people called him Wisebrain, not necessarily out of envy or disrespect. Like John Wayne, Enrico Caruso, Al Capone, General MacArthur, Marilyn Monroe, and Charlie Chaplin, Weisborn carried the cross of having become a legend in his own time, at least among those Washingtonians in the know. It should be noted that he carried it with a great deal of dignity and wit.

So, whenever the president got tired of listening to the carefully researched and well-balanced advice offered by his closest advisers; whenever he needed some inspiration, a vision, he'd call for his brainy counselor, just as he had done this late Sunday night. Weisborn had arrived shortly after eleven, and their animated conversation had been in progress for over two hours now. The antique carriage clock on the mantelpiece above the fireplace—the same clock that had tolled its fateful hours for Abraham Lincoln—now indicated ten past one on Monday morning. In Europe, people were up and getting ready to go to work. If they had a job, that is.

The president set a glass of bourbon from which he had not drunk on a coffee table placed slightly off-center between three armchairs. "Let's get serious, Jack," he said, "tell me straight out— what're we doing wrong in the Middle East?"

"Well, sir, if you ask me, we've been had—by both Qaddafi and Hussein. To stay in power over there, you don't need terrorism, or oil, or some cockamamie Praetorian Guard that can't punch its way out of a wet paper bag, electronically speaking. What you need is us!"

As usual, Weisborn was speaking in the low tone of voice the president had come to identify as passionate restraint.

"We're faithfully stuck in the role of villain," Weisborn explained. "As the bad guy we help them divert attention from their domestic problems. The people in these countries are far from stupid, and they like a strong leader—"

"Isn't that what people in the West want?"

"Certainly, sir, but when you look at Western leadership, what do you see? The same washed-out types with the same gray hair! At least the Libyans and Iraqis aren't led by paler-than-life upper-management bores in dull-looking suits. If we continue demonizing every colorful, heavy-handed head of state in the Middle East, all we'll do is get the people to stand up even more fiercely for their Husseins and Qaddafis."

Instead of drinking from his glass, the president was slowly turning it this way and that on the table, making it move to the baleful ticking of Abe Lincoln's clock.

Weisborn continued, a faraway light in his eyes. "So, since people everywhere want strong men and women in power, the ideal leader for today would be someone charismatic and laid-back. Someone to lead the children of the world out of the mess, a blend of Indiana Jones, Einstein, Don Juan, and Moses."

"Or Schindler," the president smiled.

Undeterred by the president's pitiful attempt at post-topical humor, Weisborn added, "When you come right down to it, we actually envy the Arabic states their potentates."

The president still had not made up his mind about the bourbon before him. As the seconds ticked away and his hands kept twirling the glass, the question of to sip or not to sip began to loom hugely out of proportion. He was tired to the marrow of his bones. A slug of this stuff would either revive or kill him. As a man he was ready to take that chance. As the president of the United States he hesitated.

Making himself sound casual, he said, "The other day you talked about Iran trying to develop a nuclear capacity. Anything new on that front?"

"Yes, indeed. They're working on putting two German-made 1300-megawatt reactors on line in Bushir, and they're repairing two more reactors that were damaged in the war with Iraq. They've got uranium enrichment facilities in Isfahan, Tehran, Charg and Darchovin. China is delivering a neutron reactor and an isotope separator to them. They're getting a 300-megawatt reactor from North Korea. French companies are delivering enriched uranium, which means . . ."

"Scary, Jack, ain't it?"

Weisborn gave a shrug that indicated he hadn't been scared, or even alarmed, for some time. "They've also hired a couple dozen unemployed nuclear scientists from the former Evil Empire to work on the program in Tehran."

"What program?"

"Their program to develop a nuclear strike capacity. The Agency—I mean the CIA—estimates they'll go nuclear in a couple of years, at most three. In addition . . ."

"In addition?" The president's hands stopped fondling the glass. He lifted his head, displaying features that would serve well as a case study on the effects of long-term sleep deprivation in any major medical journal.

"In addition, sir, in 1992, Kazakhstan delivered two tactical nuclear warhead sections into an Iranian port on the Caspian Sea. As far as we know, their specialists still haven't been able to crack the lock-code, so we assume there hasn't been any warhead mating. But they're certainly trying to join the nuclear club through the back door."

"You're hedging, Jack. Let's have it! What do you see as the main threat to our security?"

"The main threat, Mr. President? Probably that we don't know who our friends are anymore. Or our enemies. The collapse of the Soviet Union seems to have pulled the rug out from under all the leading nations."

"Quit stalling, Weisborn. Who or what is the threat?"

"You know my answer, sir. The drug syndicates are at the top of the list. They feed crime, corrupt our youth. Drug and drug-related crime has turned the entire nation, including the rural areas, into an urban cesspool. Look at us! We're barricading ourselves in our homes while terrorists run amok in hospitals, movie theaters, shopping malls. Places where we used to feel perfectly safe, sir. Family places! Pull it all up by the roots, is what I say. Smash the drug production centers of South America!"

The president nodded, either in agreement with Weisborn's definition of the problem or with his solution. It would have been hard to say which.

Weisborn continued, "Right after drugs, I'd list Islamic terrorist activities as practiced or planned in Tehran. Drug cartels and Muslim fundamentalist fanatics—either or both—could resort to nuclear terrorism."

It was the glass of bourbon that finally made up the president's mind for him. The ice cubes had melted; the drink was growing warm. Since he hated room-temperature bourbon, he now lifted the glass and drank about a third of the liquid. It didn't kill him. Quite the contrary; a mellow warmth spread down his throat and throughout his chest. He eyed his adviser with something resembling renewed interest. Funny bird, that owly old Weisborn with those heavy, hooded lids of his! Never knew where you had him.

"All right then, what about Libya and Iraq?"

"Let's face it, Iraq's spine was broken in the war, so Iran is the real danger. Oil power and Islamic fundamentalist zeal combined with nuclear ambitions—that's an explosive mix, Mr. President. I think it's high time we subject our current relations with Iran to what used to be called an agonizing reappraisal. Are we going to stand idly by while they stockpile nuclear warheads, purchase delivery systems from North Korea, buy up nuclear specialists in Russia, and generally busy themselves developing a formidable nuclear strike capacity—all of this with a cash flow amounting to approximately four billion dollars a year, from American oil trade?"

"Aren't you exaggerating a little?"

"Pardon me, Mr. President, but I may just be understating our case here. I should mention that, while Baghdad is clearly out of the picture, Tehran is doing its best to rekindle our conflict with Iraq, trying to keep it alive by any means necessary. My best guess is Tehran will try to provoke us into some sort of hostile action targeting Iraq."

"I'm with you. But how?" The president was still nursing his bourbon, telling himself that just about anyone could sooth an off night with Kentucky's pride and joy.

"There are some, I say some, indications that Iraqi commandos may be planning a massive terrorist operation in this country. Again I'm guessing, but I believe such an operation would be planned not by Iraq but by Iranian extremists trying to get us to commit against Iraq. The head of secret operations is a man named Reza Fahimi, Colonel Fahimi. He's based in Tehran."

"Fahimi?" The president's brows slowly went up. "How come I'm drawing a blank on that name, Jack?"

The clock on the mantelpiece indicated half past one, but Jack Weisborn looked fresh as a daisy as he smiled at the weary president. "In all the hard print we put in circulation, we have a code name for Fahimi, sir, which I'm sure you'll recall in context. It's 'Blood.' "

"Blood?"

"Yes, sir, Blood."

"Like *Captain Blood*, the movie, with Errol Flynn?"

"Just Blood, sir. We're leaving out the rank."

"Fine. So, what is this, this . . . Blood's plan?"

"It's too early to tell. One scenario might have us hitting Baghdad in retaliation for an, quote on quote, 'Iraqi' terrorist attack in the United States, ostensibly to avenge their loss in the Gulf War. The Iranian fanatics behind the operation would fan the conflict, hoping to emerge as nuclear top dog in the Middle East."

The president rose abruptly, balancing his glass with a steady hand. Weisborn, who prided himself on being a teetotaler, non-smoker and vegan, was unimpressed by his superior's obviously superb physical coordination.

"That's a scary picture you're painting, Jack."

Maybe you scare easy, baby, Weisborn thought. Aloud he said, "I agree, sir, it's certainly not a pretty picture. More immediately, we've got a real problem. Let's say my informed guess is correct, how do we prevent this fake-Iraqi attack on a target in the U.S.?"

"Well, let's see now. How about cutting this Blood, this Fahimi person, off at the pass? We might implement a plan of our own before those crazy Iranians go through with theirs."

Up to this point in their nocturnal ruminations, Weisborn had had no trouble staying on top of the conversation. Now he saw himself in danger of being outflanked by this squishy, soft-skinned,

shilly-shallying master of evasion, procrastination, and appease-
ment they called the most powerful man in the world. Still,
Weisborn had to give him credit. Scorching Persia (because he
viewed nations in historical terms, Weisborn thought of Iran as
Persia) might just be a brilliant idea.

"You mean nuke 'em, sir?"

The supreme commander gave his adviser a long, searching look.
He was thinking that sometimes Old Wisebrain displayed a sense
of humor that verged dangerously on the macabre. You never knew
what was going on behind those lizard lids of his.

"I mean no such thing, Jack. Rather, I was thinking we could
initiate some sort of accommodation with Iraq. Start normalizing
relations, you know."

Stepping lively to keep up, Weisborn jumped on the idea, silly
though it seemed to him.

"A daring move, yes, brilliant, sir! We lift the embargo, offer our
assistance with rebuilding their infrastructure. We invest, make
friends, right?"

"That's the general idea. This would neutralize the sort of Iranian scheme you project. It would also be the kind of move I've
been envisioning for some time. You know I don't like all that saber
rattling over there. So let's just tread softly on this one, not even
mention the big stick we're carrying." He set down his glass and
allowed himself a huge stretch and yawn. It was getting late, too
darn late for any meaningful exchange of ideas!

Weisborn hunched his shoulders like an accountant tracing assets on a set of annual report printouts. He shook his head.

"We're still overestimating the Iraqis as a military power. They
won't know how to handle state-of-the-art weapons for quite some
time, if ever. Their soldiers are badly trained, the entire army simply not up to par. However, and this is a big however, a handful
of technologically sophisticated specialist fanatics could cause a lot
of mischief with rockets, so we should . . ."

"I was thinking of the Russians, Jack. People like Zhirinovsky."

Weisborn nodded. "Of course. They're riding a fascist wave, and
they're picking up the ball where the Nazis dropped it. When Hitler got strong on the streets of Berlin, the commies went over to
him by the thousands. Today, that phenomenon is repeating itself
in Moscow."

"Yes. Perhaps. Certainly the formative principles of a new Russian liberalism are under heavy fire over there. Right-wing extrem-

ism is clearly on the rise and beginning to inform their foreign policy. Sooner or later those forces will clash with Islamic extremism. Or worse—join with it in a common cause! The Russians have the arsenal to supply arms, like tactical nuclear systems. I'm also thinking of the radical, fanatical Muslims who are threatening Egypt and the Maghreb. I'm referring to Iran and Sudan, where terrorist operations are conceived, then exported."

"Yes," nodded Weisborn, "that's a very real threat. Extremists throughout the Middle East, in Libya, in the Maghreb, in the former Yugoslavia and in many other places might form an alliance and confront us with a nuclear capacity as a *fait accompli*."

"As a what?"

"A *fait accompli*, sir. That's French for *fact of life*."

"If you're trying to scare me with the specter of a global conflict, keep it up, you're doing just fine."

"Thank you, Mr. President," said the unsmiling Weisborn. "But that's certainly a possibility. The collapse of the Soviet Union caught us totally unawares. A lot of people think we may never recover from it. We loved to hate them so much for so long, we became addicted to it. And we're still suffering such painful withdrawal symptoms that we haven't noticed how Iran has been trying to fit in Russia's boots as the global provocateur."

Having finally downed the bourbon, the president was now chewing on a $2.95 red-white-and-blue starred and striped ballpoint pen with the image of the Statue of Liberty imprinted on its cap. Endowed by nature and a team of three superlative orthodontists with a set of strong, even teeth that had been a major asset when he was slugging his way into the presidency, he had gnawed the cap down to a point where the flame on the torch of freedom, had it been real, would have cast a very feeble light indeed.

He said to his adviser, "You're saying Islam will eventually encircle Europe, grip it in a crescent vise? Aren't you forgetting our military strength in the Middle East? Sorry, Jack, I just don't see how we can lose control in that region. Unless, of course, we want to."

"Maybe not, Mr. President. But we certainly had to fight for control in Kuwait, didn't we? Besides, the same fundamentalist fanatics that are scheming over there are now operating right here at home, in our very own cities. I saw it on the news last night— there are still cracks in the basement of the World Trade Center.

And the most powerful ally of those crazies in this country is the drug trade."

"How so?"

"Radical Muslims promote, encourage, and support the deterioration of American society. That's how they recruit. The breakdown of law and order due to drugs and drug-related crime literally drives the desperate and the destitute into the arms of these lunatics."

Weisborn fidgeted in his armchair, crossing his legs and clearing his throat before continuing.

"With all due respect, Mr. President, sir, it doesn't make sense to me for us to play global cop, enforcing law and order worldwide, while at the same time, at home, we stand idly by as drugs destroy the youth of this great nation of ours. Instead of wracking our brains over whether or not the Russians will keep their promises and withdraw from the Baltic states, isn't it high time we start cleaning house right here in the United States?"

The two men studied each other like fighters at the opening of the final round of a championship bout. They were tired; awfully, hideously tired—yet both knew that, in some fashion, one of them would emerge the victor. Weisborn was massaging the high, broad dome of his forehead. He was certain that he had laid a solid foundation in the president's subconscious. Choosing words like so many slick, sweet lozenges carrying potent time-release messages that would unfold later—the next day, and the day thereafter—was one of his most practiced and respected skills.

Still, even as he sat mentally preparing for the final assault, Weisborn felt nothing but disgust for the sad-faced, mealy-mouthed humanitarian the American people had chosen to lead them into the apocalypse. Well, it was not too late. He, Theodore Jonathan Weisborn, still stood watch on the bridge, next to this pathetic . . .

"So, tell me, Jack, do you seriously believe an act of nuclear terrorism in this country is a realistic possibility?"

Weisborn was ready. He, too, got up out of his chair. Even though in his stockinged feet he might have been a touch shorter than the president, the discreetly sloping two-inch heels of his custom-made shoes gave him a distinct advantage as his gaze met the other man's from under heavily hooded lids.

"The truth is, Mr. President, the situation has deteriorated, I mean dramatically deteriorated. We've lived for some time with the horror vision of nuclear incendiaries in our major urban centers. You will recall when Qaddafi agents attempted to smuggle a nuclear device into New York City in order to blackmail the U.S. Government. That time we escaped by the skin of our teeth! Only ten years ago even the smallest fission bomb weighed around 280 kilos, which is more than 600 pounds American weight. Today, thanks to microtechnology, a device with the same yield, say a low-yield bomb of around eight to ten kilotons, can be carried in a suitcase or a backpack. Such carry-on systems have given nuclear terrorism a rather, pardon me, impressive mobility. Our job now is to make absolutely certain these minisystems will not be manufactured, sold, given away, or delivered by anyone on this planet."

The president squinted cagily. "Not even by ourselves?"

Weisborn appeared to be in no mood for jokes. "Not by anyone, sir."

"And how would we go about implementing such a rule?"

"Any commerce in fissionable materials or fission products that can be used in the manufacture of nuclear weapons must be outlawed. We could employ the available information agencies, I mean the CIA, the FBI, the NSA and others, to monitor infractions. Let's indulge in a bit of innovative thinking, sir, use our imagination. I'd like to see our entire top-heavy information, surveillance, and monitoring apparatus divert some energy from the rut they're in. Let's face it, espionage and counterespionage are no longer the dynamic growth area they were, say, ten years ago. We need to go into nuclear regulations enforcement, an attractive and challenging new field. At the end of the day, sir, we should be able to say we're a step or two ahead of the competition, whoever and wherever they may be."

His back wearily resting against the mantelpiece, the president looked like a beaten man—or might have, to an uninitiated observer. To himself, he finally arrived at that stage where all that mattered was sleep. He had listened to Weisborn, taken in everything his clever counselor so eloquently, or was it loquatiously, proffered. He even felt the cumulative tug of Weisborn's attempt to manipulate him. Years ago he had learned that the best way to handle this brilliant schemer was to get a good night's sleep after whatever it was he recommended; then decide.

The president's tactic had been to turn his back to the carriage clock on the mantelpiece about five minutes before it would strike two, which it did a moment after Weisborn finished. First, a tiny silver bell pealed four times, to indicate the full hour; then, after a three-heartbeat pause, the large bell melodiously chimed twice. How many times, the president wondered, had the great Abe Lincoln stood like this at 2 A.M., pondering the fate of the nation, listening to this very clock ring out the hour? And how many times had he then, finally, decided to call it a day?

"All right, Jack. Thanks and good night."

"Just one more thing, Mr. President . . ."

"You heard the clock, Mr. Weisborn," said the president with finality. "Good morning and good night!"

Bern, Switzerland, Monday, July 2

Just about the time the president of the
United States was thinking of how best to
terminate his meeting with Jack Weisborn,
Stephanie Kramer lay flattened in a hollow
in the Swiss forest floor, less than a stone's throw from the site
where Peter Kern and his bodyguard had just been assassinated.
An eerie silence had settled on the scene, emphasized by the distant, rushing sound of the river. Rigid with fear and desperation,
she peered down to where the killer squatted on the path, surveying
the scene with professional calm.

She was still in the adrenaline trance of survival, her neurotrans-
mitters speeding urgent messages at an accelerated pace through
her synaptic system, suppressing nausea, cleansing her thoughts of
all but those elements that would ensure the continuing functioning of her body. Fight or flight? That wasn't the question. Flight
and fight was the best she could hope for.

She glanced at the green face of her wristwatch—twenty minutes
to eight—then down to the assassin, noting his physical charac-
teristics. He had rolled up the hood he wore. She saw strands of
black hair, coldly glinting dark eyes, pale skin, a tiny golden hoop
in one ear. The man got up, stepped close to the prime minister's

body and flipped it over with a disdainful twist of his boot so it came to rest on its back. He stooped, patted down the dead man's jacket. Stephanie's view was obscured by the killer's back and shoulders. Now he rose, stepped over Kern's body. Barely breaking stride, he gave the dead Bachmann a single vicious kick in the side. As he trotted off, he adjusted the hood to make it look like an ordinary woollen cap.

A minute passed, two, as she listened to the killer's quickening footfall on the path. When it had faded, she got up and started moving toward the bodies, stopping every few steps to calm her breathing and listen for the assassin's possible return.

She had to force herself to look at the mutilated head of the man she had loved, the man who was already beginning to lead a double existence—that of the vibrant human being she had known, and this, here, this horrible, tragic . . . thing! Almost automatically she closed her eyes, still listening for the return of the killer, ready to bolt back into the forest. Then she made herself squint at the other body.

The dead lieutenant lay on his left side, his right hand twisted under the body, the left protruding slightly, clutching a twig. A twig? She looked more closely: a wire! Forcing herself to ignore the mutilated head, she bent down, traced the wire to a yellow Walkman in the dead man's pocket. She removed it and pulled out the connections.

Silence still reigned—no time to lose! She ran along the path, back the way she'd come, then cut across a clearing, toward the road. Maybe she could stop a car. As she moved along a low embankment, she became aware of a sticky feeling in her palm. The Walkman? Blood! Kern's, Bachmann's, her own? She wiped her hands and the Walkman on her pants, then ran on: get to the car, get out of here!

Up on the road, a tractor rattled by, going in the opposite direction. Later, the vehicle's operator, a local farmer and father of four, would tell the police he saw "something that looked like a wounded deer, she was crouching so low, moving like an animal, but she was a woman all right, yes she was, anybody could see that."

Even as she ran, the loop of the past fifteen minutes played back in her head, all of it bathed in the glorious morning brilliance that fell through the trees, backlighting the scene and shielding her from the killer's insane gaze. There was a chance he and his accomplices were at Kern's house now, had discovered her car, were waiting for her. Those who did this know all about Peter—and me, she thought. Then her legs caved in and everything went into soft focus, as if she were an actress in a romantic movie.

Later, ducking behind trees, keeping absolutely still for long seconds, she stealthily approached the house, which lay deserted, the way it had when last she saw it. All was calm and quiet. Her car stood where she had left it.

A propeller plane rose from the nearby airport, drilling noisily into the summer's day. Somewhere not far away a dog barked. Large, black birds, crows that seemed to her anguished mind as fearsome as vultures, circled silently above the forest where the murdered men lay.

Getting back in her car was like slipping into a suit of armor, bestowing strength and impregnability. As she rounded the grassy rondel, guiding the Audi toward the main road, the dog she'd heard barking met her, followed by its master, who waved and called out a cheery greeting. Pastoral tranquility, she thought. Pastoral tranquility and bloody gore!

The drive back to Bern allowed her to compose herself. The adrenaline rush was over, her brain returning to its workaday mode. She'd call the police and tell them all the details. The Walkman lay beside her on the front seat. She recalled the killer's face in such detail that she knew she'd be able to identify him. It was likely he had a police record of some kind, and there'd be a photograph of him.

As a friend of the prime minister, she would go directly to the chief of police. It was an open and shut case. She could already see the headlines, blazing on the front pages: ACE REPORTER— she shook her head. Really, Kramer, she thought, how corny can you get. It should be INVESTIGATIVE, of course!

INVESTIGATIVE REPORTER LEADS POLICE TO PM'S KILLER. That was better.

Relieved now that she had imposed a modicum of intellectual control on her thinking, she leaned back behind the wheel. Ahead lay Bern, charming innocent Bern, under a cloudless sky. In the distance, a bluish haze veiled the foothills beneath snowy peaks. A thought swept like wildfire through her mind: *I left them. I left them there on the path. I left Peter there on the path. To rot!*

She was assailed by doubt. Was it really wise to call the police? You could go to the police, and the next thing you knew, you were up to your neck in trouble. A voice of wisdom intruded on her jumbled thoughts: *Cherish your privacy, protect your anonymity. Don't mix public with private business. When you gather information, let the police handle their own work. If it's murder, stay back, or they'll all be after you—the police, your colleagues in the news, the victim's relatives and friends . . .*

That was the kind of advice she needed now, and she knew where to get it. Ralph Christen! Yes, a man of infinite learning and experience, much of it accumulated in his career as chief magistrate of the Federal Court of Inquiry. She'd call him, ask him to help her. The thought gave her strength and confidence.

You'd better call Ralph, she reminded herself as she turned into the side street where she lived.

The news of Peter Kern's assassination broke around noon, plunging the nation into shock. Spontaneous gatherings of citizens expressing their sorrow and grief brought traffic in the inner city of the capital to a complete standstill. No one heard much news, just the periodic repetition of the bare facts: *Kern and his bodyguard were murdered while jogging. An automatic weapon was employed in the execution-style killing.*

Like Olof Palme, the Swedish prime minister who had been gunned down in the streets of Stockholm several years before, Kern had been a politician of considerable international stature. His skillful and dynamic leadership for a revitalization of democratic principles in Switzerland and abroad had earned him worldwide respect and recognition. In his capacity as Switzerland's minister of energy, he had initiated a broadly-based movement for codetermination in nuclear matters among the European nations.

Time and again, Kern had cautioned against the proliferation of nuclear weapons technology. In his function as prime minister, an office he held for a one-year term in accordance with the Swiss constitution, Kern had exploited his telegenic looks to fight discrimination, racism and isolationism. Only a climate of tolerance and openness could prevent a situation in which extremist fanatics felt trapped and frustrated enough to commit acts of nuclear terrorism—a danger, he had warned, that was a distinct possibility in today's world.

The fact of the executions was simply unimaginable in Switzerland. In 150 years of modern Swiss history, no crime of comparable import and savagery had been committed. Swiss ministers of state moved freely among the citizenry, attending private festivities and official functions without the type of personal security customary in most other Western countries. As had happened in Sweden in 1986, the nation now rudely woke up from its idyllic slumber, to stumble into the harsh realities of political terror in the final decade of the second millenium.

More than by the killing as such, the Swiss people were shocked by the evident escalation of murder into a tool of political expediency. In a hastily convened emergency session, the government appointed a special task force headed by Bern's chief of police Thomas Borli to investigate the assassination.

Stephanie locked the door to her apartment and stripped off her sweat-soaked clothes. She stood naked in the living room, trembling and exhausted, wondering if this must be what it felt like to be raped. Long moments passed before she stopped shaking. She picked up her soiled, stinking clothes and threw them in the washer, along with her designer sneakers. Still in the buff, she turned on the TV, picked up the Walkman and took it into the bathroom, seeing how the remaining smudges of blood on it had dried and darkened. She took out the cassette tape, scrubbed the casing clean, and dried it off with a towel.

She went into the kitchen, poured herself a glass of milk and gulped it down. She filled the glass once more, took it back into the bathroom, sipping from it as she adjusted the shower head to massage strength. Directing the concentrated rush of hot water to her shoulders, she let it loosen her tense muscles, allowed that aching tightness to drain away.

As if to counteract the brutal violation of his living flesh, the image of Peter Kern, alive and happy, ambled onto the memory screen behind her closed lids: those mischievously innocent, scheming eyes, his tender embraces, the harnessed power of his intelligent virility. Her nipples erected, as if the vibrant skin of the living man had brushed against them. Her hand, a hand, alighted at the juncture of her thighs. She tilted her torso back and let the water caress her breasts. Remembered touches slowly turned real. With a deep sigh she made herself shut off the water, pull back the shower curtain, and step out.

In her bathrobe, the glass of milk in one hand, she sat down to stare helplessly at the television screen.

"... *police and investigating government agencies remain puzzled by the events at the prime minister's compound. A government spokesperson said there was widespread concern over the possible motive or motives for the deed, especially since the popular prime minister enjoyed the respect of even his most vocal political opponents. No group has yet come forward to claim responsibility for the assassination. In a joint communiqué, militant factions of the antinuclear movement and the ecology lobby, which had recently attacked Prime Minister Kern in connection with the P-26 affair, have denounced the murder as 'the cowardly act of lunatic fanatics resulting in the death of a respected political opponent . . .'"*

Stephanie clicked off the TV and drank the rest of the milk. She put the cassette tape back into the Walkman, then realized she must have disconnected the earphones when she took it from the corpse. She pressed the Rewind button and nothing happened—battery dead! More likely, water or blood had got into it. She was still fidgeting with the machine when the phone rang. Undecided whether or not to pick up she went to the windowsill where the telephone stood. Could it be the police? Already?

Her mind racing, her gaze absently took in the street below. The phone kept on bleating. She was about to turn away, do something, anything, to get away from the grating ululation when a dark-blue Mercedes limousine caught her eye. The car was parked across the street. As she watched, her phone stopped ringing and the rear door of the limousine opened. She pulled back from the window.

A tall, muscular man in blue jeans and a leather jacket got out of the car and strolled toward a newsstand. All she could see was the back of his head trailing strands of long black hair. Even if she'd been blind, her body would have convulsed, screaming in recognition of Kern's murderer.

The man ducked to step under the newsstand awning. He pulled a cellular phone from a pocket and punched in numbers with his left hand. *Left-handed*, she registered automatically. Her phone rang again. She picked it up.

"Yes," she said, not bothering to ask the static who was calling. They listened to each other's silence until the killer hung up. She saw him put away the handset and stroll casually past the Mercedes, toward the entrance to her building. The heavy limousine pulled smoothly away from the curb and rolled away.

So they'd finally caught up with her. Neat! First Kern and Bachmann, then Kramer. Their hit man was on his way. INVESTIGATIVE REPORTER SLAIN IN KERN FOLLOW-UP KILLING.

Now there was a headline she'd be dying to see! It would happen if she didn't move—now!

As Stephanie was snapping out of her dangerous inertia, Chief Thomas Borli sat at his desk at police headquarters, soberly reviewing the situation in his mind. These days, not much surprised him, not even the killing of the Swiss head of state. So Kern was popular, so what! If a lot of people like you, some people hate you. If Kern hadn't made such a big thing about integrating foreigners, a lot of people wouldn't have misunderstood him, in which case he'd probably be alive right now, Borli surmised.

Kern had pointed out that minorities from other countries were part of the Swiss heritage. He argued that foreign workers had done more than their share to help build modern Switzerland. Muslim workers should be made to feel at home. They must be protected against pressure and manipulation by fanatic rabble-rousers and agitators. They must be allowed to practice their religion. If we ghettoize these decent, hardworking people, Kern had warned, they will fall prey to fundamentalist subversives, creating an ideal situation for the formation of terrorist cells and cadres in our cities.

The police of the Canton of Bern had received threats against Kern's life. The first was a month back, and another just three days previously. The WWF had sharply protested Kern's Energy 2000 program. Greenpeace stridently denounced the granting of operating permits for new nuclear energy production facilities. The Socialists accused him of trying to upset the existing energy balance, while the Swiss Energy Foundation claimed he was violating his mandate by deliberately ignoring the will of the people. The Green Party demanded an immediate moratorium on all new construction of nuclear energy facilities. Kern was accused of being "soft" on the question of expanding the current nuclear energy production capacity, and the nuclear lobby found his vision for the future of nuclear energy in Switzerland a constant thorn in its side.

To top it all off, a mishap at a nuclear facility located in northwestern Switzerland, officially referred to as "negligibly minor," touched off a chain reaction of public protests that culminated in tumultuous demonstrations on Parliament Square, right under the windows of the prime minister's offices. Riot police had moved in. A couple of dozen demonstrators and several police were injured and had to be hospitalized. Shouting slogans like *Kern, leave Bern!* and *Burn Kern!*, the crowd had milled about until the early hours of the following morning. Among the usual paraphernalia of demonstration tools—baseball bats, crash helmets and brass knuckles—the police had collected a number of professionally printed posters reading *NUKE KERN!* The prime minister himself had received a letter containing a bullet with the initials PK stenciled into its jacket.

While mulling things over in his mind, Chief Borli preferred to look up at the ceiling rather than face Max, his assistant. Max had been with him for, what was it now, eleven, twelve years? Whenever Borli did look at Max he had to admit to himself that the years had not been kind to the man. In fact, for all his merits as an investigator, Max had to be one of the ugliest men Borli had ever seen. Uglier even than the ceiling with its spidery cracks and fading art nouveau decor!

"We've got a variety of backdrops to look into for our killer," Borli stubbornly addressed the ceiling. "Militant Greens, pacifists, the antinuclear movement, the underground, the drug underground, the . . ."

". . . feminists?" Max ventured cautiously.

Borli leveled a thoughtful gaze at his colleague. What a beautifully practical mind ugly Max had! During Kern's election campaign, he had used his renowned acerbic wit to intellectually denude a female opponent. The radical Women to Power group had reacted violently, calling Kern everything from a meddling macho pig to a politically deranged rapist of women's ideals. Two militant women had threatened, anonymously, to blow up his residence.

"Possible," Borli agreed. Max smiled. Wrong, Borli thought.

The chief's mind was beginning to wander again. All the information available at this moment confirmed that the perpetrator or perpetrators were well acquainted with the prime minister's jogging routes. It also seemed unlikely that the victims had known the killer. The details of the crime bore that out: Kern and Bachmann had been executed with military precision, most likely by fire from a single weapon. They had not run into a familiar face or figure on that path!

Borli's gaze wandered across the ceiling, searching for inspiration in the familiar map of cracks and smudges. A quiet voice of reason inside of him intruded on the turbulent rush of facts, factoids and figures dredged up from the chief's vast reservoir of experience. Something doesn't make sense, said the voice.

What doesn't make sense? Borli asked it. Himself.

A political motive, the voice persisted.

Borli straightened up in his chair, piercing Max with an angry look, addressing him as if he were the assassin. "You don't kill the prime minister, Max, because the prime minister is simply not worth the effort. He isn't important enough. Right? Our seven government ministers, our federal councilors, are absolutely, or should I say obsoletely, useless when things are going well. And helpless when things are going badly. Right? They could never be mistaken for exponents of any particular political program, policy or plan. They function safely, and largely anonymously, embedded in our system of collective government and collective responsibility. Which means they don't become individually distinctive targets. Right? Except perhaps to some psychopathic nut in the lunatic fringe. And we know this was not the work of a psychopathic nut in the lunatic fringe. This was the work of a seasoned professional."

A young policewoman pushed past Max. "Interpol," she said, depositing a sheet of paper on Borli's desk. Borli nodded, grumpily pushed the paper aside, then grabbed it and glared at the blurred, black-and-white features in the photo. He read the accompanying text:

CUSTER, KENNETH WILLIAM, AKA >KEYCOP<. *Arrived Switzerland Sunday, July 1, Zurich-Kloten, by private charter from Newark, NJ (USA). Crime suspect. Armed professional with military expertise. Newark office FBI notified for more information and backup. . . . For physical details see reverse.*

Borli stared at his assistant.

"Don't look at me," Max protested. "I didn't do it. I had nothing to do with it." His mouth puckered up like a prune.

"That's where you're wrong," Borli muttered. "You did. I did. We all did."

Stephanie hastened into the bedroom and slipped into a white tank top and faded blue jeans. Her adrenaline was pumping wildly. She threw the Walkman into her shoulder bag, rushed back into the front room, to the bookshelf, to pull out a couple of diskettes containing recent research material. Pivoting, she tripped on a single black loafer half hidden under the bottom tier of the shelving. She fell back against the shelf, which began to give way, sagging toward the front door. The entire makeshift affair which she had put up one desperate bachelor-girl evening a couple of years ago, in a fit of homemaker-nesting mania, now swayed beneath its heavy load of recent reading material. A complete and never-opened set of the Encyclopedia Britannica teetered on the top shelf. The whole construction was turning into a cascade of falling timber.

In instant reflex, she threw herself against the shaky contraption and pushed it back against the wall, holding it in delicate suspension, glancing about wild-eyed for a solution. As she braced herself against the falling woodwork, the front door gave way to the first smashing impact of the killer's boot, his kick connecting expertly between handle and lock. Half a step into the room, he froze. The bulky-looking object in his hand gleamed dully.

"Keep still, bitch!"

Her mind, icily cold and pristine in the adrenal firestorm that engulfed her system, recognized the unintentional humor of his command. *I'm keeping still, you bastard, I'm keeping it!* she told him silently.

"I'm gonna mix a little pleasure with business. Strip, bitch! Take it off! Now!"

She heard a sobbing sound, as if from far away, produced by herself: a damsel-in-distress type of sound, though she was now feeling more like an angry leopardess surprised in her lair.

"I'll do anything you want—fuck you, suck you—anything, just don't kill me, please, please, please . . . !"

Shifting her weight to her right shoulder, still holding the great, clumsy construction in precarious balance, she pantomimed an elaborate gesture with her left hand, thrust out one hip, unbuckled the belt, ripped open the top button and began to unzip. All the while she was watching his eyes, saw his pupils widen. She jerked her shoulder back and stepped clear.

The shelf behaved the way large buildings do when expertly dynamited to cause maximum demolition with minimum collateral damage. It twisted inward as it fell, catching the killer halfway into his move toward the reluctant victim. Skirting the slow-motion disaster in three ferocious leaps, she saw one enormous volume of the Encyclopedia Britannica drive itself into the man's face. His bestial roar filled the small room as Stephanie raced out the door.

She flew up the wooden staircase to the upper floor of the duplex apartment, her seemingly perfect close escape punctuated by the muffled report from the killer's silencer-fitted gun. The bullet sliced the solid-oak bannister only inches above her head, slashing into the wall with a whipcrack noise that inspired her to a mighty upward leap through a soft shower of fragments from the neo-natural brick wall. Thank heaven for neo-natural brick, she managed to think. A second shot missed her by a mile as she burst onto the sundeck, her bag held firmly in place by a nifty shoulder clip, thank heaven for shoulder clips!

In one smooth motion she pulled herself onto the burnished red tiles of the roof, measuring with a single glance the row of identical, built-in sundeck terraces that stretched before her. She angled her bare feet to match the slant of the roof and padded to the edge of the neighboring terrace, then jumped down. She stood still, trembling, struggling to control her breath.

Later, when she replayed the memory imprint of these moments, she saw herself standing on the terrace of the doctor's office next door, leaning forward from the waist, a savage, or rather a techno-savage minus the technology (except for a rusty wrought-iron poker she picked up off the floor next to an open fireplace), reduced to fighting for her naked life in the urban wilderness. When she heard the black-haired, golden-earringed killer scramble up onto the roof only a few meters away, she stood poised in the shadow of the countersunk terrace wall, ready to receive him.

His shoes touched the floor only two steps away from her. She ripped the poker upward into his crotch, screaming, "Bye-bye, balls!"

The gun cluttered to the tiled floor, slid far to the opposite side. Grabbing his crotch with both hands in a clumsy Michael Jackson impression, the man stumbled backwards and went crashing down amid the sundeck furniture. A bosomy doctor's assistant became an Edvard Munch blur on the threshold to the terrace as Stephanie hurtled past her, shouting, "My boyfriend—that's how he gets his kicks!"

Moments later her Audi roared to life. She punched it into first gear, churning up a rooster tail of summer dust as she pulled away from the curb.

She found herself barreling up a one-way street in the wrong direction, the Audi's careworn valves screeching in protest. She made an illegal left turn and compounded the infraction with an outrageously wide U-turn, scraping the side of a parked car. Finally, she found the approach to the big bridge leading into the heart of Bern. She felt desperately confused: Who were the people that were trying to kill her, and why?

Kern's killers, clearly, but who were they? They knew she knew Kern, but Kern knew—had known—hundreds of people, many of them closely. So why just her, what made them single her out?

Well, for one thing, I'm a journalist, she mused, giving in to the slow flow of traffic. Yet, again, Kern had known dozens of journalists. What made her so special?

Her hand tightened so hard the knuckles turned white on the steering wheel as the answer hit her: The nuclear conspiracy! Of course! Was it really possible that old man Arik's doomsday predictions were closer to the mark than she had dared imagine? And if that was true, didn't it stand to reason that Switzerland's secret services were already involved? Am I the first eager-beaver journalist to poke her nose into this Pandora's box? And now someone wants to bury that nosy proboscis!

Her own strangled groan made her shiver. She stared at her face in the rearview mirror: pale and drawn, lips pulled back in an animal snarl, beads of perspiration glistening on the forehead. She downshifted, switched on the radio:

"... *still in the process of securing and examining evidence. A woman, thought to be approximately 172 centimeters in height, in her late twenties or early thirties, slender, with blonde hair, wearing green-and-black sports coveralls and white sneakers, was observed near the scene of the crime. This woman is urged to contact Thomas Borli, head of the assassination task force at police headquarters, or report to any police station. Anyone who has seen or believes to have seen this woman, or anyone with other information relating to the crime, is urged to contact police headquarters, or any police station or individual police officer. The following telephone numbers are open for immediate ...*"

She switched channels as she pulled into a small parking lot next to a drugstore not far from Ralph Christen's home. The tune she cut into was "The Power of Love." Sentimental trash! Still, she continued listening, scanning the area with a suspicious, wide-angle gaze. Yes, kitschy, simple-minded, trashy pop, calculated tearjerkers!

... she was looking up into the friendly eyes of her house doctor, who gently patted her swollen abdomen, then produced a scalpel from behind one ear. Mischievously waving the gleaming instrument in front of her nose, he announced: "We'll have to operate, Stephanie. Your appendix is about to burst."

She felt no fear, yet the doctor's kindly face stirred her profoundly. How could this be? What she was experiencing had actually happened more than twenty years ago, shortly after her tenth birthday. Had she traveled into the past?

The physician would die a few months later, she knew. His ancient Riley would be smashed by an express train at a railroad crossing where a defective gate failed to close. Should she warn him? She hesitated. Suddenly Grandpa Enrico, her maternal grandfather, who'd taught her how to handle wood and tools, appeared at her bedside. A sob caught in her throat as she remembered that he died in an accident in the mountains only a couple of weeks after her appendix operation.

She tried to push herself up to hug him, but Grandpa Enrico raised his powerful peasant arms, soothing her with a gesture that radiated unshakable confidence. "Don't worry, Sweet, everything will be all right." His voice shifted to a strangely remote tone,

"Why aren't you with a younger, more potent man? Why choose a gray-haired, balding fellow with a beer belly?"

"Come on, Grandpa, Peter doesn't have a beer belly, and as for his hair . . ."

She broke off, then continued slowly, with a tremendous effort, "Maybe simply because my generation of men is so boring and indifferent. Men in my age group, thirty-something guys, well, either they stretch out on their back and wait to be serviced, or else their lives have been so dull that a relationship and sex with them can't possibly be exciting."

Enrico Ravelli skeptically tilted his eyebrows, which was all she needed to blurt out her confession, "I'm ambitious, Grandpa, didn't you know? I need Peter Kern's power, his connections. I'm trying to make it big. And my next piece will make me famous. . . ."

Her right hand flew to her mouth. She bit down on her index finger, embarrassed by her own candor.

"There's nothing wrong with being calculating," Grandpa Enrico said calmly. "To fight evil, you have to be hard and cold. But that alone isn't enough."

"I'm trying to survive, Gramps, I'm being hunted. If I don't keep my cool, I'll . . ."

Her grandfather nodded benevolently. "You're a young, beautiful woman. Don't waste yourself. What you need is a real man, or perhaps I should say a *true* man."

"Yes, I know. Don't you think that's what I'm looking for—a true man, a gentle man, a man with imagination? Do you think I give a hoot about a man's position, or what he does? Just as long as it's the unexpected, just as long as he does it with all his heart and strength and courage!"

An ethereal smile began to suffuse Enrico's features, spreading wider and wider, making them fade.

"So you're looking for a hero," she heard him whisper. "Is there such a one, a hero to conquer your heart? All things considered, yes, there may well be. But you must look for him. So go on, start looking for your . . ."

She glanced about, astonished: Where had Grandpa gone, and what had happened to the doctor? She saw the couch as if it were standing amid bushes profusely blooming with yellow flowers. The glacial green waters of a river washed around the edges of the pillow. Someone bent over her, bearing the chill of the grave that made her shiver: Peter!

Peter Kern. His lips parted as if he was about to whisper something. An ugly hole gaped where his right eye had been. Half his skull was missing, and most of the brain. Not a word crossed his lips. She managed to grab him by the shoulders, pleading desperately, "What is it, Peter? Talk to me, please!"

For the fraction of an instant, a malevolently grimacing, gargoylelike face appeared to her view above Kern's smashed skull; a face with boldly hewn bird-of-prey features, triangular chin and black, slicked-back hair. She knew this face, wanted it to linger so she'd be able to identify it. It vanished, and her grandfather's calm, confident voice continued, "Watch out for that fellow! Trust no one! Remember Papa!"

"Papa," she sighed. "What about Papa? Where is he, Grandpa?"

Now the river flowed past her, smooth and dark. A face with the pallor of death upon it slid by her just below the surface. Was that her father? Someone whispered something in her ear. The phone rang, so she couldn't understand what was being said. The phone kept bleating, on and on. Would someone please just answer the damn thing!

She threw herself forward, her impact with the carpeted floor jarring her awake. The phone in Christen's apartment finally stopped ringing. She pulled herself up off the floor, back onto the couch, and sat staring vacantly ahead. Slowly, she began to reassemble the components of her workaday self, never for a moment allowing the imprint of that face to slip from her mental grasp.

She knew it, she had seen it! *Connect, connect,* she commanded her brain. But her memory refused to obey.

She sat quietly for a while, happy to have woken, happy to be alive, her eyes resting dreamily on the wall of books opposite the great windows. Now she focused on Christen's collection of Dürrenmatt's works. She got up, went to the shelf and picked out a volume with a greenish blue jacket: *Justice.* That novel had started her friendship with Ralph Christen.

They'd met when the book was being made into a movie, both working as extras on the set. Christen had come on a lark, a dare from a friend, while Stephanie was supplementing her income between jobs. A murder scene took two long nights of shooting. The morning after the second night, Christen had offered her a ride back home from Baden, where they'd been filming in a rambling old hotel. The bleary-eyed Christen drove off the road, down a steep embankment, into a river. Stephanie was thrown out, unhurt.

She pulled him out of the car, which had rolled over on its roof and filled with water. Christen insisted she had saved his life. He had sworn eternal gratitude and friendship.

Maybe now he'd have a chance to return the favor, she thought as she slid the book back in place. Christen wielded considerable power. In a moment of weakness he had proudly told her that as chief magistrate of the military court, he lived in a world where all doors were open. The "potentiation of authority," he'd called it.

"An examining magistrate, empowered with all that military authority, that's a combination people will stand at attention for!" was how he put it.

She was certain Christen would know what to do. He had the clout to make even the police "stand at attention" if, for example, he told them to leave Ms. Kramer alone. And he had direct access to all government agencies, enabling him to find out just who was behind the entire horrific scenario. Yes, Ralph would give his right arm to help her. Reassured, she settled back.

From outside the window came the sound of workers hammering away on a construction site. The hum of a crane's electric engine mingled with the excited chirping of two sparrows on the balcony railing. Suddenly, all of this seemed unreal to her: too ordinary, too pointedly casual! She got up, nervously started pacing the room. The pleasant routine of her life was shattered. Ever since she'd had that visionary view of herself in the forest, running along the luminous path of her life, nothing was as it had been. The gruesome killing had shocked her into a heightened sensitivity. And now this dream of her grandfather! Warning signals everywhere!

What was she doing here, reminiscing about her friendship with Ralph? And what about him? Did she have the right to compromise him like this, draw him into this mess? As a military judge he would naturally be obliged to turn her over to the police. Even if he decided to let things run their course, pretended it was none of his business, why should she impose on him?

Then there was a good chance some secret government agency was behind all of this, which would mean they knew all about her and were only waiting for her to turn herself in. This was simply too big! She'd be a fool to trust anyone. She was on the run, and she'd better keep on running!

Indeed, the police were proceeding on the assumption that Stephanie Kramer was still in Bern. An APB had been issued, initiating maximum surveillance of all train stations, bus terminals, exit routes and airports. Hotels and car rental agencies were instructed to report on all clients.

A man who'd gone for a stroll near the Kern residence, accompanied by his dog, had identified Stephanie and her car. A woman told police officers that someone whose appearance fit the televised picture of Stephanie Kramer had run into her while she was bicycling past a local drugstore. The men under Thomas Borli had all reason to believe Kramer would soon be in custody.

They might not have been quite so optimistic had they been aware of the existence of a man named Matak, who was seething with anger over the way his target had eluded him. His anger grew with every twinge of the pain that flashed through his crotch and groin each time he took a step. I'll show the bitch! he promised himself, limping grim-faced through the train station, one hand jammed in a pocket cautiously cupping his genitals to shield them from further injury.

He'd done some of his best work in train stations. For snuffing a body in a crowd, soccer stadiums and train stations were among his favorite locations. Surveying the milling crowds in the vast, domed hall, Matak figured he might get lucky again. A slicky little chicky, that one! Next time they met she wouldn't be so lucky, no sir! He surreptitiously touched the spot under his right eye where the Encyclopedia Britannica had struck him. The flesh was puffed up and felt sore.

Slowly, he made his way to the escalators leading to the aboveground parking and the university. Yes sir, it was better when they fought a little. Made it more challenging.

The plastic bag with the drugstore logo lay on the floor by the couch. Seeing it brought her back to reality. She picked it up, carried it into the bathroom. It would have been nice but, finally, Ralph was not the solution to her problems. With a shrug and a sigh, she unpacked the bag and began to busy herself with scissors, hair dye, and mascara.

After an hour or so, when she finally examined her handiwork in the mirror, she barely recognized herself. Jet-black eyes returned her gaze with laser intensity; gamin-styled black hair signaled a street-smart toughness; long eyelashes hinted at sensuous cunning. A combative femme fatale! She winked at her new image. "Perfect! This'll scare the dickens out of them!"

In a closet she found a dark-green T-shirt with the West Point motto *Duty, Honor, Country* emblazoned across the front. She pulled it over the conspicuous white tank top; it fit perfectly.

She sat down at Christen's desk, found pen and paper, scribbled a few words. She folded the sheet and placed it in an envelope, which she marked *Ralph.* Then she left the magistrate's flat.

In the street, anonymous in the shade of the arcades, she hailed a taxi and told the driver to take her to the university. Once inside the entrance hall she hesitated, trying to decide what to do next. In the library she could fade inconspicuously among the students and have plenty of time to think things through.

Inconspicuous as a sitting duck!

No, what she needed was movement, not contemplation. Better to get out of town. By train.

She left the university and walked toward the enormous platform high above the railroad tracks. Beneath her, row upon row of roofs with reddish brown tiles meandered down to where the historic center of ancient Bern formed a peninsula in the great bend of the river. In the distance, floating like a mirage above the picturesque panorama, the dazzling white summit of the Eiger's north wall challenged the skies.

She stepped onto the down escalator heading to the station. Where should she go to be safe for the next few days? Wrack her brain as she might, nothing occurred to her. Scanning the crowd, between blinks, she spotted the killer. He stood at the bottom of the escalators, with his back toward her. Now he turned and limped to the up escalator.

Already on her way down, she turned sideways: inevitably, they would meet halfway. Unless . . . She slid down to a sitting position, pretending to be adjusting her sandals. Then she stretched out full-length. The serrated metal tiers cut into her tightened thighs, scraped her back and shoulders. She lay close to the inside wall and squinted apprehensively up beyond the handrail but, with a silent prayer, she passed him undetected. Just before she reached the bottom she got to her feet, using a fellow passenger for cover.

The portly elderly gentleman eyed her curiously. "Are you all right, Madam?"

"Oh, absolutely." She flashed him a smile. "It's called escalatrics, very popular in the U.S. right now. Try it some time, it does wonders for your libido."

Without turning to see what happened to the assassin, she left the escalator and found herself heading straight for a couple of uniformed policemen, equipped with walkie-talkies, scanning the crowd. She veered off sharply, walked to the nearest platform and managed to slip into the El just before the doors closed.

Two stops down the line she got off and took a cab to the Convention Center where she rented a car, using plastic to pay. Ten minutes later she was driving west out of Bern. Every few kilometers she turned off the freeway, then drove back on, keeping an eye on the rearview mirror. As far as she could tell, no one was tailing her. Tailing? She frowned at her new and fierce-looking Italianate face in the mirror. Listen to that lingo, she told her mirror image. You not only look like a Mafia moll, you've even started thinking like one!

As Stephanie drove steadily west, a young car rental clerk with neo-natural blonde hair thumbed through half a dozen contracts copies. The stack included the one for the Volkswagen Golf she had assigned to that cheap-looking trollop with the black wig and the Prince eyelashes. She pursed her lips and tilted her head indecisively. It would take at least ten minutes to fax all this stuff to the police number her boss had handed her, using his free hand to cop an unusually close and drawn-out feel. Maybe the assassination turned him on, the pervert! She threw the sheaf of papers in the *Pending* basket.

"Too bad, Fatso, you'll have to do this yourself in the morning," she muttered. "And by the end of the month, you can do everything yourself. Because I won't be here to do it for you!" She sat down, crossed her legs, and lit a cigarette.

A mountainous cloudscape loomed high to the west, with the broad, ascending band of freeway heading straight for it. A frayed, murky piece of cloud drifted away from the main white-and-gray bulk. The Golf ran smoothly, its engine humming monotonously. Stephanie sat far back in the seat, her arms extended to the steering wheel. Deep in thought, her eyes relaxing in contemplation of the dramatic sky, she at first didn't notice the subtle changes occurring in the dark, wispy fragment of cloud that drifted slowly through her field of vision.

Gradually, the semblance of a face emerged: predatory features like those of an eagle or hawk, though in a human face. She stared in fascination as the features became more and more distinct against the intense blue of the afternoon sky. What might have been a nobly aquiline nose, worthy of a senator in ancient Rome, was vulgarized by a coarse, flat base set between eyes that were spaced too far apart. The chin, too, might have been thought of as dynamic, had it not come to an aggressively wedgelike point that threatened—

Stephanie blinked a couple of times. Already, the cloudface had begun to look innocuous. Yes, of course, she herself had projected a remembered face onto a convenient bit of the landscape. And yet, the image was real, there was such a face!

"I've got it, that's him!"

She drummed a staccato victory beat on the steering wheel and started looking for a turnoff. She took the next exit and found a rural train station with a telephone. Her hand trembled as she dialed Christen's number on the battered, antediluvian set mounted on the station wall. Just then a gleaming, spanking clean train rolled in, completing the picture of peaceful efficiency: *Switzerland, Country of Contrasts*, she wrote in bold letters in her head.

"Come on, pick it up!" she murmured. The pauses between rings seemed interminable. Beads of perspiration appeared on her forehead.

At last, a calm, male voice said, "Christen."

"Ralph! It's me, Stephanie. Am I glad to hear your voice. Now Ralph, listen to me, please. This is very important." While she waited for a word of affirmation, the station's PA system boomed out a message. The telephone receiver conveyed only white noise.

"Ralph? Are you still there?"

"Of course I am. Where are you? Wherever you are, stay there. I'll come and get you. I read your note and you're right, it looks bad. But don't try to run from this, I know we can work it out. Where're you calling from?"

"Forget it. I'm under a lot of pressure, but I'm doing fine."

"Stephanie! The police are looking for you. They'll—"

"Don't you think I know that? I need a particular piece of information. It's urgent, okay?"

"Yes, but . . ."

"Listen carefully now, please! About two years ago, there was a demonstration against a nuclear dump in some hole in west Switzerland, Canton Waadt, I believe. Can you remember the name of the place?"

"Yes, I think so, let me see. Oll . . . Ollon. Yes, Ollon."

"That's it, Ollon! The whole town was up in arms about government plans to build an underground depository for nuclear wastes. The demonstration was a big event live on TV, remember?"

"I heard about it. Why? Does this relate to Kern?"

"Ralph, listen. There was some big shot at this demonstration, a politician or celebrity, a public figure. He was talking to the police, waving his arms at the demonstrators. Paint bags were thrown, a free-for-all started. Now, this fellow had pomaded hair, black hair, slicked back thirties style, and a beak of a nose. Ring a bell?"

"No, not really. I must have missed it on television."

"That's him, Ralph."

"Who is him?"

"That's the man behind the killing. Don't ask me how I know, but I'm absolutely certain. Get his name, find out who he is. An imposing personality, well-known, distinctive looking. Call the TV station, they'll tell you."

"Wait a second, Steph, hold it! This is serious. Are you sure you know . . ."

"Look, Peter Kern was blown away this morning. He was my friend. And you think I'm joking?"

"Don't get me wrong. I wasn't—"

"I saw his face, back at your place when I took a nap. Clear as day, in a dream. And a few minutes ago—" She stopped just in time to avoid blurting out her fantasy cloud vision. That would really make Ralph send the men in white coats after her!

Meanwhile Christen, in his apartment, swallowed hard and sat down. Then he said in a calm voice, "Are you sure you're all right? Let me come and pick you up. You're under terrible pressure. You need help, get some rest. Then we can talk about this . . . uh . . . dream. But right now, you know, there isn't much I can do with a . . ."

"Ralph!" Her tone stopped him cold. "I need information, not therapy. Get me the name of that man! As soon as you can—like, immediately! If not, I'll call the head of the . . . I'll call Borli. I'll tell him I've been hiding out in your apartment. Am I making myself clear, sir?" She was close to tears.

Christen said nothing. Memory of two or three serious attempts to blackmail him stood out in his long, sometimes turbulent career. He remembered one in particular, when a man who claimed he had turned himself into a human bomb telephoned and threatened to blow himself up unless Christen destroyed a certain piece of evidence he had in his possession. Christen refused, and the caller was never heard from again. He had felt it was a tricky situation.

He hated to give in to this type of emotional bullying. But this was Stephanie . . . she really was in a jam, wasn't she?

"All right, Stephanie," he said, slowly, soothingly, "but—"

"No ifs or buts about it!" She was down to her last reserves of strength. "I will call you in one hour and you will tell me the man's name. If not," she paused, her heart beating steady as a jackhammer, high in her throat, "you can go have sexual congress with yourself."

"Steph, please . . ." he pleaded, but she hung up.

Christen checked his watch. He pressed the Rewind key on his telephone recorder, then touched Fast Forward for an instant, cutting in where Stephanie's voice said, ". . . listen to me, please, this is very important." With his ear close to the machine, he listened intently to the public address system announcement, then shook his head, rewound the tape, and listened again. After several repetitions, he called Steiner. His senior investigator listened attentively, assured Christen he'd attend to the matter immediately, then set about locating the train station or stations where an express train had left for Lausanne at 1635 hours.

"Bloody bother, this!" Christen cursed. He didn't often get excited enough to regress to the language of his merry student days at Cambridge. He opened a phone directory and found the number of Swiss Television. Still cursing like a trooper, he started tapping it out on the telephone keys.

"Dreams, by Jove, the silly wench trusts in dreams," he growled, beginning to ease back into a more earthy, regional Swiss speech. "She's gone off her rocker for sure. What kind of goatshit is this anyway! What kind of stupid, stinking, nuclear mountain goatshit . . . !"

"Sir? Would you repeat that name, please," said the operator at the Swiss Television offices in Zurich.

"Ch-Christen," he stammered. "Ralph Christen. Put me through to the newsroom! Please."

When Borli looked up from his desk, he saw with some surprise that the assembled members of his closest staff were staring at him.

"Anything new?" Max asked.

"Well, what about the feminist connection?" Borli rasped back defensively.

"We're working on it, sir. I believe . . ."

Borli flapped a hand. "Never mind what we believe. We need reliable information. This isn't some simple crossword puzzle in the morning paper, it's a big mosaic. So we look for tiles, one at a time."

Borli nodded at Steiner, his deputy. "I want every available man and woman on this. I want all government and public agencies, police, administration, army, border patrol, air force and air space security, train stations. Plus all the relevant civilian and private enterprises—hotels, restaurants, nightclubs, car rentals and travel agencies. I want total monitoring and surveillance on all of that. Steiner, if I've left anything out, use your imagination! You know the procedure. You're in charge of analysis. And spare me the details, just give me the summary, yes?"

Satisfied with the humble nodding of heads from his staff, Borli softened his tone as he made the introduction. "Our work depends on friendly relations with the military. This is Ralph Christen, chief magistrate of the Federal Court of Inquiry. Chief Magistrate Christen will be cooperating closely with us."

Christen, discreetly seated on the visitors' couch under the windows, half rose, nodded in the round, then slumped back again. Half a dozen pairs of case-hardened eyes skeptically followed his every move.

Borli was in no mood to waste time with etiquette. "We'll meet every morning at nine sharp in this office. Now, ladies and gentlemen, shall we crank?"

The phone beeped. Steiner picked up an extension, listened and, with a shrug, handed the receiver to Borli.

"Borli."

"Commander Borli, Adam Schlammer. I take it you haven't got anything yet, otherwise you would already have let me know. I want to be kept on top of this development, right up to the minute. Is that understood?"

"Of course." Borli sounded cool and detached. "I'm in a meeting right now. . . ."

Borli frowned into the receiver as he listened. "Okay, yes, tomorrow morning. I'll do what I can. Yes. Bye."

As he hung up he gestured at Max, Steiner and the others. "I thought I told you to get going. So, please, everybody!" With Steiner in the lead and Max bringing up the rear, his staff filed out. Muttering softly under his breath, Borli turned to Christen.

"That was Schlammer. Adam Schlammer, on the Committee for Internal Security."

"I understand," Christen said.

"He's throwing his weight around. Wants to be kept up to date on the investigation. And the names of everybody on the team."

Christen produced a casual smile. Seeing Borli's puzzled expression, he said, "These CEOs are all alike. They simply have to call all the shots!"

Borli turned back to the phone, while Christen mentally recapitulated: Adam Schlammer was president and CEO of the Schlammer Group. Swiss Television just confirmed he was the man who had negotiated with the demonstrators at Ollon. And Stephanie's premonition, which he'd dismissed as the fantasies of a hysterical woman, was right on target! Every minute counted now.

He crossed his legs, giving the impression of a man casually in control of the situation, but inside, he was ready to explode. What a woman! If only she'd call! Stephanie's "premonition" was worth every second of the frustration she'd caused him earlier.

Christen uncrossed his legs and leaned forward, noting that he was no longer smiling and that his face felt hot. Well, the situation was unique! But as examining judge on the highest military court in the land, he had optimum security clearance. Which meant he had access to the top-secret files of the UNA, the Subdepartment for Defense Intelligence—the Swiss counterpart to the National Security Agency.

To show he was in a hurry, Christen got up and leaned on Borli's desk. When Borli cupped the speaking grate of the receiver and looked up at him, Christen said, "If you need me, I'll be in my office."

Fifteen minutes later he was feeding his rather elaborate clearance code into a computer. When the screen indicated access granted, the chief magistrate began tapping the UNA files for everything they contained on one Adam Schlammer.

Nucleanne, Monday, July 2

In the high-rise command center of the Schlammer Group, President and CEO Adam Schlammer gently replaced the receiver. The long, intense gaze he directed at the man with him caused havoc in the attorney Geigel's mind. When the tycoon finally spoke, his voice was smooth as velvet:

"So my bombs trigger a nuclear war, so what! They'll explode thousands of miles away. Who cares if a couple of million peons in the Third World go up in smoke? Honest, Geigel, who gives a shit?" he mused, tucking his chin on his chest. Behind him stood a black-haired, dark-eyed young woman, her plump lips painted fire-red, massaging the tycoon's head. "Worldwide overpopulation is our biggest problem. It's choking us to death. And what do we do about it? Nothing! *Nada*, as our Latin American friends would say."

Shrugging off the masseuse's hands, Schlammer stood up. Moving swiftly, confidently, he went to the paneled wall, where an electronic map of the world pulsated in a profusion of colors. Once again, Geigel felt the man's powerful charisma like a physical force that filled the room. Schlammer turned his buccaneer's face toward the shimmering green of the Asian continent on the map. Reflecting the electronic gleam, his dark eyes blazed with volcanic energy and determination. The ridge of his nose jutted out sharply above a triangular chin that pointed like a spear tip at the map.

"Just a show, Geigel, pure hypocrisy, all of it! When you come right down to it, aren't we actually glad that AIDS is wiping out the blacks in Africa, or when an earthquake kills half a million Chinese? On this planet, survival of the fittest is what counts. The more people there are, the harder people like you and me have to fight to survive. Why, eventually, just the population overflow will destroy our living space, that's as certain as the amen in church! One day in the not too distant future the armies of Allah will be at the gates of Europe, just like the Turks once stormed the gates of Vienna."

Schlammer clenched his fists, his eyes narrow slits.

"Tell me, Geigel, are we just going to stand idly by and watch that happen? Let's get real about this. What we have in our government is a bunch of clowns who don't have the faintest idea what is going on in the world."

Schlammer seemed to be looking through Geigel into another world. Neatly slicked back, the CEO's shiny, black hair made the top of his head look like the glistening back of a seal. His tailor-made, dark-blue, pinstriped, double-breasted suit with the narrow lapels was of the latest cut. The impeccably starched collar of his white shirt elegantly shaded the perfect knot in a yellow silk tie. Built solid, not stocky, Schlammer seemed taller than his real height of 180 centimeters. Anyone trying to guess his age would be amazed to learn he was actually fifty-eight years old.

Schlammer was rubbing his long-fingered, well-manicured hands. Geigel cleared his throat and said, "But what can we do, Professor? We fold our hands in our laps and look on while the pope outlaws birth control and the use of condoms. Believe me, I agree with you. We must do something."

Schlammer looked at Geigel, disgusted by the man's servility. Fixing him in his dark gaze, he wagged a threatening finger.

"Almost one out of ten people living in Germany today is a Muslim. The situation in England and France is similar. There are some ten million Muslims living in Western Europe today, right here among us. And what are they doing here? Getting ready to wipe us out, that's what! Ten million, Geigel. *Ten million!*"

Geigel timidly craned his neck. "Those certainly are catastrophic figures but, you know, there've always been Islamic communities in European countries. Even in Switzerland . . ."

Schlammer's right hand cut the air like a scythe.

"For chrissake, Geigel, I'm talking about now, not the fucking Middle Ages! Soon, Switzerland will be like the former Yugoslavia. Do you think our unemployed will always sit on their asses and let those *lumpen-immis* snatch up jobs from under their noses? One out of ten Muslims in this country is a religious activist drumming into his brethren's heads how badly off they are, how they've been sold down the river by a corrupt government at home, and how they're being exploited by Christians and Jews in Europe. I'll put it like this: the Muslims we have now are just the tip of the iceberg, they're just the first wave of a veritable deluge. And what are we doing while Muslim fanatics are stirring up their own to commit acts of terrorism against our nation and our culture? Nothing, that's what!"

He paused briefly to catch his breath. "But don't worry, that's not going to happen. We will act. We will stop it!"

Geigel made bold to ask, in humble tones, whom Schlammer had in mind when he said "we." But Schlammer allowed no interruptions.

"We're talking optimum solutions here, Geigel, I hope you understand that. And by optimum I mean nuclear. We'll bomb them to kingdom come. You know what my favorite German general, Guderian, used to tell his staff? *Don't fart, gentlemen, shit!* I say thank God we've got the power to shit, and shit big!"

Now the inner glow of Schlammer's eyes was competing successfully with the reflection from the electronic board.

"Descrambled, Geigel: we will use nuclear devices."

The attorney recoiled inwardly before Schlammer's horror vision. He looked at the tycoon, cowed, careful not to contradict him. If you chose to oppose this man, you did so at your own peril. Geigel reminded himself that some who tried were never heard from again, others had committed suicide. Schlammer wielded tremendous power.

And money, obscene amounts of it! Schlammer had more, in fact, than all the wealthiest Swiss combined, those men and women who each year posed foppishly for ridiculous pictures in *Swissiness*, Switzerland's leading business weekly.

*   *   *

Stephanie Kramer felt a surge of fresh optimism as she drove away from the station where she had phoned the chief magistrate. Once back on the freeway, she pulled the Walkman from her shoulder bag, plucked out the cassette tape. She inserted it in the dashboard deck and pressed the Play button. Rustling noises emerged from the speakers, then panting sounds, then a muffled voice—Kern's. She turned up the volume.

"...yesterday...I lucked into...unannounced inspection... them totally by surprise...always...an uncanny feeling, call it a hunch...decided to take a look, so I..."

A burst of strenuous coughing smothered Kern's words. "... anne, in western Switzerland...unofficial visit..."

The name of the town he referred to was only partially intelligible. Biting her lips, she activated Rewind, then Play. Again, Kern's voice gasped: "...call it a hunch...decided to take a look, so I ...anne, in western Switzerland...unofficial visit..."

A town that ended with ... *anne!*

The tape continued, "...imagine, Bachmann...all that beautiful countryside...bombs...place of death...get to the bottom of..."

A sound like giant fists ripping sheet metal apart cut into Kern's voice.

Stephanie screamed, "That's the gun!" The tape faithfully transmitted the eerie sounds of two men in the throes of sudden, violent death. There were two more bursts of gunfire at short intervals, then silence.

She pulled over and stopped on the soft shoulder. Covering her face with her hands, she was wracked by dry sobs; no tears would come. There simply wasn't time for tears, and tears were not what she owed Peter anyway. What she owed him was to put her nose to the ground and pick up the trail.

That was simple. After all, she'd learned from the best. So what about that word fragment ... *anne?* Western Switzerland—yes, of course: ... *anne* stood for *Lausanne!*

She stepped on the gas pedal, floored it. The Volkswagen indignantly lurched forward. Yes, she smiled, Lausanne. On the rustic shores of Lac Léman, where the glacial Rhone river is born again!

Not far from where Stephanie was pushing westward, Schlammer raised his left fist before Geigel in a gesture of power.

"We must take control! What is happening in Europe now is a

defilement of everything our ancestors stood for. Take that idiot Kern—may he rest in pieces!—preaching all over Europe how we're supposed to integrate foreigners, Muslims to boot, hand them our sacred Swiss citizenship on a platter—"

He shook his head in disgust. A strand of pomaded hair cleaved to one side and slid down across his forehead. He pulled a small comb from the breast pocket of his suit and carefully combed the hair back in place.

"Listen, Geigel! When our deal with the South Americans is in the barn, you'll get a juicy share. I don't expect any hitch at all. This is a seamless, professional operation."

He walked back to the big desk with the heavy black marble top. Staring absently through the attorney, he said, "We're talking money here, Geigel. Approximately one thousand five hundred million dollars. A billion and a half, man!"

At these words, a mild, electric shock sweet as gold dust tingled up and down Geigel's spine. It created a thrilling sensation of organic heat that made the lawyer press his knees together and snuggle his buttocks deeper into the red leather upholstery of the armchair in which he had taken refuge from Schlammer's scorching visions. He wondered discreetly how much of this awesome amount would be diverted in his direction. Enough to make him rich, he figured. Forever!

"And when I say juicy, I mean juicy!" Schlammer added.

The attorney roused from his dreams of glory. "Yes, Professor, thank you. I . . ."

But the president and CEO of the Schlammer Group, paymaster for more than 250,000 employees worldwide, was smiling into himself, remote from all mundane human concerns. His ecstatic gaze swept over Geigel's balding pate, through the palatial windows, and into the distance, where great fortresses of white clouds bulged above the horizon. Yes, the fine, stable summer weather continued.

As he contemplated this blessed Swiss countryside, Schlammer's mind turned to his historic mission. After all, he was not just another billion-dollar player in the international marketplace: he was a patriot! He loved the valley he now surveyed. He loved Switzerland. And he hated everything that wasn't white and Christian. Or at least controlled by white Christians!

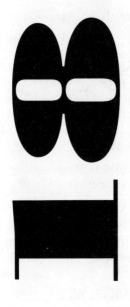

Driving along, Stephanie remembered how she had celebrated her birthday with Peter Kern and a bottle of Taittinger at Les Vacances, a posh Bern nightclub. In splendid spirits, Peter had raised his glass and toasted, "To you and to a happy future!" Their glasses touched and they drank.

Kern then waved an eager waiter aside, expertly wiped moisture off the bottle with an immaculately white champagne towel. He refilled their glasses. He said abruptly, "I've been thinking how much better women handle crises than men do. And why? Because they're used to acting intuitively. They don't feel they need to control a situation, the way men do."

At the time, she had laughed and promptly forgotten his remark. Until now. As she drove through the terraced wine country that slanted down to Lake Geneva and Lausanne, his words came back to her. She took a turnoff that led down to the lakeshore, pulled over to the side of the road. Across the lake on the French side, snow-capped alpine peaks glistened in the summer sun. Propelled by a gentle breeze, a windsurfer slowly drifted along beyond the small harbor. Farther out on the lake, spinnakers in bright colors billowed like so many historical banners. Sun worshippers and swimmers were enjoying the fine weather. In the shadow of an old chestnut tree, a fisherman busied himself with his nets.

She decided Peter had been right. All she had to go on was her intuition—plus one syllable from a garbled word on a cassette tape: . . . *anne.* That was where the trail ended. She closed her eyes and tried to calm her mind. Even if Lausanne was the place, and even if this city was not very large, how could her feminine intuition be expected to conjure up a specific location in this elegant old town?

A kid on roller skates, with long, flowing hair, wooshed past her, spun around and, skating backward and hunkered low, rattled down a dozen steps to the harbor basin, where he swung into an elegant curve. Stunned, Stephanie stared after the crazy daredevil, who was now airborne, flying in a low arc across a bannister. Not into the water, good God! No, onto a jetty with boats tied up at its end.

Smiling resignedly to herself, she had to admit that, right now, her female intuition appeared to be on hold. Disappointed, she decided to drive back. She turned the ignition key, guided the Volkswagen back onto the road, up a gentle grade, past stately mansions and villas. Deep in thought, she missed the freeway entrance, which was just as well as far as she was concerned. Why not just enjoy the scenic drive back to Bern!

Well, Peter, she mused, for all that wonderful intuition of mine, here I am, rolling aimlessly through the countryside!

Half an hour after she decided to head back toward Bern, she passed a road sign that said *Nucleanne 3 km.* Wavelets of excitement rippled through her body, up the spine, through her head: *Laus . . . anne, Nucle . . . ANNE!* She tried out the sound of the words. Lausanne was past history, while Nucleanne . . .

For one thing, Nucleanne was a small town. And what did she have to lose? She smiled to herself: Feminine intuition, Peter, you don't know the half of it. Oftentimes, what it really amounted to was an admission to oneself that anything at all might be better than nothing.

So she drove into Nucleanne and parked on the town square. Not much of a place! Lausanne at least had a history, if only due to its proximity to Montreux, where famous men like Charlie Chaplin and Vladimir Nabokov . . .

She stopped dead in her thought tracks. That man over there, that ominous, stooping scarecrow with a golden hoop in one ear, and those rotting teeth! The killer! So much for feminine intuition.

It had guided her to within sixty feet of the freak who blew away two good men and now moved about with arrogant disdain, openly, as if nothing had happened.

"I must be dreaming," she muttered under her breath. This can't be true!

But it was true. And as she shuffled the pieces in her mind, it made perfect sense. Not Laus . . . anne, *Nucleanne* was the deadly trap Kern had talked about to Bachmann. Panicking, she ducked low out of sight, as the long-haired hit man strolled toward her car.

Not far from where the intrepid reporter once again confronted a particularly dangerous component in her recent nightmare existence, the great ten-story steel-and-glass headquarters of Schlammer Engineering stood gleaming in the afternoon sun. Its bluish, mirror-smooth facade reflected the outline of the gently hilly countryside around Nucleanne. A discreetly proportioned variant of Geneva's famous jet fountain threw sparkling cascades of water into the air. A large parking area shaded by a dozen stately ash trees delineated the Schlammer property's frontage on the road, where a converted aluminum container with windows of tinted glass served as a guard house overlooking a mechanical red-and-white boom that controlled vehicular access to the area. From the main structure, a gracefully curving canopy, unobtrusively held in place by two delicate fiber-glass cables, swung out over the entrance area in an elegant arc. The Schlammer headquarters exuded an unmistakable musk of modernism and big bucks.

The boom by the guard house was being raised for a black Mercedes limousine. The car rolled up the driveway toward the big building, through a mist of spray from the fountain, then came to a stop where the red-brick tiling of the drive met the white marble of the entrance hall. A chauffeur dressed in a dark-gray suit of military cut jumped out, jogged around the rear of the big car, and officiously yanked the back door open.

Out stepped Adam Schlammer. He bounced a couple of steps up toward the grand entrance, then pivoted to cast a long, appreciative look at the compound he owned and commanded.

The boss of more than a quarter of a million employees had every reason to be proud of what he had achieved during the worldwide recession of the early nineties. Along with just a handful of Swiss industry giants, he had been smart enough to initiate restructuring measures as far back as the late eighties, when economic barometers were still predicting neverending fair weather.

He had done this mainly by drastically trimming top and medium-level management. In addition, he had delegated decision-making powers downward to lower management, while shifting to a modular structure comprising four thousand operating units of fifty employees each, whose managers now reported directly to the president and CEO.

Satisfied with what he beheld, Schlammer turned and skipped up the rest of the stairs. He walked through the immense entrance hall toward the elevators, one of which was held open for him by a liveried doorman.

In a few short years, Schlammer's burgeoning technology group had made a tremendous leap forward when it managed to corner the Swiss market for nuclear waste management, such as it was. Where other, more conservative entrepreneurs had hesitated, Schlammer had dared to seize the iron and forge it while it was still hot and controversial. In a string of brilliant presentations he had personally sold the Swiss government on allowing privatization of the hazardous waste management area, thus throwing it open to business from all the European nations.

Initially, the news of a dump for nuclear wastes in Switzerland had been received with much skepticism by the European nuclear community. Whenever and wherever other European agencies had previously attempted to implement such programs, they had encountered immediate, stiff opposition from the residents in the designated areas. Now, as it became apparent that Switzerland indeed had thrown open its gates to radioactive garbage, a great sigh of relief was heaved by one and all. No one worried in the least that the name of the gatekeeper would be Adam Schlammer.

As he stepped out of the elevator into his penthouse suite, Schlammer reflected with relish on the important role chance had played in his life. He didn't mind at all being called an opportunist by his detractors. The way he saw it, opportunity was the lifeblood of business. And, more often than not, opportunities arose fortuitously. Chance, good fortune, creative errors and failure—these were vital components of progress, as he perceived it. Rational analysis alone will only take you so far, he liked to say. It was important to think laterally, and to accept unplanned developments as they occurred. Make them the springboard for forward leaps.

Nor, in Schlammer's view, was progress possible at all unless one was willing on many occasions to intelligently sidestep or disregard existing rules and regulations. Frankly, whenever necessary, not to give a hoot about them.

Feminine intuition! Stephanie Kramer softly cursed this mystical ability women were supposedly endowed with as she watched the killer advance upon the Volkswagen. At the last moment, she grabbed the shoulder bag off the passenger seat and held it up in front of her face. But the hippie-haired freak simply climbed into a Japanese 4WD parked in front of her. Maybe he wasn't the killer after all. Maybe she was caught in some sort of twilight zone, disoriented by the unreality of it all!

Yet, as the man unlocked the car door, slanting a shifty look backward in her direction, there was no mistaking that pockmarked face, the bobbing motion of the shaggy head, the stoop, the slight limp. It was him, all right: the man on the path, the man in the street, in her apartment, on the roof, on the escalator in the railway station. Oh yes, it was the killer!

During the sixties, Nucleanne—Switzerland's first experimental nuclear reactor—malfunctioned due to a flaw in the cooling system. As a result, the Swiss administration shut down the facility. At that time all radioactive components at Nucleanne were sealed away in six containers, weighing from seventeen to ninety tons each. These were then stored as inactive waste deep inside a former munitions dump in the mountains.

About this time, during a tedious reception at the Romanian Embassy in Bern, Adam Schlammer bumped into a man named Roger Ingramm, who was an upper-echelon civil servant working in the Swiss Department of Energy. Halfway through their second vodka gimlet, Ingramm suggested that Schlammer lease the entire underground complex at Nucleanne for use as a storage facility. Schlammer, who had been listening keenly, finally inquired who would then be in charge of the nuclear waste deposits already stored there.

"Well," the official shrugged, "that would be a fine point. Perhaps too fine a point to bother anyone with, should you, for example, Herr Schlammer, wish to assume that responsibility."

Predictably, Schlammer soon negotiated a long-term contract, valid until 2011, that gave him the right not only to utilize the storage facility but also to make any structural alterations he saw fit. The leasing fee quoted by the Swiss Nuclear Authority was indecently high, but Schlammer, not by nature inclined to disapprove of highway robbery, paid without blinking. Experience had taught him that extortionist fees often metamorphosed into blue-chip insurance: if ever the government decided to inquire into the goings on at Nucleanne, the lofty price tag would surely tend to discourage too close a scrutiny.

Or, as he himself put it: What goes up must come down—usually with a bang.

Indeed, Schlammer's Nucleanne acquisition turned out to be a knockout bargain. The immense cavern, hewn into solid rock, reached several floors down into the mountain. The Hole, as insiders dubbed it, featured an immense, domed central hall that housed the burnt-out reactor. Structurally, the facility resembled any one of the numerous fortified installations located throughout Switzerland, designed to serve as underground shelters for long-term occupancy during national emergencies.

The Hole had been designed to function as an autonomous, closed system, capable of being hermetically sealed off from the surface. Capable of generating its own energy, it included primary and secondary water purification and air conditioning systems. In addition, there was virtually unlimited space for communications equipment and a wide range of other technological gadgetry. Schlammer gleefully figured that the ten million Swiss francs rental fee he paid each year for the Hole amounted to no more than a flea fart in a hurricane. If that!

The moment the killer at the wheel of the 4WD finally got around to pulling out from his parking spot, Stephanie had a vision. Time slowed down. She beheld an enormous wave, a glassy wall of water of turquoise transparency, rising slowly, so high that it blotted out the horizon. A ceremonial tidal wave, this, festooned with plumes of white ocean spray, bearing down on her. Instinctively, in her waking body, she brought up an arm to shield her face. The vision faded. Her arm remained at rest on the wheel. Automatically she cranked it to the left and started up the engine. She slipped out of her parking spot and fell in behind the assassin's gleaming Mitsubishi.

They drove through the ascending terrain in tandem, the white 4WD at a comfortable distance in front of her. Now it crested a rise and was momentarily hidden from view. When she got to the top of the hill, the Mitsubishi had vanished. She stared incredulously at the mountainous hillscape dominated by a huge cube of a building whose glass-and-steel facade reflected the nearby mountain and the surrounding pastel-colored factory compounds.

If he'd parked his distinctive-looking vehicle on the parking lot, she would immediately have noticed it. She decided he could not have got very far, and pulled the Volkswagen over onto the asphalted soft shoulder, with nothing but emptiness and failure staring her in the face. Just as she prepared to turn back, something at the far side of the concrete parking area caught her eye: an arched gateway. Which moved!

Large, gray-mottled portals parted, slid back to blend almost seamlessly into the brushy, rocky mountainside. She squinted, straining to peer into the gaping black opening. No use forcing herself to search for the Mitsubishi's tail lights glowing in the dark passageway. In fact, she saw nothing. The killer had been swallowed up by the mountain. Now the portals closed, locking her out. Once more, nothing moved.

She decided to continue along the roadside frontage of low factory buildings. The *Schlammer Engineering* logo glinted in the late afternoon sun as she took the Volkswagen up the narrowing road until she came to a stretch of level ground. There she stopped. Ahead, in solitary splendor atop a hill, lay an ancient country estate. Around it were meadows and pine groves. Very charming, very picturesque. She frowned, just another damn dead end!

So the great Stephanie Kramer, ace investigative reporter, sat in her pathetic little car, head tilted back on the backrest, trapped in a waking nightmare, spent. She closed her eyes. Once again that monstrous wave rose against the horizon, white spume frothing along its top curl. She was too exhausted to fight the terrible vision that blotted out an even more terrifying reality.

"Great, this, all of this here," Schlammer congratulated himself as he gazed out at the mountain from behind the glass walls of his immense study. "The crowning glory of my life's work. So far!"

Concealed deep inside the forested massif whose far flanks plunged spectacularly into the savage depths of a dark ravine was the very cutting edge of Schlammer microtechnology. This was where Schlammer Engineering specialists designed matchbox telephones, transceivers, miniclockworks and telecommunications equipment. This was also where they designed and manufactured microchips and used sophisticated laser technology to coat superconductors.

With all of these activities, by far the largest portion of the vast subterranean space was taken up by the nuclear waste disposal facilities. In addition, the mountain housed the R&D laboratories of Schlammer Engineering, as well as a now defunct observatory Schlammer had inherited in the bargain. The tycoon smiled at the improvisational logic that had inspired him to upgrade this facility into what, for wont of a better term, he had come to think of as his very own private astrolab—well, not quite, but . . .

Schlammer approached a multifaceted board of computer screens. He punched a sequence of keys. One of the screens fluoresced to life: a view of conveyors, turntables and transport systems coalesced into being. As he watched, the conveyor system transported a bright-yellow barrel to the docking station. Along the top edge of the screen oscillated the legend 18:34 HOURS/BETA-GAMMA-BOX/RAW WASTE CONTAINER NUMBER 14.

Protected by an arrangement of radiation baffles, a coveralled operator manipulated the claws of a remote-controlled crane to position the barrel, then push it onto another conveyor. The adjoining screen on the board showed a second container as it slid onto a turntable, then moved toward a lifting robot. Two carts with thick rubber wheels, each carrying two of the bright-yellow containers, now moved from right to left through the foreground of the monitor display. The computer noted and registered each container according to whether it was empty or filled with raw waste. Work-in-progress digits, along with a running total, reeled off at bottom left on the monitor screen.

Schlammer activated a screen on the bottom tier of the display board. Pale electronic mists condensed into a wide-angle view of a large laboratory area enclosed by bare walls of bluish-gray color. In the background, a silvery figure was moving back and forth on a stainless-steel platform that was sealed off from its surroundings by a massive radiation lock.

Schlammer zoomed to a closeup of the mechanical figure at work on the platform. Its helmet bore the inscription SMARTY in bold black letters. Smarty was a third-generation biomimic robot, designed by Momoto, the Japanese robotics giant, which probably accounted for its vaguely Asian appearance. With humans strictly banned from the high-intensity radiation environment on Subfloor 3 of the former reactor facility at Nucleanne, electronic coolies like Smarty handled all of the hazardous work. This type of robot was particularly adept at mixing radioactive waste materials with glass, a job that would have caused the immediate malfunction of any human organism.

Even though Schlammer himself had had absolutely nothing to do with developing the principles his robots implemented, he felt inordinately proud to have learned that the molecular structure of glass made an excellent binding agent for radioactive materials. Physiologically highly inert, glass retained its structural integrity for thousands of years before disintegrating. Once absorbed into its crystal grids, radioactive waste materials were safely locked away—

virtually forever. Leakage into the environment, especially into the ground water, became impossible.

So impressive had Schlammer found this state-of-the-art technology that he created a company he named Schlammer Green Please Corporation, expressly designed for the purpose of nuclear waste disposal through glass bonding. Smarty robots poured the radioactive waste and glass admixture into 300 × 60 cm stainless-steel cylinders, which were then buried in a vast, thickly insulated cryptlike hall directly beneath the service level. Using his index finger, Schlammer touched a key that activated the totaling function. The computer indicated a current grand total of 20,560 cylinders placed in storage.

"Let's see how much that comes to," Schlammer muttered. Whenever thoughts of large sums of money crossed his mind, which happened frequently, the tycoon felt a syrupy sweetness spreading through his abdomen and into his loins. Occasionally, as now, such associations actually resulted in an erection. Staring fixedly at the columns of digits rolling across the screen, he unabashedly adjusted his Armani trousers to create more space in the genital region.

According to the multicolored graphics, his nuclear waste disposal operations had earned a total of U.S.-$534 million, with rental income from cylinder storage operations amounting to U.S.-$203.5 million per year. Reclining voluptuously in the contour chair, his eyes never leaving the screen, Schlammer absently reached for a crystal bowl in the shape of a curled-up iguana with the initials C de C etched into its elegantly ornamented lid: a gift from Don Cali de Cali, filled to the brim with the finest Colombian cocaine. He took off the cover, unceremoniously dipped thumb and middle finger of his right hand into the snowy profusion of powder, and, with two elegantly practiced flicks of the wrist, stuffed both nostrils full of Don Cali's bounty. After some more noisy snorts he pushed the bowl aside, closed his eyes, and allowed his mind to billow and bloom in the smooth rush of superior coke.

The wave that was towering over Stephanie, threatening to bury her, turned out not to be a wall of glassy green water, but a huge harvester of yellow steel bearing down on her from behind, seemingly out of nowhere. Caught floundering between her vision of the ethereal wave and the very tangible threat of being crushed by a monster machine, she waited, gasping, for the crunch of metal on metal as the harvester would squash her Volkswagen like a sardine can, with herself in the unglamorous role of the sardine. When nothing like that happened, she pulled herself together to poke her head out of the window for a cautious glance backward.

High above her in the cabin of the monster the handsome young operator grinned happily down on her. He wore a black baseball cap with a net top, a horse mane of blond hair pushing through the opening in back. He seemed to have all the time in the world as he caressed her outrageously with hungry eyes. The logo on his cap proclaimed: *Need a Charmer? Try a Farmer!*

On the harvester's windshield big decals spelled out another slogan: *Farming Is Everybody's Bread and Butter.*

The laid-back posture of the young buck atop his grimy, noisy monster, his casual wave and ready laughter pulled her back into the real world. The kid up there really liked her—and his innocently horny appreciation of her confirmed her very existence in the world of flesh and blood. Smiling happily, she paraphrased: I think he's giving me the eye, therefore I am!

Blood rushed into her face, a warm sense of human comradeship flooded her, all of her. What was she doing, waving back at him? Especially waving back at him as she imagined his powerful thighs, his . . .

Thank you, Mr. Youngbuck Farmboy, for restoring me to the world.

She started up the car and unhurriedly pulled out into the road. She drove back up to where she had first seen the old country estate, turned and rolled back down, passing the kid in the harvester. One last time their smiles met, merged, turned to laughter.

Again she drove by the Schlammer Engineering spread. Clouds covered the sun, softening the light, reducing the glare. There, the cave's steel portals parted again!

Startled, she hit the brakes and slid to a stop. A red minibus emerged at high speed from the cave. She caught a fleeting glimpse of a face, auburn hair, a mustache perhaps: not the killer, in any case. This was someone she had never seen before. Whoever he was, he'd already turned onto the road, roaring past her down into town.

If she hadn't already been noticed, she soon would be. Time to get out of here—but slowly, casually, like some aimlessly sightseeing visitor admiring the mighty castle with the great bear coat-of-arms on its fortress walls across the valley. Easy now, she told herself, be inconspicuous, move casually, a slow coast down into Nucleanne. The most fascinating town in the world. Right now it was, as far as she was concerned.

While Stephanie labored to recapture her joie-de-vivre, Schlammer was back on the speaker phone. Listening impatiently to the endlessly slow signal tone at the other end, he paced up and down, fists clenched in his trouser pockets. Outside the enormous facade of glass, a Turkish window washer slowly cranked his platform through Schlammer's field of vision. The tanned, wiry-looking worker waved casually back at two teenage boys and a dark-skinned girl who whistled up at him as they bicycled through the inner court. Even though his mind was elsewhere, Schlammer absently registered everything until a harsh, familiar voice rasped through the speaker.

"Hannibal here."

"There's this woman, this reporter," Schlammer said, "that cunt who's always poking her nose into other people's business. A friend of Kern's, I think."

"Stephanie Kramer, boss. A real looker if you ask me—"

"I didn't," Schlammer cut in. "I want you to search her place, see if she's made notes, anything. She was close to Kern, maybe working on a story. Like the thing she did on that fast breeder near Lyon, what was the name, Cray . . . Cray . . . Cray . . ."

"The Creys-Malville Super Phoenix," Hannibal supplied dutifully.

Yes, of course, Schlammer remembered it well. Practically still a teenager, Kramer, the budding journalist, had broken through overnight with her story of seriously deficient safety at Creys-Malville. She'd spiced her account with a wealth of well-researched detail about what might go wrong in the handling of plutonium, and what would happen if it did. Scared the shit out of people, she had. Scared them into shutting down the whole thing in 1990.

Schlammer flapped his arms like some great bird of prey preparing to launch himself from his lofty perch to plunge down on a tiny speck in the valley below. A speck his peerless sight had identified as warm, bloody cunt meat.

"Where is she now?" he asked. "Maybe Kern managed to talk to her before he kicked the bucket. That would not be nice, not nice at all. You appreciate that that wouldn't be nice, don't you, Hannibal?

Of course Hannibal appreciated. He was the chief security officer at Schlammer Engineering, wasn't he? It was his job to appreciate security hazards. Mainly, he appreciated that the question as to whether or not he appreciated had been a rhetorical one. Which meant Schlammer was in one of his nasty moods. Which in turn was something Hannibal didn't appreciate at all.

"We'll take care of her, boss," he said. "I'm sure she was having an affair with Kramer."

"So?" Schlammer coldly cut him off. "What do you care? But if they were fucking, she probably knows more about him than just the size of his dick. Like inside information, explosive stuff. Go in and find out. And do me a favor—neutralize the bitch!"

"Neutralize? Didn't you . . . I mean, uh, I thought we were just going to have Matak bring her in. Have a little chat with her, a little fun. She may decide to cooperate. If not, well, we can always . . ."

With a couple of bounding steps Schlammer was at the phone, growling directly into the speaker grate: "Yak yak yak! Do whatever you like. Stop yakking and get to work!"

He pounded the Clear key so violently that the entire unit hopped an inch off the desk, emitting a jangling screech. On impulse, Schlammer punched Redial. Hannibal came on again.

"One more thing," Schlammer hissed icily. "You call me boss one more time, just one more time, I'll feed what's left of your manhood to my pitbull, even if I don't have a pitbull. I mean your *dick*. To my pitbull. For breakfast!"

Stephanie immediately spotted the red minivan parked on the right-hand side of the street, away from the supermarket. She passed it slowly. Farther down the street she found a larger parking area where she put the Volkswagen, then strolled back to the minivan. Nobody paid any attention to her. When a truck rumbled by, she tried the van's sliding door: it gave. Summoning all her courage, she slipped in and pulled the door shut behind her.

Inside, tinted windows created a protective twilight. She pushed herself up over the rear bench, slid down into the hold. There she knelt, her heart beating high, holding her breath: She had to be crazy to be doing this! Who did she think she was, Joan of Arc? She was still smiling at her little joke when the driver returned. He pulled open the side door, threw some stuff in, slammed the door shut. She heard him walk around the front of the van. He got in, turned on the engine, then the radio. As they pulled out, thanks to the radio broadcast, she was given the benefit of the latest news on the Kern assassination:

"*. . . conducted on an international level, with all governments cooperating. At this hour, the killer or killers are still at large. And police are still looking for the woman who was seen near the assassination site. She is believed to be able to contribute vital information. Police would not confirm, or deny, that the woman is a suspect. The Swiss daily* Blick *reports today that she may be Stephanie Kramer, the well-known journalist, a close friend of the late prime minister, known to frequently accompany him on his early-morning jogging rounds. According to* Blick, *Kramer disappeared at about the* *time of the assassination. A source close to Police Chief Borli speculates that Kramer herself may be the victim of foul play. All-out efforts to locate the journalist are under way. Kramer is approximately 172 centimeters tall, with long . . ."*

At this point the driver switched stations. Eric Clapton broke in with "Tears in Heaven." Sensing the route she had taken earlier, Stephanie felt the minibus approaching the Schlammer Engineering complex. A couple of minutes later they bumped over a grate. The hum of the engine reverberated hollowly from tunnel walls. She pressed her fist against her lips to stifle an urge to cough. Or scream. Once again Stephanie Kramer, reporter extraordinaire, had penetrated a top-secret installation.

No! Stephanie Kramer, extraordinary fool! Once more she had jumped from the frying pan into the fire.

From the Schlammer highrise, Hannibal watched the minibus drive through the cavern entrance and disappear from view. Assuming it was Matak with Kramer inside, he tapped in Matak's cellphone number. Almost six foot seven, with a pale jelly-face, the towering Matak looked as if he couldn't hurt a fly. But hiding behind that innocent facade was a professional hit man. Where the hell was he!

Hannibal hit Clear and again punched in the number: Matak's phone was off. The pig was probably having a ball with the journalist, Hannibal thought. Then he punched in the number of his contact in Bern.

Outside, two guards with German shepherds on short leashes were patrolling the yard. Soon they moved over to the cavern entrance and disappeared inside.

The Iraqi with the pencil-thin mustache stared fiercely at Schlammer, who ignored him. As far as the Swiss tycoon was concerned, a camel driver by any other name was still a camel driver.

The Iraqi's mellifluous tones belied his angry facial contortions as he said, "My dear Mr. Schlammer, I'm sure you will agree that my principals have shown you the very greatest consideration and patience. We expect product delivery no later than tomorrow. We will pay cash, as agreed." He patted his black Vuitton attaché case as if the cash was already in it.

His companion, who had been introduced as Dr. Krauthammer, was busy fingering the sorry imitation of a Vandyke beard that grew on his recessive chin. Above the scientist's furrowed brow, strands of wispy hair fought a losing battle trying to cover up a pinkish, pointy pate.

Schlammer disdainfully ignored the Iraqi's impertinent gaze. He hated having to deal with ugly Hussein trash like this. The fellow's stocky build and yellowish skin annoyed him, as did the impeccably cut designer suit, the gold Rolex, the designer attaché case. Frosting on the cake was the creep's command of a grandiloquent, accent-free German.

Schlammer's voice betrayed none of these impressions. "Perhaps we're going a little too fast at this point in time. Considering the sum involved, I'd feel a lot more comfortable if I had some sort of indication, beyond the minimal advance your principals have deposited, that such monies can indeed be paid by your group. Let's go downstairs and talk some more about all of this, shall we?"

At a touch of his hand, a stretch of polished-brass wall in a corner of the room swung open, revealing an elevator door.

"Mr. Schlammer," the Iraqi said sharply, "I must remind you that for years our by no means negligible down payment has been accumulating interest in your account. We are talking not of a minimal advance but substantial sums of money."

Ignoring the obnoxious foreigner, Schlammer simply walked to the elevator and stepped inside, so the Iraqi and his disheveled sidekick had no choice but to follow. As the doors closed, Schlammer caught a passing glimpse of a silhouette outside the see-through walls of his office. It was that Turk, the window washer, looking like a cardboard target at the receiving end of a shooting range. Hadn't that hash-smoking drifter already done this stretch of windows today? Dismissing this observation with a shrug, Schlammer turned his attention back to the Iraqi.

"Mr. Hazmoudi," he said, "you know very well that the planned transactions would have been carried through long ago if your government hadn't chosen to wander into Kuwait, which in turn resulted in the embargo that has held up our plans."

Hazmoudi raised his palms in a placating gesture. Dr. Krauthammer nervously smoothed a lonely, oft-patted tuft of hair on the crown of his cone-shaped head. The elevator door slid open and Schlammer walked to a golfcartlike vehicle on a nearby track. The two men followed silently.

As they moved along on one of the lower levels, Schlammer gestured at the cart and the rails. "If you're wondering at the smooth ride, we're being wafted along by means of superconductors that have been developed as part of our in-house research program."

Krauthammer promptly leaned sideways, thrusting his nose out over the rails, like a ferret testing the air for the veracity of Schlammer's statement.

Schoenhof was waiting for them in the demonstration area. He wore a white lab coat and had positioned himself next to a dark-green, boxlike container. With a gesture that subtly managed not to include his employer, he invited the group to seat themselves in the luxuriously upholstered sea-green contour chairs. Repeated throughout the entire area, the sea-green color scheme introduced a soothing note into the chaotic profusion of monitors, screens, video cameras, control panels and other electronic gadgetry.

Schoenhof touched a sequence of color squares on a display, and the lights dimmed. On one large screen appeared the image of a container identical to the one that stood on the table before them. Three cameras recorded what was happening in the demo room, while Hannibal, the security chief, watched through a concealed surface from the control room.

The container's measurements were now displayed on the screen. "That's about the size of a TV set," Schoenhof lectured. "Including the fission pack, this box weighs 73.9 kilos, the weight of the fission pack accounting for 26.5 kilos of the total. The two units can be transported separately and joined in a matter of minutes. Any adult of normal strength would be able to carry the fission-pack unit in a backpack or suitcase."

On the screen, two men in combat outfits were busying themselves with the container.

"What you see here has been given the designation SADAM, which is short for Special Atomic Demolition Ammunition," Schoenhof continued. "You are looking at the smallest operational nuclear device currently available, meaning the smallest unit in weight and cubic centimeters of space occupied. Specifically, we call it the SADAM-54-SL93. For a bit of history, the first devices in the SADAM lineage were developed in Los Alamos during the 1960s. The Americans called that weapon the W-54. At that time, some three hundred such units were allocated to the U.S. Army and the Marine Corps. Later the Soviets tried, unsuccessfully, to copy these weapons. Eventually, the Soviet team asked us for help with one of their nonfunctioning prototypes. We were then able to improve on the American original, mainly by improving the trigger and detonator functions."

Dr. Krauthammer ostentatiously cleared his throat. Affecting the air of an old hand at this game, he croaked, "So what kind of punch does this thing pack?" He impatiently waved his eyeglasses, giving a provocatively comical impression of a mad scientist trying to appear perfectly rational.

"The precise yield is .25 kilotons," Schoenhof replied, then turned to Hazmoudi.

"That is approximately the equivalent of the explosive power of 250 tons of trinitrotoluene. I should point out that 250,000 kilos of TNT,"—he pursed his lips just enough to indicate respect— "well, 250 tons of TNT blowing up is not just a couple of firecrackers going off on New Year's Eve."

Unimpressed, Hazmoudi asked, "How do we know this device actually works?"

Schoenhof's fingers lovingly stroked the monitor display, then pointed at the big screen where the two soldiers were maneuvering the SADAM unit into position. The next sequence showed a panoramic view of a desolate desertscape. A flash momentarily blanked out the entire scene; then a giant fountain of dust, dirt and debris rose skyward. In an instant, it had formed a broadly based, almost rectangular pillar of black smoke that took up the entire center portion of the screen.

"This weapon was tested by us in the Soviet Union," Schoenhof explained laconically. "All systems worked perfectly."

The Iraqi nervously knotted and unknotted his fingers. Small beads of sweat on his upper lip made his mustache glisten. "And where is the mushroom cloud, may I ask? Every child knows that there must be a mushroom cloud. I venture to say this is no nuclear explosion."

From his hidden vantage point in the control room, Hannibal studied the Iraqi's greedily puffed-up visage. With his transfigured stare at the nuclear package, Hazmoudi looked like an addict desperate for a fix. Hannibal nodded with satisfaction as Schoenhof continued his lecture.

"Due to the design of the device it can be detonated only at ground level, which means a zero altitude blast. Unlike those nuclear devices detonated at higher altitudes, a ground-level blast does not produce the classical mushroom cloud. A zero-altitude blast is a dirty business, gentlemen. Thousands of tons of earth and dirt and dust are sucked up into the atmosphere and distributed over a vast area, later to settle back on the surface. Each and every particle of this literally atomized earth and dirt is radioactive and will contaminate the affected area for decades or even centuries with lethal agents such as cesium and strontium 90. However, the ground-level A-blast you just witnessed does produce a sort of chopped-off mushroom cloud effect. As you can see, the diameter of the pillar of smoke almost approaches that of the type of mushroom cloud that would result from a high-altitude blast."

At about the time Adam Schlammer's physicist was nasally lecturing Hazmoudi and Krauthammer, four men were leafing through identical copies of a thickly bound report compiled by the National Security Agency. The four had gathered that morning at a round, gunmetal-gray conference table in a soberly white-walled room on the 35th floor of the Trump Park Building in Manhattan. Three of them were case-hardened operatives.

The fourth man would not have objected to being called a case-hardened *amateur*, as certain pros in the intelligence business indeed sometimes did. He was Harald Wagner, chief of intelligence in Vienna for IAEC, the International Atomic Energy Commission.

In the considered opinion of the National Security Agency's Bill Conklin, Wagner constituted a distinct security risk. Conklin believed that what the IAEC called its Intelligence Division was no more than a pathetic, dilettantish exercise in futility. No wonder Wagner had never learned the rules of the game! On the other hand, since the Austrian had been placed at this table on White House authority, he'd have to be tolerated—though not necessarily accommodated.

Conklin decided that the spy business wasn't what it used to be. Aloud, he came straight to the point.

"Gentlemen, I don't have to tell you that there are too many in the world today with their itchy fingers on nuclear triggers. Take a look at the charts in your folders, if you will. As you can see, we now estimate that some twenty-five nations on this planet have developed or are engaged in developing nuclear weapons."

He adjusted a transparent sheet in the overhead projector, then switched it on. A statistical table appeared on the white wall, under the heading:

FIGHTING OFF DOOMSDAY
The Global Arsenal

Declared nuclear weapon states
(longest known range in kilometers)

Great Britain	4,600	**
China	15,000	**
France	5,000	**
Russia	13,000	**
Belarus	10,500	**
Kazakhstan	11,000	**
Ukraine	10,000	**
U.S.A.	14,800	**

Undeclared nuclear-weapon states

Israel	1,500	**
India	2,500	
Pakistan	300	
Switzerland	???	

**capable of carrying nuclear warheads

Nations working on obtaining nuclear arms capacity

Algeria	65
Iran	500
Iraq	300
Libya	300
North Korea	500
Syria	500

Shrugging, Conklin looked around the room. "As we know, the United States, Britain, France, China, Russia and Israel all have carrier systems—missiles, rockets, bombers, submarines, artillery, and other types—that are capable of delivering a nuclear punch on target." He pointed at the lower portion of the chart. "The other countries listed here are trying to develop or acquire such systems."

"Yeah, like North Korea," interjected Simon Golan, a wiry man with black, crew-cut hair that was graying at the temples. Muscle chords reached from his neck all the way up to the jawline of his weatherbeaten face. There was a strangely casual, cutting edge to his voice. "Face it, North Korea has enough plutonium to manufacture two to four bombs. They've already tested a carrier system, the Nodong 1 missile, which has a range of 1,000 kilometers. Everybody in Israel knows that these missiles are being developed for sale to Iran. Which means my country will be inside the range of target-true, state-of-the-art missiles capable of carrying nuclear warheads."

Golan paused, his bright blue eyes sizing up the others at the table. When he continued, he spoke in a low, persuasive voice. "Iran is systematically engaged in developing a dangerous nuclear potential. This clandestine operation is headed by Colonel Reza Fahimi, an ambitious, power-hungry, highly intelligent strategist who won't rest until his country commands an operational nuclear strike force. As chief of covert operations, he reports directly to the prime minister. Fahimi is a dedicated, unscrupulous soldier—a lethally dangerous adversary."

Wagner was still jotting down notes after Golan had finished. Krutov, the Russian delegate, gestured affirmatively, as if he knew Fahimi personally.

Conklin took only a moment to digest the input from Golan. Both elbows on the table, his chin resting on his hands, he said, "From what you're saying, Colonel, it seems to me the current trend of defense cutbacks in Europe is premature, to say the least. Why limit our vital strategic considerations to accommodate budget reductions? Doesn't make sense to me at all. Crazies or ruthless criminals in uniform, like this Fahimi, aren't even noticed, let alone taken seriously. It seems to me the West today is more vulnerable than at any time since just before World War II."

Silence descended on the group. Wagner stared up at the *Fighting off Doomsday* figures on the screen, his hand twirling a pen. A moment later he was back to scribbling notes on IAEC letterhead paper. The Russian delegate looked miffed as he pondered the significance of clandestine transshipments of nuclear products through Crimean ports. There was a glint of amusement in Golan's eyes as he watched Conklin pace the room like a caged tiger.

Friends of long standing, Golan and Conklin had made a highly efficient team during the Gulf War. Just before the air strikes started, they had managed to spirit a SAM-7 right out from under the noses of the Iraqi generals. As a result, the Russian-made targeting equipment, which included frequencies and target data for the feared SCUD-C rockets, eventually ended up in the hands of the Saudis.

"Well, gentlemen," Conklin continued, "I can't stress enough the devastating potential of a black market for nuclear weaponry." He paused briefly, for emphasis. Then, "I want to show you a little movie we've put together, a dramatization of how a terrorist group might get a hold of a nuclear device, deliver it to target, and detonate it there."

He activated the video deck. The film opened with a picture of *Fat Man*, the atom bomb dropped on Nagasaki. This was followed by a group portrait of a smiling crew posing in front of the plane that dropped the bomb.

While the four secret service knights of the roundtable stared in fascination at the horror scenario dreamed up by Conklin's people, across the Atlantic Adam Schlammer uneasily studied the men around him.

It bothered him that Schoenhof had obtained disturbingly reliable information indicating that Hazmoudi might attempt to smuggle a SADAM system into the United States. One reason Schoenhof had reached this conclusion was that the Iraqi had tried to obtain from him information on ultra shortwave frequencies used along the East Coast of the United States.

The mere thought of one of his nukes being introduced into the U.S. gave Schlammer the shivers. Key companies over there were among his major clients. He'd allow nothing, certainly not the false prospect even of enormous profits, to disturb the harmony of the cherished business relations he had built up over years.

The Swiss tycoon squinted hawklike at Hazmoudi. He had serious doubts if this camel-driving bastard son of a camel driver actually commanded six hundred million U.S. dollars, cash on the table—or the equivalent of a table—to pay for one complete, operational SADAM system. No, it would be expedient to keep negotiating a little while longer, then abort the whole thing. Contractually, the downpayment of U.S.-$ ten million would go to Schlammer, as was only fair, since the Iraqi had been allowed to pick up valuable inside information on the evolving market for carry-on nukes. Bored with having to look at the repulsive foreigner, Schlammer decided to visit his security chief. He produced a dangerous-looking eagle yawn, flashed a semi-apologetic smile at Hazmoudi and Krauthammer, then simply walked out.

When Hannibal saw his boss coming, he yanked his feet off the computer console and jumped up. What he feared especially was being pinned to the wall by the tycoon's laserlike gaze, like some bug.

"I'll tell you something," Schlammer announced as he arrived, "I wouldn't sell a pound of goat shit to those people. It's a matter of principle. I don't want to deal with people who make my skin crawl."

Hannibal was careful not to nod in agreement: Schlammer loved to pounce on brownnosers.

"Besides, I already have a much better offer. I'm talking to megamoney now, not like these Iraqi small-timers. All they're finally good for is trying to pan their greasy camel oil off on us for cash. I'm meeting a new negotiator, an American, Kenneth W. Custer. Get on it immediately. I want full details on this man. Today!"

"Yes, bo . . . I mean, sir. I like a little action myself, sir." Hannibal was keeping his eyes glued to his monitors.

Schlammer snorted combatively. "In that case, what's the action on Kramer?"

Crouching in front of the monitors, Hannibal obediently ran down his recent intelligence developments. The reporter had used a credit card to rent a car. The security chief's contact at Eurocard had immediately informed him of this. One of their men had then paid a visit to the rental agency. Apparently, Kramer had purchased a map of western Switzerland, so he assumed that's where she was heading.

"She gave us the slip, sir," Hannibal finished, looking just concerned enough not to provoke the tycoon's disdain for self-pity. "She's a real pro, sir."

As so often recently, he had misjudged Schlammer's mood.

"What is this, Hannibal?" The president and CEO of the Schlammer Group roared. "Am I paying you to let some two-bit feminist tramp walk all over us? What the devil happened?"

"She kicked Matak—"

"That's it? She *kicked* poor old Matak?"

"—in the balls, sir."

"*What* balls? Since when do robots have balls?"

"I don't have all the details at my fingertips, sir, but somehow she got away from Matak. The police think she made a stopover at Ralph Christen's apartment, the military judge, you know."

Schlammer's voice dripped venom. "I know, Hannibal, I know."

"We underestimated her, sir, but we won't let her get away again."

Schlammer slapped his thighs with both palms. Laughter exploded from deep inside his chest.

"Kicked Matak. In the balls! A real ball buster, that one, eh? Just the kind of kick I like in a filly. Wouldn't mind getting a little of that action myself. . . ."

The security chief made the mistake of chuckling as if he, too, appreciated the humor in the situation. Schlammer's voice cracked over him like a bullwhip.

"You think that's funny? She's a troublemaker, that woman! I want her here, you understand? That's your job, Hannibal. I'm holding you responsible! I want her here by tomorrow, before noon. Don't fail me again! And I want Christen watched round the clock. Full surveillance. That man is unpredictable. Stay on top of him and keep me informed. On everything, understand? Every hour. If you have a problem with that, just remember what I feed my pit-bull for breakfast! Now get on it!"

He stalked off as if Hannibal had never existed.

The film Conklin was showing in the Trump Park Building had concluded. Krutov braced himself against the back of his chair. His broad shoulders swayed impressively. Above the mongol cheekbones, the narrow slits of his eyes gleamed dangerously as he spoke.

"Russia's most urgent problems are with the Ukraine. We're doing everything possible to gain access to the Ukraine's nuclear arsenal, which currently includes 170 pieces strategic missiles, 30 units nuclear bombers, and approximately 1,600 pieces nuclear warheads. We're considering implementation of military measures to ensure control of this powerful arsenal. The Ukraine has threatened to employ these very same weapons against us if we try to use force against them. As you can imagine, this is a tricky situation."

Krutov was an officer in the KGB, or what was left of that organization—and that, insiders claimed, was virtually everything. His job was trying to collect leftover nuclear weapons throughout the territory of the former U.S.S.R. which, as far as he was concerned, would soon be the territory of a reunited Holy Russia.

"My dear Vassili," Conklin said soothingly, "don't you miss the Cold War, when we all knew precisely where the front lines ran?

When our mutual deterrent capabilities guaranteed the balance of power? Weren't those the days!"

A communal sigh rose inaudibly from the assembly. Conklin offered a resigned shrug.

"Yes, gentlemen, we live in a topsy-turvy world, with danger lurking everywhere. Everything has become unpredictable. Spiteful potentates and lunatic fanatics obsessed with power are playing with the fire that may ignite a nuclear holocaust. If it isn't the Holy Q'ran that sounds the call to action, it's some other religion. People everywhere are again screaming for what Hitler called *Lebensraum*. Only this time the finger is on the nuclear trigger."

Wagner emitted a throaty moan. "Really, Mr. Conklin, isn't that a little ridiculous! Are you trying to tell us that the United States, the world's megapower, can't or won't contain these upstart nations? Who are you trying to scare with this sort of propagandistic garbage?" He looked pointedly past Conklin, through the window, and out over the verdant expanse of Central Park.

Conklin gave no indication of being in the least disturbed by the Austrian's remarks. "All right, Mr. Wagner, I'll be more specific. You see, now that the era of global confrontations is behind us, because the enemy we loved to hate, the Evil Empire, has pulverized itself . . ." he darted a quick glance at Krutov, then leaned across the table ". . . a whole slew of crazy totalitarian types have crawled out of the woodworks in brand-new power situations everywhere. These are utterly unscrupulous people, believe me, who won't hesitate to use nuclear or chemical weapons if they can get their paws on them. Saddam was the first to reach out for nukes, and we slapped his wrist in the nick of time. Others will try. As long as obtaining nuclear weapons is as childishly easy as it is today, the disaster of nuclear action is only a hair's breadth away."

Golan took a deep drag on an emerald-green cigarillo, then carefully blew three perfect smoke rings into the air; they rose to the ceiling like miniature copies of a mushroom cloud.

"I agree wholeheartedly," he said, "the nuclear threat is back in business. Especially these, uh, carry-on nukes, which I'm told are easy to obtain, provided you've got the cash." He demonstratively ground his right thumb into his left palm, in a money-counting pantomime. "It's childishly easy, all right!"

"Yes, indeed," Conklin nodded earnestly. "Now, let me remind you again that we're here to discuss ways and means of combating the threat of nuclear terrorism. That's the job our governments have entrusted us with. On the premise that four brilliant brains are more effective than one, I guess."

"Some premise!" Golan grinned. The others made appreciative noises.

But Conklin hadn't finished yet. "Among the measures implemented to inhibit the spread of nuclear technology is the creation, by the CIA, of the Center for Weapons Transfer—CWT for short. This is a nonaccountable organization with covert operations, designed to prevent the unauthorized delivery of nuclear weapons, by force if necessary. In addition, gentlemen, there is COCOM, in Paris, which cooperates closely with IAEC in Vienna, as Mr. Wagner can tell you. Its purpose is to stop unauthorized delivery of components needed for the manufacture of nuclear weapons. Also, the U.S. Government is spearheading a move toward achieving an international agreement banning all unauthorized commerce or trade in fissionable materials worldwide, especially of plutonium. The objective of our task force is to hunt down black marketeers in weapons and plutonium and put them out of business. Everywhere. And without mercy."

From under the stack of papers in front of him, Conklin fished out a sheet, dangling it nonchalantly between thumb and index finger. "I have here a report from the BND, the German Intelligence Service," he said portentously. Bracing his elbows theatrically against the tabletop, he used both hands to lift the sheet to his face. "During the past year alone, gentlemen, a total of fifty-five criminal incidents involving nuclear or other strategically relevant substances were reported throughout Europe."

Squinting across the top of the sheet at Krutov, he read, "Murmansk: three fuel rods for use with nuclear submarines stolen . . . Moscow: radioactive radiation used to murder businessman. A source of radiation had been concealed in his desk chair . . . A Bosnian action group announced it would detonate four nuclear devices in European capitals on New Year's Eve, unless its demands were met. Further: weapons dealers acting on behalf of North Korean interests are said to have delivered seventy-five kilograms of plutonium from Russia to the Philippines. Or how about this— four kilos of cesium-133 seized at the French-Swiss border . . . and this: more than ten kilograms of uranium oxide and three hundred grams of barium nitrate confiscated . . . and so on . . , ah, here, one more item." Conklin's brows contracted as he continued, "The

Serbs are said to be holding large quantities of uranium, as well as—get this—a suitcase-sized neutron bomb!"

Golan threw up his hands, "I don't believe it; that's a bluff, nothing but targeted disinformation."

Shrugging, Conklin tapped a middlefinger against the sheet. "BND," he said drily. "They didn't pick all this out of thin air. We'd better take them seriously, Simon. The situation has clearly deteriorated." He got up, went to a copying machine positioned against the wall and fed it the BND report. Gathering up the copies ejected by the machine, he went from man to man, handing one to each.

Adam Schlammer took his guests back along the same route they had come. Once they were settled in his study, he made a show of continuing to negotiate price, payment terms, technical details, even though it meant nothing to him. As far as he was concerned, he held an unbeatable hand. If a hawk could be imagined with a poker face, that was Schlammer as he stared over the heads of Hazmoudi and Krauthammer at the greenish donkey in a Chagall painting he had recently acquired.

Hazmoudi was tired of beating around the bush. "Mr. Schlammer, we will not tolerate any further slip-ups. Let me show you something."

The Iraqi opened his attaché case and extracted a video cassette, which he inserted into the tape deck. The Venetian blinds, lowered across the entire broad front of floor-to-ceiling windows, created a cool, muted twilight in the enormous room. Through the slats one could glimpse the jagged contours of a large, well-tended lawn surrounding the weatherworn wall of an old well. Schlammer lazily shifted his gaze from the Chagall to Hazmoudi. The impertinence of the man, not to bother asking for permission to use his equipment!

Hazmoudi touched the play key. Flickering mists appeared on the screen, then the ashen face of a man, set stiffly against a gray wall in an anonymous room. Schlammer blinked—once—involuntarily.

Hazmoudi touched the Pause key. "You know this man," he said.

Schlammer managed a shrug. Beads of perspiration glistened on his forehead. Of course he knew the man.

"Cohon . . ."

"Excellent. Germain Cohon. Who, in 1984, was in business selling Exocet rockets." Hazmoudi held the frame.

His throat parched, Schlammer croaked, "That was a long time ago."

The Iraqi reactivated the tape. Offscreen, someone shouted an order. There was laughter. Cohon began to undress. More laughter. Cut to a bright interior with white-tiled walls—a torture chamber, Schlammer decided, complete with the type of paraphernalia found in S&M dungeons. Two men pushed the naked Cohon into the picture, shoved him against the wall.

"A lesson in moral hygiene, Mr. Schlammer." Hazmoudi's voice was no more than a whisper. "Watch carefully. This is what we do with people who try to double-cross us."

He touched Fast Forward. An accelerated rush of frames showed Hazmoudi's goons spreadeagling the hostage, whose ankles and wrists were cuffed to the wall with absurdly comical speed. What Schlammer needed was a glass of water, a piece of bread, anything to distract his stomach from churning up its own nauseating juices.

Now they heard a high-pitched warble that Schlammer interpreted as a shouted order. Weirdly speeded-up cranks and pulleys began to stretch Cohon's legs and arms. Zoom to closeup of Cohon's face, distorted by pain. Using the remote control, Hazmoudi cut the volume to zero. One of the goons jerkily stepped up to Cohon. The knife in his hand flashed—one, two, three times. At the breakneck speed of the tape, Schlammer did not actually register Cohon's ears having been sliced off until he saw blood spurting from both sides of the Frenchman's head.

This, at last, was enough to propel the tycoon out of his chair. He grabbed the entire tape deck with both hands. One violent, wrenching yank and he lifted it, threw it at Hazmoudi, screaming, "You crazy sadist maniac! I'll—"

Anticipating Schlammer's move, Hazmoudi bent lithely at the waist. The deck missed him and crashed to the floor. The Iraqi calmly straightened his silk tie. "Just in case you were wondering what will happen if you try to pull our leg, Mr. Schlammer, we will pull yours!"

Schlammer took two steps to the deck on the floor. He lifted his right foot and brought it crashing down on the machine. The tremendous burst of kinetic energy generated by this eruption compelled one last response from the video player: the eject function spat out Hazmoudi's tape. Schlammer seized the advantage. Once again his Italian-made boot descended, this time on the narrow portion of tape that protruded from the aperture, neatly smashing it.

"And that's what I do with stupid videotapes like this one, Mr. Hazmoudi! Just in case you were wondering."

The Iraqi spread both arms in an effusive, conciliatory gesture. "Why quarrel, Mr. Schlammer? If I have offended you, please accept my sincere apologies."

Still gasping, Schlammer managed a few words. "All right. Accepted, Mr. Hazmoudi. And forgotten. Let's stick . . . to business . . . shall we?"

They shook hands, paying no attention to Krauthammer, who pretended to be nursing an invisible cut on his cheek, where one of the cables on the tape deck might have nicked him had he been anywhere near its flight path, which he wasn't. Schlammer and Hazmoudi, closer to each other now, were already walking down the corridor. Just before they got to the elevator, Hazmoudi stopped to admire a large painting. Pompously thrusting out belly and chest, he exclaimed, "Ah, a Goya! How I love the Spanish masters!"

Schlammer winced. What could this camel-driving peasant possibly know about the great Spanish masters! His equilibrium at last fully restored, he lectured patiently, *"The Four Horsemen of the Apocalypse.* By an anonymous Flemish master."

"Of course," Dr. Krauthammer managed to get in as the two stepped into the elevator.

Schlammer stood squinting at the closing elevator doors. Idiots! To imagine they could scare him with some silly torture tape. To imagine that he, Adam Schlammer, would identify with street vermin like Cohon!

Back in his study, he tightened the Venetian blinds, further toning down the indirect lighting, then called for the masseuse, Rosalia. By the time he had undressed, stretched out on the couch and closed his eyes, he heard her entering the room. At the first touch of her small, strong hands he thrust up his pelvis. All his pent-up tension and fear released itself in a garbled gush of verbiage: "Yes oh good so you good the way this makes you feel me yes yes now this soft don't there that's good right there don't stop my little bitch . . ."

Young Haluk, the window cleaner, was well liked around Schlammer Engineering. For a couple of years now he'd been steadily employed cleaning glass surfaces—small, large, and enormous—a neverending job, it seemed. He was always on time, a helpful and adaptable kid who often praised his good fortune for being allowed to work in such a wonderful place as Switzerland. No one could have suspected that this carefree and gregarious young man might be a member of the PKK, the militant workers' party of Kurdistan. Nothing in his calm, polite demeanor indicated the volcano of hate that seethed and churned inside of him: his three brothers had perished in the massacres Saddam Hussein inflicted on the Kurds after the Gulf War. His sister had been kidnapped by Iraqi regulars from a village in Northern Iraq, her fate unknown.

The leaders at PKK headquarters in Switzerland used Haluk in their intelligence operations, which were directed from Center 1 of the Frontline Committee of the ARGK, the PKK's armed-action unit. Haluk's job was to keep eyes and ears open and to report on everything he saw and heard. At first, he had looked at the assignment as a demotion. He loved action, combat—and what kind of combat action was watching and listening while you shimmied up and down great glass surfaces like a monkey? What sort of weapons were window rakes, sponges, pails of water and soggy cleaning cloths?

Soon, however, he began to realize that he'd been entrusted with an important mission and that polishing the Schlammer Engineering Building's facade to crystal splendor might just be as important as setting the timer on a plastic pack. Earlier that Monday, Haluk had watched Hazmoudi and Krauthammer arriving in a Mercedes limousine: just the sort of event that would make interesting reading in his next report. As he made his way across the facade of the building, he casually observed Schlammer and his guests in one of the conference rooms, then slowly steered his platform downward, carefully timing his descent to coincide with the re-emergence of the two men some forty-five minutes later.

He positioned his gear against the building, behind a double row of dwarf conifers. When Hazmoudi and his cone-headed companion came walking out of the building and stopped under the high-tech canopy, Haluk was well hidden from view. Still, just in case they caught sight of him, he pretended to be tightening a pulley cable with a pair of pliers, all the while remaining intensely focused on listening.

"The bastard wants to put one over on us," Haluk heard an excited voice babble in near-falsetto.

"Worse than that," came the calm reply, in a lower register, "he has no intention of delivering at all. He's looking down on us and our money. As a matter of fact, if he could have his way, he'd piss on us. So, my friend, we'll just have to take what is ours!"

As the two men moved away toward the parking area, Haluk caught one more fragment of conversation: ". . . tomorrow . . . we have reliable information . . . preparations are underway."

Sketchy, sketchy, to say the least, Haluk muttered to himself as he jotted down what he'd heard. He'd pass it on to his superiors. Let them analyze it. Probably some routine arms deal of no great urgency. He began to crank himself upward, slowly emerging from the conifer grove.

Below, the limousine was rolling slowly toward the road. Hazmoudi gestured disdainfully at a flower-fringed pedestal that supported a large cube of jade-green granite. One of the four faces on this tombstone of a clock, the one marked *New York*, indicated 08:15.

"How do you like that, Krauthammer," the Iraqi teased, blithely ignoring his companion's academic title, "the marvelous world clock, made of superior Swiss granite!"

Eager to expose his knowledge of worldly affairs, Krauthammer quickly informed his employer that one just like it stood in front of the U.N. building in Geneva. "For the life of me I can't see what's so great about these weird clocks," he said huffily. "They're everywhere—in front of museums, cluttering up public squares. A couple of months ago I saw one in front of the main post office in Singapore. And that hideous green! I don't know what people see in it. Maybe the combination of something as solid as granite and something as ethereal as time symbolizes control, strength, precision. Who knows or cares!"

Hazmoudi cared: a lot more than Krauthammer could have imagined. It was in precisely one of these green granite monsters marketed under the trade name of Rock'O'Clock, Clissot's answer to the Swatch, that Schlammer was using to house the SADAM device he had pretended to be selling to them.

Reclining comfortably on the luxurious back-seat upholstery, his eyes half closed, Hazmoudi's mind was bright and alert as it skipped over some of the details of their back-up plan, which was designed to cope with just the kind of situation they now had on their hands. His informants had given him the precise location where Schlammer guarded the dummy clock that contained the nuclear charge: an abandoned mine shaft in a cave high up in the mountains. Even though the information was reliable, his contact would confirm details of the location just before they went into action.

Meanwhile, a small, compact assault unit was in training in a remote mountain valley. Its leader, an experienced Hamas terrorist with a brilliant record in precision-targeted assaults on command posts and ammunition dumps, had arrived yesterday at Zurich-Kloten. He had immediately linked up with the two other members of the commando. The team had then picked up the helicopter, a black Cobra, which Fahimi's people had placed near Bern, then moved up into the mountains.

The Hamas hit man, known and feared as The Avenger, was now in place, awaiting action orders in their base camp. On instructions from Colonel Fahimi, the Iranian Embassy in Bern some time ago had placed an order for one Rock'O'Clock. A photograph of this unit was in the hands of The Avenger.

Hazmoudi squinted lazily at Krauthammer, who was busy biting his fingernails. Since all his nails were chewed down to the quick, Hazmoudi sustained some mild curiosity as to where the next point of attack on that ravaged fingerscape would be launched. At the same time, he was thinking that once Schlammer's carry-on nuke had been pirated, there'd be no further obstacles blocking the day of reckoning.

He once more glanced at his gold Rolex to assure himself of the date: Monday, July 2. Two more days, and the apocalyptic bonfire would light up the skies over Philadelphia. Such was the macabre surprise party planned by his principals for Independence Day in the United States. To avenge the humiliation inflicted on Iraq during the Gulf War—at least so the world would reason. Late, sweet vengeance it would be!

Finally disgusted with Krauthammer's cannibalistic chewings and spittings, Hazmoudi casually reached out and slapped the scientist's wrist. Shocked, Krauthammer started up, then thought better of it, muttering something into his beard. He sunk back into the upholstery, while Hazmoudi savored a gaudy visualization of how the nuclear charge, detonating only a couple of hundred meters from the site of Liberty Bell, would tear the very heart out of the American nation and its so-called dream. Perfectly concealed as it was in the world's favorite Swiss outdoor clock, protected by the Clissot quality seal! But this timepiece would contain two clockworks: one that drove the Rock'O'Clock, the other that would drive the world to the brink of despair.

Two days from now. A plan so satanic it out-satanized even the Great Satan America!

"Instead of biting your nails," Hazmoudi mildly admonished Krauthammer, "you should try a little harder to chew on reality. Memorize those circuits. Focus on faultless progamming."

Krauthammer affected a bored expression as he turned his face to the window and said, "There is perfect order in my mind, sir, you have nothing to worry about." As he finished, he managed to sneak his left hand up to his mouth and start gnawing on the thumb, which promptly started bleeding.

Hazmoudi wasn't worried in the least. In fact, he was silently congratulating himself on the brilliant idea of provoking the United States into launching a massive retaliatory strike against Iraq. Well, it was Fahimi's idea, actually . . . but he, Hazmoudi, was the key player in it, doing all the back-breaking work in the field. Without his intricate network of reliable contacts and connnections this, the greatest conspiracy of all time, could never have been undertaken. Tomorrow he'd modem a coded, cryptic message to Tehran: *SA-DAM is ours.* What an accomplishment! Even if Baghdad intercepted and managed to decode it, no, especially if they did, it might just send a bit of a chill down the spine of you know who.

Elated, yet suddenly enraged by Krauthammer's continued fingernail-biting, Hazmoudi sneaked a vicious little punch into the scientist's side. Squealing like a stuck pig, Krauthammer doubled over. Momentarily distracted, the driver almost sideswiped a red minivan that was coming up the hill. Both passengers flew to one side, against the backrest, as the driver wrestled the limo back across the dividing line. Hazmoudi was the first to crawl back up onto the seat. He sent a guttural string of choice Arab expletives after the minivan, then cursed his driver to vent a darkly unpleasant feeling that swept through him.

Stephanie Kramer, flattened into the darkest corner inside the van, heard only the squealing of the limousine's tires. Neither she nor the Iraqi had any conscious awareness that their paths had crossed. Yet, somehow, both had seen the searing flash and heard the clash of steel on steel.

As Hazmoudi's black Mercedes with its small red-and-green standard on the right front fender rolled out of the Schlammer Engineering compound, the sworn members of Adam Schlammer's general staff were congregating no more than a couple of hundred meters away, deep down in the rocky recesses of the nearby mountain. In the center of the oblong conference hall with its sea-green walls stood a large, oval conference table with a black-and-white speckled granite top. Just then only four, rather than the customary six, of the ten black-leather contour chairs were occupied.

In a few moments the president and CEO of the Schlammer Group in person would be seated at that end of the table he habitually referred to as "the top," commanding their full attention. Chair number six would remain unoccupied today.

To the right, seen from the "top," sat General Breckerlin, solid as a weathered rock in the corporate surf. His gaunt, imposing figure was covered in skin that looked as if it had been transplanted from a polished old riding boot. The black leather holster of a nine-millimeter service automatic bulged below a black leather belt drawn tightly around the old general's scarecrow waist. He wore combat coveralls with a green-black-and-yellow camouflage pattern.

His bony skull, whose sparse, closely cropped gray hair featured a razor-thin, razor-straight part, was dominated by greenish eyes, a sharp-ridged nose and thin, bloodless lips. With his elbows resting on the granite tabletop, Breckerlin thrust his cleanshaven chin forward, keeping his eyes steady on the door.

In fact, Dr. Dr. Adolf Breckerlin was not a general at all. When he deserted from active service in the Swiss Army to join Hitler's Waffen-SS in 1942, his rank was that of lieutenant. He fought in the eastern theatre, attaining the rank of Sturmbannführer, and was captured by the Soviets. Immediately after the war, he was inexplicably turned over to the French, who passed him on to the Swiss. While other active servicemen in the Swiss Army had been executed by firing squad for what amounted to minor infractions, Breckerlin got off with a ridiculously lenient sentence of three months in the stockade. He was able to continue his studies and eventually achieved doctorates in both history and economics.

Something of a dandy, Breckerlin frequently wore custom-tailored double-breasted suits and affected a monocle. He might have passed for a wealthy, charming gent of the old school, if he hadn't been fond of posing as a dashing officer type and maintaining close ties with the still sizeable clan of ex-Waffen-SS men. During 1992, for example, Breckerlin paid several visits to Rostock in the former German Democratic Republic, where he made substantial cash donations to the neo-Nazi movement, while expressing his profound appreciation of the firebombing of Vietnamese homes and refugee facilities.

For Breckerlin, Schlammer's nuclear waste management operations were a dream come true. He had organized the cavernous underground facilities like a mountain fortress, establishing his personal command center in the abandoned observatory that Schlammer thought of as his astrolab. The general's retreat came complete with an enormous weapons cache. His post was secure, for what Schlammer appreciated most in the fanatical old Nazi was Breckerlin's unconditionally blind obedience.

Across the table from Breckerlin sat Schoenhof, one arm draped casually over the backrest of his chair, the other extended, fingers tapping out a nervous drumbeat on the polished granite surface. He wore black cotton trousers, a wrinkled white lab coat over a blue shirt. The white collar framed a toxic-green tie bearing a pattern of bright yellow champagne corks that seemed involved in an intricate dance of absolutely no relevance whatever. The effect, if not the purpose, of this gaudy piece of apparel was to add a bold touch to Schoenhof's sullen, pockmarked face, as well as perhaps to distract from a rather prominent concavity on one side of his nose where some sort of miniature meteorite appeared to have impacted some time ago, judging by the scar tissue.

What the physicist lacked in comeliness he more than made up for with acuity. Schoenhof was considered the genius at Schlammer.

A cigarette dangled casually in one corner of his mouth, absently held in place by tiny furrows in his dry, flat lips. Schlammer's legal counselor, Geigel, who was busily arranging notes to the left of the scientist, emitted a series of eloquent coughings and throat-clearings as clouds of smoke billowed from Schoenhof's cigarette to waft past his crinkled nose.

Next to the general sat Hannibal. He wore flannel trousers, a windbreaker and a leisure shirt, all in earthy shades of brown and beige, which imparted to his athletic appearance a touch of the nature boy. Hannibal's alert, dark brown eyes shifted back and forth between his companions at the table and the windowlike board of monitor screens with their multifaceted view of the Hole's interior as well as of its topside surroundings.

Conspicuously absent from this secret assembly was Number Six, Viktor Gisling, former deputy chief of UNA, Switzerland's Department of Defense Intelligence. Disgraced after being linked with the government's secret militia organization, P-26, Gisling had fallen straight into Schlammer's welcoming embrace. The former UNA chief's turncoat switch to a rather opaque but no doubt lucrative position in Schlammer's megagroup had been viewed as treasonous by his former colleagues at UNA, who promptly nick-named him *Adam's Quisling*, in reference to the Norwegian fascist leader who had collaborated with the Nazis during World War II.

The P-26 affair, which involved clandestine efforts to build up a secret resistance force in the event Switzerland was taken over by a foreign power, broke in the wake of the collapse of the Soviet Union when public tolerance for clandestine military efforts had sunk to nil. Gisling realized that his former UNA colleagues would have no choice but to swallow their pride. Like himself, they too had only done their duty by attempting to build up a secret organization along the lines of similar groups already operating inside NATO.

The Swiss media criticized such clandestine efforts as Rambo games played by die-hard hawks, but were careful not to mention that preparation of defensive measures in the event of occupation by a foreign power were standard components in the wartime strategy of most responsible governments on earth. If at one time they had been prepared to sacrifice everything for their country, the P-26 patriots now felt betrayed and humiliated. Gisling found it easy to recruit most of his old buddies for his own private intelligence network. As Gisling's novel business concept caught on, public catcalls magically began to fade away. The exonerated traitor was paying double the money his associates made in their government jobs. The newly established network focused on gathering intelligence concerning refugees, activists among the foreigners in Switzerland, refugees, terrorist groups supported by Iran and Islamic fundamentalists in general, not to mention left-wing intellectuals, religious sects, environmentalists, and opponents of nuclear power.

All intelligence data obtained were transmitted in the professional mode, as practiced by Switzerland's secret agencies: in coded fragments, using microtelephony and computers. Dubbed *Lomoro*, Gisling's network soon functioned more efficiently than UNA, which was hampered by antiquated methods and certain constitutional restrictions imposed on it by bleeding-heart liberals in the government. To the embarrassment and chagrin of UNA, Swiss police agencies soon began to turn to Lomoro, paying hard cash for vital information.

While Adam Schlammer's four lieutenants, deep inside the recesses of the Nucleanne cavern, were waiting impatiently for their boss to arrive, Colonel Golan in New York pointed at the chart projected on the wall and demanded to know why Switzerland was listed in the same category as Israel. Conklin set down the glass from which he had been drinking.

"Well, Colonel, we're quite certain that someone or some group with an operational base, either in Switzerland or in neighboring France, is offering small-size and miniature nuclear devices for sale." Pointing at a stack of documents on the table, he added, "As far as we can tell, the bombs now available on the marketplace were obtained from the weapons arsenal of the former Soviet Union. Actually, we're practically certain this is so."

Krutov objected violently, "Absolutely not! No nuclear weapons have been delivered from CIS states to other countries, certainly not to Switzerland. Just think how ridiculous! Cheese, chocolate, clocks, 'The Swiss Family Robinson'—fine, but nuclear bombs? What a joke!"

Harald Wagner made no attempt to hide his irritation at Krutov's remark. In the Intelligence Division of the IAEC it was common knowledge that since the collapse of the Soviet Union a vigorous black market for enriched uranium, strontium, red mercury, and plutonium had sprung up. Contrary to what Krutov claimed, business was booming, with Switzerland functioning as a turntable and port of transit. Fission agents, such as plutonium and uranium, were taken into Switzerland's reputable testing laboratories for authentication and quality control. So real were the hazards of dealing in radioactive materials that Zurich banks regularly used Geiger counters to check their vaults for plutonium caches.

Still, even though Wagner knew that the Swiss had the technological know-how for manufacturing nuclear weapons, he doubted that they were using it. They had signed the Anti-Proliferation Treaty and, to the best of his knowledge, were sticking to it. Respect for international law and international agreements was nearly as sacred to the Swiss as was their dedication to keeping the Swiss Franc one of the world's truly hard currencies.

By contrast, in the meeting room beneath the mountains of Nucleanne, there was little disagreement among the members of Schlammer's general staff. They all knew why they were gathered for an emergency session at the granite-top table.

Despite Sunday's turbulent events, Schlammer had slept like a log. Now he was looking each and every one of his men straight in the eye. Schoenhof responded by lighting his third cigarette. Geigel's hands trembled noticeably as he pulled a pair of bifocals from his breast pocket; the magnification made his eyes look enormous, and enormously frightened.

Breckerlin's right hand fussed with the stiff, military-style collar of his hand-tailored, monogrammed silk shirt. Beads of perspiration glistened on his forehead. Still, he unflinchingly returned Schlammer's gaze and said, matter-of-factly, "Eliminating Kern was a mistake."

Schlammer angrily turned on him. "Listen, Breckerlin, I've invested millions in this operation. Our facilities are the most sophisticated in all of Europe. We're the best. And in case you've forgotten—" he gestured violently at the monitors where the cavern's various sections oscillated palely on a dozen screens "—we're making hundreds of millions with this stuff. I'm not going to let some green-tinted politician who thinks it's his duty to turn the nuclear energy sector upside down mess around with the century's most profitable business. He signed his own death warrant with that idiotic surprise visit yesterday—"

Undeterred, Breckerlin broke in. "This thing could turn nasty. The police will find out that Kern was here yesterday. They'll start snooping. I suggest we get ready for a police investigation, a search of these premises. Maybe even an outright raid!"

"We're prepared," Schlammer said calmly. "All weapons and related materials will be flown up into the mountains. Including the SADAM package the Iraqi is trying to buy."

Breckerlin combatively shifted his weight and said, "Why don't we hand it over to Hazmoudi right now? That's six hundred million in the kitty, and we'd be rid of some evidence."

Schlammer thrust out his chin. "No! No nukes for Arabs. Those camel-driving mongrels aren't playing with an open deck, so the deck is off. Tomorrow morning we're receiving blue-chip clients, a man from the drug cartel. That, gentlemen, is heavy South American money, and they're seriously interested in our carry-on line. With a little luck, they'll get here just in time to take that load off our hands. But, just to be sure, I'm still flying everything up into the mountains."

He jumped up and hurried toward the exit. In confusion, the others bolted from their armchairs and followed him. As he jogged along the corridor, Schlammer sliced the air with cutting gestures.

"Organizational stability is our first priority. The nuclear business must continue to run smoothly and grow. Anybody who gets in our way will be eliminated! That the prime minister managed to penetrate security is a damn sloppy piece of incompetence," he raged. "If you'd done the job I'm paying you for, Hannibal, this mess would never have happened. I want you to go after Kramer and Christen, right this minute, and no more fuckups, understand?" He angrily kicked the door to the personnel lock open.

"And you, Breckerlin, you're launching our PR campaign today! Get those ads out right now. Kern is dead, long live nuclear energy!"

He snorted at Geiger. "We don't want to lose our license, do we? Especially our cylinder storage business and our intelligent-bombs production. . . . Now listen, Geiger, the minister of justice is on our side. Make sure this Borli fellow doesn't bother him. That chief of police is a real rabble-rouser. Threaten the minister with cutting off our contributions to the Neutron Resource Fund. That's one hundred million Francs. Tell him we might decide to relocate the Schlammer Group abroad. That would cost them hundreds of millions in tax revenue. Get on it, Geiger, explain to the fellow what we want done!"

From somewhere behind Schlammer, Hannibal rasped, "No more slip-ups. I'm running an in-depth check of all security functions immediately. The entire system needs tightening. We need airtight controls, inside and out. All access points will be put on dual-control security alert. Slackers will be eliminated. Breakdowns in discipline mean the beginning of the end."

Schlammer stopped abruptly, pivoted. One arm shot forward, the fist connecting with Hannibal's chest. "I want that Kramer woman neutralized. I know the little bitch spells trouble."

Under Schlammer's penetrating gaze, Hannibal blushed. "I understand, sir. The police believe she has been moving west . . . uh . . . it's possible Kern dropped a hint about Nucleanne. But apparently she is acting independently, on her own initiative. The information we have indicates that she's been in contact with Chief Magistrate Christen. It seems she doesn't want to turn herself in to the authorities. Gisling and the Lomoro people are running tight, round-the-clock surveillance on Christen. If she tries to rendezvous with him, they'll grab her. I'm personally—"

Schlammer turned away, irritably mumbling his consent. Schoenhof suggested he now brief the executive staff on the new carry-on type nuke that would be shown to the drug cartel's emissary tomorrow. The men silently marched into the laboratory. Hannibal, who had dutifully hurried ahead in order to unlock the electronic safety door, felt Schlammer's laser gaze impacting in the back of his neck—or was it fear?

"The Kramer bitch," Schlammer snarled at him by the door. "Don't come whining again with excuses, or else. Remember my pitbull's breakfast treat?"

"Yes, sir," Hannibal stammered, one hand involuntarily clutching his crotch.

New York City, Monday, July 2

Wagner gave Conklin a long, irritated look, then ostentatiously glanced at his watch.

"Mr. Conklin," he said, "I for one haven't come all the way to New York to waste time with rumors and speculation. Let's have some facts, if you don't mind."

Conklin, who still hadn't warmed to the Austrian, made a show of getting up and slowly walking to the window. Never taking his eyes off the impressive Central Park panorama, he told them that it all went back to the days of Brezhnev.

At that time, a number of small-size nuclear weapons were delivered into Switzerland under the auspices of the old-guard Communists. In those days, Soviet leaders were crazy for state-of-the-art U.S. technology; they needed high-tech products for their armament industry, for rocket and missile guidance systems, for space exploration. You name it, they didn't have it. Much of this material passed through Switzerland en route to the Soviet Union.

Pausing dramatically, Conklin turned to address them. "You may ask: Why Switzerland? Switzerland is a neutral country, not shackled by political alliances. Switzerland is also known as a free country, one of the earliest modern democracies on earth, whose government prides itself on not interfering with business and the economy. This latter was the factor the Soviets exploited when they secretly used Switzerland for transshipment of U.S. technology."

"Just one moment, please," Wagner objected. "How about France and Japan? They weren't doing too badly in that department either."

"A point well taken, Mr. Wagner. But remember that Swiss firms themselves were, and continue to be, manufacturers of superior technology products. Which meant easy access to U.S. suppliers, who in turn trusted their Swiss business associates. Which created an ideal situation for this type of hanky-panky."

Conklin marched back to the table and sat down. Colonel Golan squinted intensely at the tip of his cigarillo.

"Come on, Bill," he jeered amiably, "that's old hat. Get to the point!" Wagner and Krutov made affirmative noises.

"As far as we can tell," Conklin answered, "official Switzerland was never involved with any of this. We believe the government of Switzerland never even knew it was going on."

"So?" Golan continued, still playing devil's advocate. "I still don't see the point."

Conklin told him that the U.S. Government had been far from blue-eyed in this matter. Contractually, Swiss buyers were obliged to assure U.S. suppliers that no sensitive technology would be processed, sold or otherwise passed on to any Communist nation. Any violation would result in the imposition of massive sanctions including, ultimately, a total ban on technology sales to the violating country.

"Which is exactly what happened, isn't it?" Wagner interjected with unbridled enthusiasm, gleefully recalling some of the conversations in Austria at the time.

"Exactly, yes," Conklin replied. "By the end of the seventies, we had a pretty good idea that there was a particularly huge hole in the Swiss cheese—a hole through which skillful intermediaries were funneling sensitive state-of-the-art technology from the West into the Soviet Union."

Krutov peered suspiciously at his newfound Western colleagues. "And what, if anything, did your government *do?*" he asked.

"We filed protests with the Swiss Government, naturally," said

Conklin. "Ostensibly, they had no idea this was going on. Not a single government agency could, or would, explain the technology leak. They left us no choice. We got tough."

"Wasn't that around 1976?" Golan inquired with feigned innocence.

Conklin nodded. "The exact date was March 11, 1976. The Senate Subcommittee on International Trade and Commerce issued a statement which, in relation to technology transfers, assigned Switzerland the status of a Communist nation."

"Which meant what?" Wagner asked.

"It meant," Conklin explained, "that the Swiss received as much as Albania or Poland, namely nothing. Not one screw, not one computer, nothing, until they had managed to plug up the leak."

"This high-tech embargo was lifted when a general in the Swiss army was exposed as a spy," Golan said soberly. "That affair stirred up a lot of dust. John le Carré even wrote a book about the good soldier, *The Unbearable Peace*. In Switzerland they called this Grandmère, that was the name of the general, the 'Spy of the Century.' "

Wagner chuckled at the graying colonel's youthful enthusiasm. "Jeanmaire," he corrected.

"All right, Jeanmaire, whatever." Golan ignored the interruption as he warmed to his subject. "He was sentenced to twenty years of hard labor. In 1977, I believe. A lot of people thought he was innocent, the poor bastard. Victim of an ugly little conspiracy, probably just to get the CIA off their backs . . . huh!"

His eyes were narrow slits, his lips compressed, head moving from side to side like that of a cobra ready to strike. The Israeli was talking himself into a dangerous mood.

"Take it easy, Simon," Conklin tried to calm him, "that's all water under the bridge. Let's focus on those nuke makers!"

Wagner lightly slapped the tabletop. "Yes, what about those nukes? What has this high-tech story to do with the nuclear bombs allegedly stored in Switzerland?"

Conklin poured more water into a glass, drank most of it, then addressed them with renewed vigor. "The CIA found the answer in Moscow. Long before the Berlin Wall came down, we received reliable information from a Soviet double agent—to the best of my knowledge the last of a dying breed. According to this man— actually I believe it was a woman—an outfit in Switzerland was trading sophisticated Western arms technology for nuclear weapons. A nice barter economy, if I do say so. Lacking a hard currency, the Soviets used nuclear arms for payment. Apparently, several dozen operational nuclear warheads were smuggled into Switzerland in this manner."

The silence that settled on the assembly was becoming oppressive when Wagner spoke. "And this mysterious double agent of yours, the last of a kind, did he, I mean she, tell you the name of that Swiss outfit?"

Conklin had anticipated the question; it went straight to the soft heart of his theory. He gave the Austrian a sour grin. "If we knew that, sir, there'd be no need for this meeting. We could have taken care of the situation long ago."

The Israeli shrugged indifferently, while the stocky Krutov made no bones about his opinion that this type of conspiracy was impossible in tiny Switzerland. He told them that they were wasting their time and energy and that their approach would lead to nothing.

"Once again, Vassili," Conklin repeated patiently, "the nuclear proliferation threat has intensified by leaps and bounds. Does the idea of terrorists actually using nuclear weapons seem far-fetched? Use your imagination, gentlemen! Look how much damage was done in Oklahoma City by a couple of farmboys with a truck full of fertilizer! And that jumbo bomb the Islamic extremists set off just a couple of blocks from here in the World Trade Center may be no more than a foretaste of what is to come—unless we act. Take a look out the window! What if those crazies set off a nuclear charge in Central Park? That would make the World Trade Center bomb look like a string of Chinese firecrackers on New Year's Eve."

Conklin's left hand abruptly flicked at his eye, wiping away a drop of moisture, then a second one on his forehead. He looked up, squinting at the ceiling. A third drop impacted on his forehead. He found a crumpled-up Kleenex tissue and wiped his face.

Golan guffawed, "Another leak, Bill!"

Keeping his eye on the dripping ceiling, Conklin moved his chair away from the impact area. The drops narrowly missed the table. Wagner got up, picked up a wastebasket of brown plastic, and positioned it under the leak. Krutov impassively watched the action.

Grinning valiantly, Conklin said, "Must be the air conditioning. Okay, let's move on. As I was saying, it's our damn duty to do everything in our power to prevent crazies like Fahimi or other lunatic power players and religious fanatics from getting hold of such nuclear weapons. We're following up each and every lead we have, wherever it may take us. I appreciate your skepticism, Vassili, believe me, but there's definitely something rotten in the state of Switzerland."

"Why don't you simply inform the Swiss Government?" growled Krutov.

Conklin's reply was punctuated by the slow drip of fluid from the ceiling. "That's precisely what we did. We sent a strictly classified brief to their Federal Council—that's the Council of Seven, Switzerland's highest governing agency. What we got was not what we'd hoped: Bern was clearly put off. They thought the whole thing was absurd, and they told us in no uncertain terms to stay out of their internal affairs."

The Russian got up, took a few steps toward the drip. He thrust his hands deep into his pockets and stood, watching the slow, arrhythmic fall of drops into the improvised bucket. Wagner used a bit of moisture from his coffee cup to draw a circle on the speckled tabletop, while Golan watched Krutov watching the drip.

Conklin felt a surge of frustration. Even though he was saying everything he wanted to say, he didn't seem to be getting through to them. And being dripped on like this had done nothing to improve his mood, or his image.

Golan finally released them from the awkwardness of the moment by asking Conklin what he thought should be done now. Conklin held up a thick folder with a bright red cover.

"Well," he said, "we're working hand in hand with the CIA and the State Department, of course. This here is a detailed analysis of possible scenarios, which I'm sure you've all read. For now, gentlemen, that's our best shot.

Wagner's frown steepened. "Mr. Conklin, please! Let's not turn this into a Hollywood story conference. You know very well that these scenarios are mostly pure speculation, elaborated upon at will. According to your theory, anybody can obtain a nuclear weapon—in Switzerland, in Russia, anywhere—and strike wherever they choose, in order to achieve some goal or other. To me, this means that we are totally exposed and that there's nothing we can do about it."

Conklin shook his head. "Not at all, Mr. Wagner. All these scenarios have a common denominator: each one of the target groups we've identified is motivated to act by some political or religious mission. However, wishful thinking and a cause by themselves won't get you nuclear capability. Cash is the key factor. You need cash for payment and for bribes. That eliminates a lot of poverty-stricken fanatics, factions and splinter groups. The drug cartels, on the other hand, are loaded with cash. The same goes for splinter governments and regimes. Without cash, you have no connections, no access to restricted raw materials, equipment or technology. No cash, no nothing!"

Wagner pondered this for a moment, then asked, "And how can we trace the flow of this big money?"

"Well," Conklin drawled, suspiciously peering at the continuing drip over his left shoulder, "we believe an ex-CIA agent is out there trying to penetrate a nuclear cache." He hesitated briefly. "Langley views this man as a traitor. They want to bring him in." Again he paused, this time for more than a couple of heartbeats. "Dead or alive! This is a former NSA man who joined the CIA. Later, he turns up in Panama, as chief of intelligence in Noriegas secret service, G-2. From there, he established close ties with the drug cartels. He is believed to be based in Colombia, Brazil or the United States, maybe in all three of those countries."

"That's a pretty wide range of options," Golan taunted him cheerfully. "And how did he manage to get on the CIA hit list?"

Snorting irritably, Conklin put out one foot and adjusted the wastebasket even though it had been perfectly positioned. He said, "The man is in possession of bank codes that enable him to access large amounts of cash which he can then use to purchase nukes. His code name is >Keycop.< The NSA confirms that he's in charge of directing the money flow for powerful South American drug interests, and that he's using highly sophisticated money laundering techniques. Some of the NSA and Treasury top specialists have failed so far to even make a dent in his system."

Conklin gave the pail another push that almost put it outside the drop range. Wagner jumped up, readjusted the receptacle to its original position, then returned to his chair. Krutov let out a short bark of a laugh. Clowns in the American circus, he thought. Yes, they would be good for many laughs!

Conklin continued evenly, "In 1989, during our 'Just Cause' police action in Panama, an attempt was made to capture this rogue operative along with General Noriega. I'm afraid it failed rather miserably. >Keycop< got away clean. And then he had the nerve to fax CIA headquarters from Costa Rica! In the fax, which was addressed to the director personally, he called . . . let me see . . . he called the failure of 'Just Cause' a triumph of 'Just Rewards,' or something like that. Very clever!"

"Adding insult to injury," Golan observed.

Apparently undisturbed by the dismal failures he was describing, Conklin smiled as he announced his immediate plans. "We're convinced that this >Keycop< is planning to meet with these clandestine nuclear operators in Switzerland, and that this might happen at any time now. So, later today, I'm flying over there."

He looked expectantly around the table. Seeing no earthshaking response to his travel plans, he told them that he would stay in touch over the phone, from Bern, to keep them abreast of developments. Possibly another meeting, this time in Switzerland, would be called for. A detailed cv on >Keycop< was included in their folders. "By the way, gentlemen," he concluded, "this >Keycop<'s real name is Kenneth W. Custer. You might like to know that he was decorated with the Silver Star for bravery in action, and some other medals for saving a number of men in his platoon. All of this in 'Nam. Now, I suggest, we adjourn until further notice."

At last Conklin was alone in the conference room. He stood by the window gazing absently out over the park. This time Custer would not get away! They couldn't afford another fiasco like in Panama! He went back to the table, pulled a cellular phone from his briefcase, and instructed his driver to bring the car to the front entrance. Then he used one of the telephones on the table to inform building maintenance of the leak in the conference room.

As he stepped into the elevator he realized, with a sinking feeling, that he had dedicated his life to doing precisely what he always did when he left a place: cleanup and damage control. He smiled wrily at himself. It was a tough job, but somebody had to do it!

Secure in his cozy love nest above the experimental laboratory, Schoenhof slowly
lowered his intensely private fuel rod into
the most magnificent and fieriest of all en-
ergy chambers. All his senses were focused in anticipation of the
great moment; even his breath was held so tightly that one could
have heard a pin drop.

Meanwhile, Rosalia, the owner of that delicious chamber,
squinted furtively at the night table where her loverboy had carelessly dropped her tiny, pink-and-white lace panties on top of a
crumpled-up piece of paper that bore a most intriguing sketch.

The gentle fingers of her internal musculature suddenly clutched
and held Schoenhof's rod. He paused, moaning with pleasure, as
he felt himself grow even bigger inside this most lascivious of
wenches. His eyes were closed to squeeze every last ounce and drop
of pleasure out of her corruption, giving Rosalia the opportunity
to slide the paper out from under her panties on the night table.
The sketch showed a Rock'O'Clock granite clock unit with an open
cover. Beneath it, Schoenhof had scrawled: *Tuesday, 18 hours.*
Transport.

Rosalia's thieving hand returned to Schoenhof's shoulder. She pushed him up at the chest, started covering first one, then the other of his nipples with quick, feathery licks. Then that magical circular clutch of hers segued into a steady rhythm of internal stroking and sucking. Schoenhof's eyes were still closed, the unexpected sucking action making him grow to what felt like mastodonic size. In an involuntary reflex he began to move up and down.

"The boss was fuming at the Iraqi," Rosalia purred to Schoenhof's hairy chest. "He even wants to hide the clock unit."

"Aaaahmmnnnh . . ." Schoenhof moaned, ". . . fuming, did you say? Fuming in his pants, you mean. He's scared shitless, the old Slamdam. Afraid the cops will raid the place, after what happened with Kern. . . ." The ardent lover was beginning to overheat, his reactor close to the meltdown stage.

"Will you too fly up into the mountains?"

"What . . . when, tomorrow evening?" Schoenhof grunted, half gone.

"Right. With Summermatter, in the copter?" she ventured, thrusting up her buttocks, bringing Schoenhof up against his ultimate destination.

Twitching uncontrollably, he muttered, "No way, what'd I be doing up there? No no no I'll . . . unnnhhh . . . stay here with you, my little honeypot . . . yahhh . . . it's crazy uh up there . . . too dangerous . . . unnnnhhhhhhnnnnnn . . . ," he howled, his body jerking up and down. He collapsed on top of her and rolled to the side.

Just when she thought he'd fallen asleep, he abruptly spoke up. "It's Breckerlin's boys who'll be doing most of the work tomorrow when they fly all that junk upstairs."

He sat up, fumbled with his trousers, then handed her a folded-up paper. "Take a look at that, Rosalita, that old fart in uniform has gone totally bonkers. Go ahead, read it—the manifesto of a madman!"

She smoothed the paper out on her belly and read aloud, ". . . *when that nuclear bomb goes off in the United States, it will be the dawning of a new era for us! And we will not shrink from telling the world who is responsible. . . . Great waves of fury will be unleashed. The flames of racial hatred will reach to the sky . . . illuminating the night of apathy, shaking Germany awake. Our people are ready and waiting for the signal. We will thrust the sword of vengeance deep into the old, festering wounds. The new party will ride to power on a landslide. The new Führer stands ready, well prepared for his sacred historical mission. . . ."*

Rosalia pushed the paper aside, jumped off the churned-up trysting place, and stepped into the tiny shower stall in one corner of the gallery platform. She turned on the water, adjusted the temperature, and pushed the dainty showerhead up between her glistening thighs.

"But it won't . . ." she heard Schoenhof shout happily, "won't go off—the old latrine general is gonna shit with fury. Hah hah hah!"

Early in the morning, von Alp had driven the dark-green van uphill to the Nucleanne castle and parked it in the shadow of an old linden tree, hard by the steep drop of the fortification wall. It had taken a little while to fine-tune and focus his equipment, training the high-resolution camera and its powerful telescopic lens on the cavern entrance in the Schlammer Engineering compound. The monitor screen on the console behind the driver's seat now displayed a perfectly focused view of the heavy, camouflage-patterned sliding door to the cave, as well as the concrete area with its battery of powerful floodlights just outside the entrance.

Surveying his setup, von Alp nodded with satisfaction. Yes, this would do nicely! He unlocked and opened an aluminum case and lifted out the nightscope. He set the dull-green unit on a tripod, tightened the screws, then plugged a dangling cable into the van's electric power source.

Built into the paneling above the monitor console was a small, high-frequency transceiver. Von Alp flipped its master switch, adjusted the frequencies to the desired level, then clicked the static-control lever to ON. He looked around, pulled a flat, black metal box closer to himself with one foot, and lifted the cover, gazing inside with childlike enthusiasm at his favorite toys: a directional mike and a combination voice detector/amplifier. It was all there, in fine shape! He let the cover fall back, opened the door to the compact fridge, and took a moment to marvel at the stacks of sandwiches and rows of soft drinks thoughtfully provided by his angel Claudia.

He grabbed a jazzy-looking bottle of Citrus Obsession, held it against the edge of the console counter and brought his right hand down with a practiced chop. The cap flew off and von Alp took a thirsty swig, put the bottle down, then turned back to his equipment. He panned to the parking area in front of the Schlammer Engineering Building, where a silver-gray BMW had just rolled to a stop. The close-up zoom showed a haggard-looking man with horn-rimmed glasses, carrying a leather briefcase, getting out of the car.

Looks like an ambulance chaser—must be Geigel, von Alp told himself as he sipped his Citrus Obsession. As he jotted down the BMW's license number, just to be sure, Claudia's cheerful voice crackled through the speaker.

"Everything's a-okay, Theo. I've got the blueprints. Anything else you need?"

"Yeah. How about a cold shower?"

"You must be itching for a coronary," she laughed and signed off.

They'd started out early that morning. Finally on the road, they had turned west. Muted sunlight fell through the tinted rear window of the van. On the passenger seat in front, Custer idly played with the thin sheaf of hard copy the laser printer had spewed out. They were making good time in light traffic. Von Alp took the opportunity to brief Custer on Schlammer, while Custer listened intently, his eyes half closed behind extra-dark sunglasses, his face expressionless.

"To begin with, Schlammer used questionable means to buy into Clissot, the clock and watch manufacturer," von Alp said.

"What do you mean, questionable?"

"Well, as a young man, Schlammer was an engineer, later a physicist, working for the original Clissot company. After old man Clissot died—of natural causes, cancer—Schlammer quickly gained the trust of Clissot's widow. He pulled rank and renamed the company 'Clissot Veuve,' then made a proposal."

"Not of marriage, I hope!"

"Oh no. He proposed to acquire the company. After that, everything happened very quickly. Madame Clissot granted him an option to buy, probably just an oral agreement, and Schlammer immediately started plucking the raisins out of the cake."

"Meaning what? Stripping the company of its assets?"

"Right. Stripping, cannibalizing, gutting, whatever you like to call it. He pulled raw materials and finished products out of storage areas and warehouses, and carted them off to someplace else. And he purchased new machinery and equipment which, for some strange reason, never seemed to get as far as the Clissot plant."

"What kind of machinery?"

"Good boy, interesting question!" von Alp grinned, gunning the Ram down a straight stretch of road as if he were testing it on the salt flats of Utah. "Schlammer happened to have a nose for the latest trend. The Swiss watch- and clock-making industry was floundering in a deep recession. Like Clissot, a lot of firms were heading straight for the graveyard. But our clever friend, who'd spent a year or two in California, working for Fairchild, I believe, remembered a little line of items called semiconductors. What an opportunity! Using funds he had syphoned off from Clissot, he secretly set about building up his very own high-tech company. Featuring—you guessed it—semiconductors."

Custer emitted a soft, strangled moan that surprised his friend. It sounded as if this seasoned veteran of international intrigue and mayhem had actually been hurt to the quick.

"I still can't see it," Custer said, frowning. "How could he have? With Mrs. Clissot still owning the company?"

"Okay. When she reminded him of the option and asked him to make up his mind, Schlammer simply backed out. As I understand it, he told her he was no longer interested, the bottom was dropping out of the market, the company had terminal cash-flow problems, and who knows what other kinds of cock-and-bull stories."

"So Clissot went bankrupt."

The way Custer said it, it was not a question. Von Alp elegantly passed a tank rig that seemed two blocks long. It was marked *Fresh Milk from Happy Cows.*

"How did you guess? Madame Clissot remained blissfully ignorant of what Schlammer was doing to her company until the day a man from the State Receiver's office turned up and notified her that bankruptcy proceedings were impending. When she found out that her trusted manager, whom she'd always treated like her own son, had ruined her company, she suffered a nervous collapse."

Stretching in his seat, Custer adjusted his sunglasses. "A cheap gimmick that didn't cost him a dime, and the bastard made millions that cost her everything!"

Von Alp shot a glance at his friend. Custer's vehemence surprised him.

"My sentiments precisely. Old man Clissot's once sparkling Chronometer and Timepiece Factory had been turned into a rusty pile of redundant machinery. And his widow never got over Schlammer's treachery. She died a few weeks after Clissot Veuve went bankrupt. And Schlammer got away scot-free. Not only that, the slick sonofabitch put in a bid and ended up buying the whole kit'n'kaboodle from the Receiver. Dirt cheap, of course!"

"Nice work if you can get it," Custer mumbled. "Who else'd buy a pile of junk like that? Only it wasn't really a pile of junk, was it? I bet Schlammer rode in like a knight in shining armor." He removed the sunglasses and stared angrily ahead.

Von Alp grunted a Yes.

Traffic thickened as they entered the periphery of a town. Von Alp shook his head in exasperation, scanning the action on the road.

Custer's gaze traveled through the window on his side, across summery meadows to the distant, misty silhouette of the mountains. "I've yet to see the prosecutor who'd jump into a situation like that in order to transform a shining hero into a dastardly villain," he commented.

"That just wasn't in the cards," von Alp acknowledged.

"And the heirs?"

"Negative again. There weren't any. The Clissots lost their only child, a son, in an accident. After that tragedy, Madame Clissot's health was never the same. And then the bankruptcy . . ."

Custer idly checked in the rearview mirror, but saw no sign of the Lancia. After a long silence, he told von Alp, "I've got a strange feeling this is not the end of the story. Something is missing. Like retribution, an avenger? You mean to tell me there really wasn't a single person, not one human being, who stood up for justice? Fought Schlammer on his own terms . . . ?"

Custer's voice had dropped to a whisper. Strange, distorted images whirled through his mind. A thought came. Went. Came again. He tried to hold on to it. It slipped from his mental grasp: an elusive yet persistent wraith of a thought, some preposterously painful fragment of memory. . . . He shook his head. Talk about jet lag. This one was a real humdinger!

Nucleanne, Monday, July 2

The Lindenegg team arrived in Nucleanne early in the morning. While Claudia joined Theo on the hill, Custer parked the Lancia with the Bern license plates on the square by the church, which he figured had to be the center of town. He strolled across the square to the main street, looking for a spot from which to survey the territory.

A young woman on the opposite sidewalk attracted his attention. It was the way she walked, or rather sidled, toward a red minivan parked directly across from where Custer was standing. For a moment, she was obscured by the vehicle; he expected her to emerge on the far side. She didn't. What was she doing, furtively peeking up over the top, then ducking down? He sensed her monkeying with the side door.

Suddenly, she was gone, had ducked inside. For a fraction of a second, he glimpsed her silhouette in the cargo hold.

If it hadn't been for the grim, determined expression on her face, he might have shrugged the whole thing off. Who knows, she might be the eccentric owner of the van. But an eccentric who sneaks into her own car? How eccentric can you get! Besides, why would a sophisticated young woman like her own a fire-red minivan that looked as if it belonged to Mr. Fixit?

Ah, now, here comes the answer. A rather sloppy-looking Mr. Fixit shuffled up to the van and climbed in the driver's seat. Surely any second now the surprise bunny behind him would jump up, clasp her hands over his eyes and shout "Peekaboo!"

Custer watched the van. Nothing like that happened. The woman stayed down, hidden. If this was a game, Custer figured, more likely it was Stowaway, or The Secret Sharer!

Responding to his years of conditioning, Custer found himself sprinting through a narrow lane, across the church square. He threw himself into the Lancia, started up and accelerated across the open space, then swung right on main street. Only then did he see the minivan, in the rearview mirror, going the other way. Shit!

He wrestled the Lancia through a tight U-turn and quickly made visual contact with his target. A small Japanese car conveniently emerged from a side street and fell in between them.

Just out of town, as they started climbing the winding road across the valley from the castle, a black Mercedes limousine on its way into town got briefly out of control, crossing the dividing line and missing the minivan by inches. Then it recovered. As it passed the Lancia, Custer noted a small standard with the colors of Iraq on the right front fender.

Cresting a hilltop, he saw the minivan turn off onto a private access road that led to an open area with some buildings at the base of a sheer rock face. As he slowly passed the turnoff, a big steel door recessed into the mountain slid back, and the minivan drove through. Just before the door closed, Custer glimpsed a dimly-lit tunnel. From the way the van gradually shrunk in perspective, then vanished, Custer guessed the tunnel slanted downward into the interior of the mountain.

Good old CIA programming, he told himself, noting a wealth of other details. Four floodlights, each fitted with a scan camera, stood atop tall steel masts. The lights illuminated a large, concrete area in front of the cavern entrance. To the left, a wind sock at the tip of another mast billowed in the morning breeze. A large letter H, painted a brilliant white, marked a helicopter landing pad. To the right was a low, flat-roofed, barracklike building with six shuttered windows. Nearby, in front of a second, larger, building, men were at work positioning drumlike containers, which were picked up and carted off by a fork lift. Custer slowly passed the Schlammer Engineering Building, following the road to the top of the hill, where he briefly marveled at an old country estate. Then he turned back toward Nucleanne.

He couldn't get the woman in the minivan out of his mind. What was it that caused her to sneak into the cavern in this fashion? Could she be unaware of the danger she put herself in? She looked like a girl, oops, woman, no, girl, he corrected himself, girl was the right word here: She looked like what they used to call a "girl from a good family." How on earth had she got herself into this, and what could he do to get her out?

The truth was, her daring action stirred up the ancient responses in him. Imagine, a total stranger and he felt protective about her! Absently accelerating, he almost ran into a yellow mail truck. Gazing down at Custer, the mailman at the wheel slowly placed the top of a middle finger in the center of his forehead and wiggled it, indicating a serious mental dysfunction in the object of the gesture.

Mail carriers, Custer murmured, carrying out mail, that's the solution! Milkmen and mailmen came and went freely almost anywhere. No one paid attention to the face above a uniform.

He pulled over to the side of the road, allowing the mail truck to precede him into town. Wide awake, buoyed by a mild rush of adrenaline, Custer experienced the phenomenon of time dilation so familiar to people with his type of lifestyle. He watched the vehicle pull slowly, oh so slowly!, into a slot between two service trucks that were parked in front of what looked like City Hall. Since everything seemed to be happening in slow motion, he had no trouble finding a parking spot for the Lancia and catching the mailman just as he was about to close the rear gate on his truck.

Custer shoved the barrel of his Walther PPK into the small of the man's back and, in his most professional tone, ordered him to climb in unless he preferred to have his spine scattered through his guts. They climbed in and Custer drew the gate shut. He showed the man his handgun and, in passable German, announced, "For your information, I'm a professional killer. I kill only for money. And since nobody has paid me to kill you, I won't. Unless you're aspiring to the Heroic Mailman of the Year Award. Am I making myself clear?"

"Yes, sir. I think so."

"Are you reasonably comfortable?"

"My b . . . back hurts where you poked me with your gun."

"There are winners and there are whiners," Custer sighed. Then, sternly, "Tell me your routine."

"It real nice morning, Fred," Custer said to the gatekeeper, working hard to produce the bumpy accent of a foreign worker from Palermo.

"God bless," answered the big fat guy in the guard shack, "what happened to Alois?"

Custer added an outrageous Italianate grimace and wink to his outrageous Italianate Swiss. "I tie him up in back, nice beeg package."

The fat guy roared his appreciation and activated the boom.

Custer stepped off the truck. He walked along the narrow driveway, down past the old draw well, around the corner of the great steel-and-glass edifice, then across a small, red brick square to a four-step stairway leading down to the entrance of the barracklike building he'd observed earlier. The wooden, green-lacquered door with a brass knocker shaped like a fish reminded him of his mother's summer home in Maine. A cute message, etched on a sampler also made of brass, urged: *Enter without Knocking!* Custer went in.

The room was deserted. Four café tables with black tube chairs stood against the wall to the right, a coffee and soft drink vending machine in the corner. This dull-looking rest area adjoined a corridor, where a gray-haired man wearing a white apron came into view. Slouching toward a door at the far end, the oldster pulled a piece of paper from the apron pocket and held it up to his face. Custer hurried to catch up with him.

"Moment, please," he called after the stooped figure, "still need one paper for parcel. Colleague forget."

The oldster turned, gesturing, "No, no, no. This is off limits, a restricted area. No go in there, understand? Go back outside, one door to the left, there's a window for mail deliveries. That's where you go. Understand? Outside. One door to left!"

Custer's attention was on the paper in the man's hand, which was now being stuffed back into the apron pocket. An instant later, the log book slipped from the fake mailman's hand, spilling loose receipt tags on the floor. Custer had guided the book's descent so it came to rest at the feet of the oldtimer who, having been brought up to be helpful, bent down and started gathering up the scattered tags. Squatting to give him a hand, Custer pointed at a piece of plain white paper with some numbers on it.

"That's not paper from book," he said, chuckling to himself. Of course it wasn't. With the falling book distracting the senior, Custer had simply picked the man's pocket, glanced at the numbers, then dropped the paper.

Shutting the book on the tags, Custer stood up. The oldster slouched to the door, code slip in hand, mumbling distractedly. He tapped in the code, a string of tiny electronic windows lit up green, and the door slid open. The old guy shuffled through.

Custer caught a glimpse of the interior: soft, indirect lighting gave the sleek, computer-studded officescape a futuristic aura, making it look like a construct in virtual reality. Then the door slid shut and he walked back to the rest area.

When he got to the vending machine, he stopped and turned to squint back at the code-locked door, asking himself if he was going to give up this easily. Like nature, Kenneth W. Custer abhorred a vacuum; whenever somebody or something locked a door on him, he felt excluded, vacuous, itching to open what shut him out. While he had realized long ago that this type of attitude probably reflected some deep-seated psychological problem, he'd been much too busy to try to sort it out.

Now he simply walked back and fed the door the code he had memorized. It obediently slid open. This section of the stunningly modern office environment, resplendent in hues of baby pink, lay deserted before him.

Custer turned left on soft mauve wall-to-wall carpeting and quickly walked toward an arrangement of moveable partitions that made a small office area, which he cautiously entered. The space contained a gray tabletop above a chromed, tubular support. Clamped to the table was a computer mounted on a swivel arm. A potted palm and a metal filing cabinet completed the decor.

On the black desktop lay a note pad, a pen that seemed to have been carelessly dropped, and a newspaper. Next to the telephone was a brochure, open. It looked as if whoever used this office had just walked away. To what: the restroom, a coffee break? Custer checked his watch; looking around, he listened for voices or footsteps. He noticed a hook in one of the moveable walls; a white lab coat hung from it.

Deciding he had a couple of minutes, Custer sat down at the table and reached for the brochure. It turned out to be a manual. Taken aback, Custer read:

TOP-1 SECURITY-CLEARED EYES ONLY.

Centered beneath that warning was the title: *Mikrotel 2000 Detonator, User Manual.*

Custer blinked as the second adrenal rush of the morning hit him. Hole-in-one, old chap, he told himself, absolute two-hundred-yard hole-in-one!

He quickly scanned the list of contents, stopping, bug-eyed, at "The Ignition Dialog." He turned to the indicated page and switched to speed-reading, scanning the conveniently indented and paragraphed text. Apparently any system user could contact a built-in microreceiver by telephone to activate the ignition sequence. The touch phone code was * 0 0. Closing his eyes, Custer paused to imprint the image, phonetically anchoring it by whispering: *Star Zero Zero, Star Zero Zero, Star Zero Zero.*

Once this command had been given, the timer could be accessed for direct activation or time setting.

Unable to suppress a grunt of profound satisfaction, Custer slid the manual securely in under the waistband of the mailman's tightly fitting uniform trousers. He pulled the computer closer and switched it on. The screen fluoresced briefly, then stabilized in a milky pallor as service function icons lined up along the bottom. A message demanding the entry code appeared. Custer frowned: One more locked door! How he wished he had a portable version of Theo's decoder handy! Well, there was nothing to do but admit that . . . he felt a tiny turbulence of air at his neck.

Someone laid a hand on his right shoulder. Reflexes taking over, Custer spun around in the desk chair.

The intruder was a woman; she stumbled backwards. Quickly recovering her balance, she stood, legs apart, her back against one of the partitions.

A stunning sight! Custer swallowed a couple of times, wracking his brain for something to say. Long black hair framed a sensual face, full breasts stood out firmly under a loose green silky shirt. Sleek, muscular thighs strained against a tight-fitting, short black skirt. To complete her provocative appearance, the intruder sported magenta Keds on bare feet. There was a teasing, challenging expression in her brown eyes as she looked at him steadily.

No, Custer stammered inwardly, really, you're . . .

The tip of her perfectly healthy pink tongue slowly moved forward between strong, white teeth, then curled upward to lick the already moist upper lip. A shudder that originated in Custer's groin traveled slowly up through his body and crested in his brain.

"You must be the new guy! I'm Rosalia," she said, her voice a sexy mélange of young Lauren Bacall and vintage Rod Stewart.

Custer reflexively crossed his legs, ran a hand through his hair. He nodded slowly, entranced. Turning his head slightly to one side, he ran his left thumb slowly along his lower lip.

"I'm the company masseuse," she said with a smile that reached all the way into the pockets of Custer's trousers. As if to prove her statement, she put both hands near the base of his neck and swiveled the desk chair around, so Custer's back was again turned toward her. Then she began to rub the back of his head with powerful hands. "What's your name?" she whispered, massaging his shoulders.

"Ken," he heard himself say, shocked by the intimate tone of his voice. Reaching down from behind, she pulled the shirt up out of his trousers.

Her powerful fists pressed deeply into his flesh, moving up and down his bare back on parallel tracks along both sides of the spine. Again, a delicious chill swept through his body.

Then she stepped away from the chair and took him totally by surprise. Putting both elbows down on the tabletop, she leaned forward and thrust her bulging buttocks high into the air. She wasn't wearing panties.

Zombielike, Custer rose to the challenge. Positioning himself behind her, he began caressing her back through the thin fabric of her shirt. Slipping his hands in under the shirt, he cupped her heavy breasts and gently lifted them, feeling their weight, his middle fingers stroking, teasing the nipples.

Rosalia impatiently undulated her buttocks in small, circular movements. "Take your time," she whispered. "They're all at the Monday meeting."

In response, Custer slid his hands down along her hips, to the knees, then slowly moved upwards again, his thumbs kneading her flesh, until he reached the juncture of her smoothly muscled legs. First cautiously, then more boldly, he began to explore the softly pliant, supple entrance to her vagina, caressing the labiae, tracing her clitoris, his fingers immersed in Rosalia's creamy love juices.

Mumbling unintelligibly, she lifted her buttocks even higher and reached back with one hand, which she turned upward and opened. On her palm lay a condom.

Trying to unzip, Custer discovered that the Swiss Mails kept its carriers buttoned. Wild with desire, he ripped both hands down the full length of the fly. Buttons popped. His eager rod needed no help; it had already pushed through his black boxer shorts and stood trembling at the ready. He tore open the condom package with his teeth, rolled the blue sheath down over that eager shaft. All he had to do was take a quarter-step forward.

Rosalia groaned as she received him, for Custer was wasting no time with further preliminaries. Under his powerful, steady thrusts she started moaning, "C'mon c'mon c'mon c'mon . . ."

And, "Yes yes yes yes . . ." as he lightly slapped her buttocks to the rhythm of his pumping thrusts. It was a fast, dizzy ride for both of them. Custer felt all of the lust that trickled from brain and heels into his loins contract and explode forward. Rosalia's body shivered; she gasped and bit into her index finger but made no sound.

Then it was over. Rosalia sank to her knees and rummaged through her handbag. She thrust a half-empty pack of Kleenex at Custer and pulled herself up. She straightened her shirt, brushed back her mussed-up black hair, and watched with an amused smile as Custer stuffed first penis, then shirt, back into his pants. A single button at the top had survived his ferocious attack, and now it had to do the work of five or six!

"Wow, that was something else!" Custer grinned, pulling at the mailman's trousers. "Lady, you've got class—a quickie for a coffee break, I like it. This outfit ain't half bad!"

She giggled, looking coyly at the floor, then dove down, picked up the manual and handed it to him. "Next time you want something, instead of sneaking in, just call me." Again, she burrowed through her bulging handbag and came up with a pink business card. ROSALIA—SEXCLUSIVE LOVE, it read. Somewhat dumbfounded, Custer made a mental note of the phone number.

"I mean it," she said, "call me. A quickie can be nice, but I really prefer taking my time. By the way, in case you're wondering, El Chopo's been wanting me to meet you for some time. This section is dangerous—drugs, guns. You're lucky everybody's in an emergency meeting. Ciao, bello!"

So she's calling Don Cali by his old nickname, The Gun, Custer mused. It was a label that served as a password to the initiated. He suddenly remembered that some time ago there'd been talk of putting a mole into the Schlammer Group. *Rosalia!* Man oh man, what a mole! he grinned to himself, wondering what else that old goofball Cali might have up his sleeve.

"Ciao," he called, but she was already at the far end of the pinkish-gray room below. He put the secret handbook back inside the waistband of the postal trousers. Moments later, he stood outside the building, caught in a post-orgasmic shudder, shaking his head, telling himself with a chuckle that you never knew what was going to happen in a small town in Switzerland.

Then, mimicking the unhurried gait of a solidly unionized postal employee, he walked back to the mail truck . . . and saw the two rough-looking characters. They were lounging idly by the mail truck, which he had parked out of sight of the guard house. One of the men, the one with the crew cut and the broken nose, was leaning casually against the windowless side of the vehicle; his buddy, whose head was shaved skinhead clean, was bobbing up and down on his heals, nervous as a pitbull tearing at the chain.

Custer whistled softly to himself. No pretty picture, this! Adrenaline started pumping, urging him to choose fight or flight. It was a matter of conditioning: Vietnam, Panama, Libya. Every fiber of his body whispered *fight*, but he smiled a casual "Good morning, gentlemen!" and walked slowly past them toward the driver's door. The neo-Nazi-skinhead knockoff with the blotchy-pink face took one step, blocking his path.

Unnoticed by anyone, a fourth party was involved in the action—Rosalia. She focused the high-powered telelens of her Canon SLR camera on the group by the mail truck. *Tsst tsst tsst* went the Canon, capturing Custer's profile.

"Hold it there, friend, what's your name? Come on, spit it out, haven't got all day!" The skinhead pointed at Custer's white-and-yellow Nikes. "Never seen a mailman wearing sneakers on the job. Changing regulations down there, asshole? Come on, whatcha doin' up here, and what's . . ."

Custer's right foot connected heavily with the man's knee, producing a sickening crunching sound. Simultaneously, Custer pivoted to the right, using the momentum to hit the wretch with a picture-book left, an uppercut that smashed his head against the side of the truck. Shaven-head was out even before he hit the ground.

Tsst tsst tsst went Rosalia's camera, catching Custer in action. Great! she enthused, like some wildlife photographer ardently involved in her work.

If crew-cut's hair wasn't already standing on end, it would have risen instantly. Custer's nasty little display of hand-to-hand combat techniques momentarily froze the goon to the spot. Too bad! The man the CIA thought of as a rogue operative was already upon him, viciously twisting his left arm behind his back. Custer's free hand dove into the man's pockets, patted down his sides. In seconds, he had collected wallet, walkie-talkie and ID badge. A quick, powerful knee kick into the behind sent crew-cut flying.

Custer jumped into the truck. The engine roared to life, Custer clutching recklessly. The truck roared past the old draw well and shot through the wide-open delivery gate to the right of the lab buildings.

Rosalia sat at Schoenhof's desk in a far corner of the lab, her face tinted by the reddish glow that illuminated this interior. Her thighs were clamped tightly together as if to retain the precious sweetness she still felt, while her mind focused on the man who'd taken her to such dizzying heights. She took the exposed roll of film out of the camera and put in a new one, then stuffed the exposed roll into her handbag.

She sat still for an instant, composing herself, then went to a metal cabinet and quickly turned a sequence of digits that opened the combination lock. Inside, papers, diskettes, folders and books were piled in a pell-mell fashion. She grabbed a slim volume with the title *SADAM-54.SL93 (Special Atomic Demolition Ammunition)*, wedged it under one arm, closed the cabinet, and spun the combination out of sequence. She put the manual in her handbag, picked the camera up off the table, and left. She felt wonderfully calm and contented, and her hips swung freely to the rhythm of a little samba tune she hummed to herself.

Rosalia was blissfully unaware that Hannibal had watched everything through the back door window. Time to have a serious talk with the bimbo, he decided.

As she pulled out of the parking lot, she saw Schlammer's security officer in the rearview mirror, walking briskly toward his white Cherokee Chief. Suddenly he stopped. The skinhead type Custer had beaten up, that scumbag who was always slobbering and smacking his lips over her, was limping toward Hannibal, looking angry and gesticulating.

Rosalia smiled. Skinhead's tale of woe should keep the security chief busy for a while.

Stephanie cowered motionless among some boxes in the cavern. The realization that she was trapped stifled her breath. Confused thoughts played havoc with her mind: I'm trapped in a dungeon! I'll never get out alive! I'll starve, no, thirst to death, my body will dehydrate, I'll turn into a desiccated mummy! The place must be crawling with rats!

She listened intently but all she heard was absolute, overwhelming silence. No scratching or gnawing sounds. Or were there? What was that? A metallic noise, far away, somewhere outside. Outside?

She fought a rising tide of panic. She cursed herself for getting into the van. She clenched her hands and bit her lower lip. Her anger at herself finally broke in a burst of crazy, cackling laughter.

It took some time, how long she had no idea, before she forced herself to start thinking straight. She had to pull herself together. Thinking straight always helps, she told herself. Encouraged by the thought, she began to take stock of her surroundings. At first she made the review purely from memory, going back in her mind to when she'd plunged into the room, before the door slammed shut. There were two rows of stacked-up containers: gray, metallic boxes. Beyond those, more of the oblong room. Again she heard the distant, metallic noise. Maybe there was another exit. The air she was breathing had to come from somewhere—she hoped.

Air! She started feeling desperate again. Maybe the door was airtight—how long would she last then? Holed up in a mountain, sealed away in an underground dungeon. No one to blame but herself. And no one to know but herself. Not a soul in the world knew she was caught in this godforsaken cavern.

Cavern? What was it she knew or remembered about caverns? A certain smell that triggered childhood memories, was that it? Where had she breathed such sweetly mouldy air before? Pictures of the distant past took shape, first vaguely, then more distinct. She saw herself as a child, no more than nine years old. Her father, a nuclear physicist, had just died in an accident at some experimental station—that's all she had been told. Later, when she was a student at the university, she overheard people whispering about how he'd committed suicide. She'd started digging on her own, spending days in front of microfilm screens, reading up on the accident. In an experimental reactor, in a cavern.

Suddenly she saw it all with dazzling clarity: the cavern she remembered contained a nuclear reactor, near Nucleanne. This cavern, here! This one!

She felt perspiration forming on her forehead. Yes, she knew it now—she'd been here, long before Schlammer, with her father! So she really was no longer alone! She started digging in her purse, found the tiny flashlight on a keyring. Its pencil-thin beam caught something yellow. She played the small pool of light along a surface, instinctively shrinking back from three yellow triangles in a field of black, arranged around a dot, like propeller blades around an axle: the international symbol for radioactive radiation.

This was awful! She was in a storage dump for radioactive wastes, caught in a mountain of nuclear garbage; fuel rods, probably on their way to Russia, to be dumped in the Baltic! Hot tears welled up in her eyes. Papa, oh Papa, all these years, all these long, long years! It was as if, for the first time, she stood at his grave, the real grave of her father, the place where the darkest secret lay buried.

Trembling with sorrow and rage, she tried to recall the numbers she had mastered as a child; remembered her father looking over her shoulder as she jotted down radiation coefficients in her notebook. Gone, Papa, all gone, she smiled through the tears, can't remember a single one. Where was the hazard line? What was the radiation level in this room? All she knew was that she had to get away, get out of this poisonous pit.

If she could find a wall, yes, that much she remembered! A certain thickness of concrete protected against radiation of practically any strength. As she moved backwards, her left heel became wedged in between two crates. Panicking, she jerked it free, lost her balance, and started falling—a slow, adrenal-searing fall. Trying to get control over her body, she told herself not to land on her back, no matter what happened. She twisted like a cat, or rather, perceived herself as twisting in midair like a cat. Her head impacted. Hard, with the front of the skull. She was drifting through an infinite universe of whirring stars, each with a tiny circle of yellow triangles in the center.

Washington, D.C., Monday, July 2

The quartz clock in the Oval Office chimed eight. Veils of rainy mist clung to the windows as Washington slowly cranked up for another Monday. DEA Director Robert Donner and the current head of the CIA, Mitchell Taylor, sat in their armchairs, looking attentively at the president. Nicholas Pozzi, chairman of the Joint Chiefs of Staff, was seated on a nineteenth-century chaise longue over by a window, while Secretary of State James Frazer lounged in a grossly overstuffed, grossly comfortable grandfather chair, his long legs crossed, one bony knee pointing at the president's desk. Rose, the president's faithful and unabashedly anorexic family retainer, had seen to placing trays with coffee and cookies strategically around the room.

"All right, Bob, shoot," said the president. "What's new on the drug front? Do we or don't we send the leathernecks in?"

The faces before him looked sober, respectable and eager—a lie, the president knew, for the men were uniformly hung over, worn out and ready to head up the coast for the summer. This was when he loved to rattle his closest staff with challenging openers like this one.

"Last year, we as a nation sacrificed nearly ten times as many lives to drugs as we did to traffic fatalities," Donner told them. "Five times more than in Vietnam. And that's just the beginning. Drug-related deaths are on the rise, to say nothing of the damage done to those who don't die. The drug epidemic is turning millions of kids into real-life Beavis-and-Butthead-type morons. Because of drugs, performance standards for individuals and for society as a whole are rapidly declining. Why? Because innocent, hopeful youngsters from all walks of life, our most precious resource, are being swallowed up by the devastating lure of cocaine, crack and other drugs. Every day of the week, gentlemen, thousands of kids who can't find a job are taken in by the tremendous potential for profit in the drug market. Drug-related crime is rampant. The nation's family infrastructure is eroding. We're not just going to seed, we're being gobbled up by drugs. Unless we take action! Decisive action, Mr. President. Not just as soon as possible, but right now!"

There it was again—the evil menace threatening our shores from foreign lands. The president sought to break the spell that had been cast over the room.

"Now look here, Bob," he said, "we were spectacularly successful last summer, weren't we? We smashed the Medellín cartel's financial base when we confiscated their operating funds, didn't we? We made more than a hundred arrests, including some of their key personnel, and we froze literally hundreds of cartel accounts in this country and outside the United States. So my question to you, sir, is: How come we still look like rank amateurs?"

Donner knew what the president was driving at. "Quite so, Mr. President," he responded, "the cartel was hard hit. And it certainly did seem as if our people dealt a serious blow to their distribution network, as well as exposing some of their large-scale money-laundering operations. However, sir, the most significant results of Operation Green Ice were in Europe, particularly in Italy. As you know, the carabinieris hauled in a rich harvest of Mafia kingpins, including one Totò Riina, the infamous pride of Palermo. He was one of the biggest fishes they ever netted in Italy."

Donner paused to sip from his coffee cup. Rain suddenly started whipping the windows, causing the tourists outside to scatter. The faint hum of the air conditioning gave impetus to the mood of efficient, professional gloom that spread through the room.

The president stealthily eyed a framed picture of his daughter at the family's ranch in Colorado, smiling down from atop a magnificent paint horse. He hated the subject of drugs, with its endless discussions that got nowhere, leading only to an endless circle of pointing fingers. Against his better judgment, he thought fleetingly that maybe he *should* listen to Weisborn's counsel and make short shrift of those syndicates.

Donner's voice interrupted the president's reverie. "The painful truth, Mr. President, is that the flow of cocaine into this country actually increased last year. We were shocked to discover that one of the most powerful drug lords in South America, a man known as Don Cali de Cali, has developed a highly sophisticated, highly computerized money-laundering system for his drug dollars. Up to that point in time, we had what we believed to be a comprehensive overview of current money-laundering operations. To our dismay this turned out not to include the Cali organization. We simply couldn't figure out how they were doing it, sir. To date, all our attempts at infiltrating Cali's operations have failed."

Transforming an incipient yawn that would have been highly inappropriate into a lazy stretching of the arms, the president leaned back toward the Stars and Stripes that hung limply from a flagstaff behind him. His mahogany desk with its neatly-ordered office tools—a space pen with an engraved autograph of Buzz Aldrin, a note pad, and a large expanse of old-fashioned blotting paper framed in brown leather—provided ample room for a collection of personal bric-a-brac and family photographs in ornate silver frames. Between a bronze bust of George Washington and miniature replica of the Liberty Bell lay a dully gleaming medal, a gift to the president from the Navy Seals. The inscription read, *In God we trust, but if He's busy call the Seals.*

Taylor, who'd been fidgeting in his chair, now joined his colleague in pointing out that aerial reconnaissance had confirmed reports that Cali was operating well-camouflaged, large-scale production facilities, including a sophisticated command center with state-of-the-art equipment. "Mr. President," said the head of the CIA, "we're seeing in Cali's operations the type of infrastructure that is normally reserved for governments: judicial, fiduciary, and taxation agencies, private police and army cadres, that type of thing. I'd say what we have here is a megacartel that has appropriated traditional state authority for private purposes, including the police, foreign policy, and the courts. In my opinion, government authority has been effectively abrogated in Colombia."

"Are you saying that drug entrepreneurs run the country?"

"That's exactly what I'm saying, Mr. President. The Cali group seized de facto power in Colombia after absorbing the weakened Medellín cartel. This rather violent merger produced an organization of gigantic proportions whose boss, Don Cali de Cali, is an unpredictable religious fanatic. The word is, he's trying to acquire nuclear arms capacity!"

"Hold it a minute there, Mitch, I have a problem with that," the president protested. "There must be millions of righteous, hard-working Colombians who won't stand idly by while their country is going to the dogs."

"With all due respect, sir, I beg to disagree. Look at what happened in Nazi Germany. A handful of determined, unscrupulous manipulators succeeded in making a thoroughly humiliated and despirited people believe they'd regain their prosperity, prestige, power, and long-lost self-respect. The Big Lie with a capital B, you'll say. Yes, we know that now. But who is to say that kind of lie won't work again?"

The president wagged his head, looking wistful. "I don't know, Mitch. You may be right. Still, don't you think historical analogies can be misleading? Hitler's rabble rode Germany into disaster, but Colombia? That's a horse of a different color. What does Colombia stand to gain from a government of drug lords?"

"Prosperity and full employment, sir," Donner replied. "The cartel generates billions of dollars through the drug trade. Some of this dough is used to pay off the national debt, acquire sophisticated weaponry. Then the drug lords build new housing, soccer stadiums, roads, bridges, all of which generates jobs. They invest in traditional industry as well, increasing the GNP day by day. Drug money improves the people's standard of living, so why would anybody want to fight it?"

He challenged the men in the room with a look, then continued, "The cartel invests heavily in soccer, the national sport of Colombia. Teams sponsored by the drug hierarchy have no money problems. Colombia's national soccer team is among the world's best. Gentlemen, the old Roman adage of *panem et circenses* in modern garb is what Cali de Cali offers his people: Bread and Games. So what more could they possibly want?"

The president's right hand briefly touched his chin. Damn, a five-o'clock-shadow at eight-thirty in the morning. He blinked thoughtfully at Taylor. "These command centers and production facilities you mention, Mitch, where're they located? Does the president of Colombia know what's going on? And why the deuce wasn't I briefed on this before?"

Taylor scratched the back of his neck with both hands, something he did only when agitated. "Our hands were tied, sir. All of this was unconfirmed until just recently, though we've been suspecting it. We didn't want to bother you with idle gossip and speculations."

The president glanced impatiently at his wristwatch, then at the phone. Should he call Weisborn now and get him into this tiresome discussion?

"Hmmnh," he asked, "and to what do we owe your sudden certainty?" He glanced again at his watch.

"Well," Taylor said, "we've been receiving intelligence for some time but didn't trust it at first."

"Why not?"

Taylor hesitated; the answer had a rather high embarrassment factor. "Well, sir, we didn't know who or what the source was."

"You mean you weren't able to determine the origin of the information you were receiving?"

"Yes, sir," Taylor admitted, raking his neck with both hands. "It was weird. First, we received e-mail messages in Langley from our consulate in Munich. More precisely, my deputy received them into his electronic mailbox whose path number is known to only a handful of cleared people, sir."

"So? Were those messages sent from Germany or weren't they?"

"No, sir, they were not. Our stiffs—I mean, our people in Munich—had nothing to do with this. We had to assume that the system had been penetrated, so we changed our modem codes."

"And cut off the flow of information. Was that the smart thing to do? I mean, I just wonder . . . ?" The president did not look happy.

"Mr. President," Taylor replied steadily, "it was a matter of principle. We simply couldn't have some hacker breaking into—"

The president cut him off with one of the more intimidating of the many intimidating gestures in his arsenal of body-language weapons. A sudden explosion of fingers shot out from a fistlike clench of his right hand.

Taylor immediately gave in. "You're right, of course, sir. But then, right after we restructured our modem code pattern, Jellyfish—that's our tag for the anonymous source—Jellyfish started e-mailing messages through our embassy in Bern."

"Bern?"

"The Swiss capital, sir."

"Ah, how perceptive, Mitch! Are you assuming then that this Jellyfish fella is operating from somewhere between Munich, the capital of Bavaria, and Bern, the capital of Switzerland?"

Chastised, Taylor produced what CIA insiders called his 'gator grin.' "That's hard to say, sir. A relay station in that area was probably used, but precisely where Jellyfish uploaded his messages we don't know."

"Okay, okay. Now about the information itself, was any of it any good?"

"That was our problem, sir. At first, we thought some computer wizkid was just showing off, pulling our leg—"

"I can well imagine, Mitch," the president said, with a conspiratorial grin at the men assembled around him, "the Central Intelligence Agency wouldn't fancy having their noses tweaked by a brilliant teenager who might go on to win the Nobel Prize in science, right?" He drank from a red-and-white striped coffee mug bearing the unnecessary inscription *I'm the boss!* in blue-star script.

"Well, sir, no, we wouldn't," Taylor parried as best he could. "On the other hand, we must guard against disinformation. The Cold War may be over, sir, but that just means that a lot of unemployed cold warriors are out there looking for work. It's still a dirty business we're in, and once burnt, twice shy. Like when the Soviets went into Afghanistan, well, sir, they led us to believe—"

"I know, Mitch," the president interrupted, "so what happened with the Bern channel?"

"Nothing, sir. This time we left it open. The information we received checked out as extremely usable, highly explosive even, although unfortunately . . ." He broke off.

The president's eyebrows went up. "Yeah?"

"We were taught a lesson, sir. Even though, actually, it didn't concern the CIA." Taylor threw Donner a desperate look, but the DEA head only hemmed and hawed, until the president urged him to unburden himself.

"All right, Bob, what's the hitch?"

"Yes, sir, well, Jellyfish tipped us off that an undercover operation we'd been running for a good long while was about to blow—"

"Blow?"

"Sorry, sir, I mean our moles, their cover was about to be blown. Jellyfish's message just said *Palm Beach operation defunct, pull out personnel immediately*—or something to that effect. We concluded the message was a targeted piece of disinformation and I made the decision to continue as planned. What we did do, sir, was add substantial numbers to our backup team. Well, we went in and it was a disaster. Both female undercover agents on the job were killed. Drowned, I should say. We found them in a coastal canal, hands tied behind their backs, and hogtied to each other, like . . . well . . . you know . . ."

The president's lips were tightly compressed; inside, he was boiling. Damn those agencies and their arrogance, always wearing blinders, never touching any food that didn't come out of their own kitchen!

"All right," he said, abruptly returning to the main theme, "now what about these drug cartel facilities and installations in Colombia, where exactly are they located?"

Breathing an almost audible sigh of relief at the change of subject, Donner eagerly replied, "Yes, we have positive identification of an area approximately the size of Rhode Island, located on a high plateau, with some archeologically challenging features that resemble Maya or Inca pyramids, including monumental boulders carved out of—"

"Never mind the mythology, Bob, can we get to the point?"

"Yes, sir. The entire area is located inside a so-called *zona militar*, a military zone. Intruders are arrested or shot on sight. The Colombians aren't squeamish when it comes to enforcing martial law, I should say. Being located inside this military zone allows Cali, the drug boss, to do exactly as he pleases with undesirable outsiders. Media people, scientific expeditions, TV teams, militant conservationists such as Greenpeace—nobody has the slightest chance of getting as much as a foot into that territory, and flyovers are just as tough."

The president got up, went to the window, and looked out on the soggy lawn. What was it Weisborn had said just recently? Why don't we just take care of the damn cartel by military means?

Sighing inaudibly, he turned on his heels and spoke. "It sounds like our esteemed friends in the Colombian Government have created this *zona militar* for the express purpose of shielding this Cali's drug enterprise. Would that be a fair statement?"

"Absolutely, Mr. President," Pozzi piped up for the first time. "And that means military action is out of the question, since we're dealing with a restricted area inside a friendly nation. In the past, whenever we've intervened militarily on the territory of another nation, we've had full support from the government, sometimes an outright request for intervention. This does not apply in the current situation. The Colombian Government has no say in the matter, since the army is controlled by the cartel. The legitimate president of Colombia can consider himself fortunate that the cartel allows him to continue in office. All this said, Mr. President, there still is an option, a measure we can take that would constitute an appropriate response to this very real and awesome threat to the vital substance of our nation."

"You're not suggesting we legalize cocaine," Taylor said, keeping his voice neutral. After all, the question had been asked before.

Pozzi turned on him, speaking vehemently, "Legalize? Out of the question, never! Here we've been preaching to our kids for decades about the evils of drugs and all of a sudden that's all hogwash and cocaine becomes no more dangerous than candy?

"No, what I'm suggesting is that we smash their production capability, stamp it out once and for all. Send in troops and destroy the cartels in their own backyard. Mr. President, I propose war! No more trade agreements with Colombia, Peru and Bolivia. Let's go in there and crush the viper's head. Then, here at home in our cities, we'll take care of dealers and street distribution. But first we've got to wipe out production, which translates as combat action, sir, war! Including one most important option."

The president fixed Pozzi with a level gaze. "And what would that be?"

"The nuclear option. I don't see where, realistically, we have any choice but to wipe out the entire production base of the drug cartels with a single blow. Pull up the evil by the root, sir!"

As it turned out, the president was standing conveniently close to his desk when the Joint Chiefs of Staff voiced his preposterous request, so all he had to do was bring the flat palm of his eloquent right hand down on the desktop, producing a nasty, slapping noise. Without as much as glancing at Pozzi, he said, "Man, have you taken leave of your senses? Are you seriously suggesting we devastate Colombia just to get rid of a couple of drug lords? Are you trying to ruin us politically? What is this nuclear nonsense? We will all just pretend these past two minutes never happened."

The men in the Oval Office maintained a grim silence as the president threw himself into his desk chair, darting angry glances at them. Looking at the secretary of state's bowed head and nervously drumming fingers, it occurred to the president that these, his most trusted men, with Pozzi as their spokesman, had just presented to him their joint plan for the solution of the drug problem.

Unable to ignore the president's challenging stare, Pozzi said, "Sir, if you'll allow me, we do have a Pentagon study, backed up in depth by Rand Corporation research and analysis. It says that a limited number of low-yield devices, high-altitude blasts with minimal fallout, would be extremely effective in this situation. Simultaneously, we'd use a neutron device, which destroys biological life only but causes no irradiation of wind, rain or dust. The soil of those damn coca plantations would be non-arable for decades to come. As a bonus, we'd smash their administrative centers, eliminate the drug lords, the laundry men, the hit men, the executioners, and all the little fish just swimming along—*finito la comedia!*"

The president's voice came back to what was normal for him when under pressure: an icy stiletto. "And make us look like nuke-crazy imperialist maniacs with a spastic twitch in our trigger finger!"

Pozzi took his time riding out the president's cold parry. Then he took his time clearing his throat. Then he took his time unveiling the core of his argument. "Yes, Mr. President, there is that possibility. Certainly the application of nuclear weapons will cause worldwide outrage. We'd be fools to ignore that probability. But the bottom line will be that we can live with it. And that's the downside. Now, looking at the upside, we'll have destroyed their growing areas for generations to come, smashed their organization, and we'll have sent a clear signal to the entire world. All of which, begging your indulgence, Mr. President, is beside the point."

"You don't say!" the president fired. "So what is the point?"

"The point is that if we don't use nukes, some crazy or gang of crazies, somewhere on this planet, will get the idea that they can start playing nuclear poker with us. Once we've lost the initiative, that'll be just a matter of time. Everything we've learned and everything we know translates into a targeted, surgical, nuclear blow. Nobody today seriously expects the United States to use nuclear force. In fact, not ever. Now this type of nonchalant disrespect in itself constitutes a substantial threat to our security. Next time terrorists plan to strike in New York, or Oklahoma City, or blow up another Amtrak train, instead of using conventional explosives, they might just figure they can get away with setting off a nuclear charge."

"That's crazy," Taylor cut in. "No one would dare risk anything like that. They know we'd retaliate, fast and massive."

"Oh yeah? Retaliate against whom?" Pozzi asked, checking an impulse to stick with the more soldierly "who." "The Lebanese Hizbollah? Breakaway republics of the former Soviet Union? Rafsanjani's regime? North Korea? Or how about some paramilitary group in northern Idaho?"

These pointed questions were tough to answer; no one volunteered.

"Exactly," said Pozzi, repeatedly nodding in self-confirmation, "we have to deter not with retaliation but with intimidation, and we have to do it across the board, so everybody gets the message."

Since no one chose to comment, not even the president, Pozzi continued. "Let's face it, Mr. President, our nuclear deterrent has been idle so long it's stopped being a deterrent. Nobody believes in the doability of nuclear strikes anymore. Nobody dares to imagine the gruesome effects of a nuclear blast. High time, then, to start thinking about the unthinkable again. What we need is a live demonstration, a fresh deterrent picture, in the interest of the security of the United States."

The president, who appeared to have been lulled into some sort of listening trance, snapped to. Moving his shoulders as if trying to shake off the effects of the devastating lecture, he looked at Frazer. "I wonder how the State Department might view such a course of action."

Frazer practically cringed. Negotiating skills were his forte; he abhorred any type of military solution. Still, he understood that good old-fashioned diplomacy could not be expected to make an impression on recalcitrant drug criminals.

"War can also be seen as a means of safeguarding our national interests," Pozzi offered heatedly. "In order to pull up this evil by the root, we must eradicate it at its home base. Or else we'll continue pouring billions every year into a losing battle against drugs."

"So, instead of a nuclear strike, why not send in troops?" Donner asked.

Pozzi gave him a calculated look of resignation. "Come on, Bob, you know that's completely, absolutely and totally out of the question. Think of the enormous cost in dollars, in time, and in energy involved in preparing for a land war far from home. What we'd be looking at here would not be an operation like Panama, but something much more on the scale of Vietnam. The American people are not prepared to sacrifice large numbers of men and women in the fight against organized crime. 'Nuke the bastards!'—that's how people feel deep down about the scum that's destroying our youth and our cities. And I don't blame them for feeling that way, Mr. President. Matter of fact, I feel that way myself. Let's get it over with. In a single, devastating surprise attack. I say, better an end with horror than a horror without end!"

"Well, I don't know, gentlemen," the president drawled, "how do we know we'd succeed in wiping out the entire drug nation, lock, stock and barrel? What if we cut off the monster's head and three new ones pop up? Bob?"

"Personally, I tend to agree with the Mr. Pozzi," Donner said, surprised at the sober, businesslike tone of his voice. "A carefully targeted nuclear strike would seem like a very effective solution. The power of the drug cartels rests on three main pillars. First, money; second, popular support; third, production capability. As for the money, we can trace certain transactions, confiscate funds in bank accounts, smash money-laundering operations. But experience teaches that the practical effect of such efforts is negligible. Dirty money will always find a way to get clean. Weakening the popular support would prove even more difficult. The drug cartels build schools, housing, hospitals, sports fields and so on. How would we go about convincing people that more prosperity is a bad thing? On the other hand, with a single, targeted nuclear strike we would destroy their entire production capability, all the coca plantations as well as the lab facilities where the coca paste is processed. With one blow we'd wipe out their transportation capacity, their planes, the drug lords' operational headquarters, the entire network of cells and cadres, large-scale distributors, everything, sir."

Donner's right hand sliced through the palpably thick air that had accumulated in the Oval Office. "In that nuclear inferno, Mr. President, the cartel's following will collapse like a house of cards. With a little luck, we'll bag their monies too. Our nuclear action will send a powerful signal to the world that we're determined to wipe out organized crime. That signal, I'm sure, will be understood and appreciated everywhere on earth."

"Now that's where you lose me, Bob," Taylor said.

"It's really very simple, Mitch," Donner said with feigned patience. "The actual use of nuclear weapons will put the fear of the Lord into certain governments, make them wonderfully cooperative. Governments in Southeast Asia whose drug control measures today range from token gestures to half-hearted enforcement will shape up in a jiffy. Nobody'll want to be next in line on our list. They'll understand that any government that tolerates drug production and trafficking can count on merciless chastisement by the United States. It's a very simple message, Mitch. One that any child in South America, or Asia, or anywhere else can understand."

Silence ensued. Wrong, thought the president as he looked up at the ceiling, then out the window. More likely, the Asian drug cartels would just step up production to fill in the gap. He realized at last the true fulcrum of his predicament. These boys boasted keen intellects and swift, analytical minds. They knew how to tackle things cleverly, even bluntly. Their eloquence allowed them to comment on each and every point of fact. But the level-headed and the wise were sadly absent from his team. The secretary of state came closest to the profile he needed. Still, Frazer was simply too civilized a diplomat, keeping all doors open at all times. Once again the president felt keenly the absence of Jack Weisborn.

In his mind, the president moved on to Pozzi, who had absolutely no political touch. Ask him for a rundown on the current situation and he'd give you a brilliantly concise view of precisely what was going on; his organizational skills were unmatched. But he was incapable of empathizing with ordinary people, with their needs and worries. Pozzi was the kind of guy who'd consider a hundred thousand people nuked out of existence in South America as no more than a statistical fraction, the nuclear blast as its common denominator. The president smiled to himself: talk about an emotional dwarf, good old Pozzi was it!

Now, as for the directors of the CIA and the DEA, their ideas rarely transcended the perimeters of their offices. They were good cops, great bloodhounds essentially, but you didn't expect bloodhounds to make strategy decisions. Gazing thoughtfully into the round, the president noted many of the fine, traditional qualities that had made and continued to make this nation great. He saw loyalty, a patriotic readiness to sacrifice oneself for the good of the nation. A fine body of men indeed, he mused. Trouble was, right now he needed more than a fine body of men.

"Gentlemen," he began cautiously, "we appear to be impaled

on the horns of an awesome dilemma. Now, as I was listening to you, I was thinking that possibly, at some future date, this country will not be able to avoid exercising its nuclear option. Mayhap destiny has chosen me to make such a far-reaching decision. It's possible. Nor will I shirk my responsibilities if called upon to act in the national interest, to ensure and safeguard national security. However, now is not that time, nor Colombia the occasion for such action. For one thing, I don't have anywhere near enough information. Also, considering the gravity of the challenge before us, it seems to me you gentlemen have been somewhat lax in your analysis of the situation. I must insist on a faultlessly comprehensive, in-depth listing and evaluation of all conceivable, and inconceivable, factors relating to this situation, including a thorough analysis of the military, political, climatic, and cultural aspects. I also need an environmental and psychological impact study for the proposed affected areas. To put it plainly, gentlemen, ain't nothin' gonna happen before I see it on paper."

Bouncing a cutting, sidelong glance off Pozzi, he concluded, "As for my own psychological profile at present, you can probably guess I have absolutely no taste for plunging into some colossally hazardous South American adventure at this point in time."

Satisfied with having delivered a devastating counterpunch, the president rose and declared the session closed. As he watched the men file out, he had to think of Jack Weisborn. Even after everyone had left and he sat alone at his desk, his mind remained focused on Weisborn. He recalled something the old fox had told him recently: "If we don't drop the bomb, sooner or later but probably sooner somebody else will. It's been half a century since Hiroshima. What the world needs now is a real and credible reminder. The American people are tired of wars where Americans die by the thousands. Sending our kids into foreign countries to die there just won't play anymore, sir. The drug problem is tailor-made for a nuclear solution."

Granted, old Wisebrain often demonstrated great vision, understood things earlier and more clearly than others, but this time . . . well, this time he'd gone decidedly too far. The president remembered how his senior adviser's eyes had sparkled when talking about his vision of nuclear destruction. How his face had shone, how he'd beamed like a kid watching Roman candles go off on the Fourth of July.

In "The Hole," Nucleanne, Monday, July 2

At first, Stephanie Kramer thought she had died, for there was no pain. Hadn't some octogenarian once remarked that if he were to wake up one morning and feel no pain, he'd be certain he was dead? As she chuckled at this, her head felt like it was about to burst. She cautiously began to move feet, knees, legs, then her hips, arms, shoulders. At least nothing seemed broken. But her forehead felt as if it were on fire. Gently probing with her hand, she felt a long scrape, like a bandage, the blood having dried. Pushing herself up on her elbows, she cautiously looked up, squinting into the darkness. In the dim light she made out the thickly insulated, four-tube pipeline that had stopped her fall down the shaft.

She began to pull herself forward along the pipeline, slowly crawling toward a brighter patch of light ahead. Suddenly panic-stricken, she hunkered down on the pipes: This was a nuclear dump! Maybe there was plutonium up there, or red mercury! Maybe she'd already absorbed a lethal dose of radiation!

When she tried to push herself up, she heard the steel door above her grinding open with a drawn-out screech.

A gravelly voice barked out an order. "We'll ship all of this out today!" To which a whiny male voice answered, "You mean all this stuff? But that's all contaminated!"

"Cut the crap, asshole, and gimme a hand with these boxes!"

Stephanie listened, barely daring to breathe. She cautiously rolled over on her left side and squinted up into the bright light that spilled over the edge above her. Up there, containers were being dragged along the floor.

Then the rough voice said again, "These ain't no bombs, idiot, they're mines, get it? Mines! Mines are smaller than bombs, easier to move. More practical."

"Why?"

"Why, what for, and how! You gettin' on my nerves, boy. I'll tell you why. Because people won't notice so much when you move these things into place. Like Buckingham Palace. Get it?"

"Is that where all this stuff is going, to this . . . palace?" the quavering voice asked. For the length of a few thumping heartbeats Stephanie heard nothing. Then the rough voice again, more softly, "Now how would I know that, asshole? Maybe it's going to Korea, or maybe Siberia. I don't give a flyin' shit where it's going."

Stephanie strained to catch every word.

". . . and stop asking stupid questions all the time. You're in this up to your ears just like me. And if you talk, you'll—ckckck! They'll do to you what they did to Fritz . . . ckckck!"

The talk petered out. All she heard was the rumbling and banging of crates, a grumbled expletive, some coughing. But now at least there was enough light to start exploring the shaft. When she stretched out her arms, her hands just barely touched the walls. So much for the width of the shaft, but where did these pipes lead? If they were steam pipes, then there was probably a power station or engine room near by. Crouching low, ready to drop back down on all fours, she cautiously set one foot in front of the other. After a dozen or so steps, her forehead brushed against a corner, scraping some of the scab off the fresh injury. She barely suppressed a shriek, then froze.

"What was that?" whined the familiar, wimpy voice.

"Where, down there? Buncha rats, that's all. Grab that end, will ya!"

Ear-piercing squeaks rang through the tunnel as they dragged a metal crate across the concrete floor.

Stephanie felt her way forward. Through a crack she glimpsed a metal cover, a door to a maintenance passage, judging by its contours. She stopped to examine her forehead; it felt as if a huge, bloody horn was growing there, like the result of some science-fiction idea of genetic manipulation, her frontal skull grotesquely enlarged for supreme intelligence. Or else she was the first human unicorn, a universal symbol of luck. Well, Kramer, she told herself, let's see just how smart and lucky you are!

Putting arm and shoulder to the cool steel, she applied as much of her weight and strength as she could, trying to push the door lever down. It didn't budge. Stuck! *Please, please open, please!* she pleaded. From somewhere above her came the scraping sounds of boots shuffling across concrete. The two lowlifes up there were returning for another container. Stephanie's face was tilted upward, her features taut, lips compressed. If only the light stayed on just a few moments longer!

Now she heard the man with the gravel voice telling his buddy to get the lead out.

"We'll make this the last one, then we'll pop a few cans. We got a break comin'."

Every fiber in her body tense, Stephanie waited. At the first screeching of metal on concrete as the men dragged the last container to the loading dock, she applied all of her sixty-kilo weight to moving the handle—and down it went! She pushed the door open just wide enough to squeeze through—and stared into a bottomless pit.

The blood might as well have frozen in her veins. A great, empty space yawned before her, and not an inch of ground for a foothold! Slowly her eyes became accustomed to the murky twilight. A faint, distant glow fought against the darkness, allowing her to make out contours, silhouettes. An enormous dome arched over black emptiness. Like pressure lines in an energy plant, the four-pronged pipeline she'd been following dropped at a steep angle down to a mass of bulky, angular construction equipment. To the right, huge scaffolds rose.

An atavistic tremor of fear rippled through her body. This was the end of the road, she might as well turn back! She could try to climb back up into the storage room, maybe get out and hide under the delivery ramp. The plan made sense, so she pulled herself back through the door, determined to make her way back along the pipeline and try to break out through the storage room.

At that instant the light went out and she heard the door to the storage room slam shut.

Once again she was plunged into darkness, found herself clinging to a bunch of pipes, what a cruel joke! Her forehead burned as if she'd been branded, her body ached as if it were being stretched on some inquisitional rack. Anger rose up in her, a nameless, senseless, elemental fury directed at the gang that had snuffed out Peter Kern. Behind it all, she was sure, was Schlammer, that ugly bastard! He'd kill her, too. He was hiding mines and poisonous nuclear wastes in this cavern. And now that she'd found him out, what was she supposed to do, give up?

"Not on your life, buster! Never!" she screamed into the murky void. "I'm getting out of here. Alive! I'll turn you in, you and all your terrorist scum!"

The outburst tapped some hidden adrenaline reserve. Fresh energy coursed through her and along with it came a strange calmness. Through her pores, she sensed her surroundings. It smelled of moist rock; unstirring, mouldy air rested heavily on all surfaces.

Coolly and calmly she began to move. Placing hands and feet with exquisite care, she felt every grip take hold precisely where it was supposed to. Squeezing back through the door, she went down on all fours, flattened herself belly-down against the pipes. She pushed her handbag onto her back and cautiously, feet first, slid backwards until she'd twisted her hips over the edge of the great pit's inner wall. Slowly, using all of her mountain climbing skills, she allowed gravity to pull her downward along the pipes.

At first everything went well. She'd be fine as long as she didn't look down into that bottomless blackness. Centimeter by centimeter, inch by inch, she descended like that, arms and thighs clamped around the inner pair of pipes. It was taking forever, the fires of hell scorching her palms. "Don't give up now, you're almost there!" she bravely told herself.

She hadn't expected the sudden bend in the pipes, would not have seen the almost vertical drop. She started slipping, faster and faster. Gravity accelerated the slide. Her belly, her breasts and nipples, the inside of her arms were being scorched by the blowtorch of friction. She tried to clutch at the pipes with her whole body. No use! She was slipping faster and faster.

"Hang on!" she pleaded with herself, bracing for the impact. Then her body sheared off the perpendicular. Screaming out her life, hoping it would be over instantly, Stephanie Kramer plunged sideways into emptiness.

Washington, D.C., Monday, July 2

As on most Mondays of the year, three men were gathered around a table in the West Wing of the White House to eat their sandwiches or their yogurt, to drink their coffee or fresh-squeezed carrot juice, as the case might be. Their conversation today would be far from incidental, since all three were members of the president's special team to fight international crime. Among them was Graham A. Rivers, the National Security Adviser. Bespectacled, unassuming, with a bone-dry sense of humor, Rivers didn't fit into the mold of his predecessors, most of whom had been career officers. Rivers's tweedy appearance bore the clear imprint of academia. Originally with the State Department, he had served in Vietnam, openly opposed the war, and later been appointed a professor of contemporary politics at Duke University.

Across from Rivers sat Michael Lutz, a bright, career-conscious official with the State Department. Lutz had an irritating habit of snapping his broad, bright-red suspenders against the blue-and-white striped shirt that stretched over his well-muscled chest. Today he traced the impeccable creases in his plaid trousers with thumb and middle finger as he inquired what the topic for this lunch might be.

"Unrest in the Middle East, South American drug lords, or the child sex trade in southeast Asia? I feel magnanimous today."

At the State Department, Lutz was in charge of U.S. relations with non-aligned nations. Having organized his duties efficiently, he found himself with a lot of spare time on his hands, much of which he spent on cultivating contacts with the ambassadors of various neutral countries. Once a week he played tennis with the wife of the Swedish ambassador. The chief secretary in the cultural section of the Austrian Embassy, an attractive young woman in her early thirties, had been spirited away to the Bahamas by Lutz on two occasions. And he made a point of planning his skiing vacation, usually in Switzerland's Valais region, while playing golf with the military attaché of Switzerland. Indeed, the fact that Lutz was born and spent his childhood in Switzerland accounted for his having been entrusted with a post that might have seemed excrutiatingly boring to other State Department careerists.

Chewing patiently on a chunk of his ham-and-cheese sandwich and ignoring Lutz's allusion to the morning's session in the Oval Office, on which they had all been briefed, the national security adviser turned to the third man at the table, John Dexter, head of the Justice Department's criminal division.

"We have good news and bad news from Bern, John. The good news is that the bad news could be worse. And the bad news is that >Keycop<, a.k.a. Kenneth W. Custer, arrived there yesterday, Sunday. His presence in Switzerland bodes ill for everyone. We suspect that Custer is there to purchase weapons for the Super Cartel."

"Or it might have to do with the assassination of the Swiss prime minister," Lutz interjected. "CNN reported this morning—"

But Rivers was not to be distracted. "We don't have any reliable particulars on the assassination as yet, Michael, though the Swiss have promised a detailed report. Now, John, who do we have in Bern? I mean someone who can be trusted to run a vital operation without messing up the way they did in that Iran-Contra business."

Not Dexter, but Lutz cleared his throat to answer. He'd made an instantaneous assessment of the situation, and decided that a trip to Switzerland suited him fine. Zermatt wasn't far from Bern. A discreet little side trip for some skiing up along the glacier, or why not a spot of golf on the naturally terraced high plateau at

Crans-Montana? It could surely be arranged. But as he opened his mouth to speak, Rivers, directing the conversation, cut him short with a wave of his hand at Dexter.

"We have a legal attaché over there, an FBI dude," Dexter said, his chocolate-dark features revealing nothing to Lutz. "Also, I understand Bill Conklin is flying over today. Bill's an NSA electronic surveillance ace who's dead set on running this Custer fellow to the ground."

Not unduly concerned, Lutz made a small show of struggling with his turkey-on-rye sandwich. He chomped into it, started chewing, grimaced as if in pain, chewed some more, grimaced some more, and finally gulped it down with a theatrical contortion of his neck that made his prominent Adam's apple gyrate at impossible angles.

"So," Lutz finally asked Dexter, "what's the NSA doing in this anyway? I would have thought this calls for FBI or CIA attention."

Carefully folding a paper napkin, the lanky African-American with a law degree from Yale wiped a smudge of yogurt from his upper lip. He'd never had any problem from people like Lutz; Lutz was easy.

"Well, Mike," he said mildly, "there's this note Ralph Christen sent to the FBI Director couple of days ago. Christen is chief magistrate at the Court of Inquiry in Bern, and he knows the FBI's head honcho from way back when they worked together breaking up Mafia entrenchments in Zurich and Boston. So, this Christen tells us about enormous cash movements into a Swiss bank." He unhurriedly consulted his notes, then added, "The name of the Bank is CTBP Commerce & Trade Bank (Switzerland) AG, with branches in Geneva and Zurich."

Dexter went on to report that, according to Christen, a humongous pile of cash had been placed in an as yet unspecified account. The Bern police suspected this was Colombian drug cartel money, to be used for arms deals of a tremendous scope. If these suspicions proved accurate, Bern expected a breakthrough on the money-laundering front, all attempts at unveiling the monetary machinations of the drug cartels in Switzerland so far having failed. Dexter also informed them that the director of the FBI had assured his Swiss colleague of their full cooperation and support. Probably Conklin and his NSA specialists were in Bern for the purpose of electronic data monitoring, and to assist in cracking the banks involved.

As he listened, the frown on Graham Rivers's forehead deepened. Whether this was because of what Dexter was telling them, or because he couldn't find something he seemed to be searching for in the lettuce portion of his sandwich, would have been hard to tell.

Affecting his best Columbo manner, Rivers told his lunch partners that there was just one little thing that bothered him. "What I don't like about this is the security policy aspect," he said. "If Christen is talking about several hundred million dollars, then where does a broken-down ex-CIA stiff named Custer, also known as >Keycop<, get that kind of moolah? And my next question is: Granted he actually commands such enormous sums, what is it he's buying in Switzerland, a cuckoo clock?"

Recognizing another opportunity to leave his imprint on the snowy slopes of the Matterhorn, Lutz eagerly proposed that he himself fly over there and take a look at the situation.

"Switzerland is one of the countries I routinely work with," he said, "I'm exceptionally well connected there. I shouldn't have any trouble at all getting close to Custer without arousing suspicion."

Rivers gazed abstractedly at his still untouched sandwich, so Lutz could not be certain the National Security Adviser had actually heard what he said. Better not push his luck; Rivers embodied the maxim of walking softly and carrying a big stick, and his big stick happened to be an unpredictable, cutting wit.

"A billion dollars," Rivers was saying, "will get you a handful of fighter planes or tanks, but Cuckooland is hardly an advantageous marketplace for such weapons systems. Which leaves me wondering . . ."

He gave his sandwich what amounted to a dirty look, pushed himself out of his chair and started pacing along a wall that served as a gallery for portraits of former vice presidents. Under a heroic semiprofile shot of Spiro Agnew he stopped.

Dexter scooped up a couple more white-plastic spoonfuls of Yoggi yogurt and said comfortably, "Bill Conklin swears there's a clandestine outfit in Switzerland that sells nuclear weapons. I would imagine a billion bucks would buy you a few of those."

Visibly impressed, Rivers returned to his chair and sat down. Lutz stopped chewing. On the other side of the door, a gaggle of tourists pitter-pattered down the hall. The rain had stopped, leaving the city sweltering and humid beneath the gray sky, but the tourist traffic had resumed.

"Bull's-eye!" Rivers' voice sounded hollow. It had just dawned on him that, yes, of course, Swiss industry had the potential for manufacturing nukes! He shuddered inwardly.

Finally satisfied with having scraped the last bit of yogurt out of the container, John Dexter looked up with an incongruous smile. He told them, "The FBI's afraid Muslim fundamentalists are in Switzerland trying to procure small nuclear devices, if necessary have them made to order. We're talking unconfirmed here, but there may be a connection with Custer."

"Fine," Lutz said in a friendly tone, satisfied that his relationship with African-Americans in the White House was not merely politically correct, but close to impeccable. "So perhaps we should inform the president."

"It's all highly speculative at this time," Dexter admonished. "I think it's too early to talk conspiracy to the president." As he smiled guilelessly at his lunchtime cronies, Dexter was suddenly and sharply aware that they, too, wore long-standing, well-practiced, professional masks of innocence.

"That's fine, John," Lutz said again. "Now we have to look for the know-how, find out which Swiss company or companies have the capability to manufacture components for nuclear weapons. And let's keep in close touch with this, uh, this Christen. Once we're sure where all that big money is going, it's a cinch we'll get to the bottom of the mystery."

Lutz pulled his chair closer to the table. He picked up the sugar dispenser, set it down, keeping his hands busy. Without looking at Rivers, he sensed the national security adviser was watching him. Deciding to play his hand, Lutz lifted his head and faced them. "The only outfit in Switzerland that comes to mind for this type of business is the Schlammer Group," he said, keeping his voice low.

Rivers abruptly set down his glass. Dexter's head jerked up. Satisfied with the impact he'd made, Lutz enjoyed letting a few pleasurable moments pass. Then he informed them that an occasional golf partner, the Swiss military attaché, who hailed from Lausanne, knew the president of the Schlammer Group personally. When the administration in Bern decided to purchase fifty F/A-18 fighter planes from the United States, Swiss companies were assured of reciprocal business amounting to billions of Francs. Lutz told them that his friend, the golf-playing military attaché, had been closely involved especially with procuring orders in the military technology area from U.S. firms. On one such occasion, he had accompanied people from Schlammer Engineering on a trip to St. Louis, to visit an aircraft manufacturer. They had fought hard, competing for business. Apparently, Schlammer had been especially keen on spin-off orders relating to NASA programs.

Enjoying the undivided attention from Rivers and Dexter, Lutz now attacked the remainder of his turkey sandwich in earnest. Chewing vigorously but still producing acceptable elocution, he said, "I have it on good authority that Schlammer Engineering makes more than rocket and space technology products. They also make components for nuclear power plants, so they probably have the know-how to manufacture a nuclear bomb. Which prompts me to suggest, John, that your people start zeroing in on Schlammer Engineering."

Dexter tilted his head in a movement halfway between agreement and negation, while still appearing to consider Lutz's startling revelations. Rivers looked approvingly at the young, self-confident Lutz, thinking that what Lutz had told them might well turn out to be the straw that broke the camel's back. If in fact it was possible to obtain nuclear weapons in Switzerland, he now had to admit to himself that his most paranoid fantasies might actually come true.

"Then it's possible," said Rivers slowly, "that some Islamic terrorist groups might be in business with Schlammer. In the past, the Muslim militants focused their activities on countries like Egypt or Syria, where they're trying to topple the supposedly secular governments they say they despise. Since the United States supports the governments they're trying to get rid of, we are their natural enemy. These militants firmly believe that if it weren't for the support we give these countries, they would long ago have collapsed under pressure from their Muslim majorities. And that's the reason why they have shifted the focus of their Holy War to American cities. Look at the World Trade Center incident, for example. And the nasty plot to blow up tunnels under the Hudson River, which the FBI managed to foil in the nick of time. So that's the modus operandi of these extremists, and heaven have mercy on us if they ever get hold of a nuclear device. We'd have to be prepared for the worst!"

Frowns of professional concern on their faces, the three men busied themselves with what was left of their lunches. Lutz went to the door and switched on the large, southern-style ceiling fan. When he returned, his lunch partners were standing by the table.

It was one P.M. and the meeting appeared to be over. Lutz suggested they send a memorandum to the Swiss Government, but Rivers decided to await further details on the Kern assassination before pursuing their concerns with Bern.

Rivers and Lutz walked out together. Halfway through the door, Rivers almost collided with one of the communications secretaries, a lady Dexter had once described as "being built like a brick shithouse." Smiling radiantly, the woman handed him a perforated sheet.

He immediately noticed the Time Received entry. This piece of news had been lying around for hours! And no wonder; in bold letters made with a blue marker, someone had penned *Swaziland* instead of *Switzerland* across the top. Shaking his head at this blatant display of inefficiency, the national security adviser scanned the message.

" ' . . . shot to death execution-style, with a machine pistol . . . ,' " he muttered, skimming over the text, " 'Bern calls it an act of political terrorism and extortion . . . Peter Kern was in charge of the nuclear sector' . . . ah, here it is . . . 'Interpol is looking for >Keycop<.' "

Rivers looked up, his face a mask of concern. "So maybe there *is* a connection," he said somberly.

In her small apartment at the foot of Nucleanne's castle hill, Rosalia turned to the
last pages of the SADAM manual. She laid
it on the table and pressed down with the
heel of her hand to flatten it out. After adjusting the angle of the
halogen lamp she had positioned near the table, she pushed her
old Canon camera aside, picked up the Minolta, and looked
through the view finder, framing one of the two brightly lit pages.
She adjusted the focus on the macro lens, checked the exposure
setting and snapped a picture: the thirty-sixth one! That was it!
She'd copied all thirty-six pages of the SADAM manual.

Happy with a job well done, she slid the brochure back in between two cookbooks on a shelf. The digital clock that doubled as
a bookend indicated one minute left to communication time. She
took a portable transceiver down from behind two books on the
shelf and stepped to the window with it, looking out across the
valley toward the Schlammer Engineering compound. The unit
emitted a series of high-pitched warbles, then the intermittent
hum of the call signal. A gruff voice came on.

"¡Diga! ¿Quién es?"

"Rosalia," she said. "Informe de situación. ¡Muy urgente!"

Impatiently biting her lips, she checked her wristwatch. She had called at precisely the agreed-upon time; Cali simply had to be there! When she recognized Don Cali's unmistakable voice, she wasted no time with preliminaries. In fluent Spanish, she rattled off a concise report on the situation: The product was ready for delivery, but the seller chose not to deliver to the Iraqi. Tomorrow, Tuesday, July 3, the product would be flown up into the mountains and placed in a former quarry that had been converted into a storage facility.

Rosalia read the coordinates giving the location of the cave from a slip of paper. She informed Don Cali that General Breckerlin would transmit the exact takeoff time for the air transport by telephone to the number he had been given. She also told Cali that she had photographed each page of the product manual. The product itself was in excellent condition, as ordered, all-granite insulation packaging as requested.

Then she added, "I repeat, one unit Rock'O'Clock will be transported up to the mountain storage facility tomorrow, Tuesday, July 3, probably in late afternoon or early evening. . . . What? . . . Oh, that's the name of the stupid granite clock. . . . What? . . . Yes. A pilot and an armed guard who works for us. His job is to neutralize the security personnel in the cave."

"Are you absolutely certain the charge is inside the clock housing?" Cali asked blithely, apparently unconcerned that he was speaking on an open line.

"Yes, one hundred percent certain," Rosalia affirmed. "I myself saw a Schlammer physicist install the fission pack and detonator. By the way, our man Custer is now in place. He is a real man and has already made some impressive moves. An excellent choice for the job. Pardon me? No, he suspects nothing."

"Good girl, Rosalia," Cali's voice came across flat and emotionless. "Just remember—no mistakes! I'm the law, and my arm is long!"

She was barely listening to Cali's pompous threat. Through the window, she saw Hannibal's white Cherokee come zipping up the narrow street, heard it screech to a halt downstairs. She grabbed the Minolta, dropped it into the garbage pail under the sink, then stuffed a couple of empty milk cartons and some crumpled-up paper bags on top. Then she put the transceiver far back on the shelf and slid the photos of Custer she had taken earlier into a cookbook. She finished just as the doorbell shrilled, jarringly, several times in quick succession. Rosalia inhaled deeply, to compose herself, then opened the door. Hannibal pushed her roughly back into the kitchen.

"Where's the manual, bitch? Give it to me! Now!" Suddenly, a straight razor flashed in his hand. He grabbed her by the hair, twisted her head back, sliced into her chin. She screamed as the blood spurted.

"The manual! Now, or I'll cut off something else!" Pressing the naked steel against her left breast, he tore off her scanty clothes. Sobbing, trembling, she pointed to the shelf, then grabbed a kitchen towel and pressed it against her chin to stop the blood.

"That's my girl!" Hannibal laughed, pulling the manual out from among the cookbooks. Then he picked up her regular phone, which stood on the windowsill. Using the razor as an all-purpose tool, Hannibal made sure the bug his men had planted in the set was in working condition. The few calls Rosalia had made these past few days had been monitored. He glanced around in angry frustration, with Rosalia praying he might overlook the transceiver. No such luck!

"What have we here!" He whistled softly to himself as he reached up behind the books and took down the handset, which was still in the active mode. He touched Redial and a strip of digits appeared in the display window. Hannibal gulped, stared bug-eyed, then pressed Clear.

"What the hell is this? Who're you calling abroad?" He took a step toward her, menacingly flashing the razor. "Let's have it, bitch, who and where? I'll slice you!"

Pressing both hands against her bleeding chin, she stammered, "My sister . . . she' studying . . ."

"Where?"

"In . . . Colombia . . . she . . ."

"You take me for a moron?"

"Honest, she studies engineering, and she speaks English. I called her . . . to help me translate a passage from the manual . . . into Spanish!" Hannibal gazed uncertainly at the unit in his hand.

"Did Schoenhof ask you to do this?"

"Of course," she said, more composed. She raised up her torso, pushing out her well-rounded breasts, moving her pelvis forward. Hannibal's dull stare rested on the place between her thighs.

"Schoenhof wanted a sample from the operating instructions in Spanish for a major client, so he asked me. I needed a couple of

technical terms, that's why I called my sister . . . the engineer."
Holding her breath, she stretched her left leg toward him.

"Don't you worry, bitch, I'll check it out," Hannibal said, squinting at her, sending needle-sharp beams into her limpid, almond-
shaped eyes, now brimming with moisture. He wheeled suddenly,
tore open the door to the closet beneath the shelves, pulled out
the drawers, upended them on the kitchen floor. The next moment, he stood as if rooted to the spot, staring at the sink. With
one step he was by the dishwasher, pulled it out. Empty! He yanked
the door to the sink closet open, stepped on the pedal protruding
from the bottom portion of the garbage pail. The lid tilted up.

Rosalia's buttocks rested against the edge of the kitchen table.
She leaned back and let out a throaty moan, her right hand sliding
slowly toward the other camera, the Canon. Hannibal took his foot
off the pedal. He blinked, taking in the voluptuous challenge of
her naked flesh. Then he saw her narrow, long-fingered hand
stealthily sneaking up on a camera.

"So, you've been taking pictures! Smart little bitch, huh?" He
wiggled four fingers in a beckoning gesture. "Gimme gimme
gimme!"

She handed him the camera and he activated Rewind. The
mechanism started up with a metallic rasp. When it had stopped,
he took out the roll, thoughtfully weighing it in one hand.

"We'll soon know what's on it," he told her, putting it in his
breast pocket.

"Nothing is on it," Rosalia said, "it's empty."

"Okay, bitch, gimme some head!" He bared his teeth in an atavistic snarl. "Your last job for the day will be a blow job!"

Rosalia slid down from the table and knelt in front of him. She
unzipped him, releasing his thick, turgid member with its bluish-
red head. She ran a fingertip along the underside of the penis,
gently massaging the groove where the foreskin was attached. The
hugely swollen glans bobbed slowly, heavily, up and down in front
of her face. She clapped her thick lips over it, sucking it in like
some enormous gourmet asparagus. Slowly, rhythmically, she began
to move her head back and forth.

Hannibal groaned. His eyes were narrow slits, his face was tilted
up at the ceiling, his hands clawing into her long, black hair. No
way the bitch would make him lose control! Still, he hoped she'd
told him the truth. Part of her story—he groaned again, louder this
time—part of it checked out: Schoenhof had told him that Rosalia

was working for him, had some access privileges, like opening the wall closet. It would be a terrible waste to have to . . . have to—he groaned rhythmically now, his teeth bared in a snarling grin—blow away a blow artist like her!

Grunting like a stuck hog, he came. Carefully, lightly, Rosalia pulled her head back from the trembling penis and wiped her mouth with the towel. Hannibal's sperm fluids mingled with blood from the deep, still-bleeding cut. Snorting angrily, he turned away from her, zipped up, adjusted his trousers, and left, without looking at her or saying a word.

When the door fell shut behind him, Rosalia collapsed, exhausted, on the kitchen floor. A few minutes passed, her shoulders twitching uncontrollably. Finally, she told herself that the bad thing was over and the good thing was that she was still alive and crawling on all fours to the sink. She pulled herself up, repeatedly rinsed out mouth and throat, gargling, spitting, coughing up water she didn't want to swallow. By the spice rack she found a half-empty bottle of cognac, took a long, deep swig, straight from the bottle. Then she remembered the Minolta in the garbage pail.

She rewound the film, took out the yellow-and-black roll, placed it in a white envelope and sealed it. Then she put the camera back in the garbage pail. She used some antiseptic ointment and an extrawide adhesive strip to dress the throbbing wound.

Ten minutes later she was in her car, driving to the train station. After parking the Fiat at the station, she bought a tabloid called *Lucky Times* and went into the station restaurant. She crossed the large room and took a corner table by the window. There she sat, sipping coffee, occasionally glancing at the newspaper. Presently a man in blue carpenter's coveralls, who also carried a copy of *Lucky Times*, sat at her table and put down his paper. She waved at the waitress, paid for her coffee, picked up her paper, and walked out.

The man in the blue coveralls watched through the window until she was out of sight. Then he reached for the folded-up copy of the *Lucky Times*, put one hand in its pages, and pulled out a white envelope, which he slipped into one of the two large hip pockets of his coveralls. Only then did he order a glass of beer, which he tossed down before walking out of the café.

Given Rosalia's practiced dexterity, even an attentive observer might not have noticed the casual switch of newspapers. Not that there were any observers, attentive or otherwise, this Monday afternoon in Nucleanne. The few people there had better things to do than to watch what was going on at a table in the corner. Much better things, such as watching the incessant Kern updates on the screen above the bar while knocking back another glass of beer. As a result, the photos of the SADAM manual and the close-ups of Custer in action had smoothly changed hands.

Hannibal had parked on a side street, out of sight of the house where Rosalia lived. From behind some bushes he had seen her get hurriedly into her car and drive off. He waited a few minutes, then sprinted to her house; moments later he again stood in her kitchen. He found the second camera in the garbage pail and, as he looked around in the mess, noticed a cookbook on the floor, with an envelope sticking out. He bent down to it. The legend *Photos in one hour* was printed on the envelope. He pulled out the color prints and marveled: they showed Baldie brawling with the mailman.

"That's the guy from before," he murmured to himself. "Can you believe it, the bitch is playing mole!" He pocketed the close-up of Custer and left the apartment.

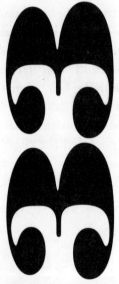

Bern, Monday, July 2

Chief of Police Thomas Borli put down the receiver with a heavy hand. So now he was head of the Kern assassination investigation unit. What kind of a job was this, that made a man break his word to his daughter, that four-year-old tousle-headed angel?

Borli stared at the dark-blue background of his computer screen, on which random lines of white were busy linking up to form rectangles. What he was looking for in the Kern case were special traits. Develop an overview, he told himself, don't think systematic, think horizontal! What he needed was information of a special sort, and he thought he knew where to get it. That morning on his way to work, the names of some ex-counterintelligence men had popped into his mind, men who voluntarily left the Service, or were forced to quit after their secret organization was exposed.

Borli activated the Search function and tapped in *P-26*. The Department was on another cost-cutting rampage and couldn't afford state-of-the-art computers. So, one day, his wife Melanie had turned up with a superfast laptop, a contribution from the computer shop she ran, to improve her husband's efficiency.

"Try this one, it's three times as fast as that old boil of obsolescence you call a computer," she had jauntily told him. Having convinced himself that she was right, Borli now routinely transferred special search data, which included information on the exspooks, from the "boil" to the donated laptop.

It took only seconds to hit pay dirt: *VIKTOR GISLING, Deputy Director of Swiss Counterintelligence, UNA, until 1989. . . .* Borli vividly recalled the electronic surveillance specialist who had defected from UNA. He scrolled on: *Since 1990, Chief Information Officer at Schlammer Engineering. Nickname "Adam's Quisling." See also Secret Army. . . .*

Borli was thinking. It was known that Viktor Gisling maintained well-established contacts in the shadow world of agents and wannabe spies; he knew couriers, informers, and other shady characters. Gisling's circle of friends and acquaintances included former Stasi agents, ex-KGB people, and CIA duds trying to survive in the turbulent world of "intelligence" with their own one-man, or one-woman, spy shops. Borli nodded; great, he'd simply have Gisling called in for a little chat. Satisfied, the chief penned a brief memo to this effect, then turned his attention to the sheaf of reports on his desk.

According to the most recent information, Stephanie Kramer had made a telephone call from a train station approximately halfway between Bern and Lausanne. The second memo reported that Kenneth W. Custer, code name >Keycop<, had spent a few hours at the Lakeview Motel just west of Bern. Too bad they'd let him slip through their fingers.

Borli absently drew a circle around each of the two locations on the large operational map spread on his desk. In the oval area framed by the curved lines of the intersecting circles lay Nucleanne. Schlammer . . . Nucleanne! Kern's chauffeur had stated that on Sunday he drove the prime minister to the head office of the Schlammer Group, where Kern got out, returning after slightly more than an hour.

Borli gazed thoughtfully at the tiny dot on the map, then picked up the next report on his desk:

An alleged U.S. Secret Service agent named Murphy had tied on a whale of a drunk the night before, and was now snoring it off in some rural jail. The man lacked all identification papers. After being alerted by an anonymous telephone call, the local gendarmes had arrested him in a state of severe inebriation at the wheel of a car. The car was found not far from a bridge, nose down, jammed into the roots of an old cherry tree at the bottom of a steep roadside ditch. Borli checked the location on his map: the accident had occurred only a kilometer or so from the site of a public shortwave broadcasting station.

The chief brooded over his map. Something about that broadcasting station irritated him; it was on the tip of his tongue but he couldn't get it out. When Max came in, Borli set his plan in motion. He designated the oval area delineated by the intersecting circles on the map as an "intensified search area." Again, he studied the map, squinting at the dot that marked the town where the shortwave station was located.

When Borli returned home shortly after midnight, he found a piece of birthday cake and two slips of paper on the kitchen table. The cake was piled high with strawberries and whipped cream, already drying. One note bore the words *Dady I luv yu*, in Julia's meticulously squiggly preschool hand. His wife's note read, *Ralph Christen and Stephanie Kramer know each other, and old love never dies! A demain! Dindin.*

Upstairs in their bedroom, Dindin lay dissolved in sleep, one long leg carelessly thrown over a pillow. Borli stood watching her for a minute or two. She was so beautiful! He wanted to feel, gently caress, embrace her. Even before his skin touched hers, she murmured something and turned over on one side, sinking deeper into her dreams. Smiling, Borli climbed in beside her and was asleep before he could pull the blanket over his shoulder, the smile fixed on his face.

Stephanie's fall lasted no more than a second. Screaming wildly, she had plunged into dark, ice-cold wetness. She swallowed water—water!—not some poisonous soup. She could swim, save herself! A few swift, powerful strokes, and she reached the wall, which was slick as slime, with no handhold anywhere. She moved sideways along the wall, feeling her way in the icy water that constricted her chest, threatening to choke her. Thrashing about, half to keep warm and half in panic, her hand touched a metal bar. She pulled up her feet, steadied herself as she gathered strength, then pushed herself up over the rim.

She was shaking violently from the cold. Hugging herself, trying to cover as much of her soaking wet body as she could with her arms, she moved toward a rounded, glassed-in protuberance that promised shelter and warmth. A door stood ajar. She went in and found an industrial-sized flashlight that had been left on the control console. Playing the flashlight beam around in the murky twilight, she saw a sign with bold, black-and-red lettering that proclaimed FUEL ROD REPLACEMENT CONTROL ROOM, ELEVATION 508.3 m. Apparently she was in the former storage cavern for fuel rods—former, because the place looked run-down and abandoned. Dirt and dust, dismantled machinery, severed connections, twisted pipes were everywhere. The beam from the flashlight caught, and held, a pair of dusty coveralls hanging on the wall.

She propped up the flashlight and stripped off her wet clothes. Gingerly poking in first one, then the other leg, she pulled the stiff garment up, pushing her arms through the sleeves. She grimaced as the scratchy fabric roughed up her nipples, but was already grateful for the warmth it gave her. She folded up her wet clothes and thrust them into the coverall's roomy hip pouches.

Squinting through grimy windows across the ominously dark waters, she made out the contours of tall racks stacked high with barrels, and a rotary crane at the basin's edge. Jagged pieces of machinery gleamed dully in the feeble light from a narrow window at the top of a staircase. She left the control room, walked along the edge of the basin to the staircase and climbed up, passing a sign: SUBLEVEL NORTH ONE, ELEVATION 511.7 m. She noticed a scaffoldlike platform along the wall that led past a row of narrow, facet-paned windows very much like the one above the staircase. Telling herself this might be her way out, she moved closer and peered cautiously through one of the grimy window panes.

Some three meters below the spot where she looked out, shockingly close in fact, stood a man in a white lab coat, happily waving a pair of panties in the air. More lingerie items spilled out of a shiny black package on a table. Half-hidden beneath the profusion of designer underwear were several large maps spread out on the tabletop.

As Stephanie stared in disbelief, a voluptuous young woman with long black hair pulled a black blouse up over her head. Wiggling provocatively, she thrust her heavy breasts at the man, who sank down on his knees in front of her. Kneading her breasts with both hands, he buried his head between her thighs. The woman spread wider, clutching his head, her eyes flashing ecstatically at the ceiling. Stephanie noted that an adhesive strip bandaged her chin. Precarious as her situation was, the scene being played out below turned her on. As she watched, heat rose from her abdomen, spreading through the body, dissolving the last chilly patches inside of her. Her moist lips slightly parted, she stared down at the woman's rhythmically seesawing pelvis, at the bobbing head of her lover, ardently bent to his task of licking. His hands now clutched the woman's buttocks, allowing her pendulous breasts to move freely, gently, back and forth, which sent more sweet bursts of pleasure through Stephanie. A wild abandon rose up in her, her hand went to her crotch, why not, what difference did it make? This, down there, was all there was, wasn't it? God, how she envied that woman!

Then she tore herself away, shut her eyes for a moment, determined to ignore the panting lovers the next time she looked. She saw a laboratory, not very large; it looked neat and scientific. There was a desk with a computer and a printer, also a drawing board with rolled-up blueprints. And a shiny, aluminum centrifuge, with a green wall rack next to it. On the rack stood a modern, brown suitcase, half-hidden by a large, cube-shaped housing made of green stone. Next to the glass door, which was the only entrance she could see, hung a fire extinguisher. Below that was a Geiger counter. An adjoining black iron staircase led to the upper-level storage space she imagined but could not see from her own, lower vantage point.

Again she looked at the cube-shaped stone housing; the side turned toward her was a clock face. A movable portion of the casing had been pushed aside to reveal the hollow interior, filled with rods, wiring and circuitry that Stephanie was unable to identify. Not far from the granite cube, metal cylinders were stacked on a cart.

At the far end of the room was a measuring station with a mass of cables, as well as more red-and-black housings. Tacked to the wall was a sketch with tube-shaped designs and explanatory text. Stacks of paper covered a large table in the center. More blueprints, she figured, making mental notes on everything she saw. Through the glass door she glimpsed an insulation chamber for personnel; to the left, in a dead angle, she suspected more furniture.

To get a better look, she stood on tiptoe and was rewarded with a clear view of the man in the lab coat. Now he got up and, pressing his buttocks against the table, made the woman ride his thrust-out pelvis. The woman's pelvis bonded with the man's in a smooth, swift, docking operation. Her arms were around his neck, her naked legs gripping his hips in a scissor-hold. Behind his back her feet, entwined, kept slipping and sliding on the spread-out map and the lingerie.

Entranced, Stephanie gaped at the action. The woman's heels jittered ecstatically up and down the East Coast of the United

States, from Florida to Maine and back again, until they came tremulously to rest somewhere in the Mid-Atlantic states. Then her gaze met the woman's.

The black-haired woman at first seemed distant, veiled and vacant, but then her eyes widened as her absent reason returned. The image of what appeared there at the window suddenly made sense.

A face!

Judging by the grimace she made, the woman might have seen a ghost. Twisting out from under the man's clutching arms, still a picture of shocked incomprehension, she pointed a stiff arm at the skylight, yanking the man out of his trance. He shook his head like a bull shaking off flies. For a moment he stared sheepishly at the woman's heaving breasts, then slowly turned his head and looked up.

Stephanie ducked down, petrified. That woman had seen her! Following her original plan, crouching low, she moved swiftly along the row of windows, until she came to the passage she had glimpsed earlier. She entered an empty corridor that widened to form a shadowy recess on each side. A feeble red glow straight ahead dimly illuminated a massive door. Stephanie reached it, leaned on the handle and pushed with all her might, but it didn't budge. Confused, excited voices reached her from below. Somebody bellowed something that sounded like: "Shitgoddamsam!" The noisy commotion came closer.

She desperately searched the niches on both sides for a way out. But there was no escaping the tunnel, hewn some thirty meters into sheer rock. Dog yips and barks sent shivers up her spine, raising goosebumps on her arms. Hearing the dog sounds gave her the ratlike strength and determination she needed to frantically burrow in behind a tall stack of sacks in one of the hollows. Shivering, wide-eyed with fear, she pressed her back against the tunnel wall, vascillating between terror and rage.

So this was the end! Just let them come, she'd fight them to the death! What a shame, what a rotten shame! Come on, dogs, I'm taking one of you with me! Except there was no room for dogs where she was going.

The barking of the dogs sounded closer. Stephanie was beside herself with fear and terrible exhaustion; an unspeakable, visceral terror had reduced her to a state of infantility in which the only release was a violent temper tantrum. Tears streaming down her face, her fists pounded against the cold, impervious rockface. Then she fainted, or at least felt as if she were fainting, stumbling, losing her balance, as a portion of the wall moved forward against her body, pressing her against that huge pile of sacks. Choking, coughing, sobbing, she desperately fought back against the irresistible force. Was this what it was like to be going crazy?

A voice whispered, "Pssst, you! Get in here!" The whites of a pair of eyes flashed at her through a narrow gap. Someone crooked a beckoning finger at her; a hand reached out. A snapshot of the scene imprinted indelibly on Stephanie's mind: a narrow iron door, opening into a chimneylike funnel. "The flashlight. Give it to me," whispered the soft voice. "I'll help you. There's a grate down here you can step on. Don't be afraid."

Stephanie shook with fear. Dogs were barking, men yelling, coming up the corridor. She squeezed through the narrow gap, took the proffered hand, and stepped into an upward stream of moist warm air.

"A ventilation shaft!" she panted.

"Right," affirmed at least two voices in the dark. Trying to control her labored breathing and the violent trembling of her body, she looked around. Three nebulous faces peered down at her in the faint light from a small flashlight.

"Who are you?" she wheezed. "What are you doing here?"

The boy whose hand had guided her spoke first. "I'm Mark. This is Tony. And Jessie."

"I'm Stephanie. You kids saved my life, you're great." Still breathing in hectic gulps, she brushed a strand of hair out of her face. The boy was struggling to lock the door with a big, square key.

"What now?" Stephanie asked.

Mark pointed up the shaft.

"Up that-away," he grinned. "This is a rescue operation. We are rescuing you. See these clamps? You pull yourself up on them, like a ladder. Plus, we've got a safety rope." He took the lead, playing the beam from Stephanie's flashlight along the walls of the shaft.

"We've been down this way before," said Jessie, her dusky features focused on the job of climbing.

"Yeah, once!" Tony chuckled.

Ignoring the remark, Jessie said, "Today, we were going to get inside the old nuclear plant. We've been working on this for months, ever since we discovered this shaft. The toughest part was breaking in here—"

"Yeah, the worst!" Tony groaned dramatically.

"Almost out," Mark called down to them. Moments later, Stephanie poked her head through dense underbrush as her hands, then her knees, sank into the mossy forest ground. Two arms steadied her. She stood upright, marveling at a wall of mighty firs. Above her vaulted a sky of intoxicating blue. She gazed up into it for long moments, silently thanking it for having sent three perfect kid angels to save her.

Breathing deeply, she inhaled her newfound freedom; it smelled to her like sage and pine resin. The mouth of the shaft lay well-concealed amid dense underbrush and bushes, atop a mountain shoulder, she guessed. She tried to orient herself; her rescue team was already pressing on.

Taking a winding path along the wooded slope, they moved down to a rocky promontory that jutted out from the mountainside. Far below, a dark, swirling river churned in a narrow bed. "What a beautiful spot!" Stephanie exclaimed. Cool mists drifted along the river's course; the vibrant green of the valley floor was already tinged with shades of gray in the afternoon light. To the west, the great luminescence of day still dominated the sky. Faraway bastions of clouds shone like snowy airborne mountains in the alpenglow.

Unabashed, the kids looked with large, clear eyes at the woman in the dirty coveralls. The garment's bulkiness only emphasized the contours of her well-toned body. The strap of the handbag she had slung over her shoulder pulled the coarse fabric tightly across the twin hillocks of her plump breasts.

Stephanie, in turn, probed their solemn kid faces with a searching gaze. What she saw, and sensed, was the kind of spontaneous, unquestioning loyalty only children can give. And the question of whether she could trust them had already been answered affirmatively by their actions. "We're partners now," she stated simply, "we're a team!"

As far as she was concerned, there wasn't really much more to say. But her youthful team members also acted like silent partners. They kept their eyes on the ground, or gazed forlornly up into the air, or squinted sideways, into the ravine. On impulse, Stephanie asked for a knife. Tony handed her a Swiss army knife with the main blade unfolded. Sure of the trio's freshly revived attention, she bravely pushed the point of the blade into the heel of her hand, pressed steadily until it punctured the skin, then made a tiny cut which started bleeding.

It was an age-old ritual, immediately understood and accepted by the kids. Three palms were presented, three cuts made: first the girl, Jessie, then Mark and Tony. Then, one after the other, they solemnly joined hands, gazed deeply into each other's eyes, as the blood of one mingled with the blood of all the others, and the blood of all with that of one. Stephanie had no idea whether this was the proper way to seal a pact of blood, but at least the solemnity of the ritual broke the ice and ignited a spark between them.

Mark stepped forward and pointed up at their hideaway, a secret cave perfectly concealed far back on a rocky ledge just above from where they stood. "Our cave," he said, with a meaningful glance at her. "No one knows about it but us. It's our secret. Which you now share."

Stephanie asked them if there was any way of reaching the cave from the river below, through the ravine. Tony took her arm and led her closer to the edge, to show her the footpath. She looked down from the very rim of the rocky overhang, then shied back, dizziness rising up in her. "I could try," she said bravely.

"You shouldn't," Mark said firmly. "There's no place for you to hide down there. But there's an old, abandoned schoolhouse on the edge of the forest. We can put you in there."

Stephanie looked doubtful. "I have to make a telephone call; that's an absolute must. And another thing—I can't afford to be seen by anyone. The police are looking for me. I have to go . . . underground." Smiling weakly at her unintended pun, she looked uncertainly at them, vaguely fearful, wondering how they would react.

They didn't draw back; weren't shocked. They just stood there, calm and relaxed, until Tony casually said, "Maybe we ought to get going."

Inside the old schoolhouse, which did not look quite as delapidated as Stephanie had expected, Mark immediately set about checking fuses, tracing wires, and testing outlets. He found an old-fashioned, dust-covered dial phone, which he connected, while Stephanie made up a list of items she needed. When Tony offered to bring her car up from Nucleanne, she rummaged through her soaked handbag and, without hesitation, handed him the keys. No doubt, the resourceful young man would be as good as his word.

Then, rather abruptly, she was alone in the house. She pulled up a chair to the teacher's desk with the slanted top where Mark had placed the telephone. She noticed that her hand shook as she dialed. The line clicked and crackled, then the familiar voice said, "Christen."

"Ralph, thank God you're there. It's me. I'm calling from somewhere near Nucleanne. Ralph, I've discovered some dreadful things. We absolutely have to meet, it's a matter of life and death."

The line crackled sharply, then Christen's clear, confident voice came through. "Calm down, Stephanie, please. And don't say any more. I will come to you as fast as I can. Wait, I'm looking for my notepad. Okay! Now give me your phone number."

She bent her head down to look at the narrow, yellowing number plate recessed into the base of the set. The number was written in ink, in a stiff, formal hand, each digit drawn perfectly and separately. She read it off and Christen repeated it.

"Very good," he said, "I expect to get there around ten, and don't you move! I'll bring along some of my men, but you stay put, okay? I'll be there soon. Now relax—and be careful."

He was about to hang up when Stephanie said, "Wait! I want to be sure you can get through on this line, so hang up and call me back."

She sat there, staring at the phone for what seemed like minutes, telling herself to calm down, be patient. When the phone finally rang, she almost jumped out of her skin, tearing the receiver from the cradle before the echo of the first ring had died down.

"Hello, Ralph?"

"It works fine," said Christen. He hung up, then dialed Information at police headquarters. Five minutes later he had the exact location of the old schoolhouse in the forest above Nucleanne.

Breathing deeply, Stephanie leaned back in the rickety old chair. Everything was going to be all right now! Ralph and his men would turn Schlammer's cavern inside out. Jessie, Mark, and Tony would be the heroes of the day.

Fifteen minutes later, a telephone rang in the command control room at Schlammer Engineering, no more than two kilometers from the old schoolhouse where Stephanie was dozing on a couch. Hannibal jumped up from his comfortable leather armchair, grabbed the receiver, gave his name.

"No!" he exclaimed. "Has this been confirmed?"

Listening closely, he hastily scribbled on a notepad, hung up. Incredible! His people in Bern had tapped in on a telephone call from Kramer to Christen. Within minutes they had zeroed in on the location of the caller: the bitch was snooping around nearby! Despite himself, he marveled at the woman's nerve.

Hannibal tapped the intercom and paged Matak. A few minutes later, the long-haired killer limped through the door. While Hannibal briefed him on the situation, Matak shifted his weight from leg to leg, then drew his automatic, a huge Beretta 92F, from a hip holster. He started slapping it from one hand into the other, grinning maniacally, licking his lips as if slobbering over a huge, juicy steak. Now that piece a shit's gonna get what's comin' to her, he told himself as he bent over the 1:25,000-scale map of Nucleanne and surroundings that Hannibal had spread before them.

The security chief tapped a heavy index finger on the spot where the schoolhouse was located, then marked it with a blue textliner. His voice was cold as ice. "No slipups this time, Matak, no excuses! This woman is dangerous. She knows far too much and she can hurt us. I want a clean kill. Eliminate her. Do you understand?"

Matak grinned and nodded.

Hannibal slapped the table, hard. "Answer me! Do you understand?"

"I get it, boss," Matak grinned, "you want me to blow her away clean, not messy. Will do, boss." Visions of the "cleanest" kill he knew—emptying the entire magazine of his Beretta into the bitch—danced in his head as he speed-limped toward the parking area.

Within an hour, young Tony Summermatter was back with the items Stephanie had asked for. There was some food, an old pair of sneakers a size too big, and a bottle of Evian mineral water. And her zippy red car was parked in front of the schoolhouse.

"Thank you, Tony, that was really nice of you," Stephanie smiled. "Till Wednesday then, up there above the ledge, by the ventilation shaft, as agreed, okay? Count on me to be there. I know you will be."

Nodding reassuringly, already on his way out, Tony said, "No problem. We'll be there Wednesday afternoon, at four, waiting. Oh, the keys . . . they're in the ignition. I'm out of here."

Warm feelings of admiration and love for "her kids" coursed through her. She raised the Evian bottle to her lips, reveled in the coolness of the water bubbling down her throat. Hope Ralph finds this old shack! she thought, stretching out luxuriously exhausted on the rickety old couch. Well, if not, he could always call. She made a final attempt to focus on the events of the past forty-eight hours, get some order into them, so she could give Ralph a professional briefing. But sleep beckoned, lapping at her feet, like a gentle version of that great wave she had seen. She yielded to a dreamless oblivion beyond time.

Ralph Christen gulped down a hastily improvised dinner snack. Even before Stephanie called a couple of minutes ago, he'd
already half decided to take on Schlammer
Engineering. As the day progressed, all the bits and pieces of cir-
cumstantial evidence had started coming together, forming an in-
creasingly clear picture. While tangible proof was still missing,
Christen was ready to swear that the great Adam Schlammer was
up the proverbial fecal creek without a paddle.

Then, when Stephanie called from Nucleanne, all the bits finally
fell smoothly into place. He'd been especially fascinated by the
irrational, supernatural elements in the dream she had related to
him. How was this possible? The woman dreams of murder, rec-
ognizes a face, then neatly links it to Adam Schlammer and a long-
forgotten demonstration at Ollon. Coincidence? Still highly
skeptical, he had started digging up what he could on this Schlammer person.

Christen was determined: the raid on Schlammer Engineering
would be staged early on Tuesday morning. The Special Unit of
the Canton Police had been alerted and was now on standby. All
he had told the task force commander was the time, 0400 hours,

Nucleanne region, and the rendezvous location. They'd strike like lightning out of a clear blue sky. Surprise wins half the prize!

The military magistrate pocketed his car keys, pulled his favorite leather jacket off its hanger, and ambled down the stairs. He turned right, out from under the archways of the old part of town, and headed uptown toward Town Hall Square, where his car was parked. Christen felt at the top of his form. A whirlwind of mental action during the past twenty-four hours had swept away all the sluggishness and inertia of recent days and weeks. The sinister events surrounding Kern's death, combined with Schlammer's mysterious machinations, had boosted the chief magistrate into an elevated state of hectic tension. He felt lighthearted and eager for action.

At last, it was up to him. He'd be the one to save the nation, perhaps all of humankind, from a terrible disaster. Impatiently, he shrugged off a faint, insistent whisper from an inner voice cautioning him not to do this alone.

But what else was he to do? Whom could you trust in a conspiracy of this magnitude? First things first, he reasoned. Before anything else can be done, Stephanie must be rescued. After that? Well, bring in Borli. Or, even better, call a press conference!

Traffic was light in Bern's old part of town at this evening hour. The ancient arcades, known as "Arbors," ran like gracefully curving corridors along both sides of the wide street. Striding purposefully toward Town Hall Square, barely taking notice of the few pedestrians he met, Christen reviewed the events of the day.

All through Monday, hundreds of tips, leads, and hints had poured in to the Special Unit. In the afternoon, Christen himself had plowed through the "promising" reports and messages. The United States agent who ran his car off the road near Bern kept insisting that the entire incident had been faked by Swiss operatives to get him out of the way.

"Which they certainly did," Christen chuckled patriotically.

The U.S. Department of Justice had notified his department of the impending arrival of Bill Conklin, a VIP from the National Security Agency. Conklin was preceded by photo warrants for >Keycop<, a.k.a. Kenneth William Custer, apparently the United States' most wanted weapons dealer, an ex-Noriega agent and behind-the-scenes puppeteer in the Iran-Contra affair.

Christen had coded and stored this information in his computer. He also made a backup copy which he thoughtfully hid in his apartment. But he felt some crucial pieces were still missing. And timing was most important: he'd drop his sensational bomb at precisely the right moment, surrounded by the susurrant cameras of the assembled media. Getting Stephanie's note was pure dynamite. Perhaps he should immediately have incorporated her eyewitness report on the murder of Kern as evidence into the investigation file, along with the kidnapping and murder attempt on Kramer herself.

How he admired this woman! And soon he, reliable old Ralph, would pull her out of the precarious mess she'd got herself into! Fairly bouncing along, he waved at a sculpted stone image of Iustitia on a pedestal by the Old Well, calling out to her, *"On revient toujours à ses premiers amours!"*

He and Stephanie hadn't seen much of each other lately. What a reunion it would be!

Christen was walking down Bärengasse, a narrow, dimly-lit side street, when his cellular phone started bleeping. Still deep in thought, he absently pulled the portable out of his jacket pocket. "Christen," he said.

On the line, Steiner from the Special Investigation Unit sounded excited. "You'd better get to headquarters fast. We've found out where Kramer is hiding. The Chief thinks . . ."

A dozen paces ahead, three skinheads suddenly bounded from a dark archway into the street. Startled, Christen lowered the phone and swung around. Two more grimacing hooligans blocked his escape route. He took a deep breath. His back against a wall, he moved intuitively to the right, fixing both groups in his unwavering gaze. They were clad in tight, black-leather motorcycle gear. The steel tips on their heavy half-length boots gleamed dully in the dim light. There was a sharp, metallic noise as one of them impatiently kicked the curb. His buddies also started kicking against the cobblestones. Their circle slowly drew tighter.

"Christen . . . Christen . . . are you there?" Steiner's scratchy little voice made the chief magistrate lift the phone.

"Help . . . I'm in Bärengasse . . . skinheads . . ."

A knee smashed into his abdomen. Grunting in pain, gasping for air, Christen doubled over. The cellular phone dropped to the sidewalk. The gang's leader, a hollow-cheeked hood with a beer bottle in one hand, snarled as he brought one armored foot down on the instrument, crushing it like a bug.

"Fuckin' copface! That's what we'll do with your head!"

They slammed him against the wall, went through his pockets, and pulled out his photo ID. The gaunt-faced leader flicked a lighter, held it close to the foldout plastic. He nodded.

"That's him all right."

He tossed the beer bottle aside, raised both arms high above his head, and smashed a double-fisted wedge down on Christen's skull. Groaning, the chief magistrate collapsed. He reflexively pulled up his knees, shielding his head with his arms.

"Oh yeah?" a square-jawed type sneered. "Does de little baby hurt? We play a little game to make de little baby feel better, yes?" He stepped back to improve his leverage. "It's called skullbanging!"

A boot crashed through the shield of Christen's arms into his face. Sledgehammer kicks pounded his face and skull. The leather punks performed a deadly sort of dance, roaring a savage, rhythmic chant: "We kick ya till we lick ya . . . we kick ya . . . "—beastly snorts, the clashing and clinking of steel-tipped boots on cobblestones—" . . . till we lick ya . . . "

At last came the distant wail of approaching sirens. Gauntface raised one arm. They let up. They turned, bolting down the dim-lit street like a scabrous pack of scavenger dogs. Not many minutes later, at nearby St. Andreas Hospital, Chief Magistrate Ralph Christen was pronounced dead on arrival.

Drowsing at the wheel of the Lancia that was parked near the public pool, Custer's thoughts revolved sluggishly around Rosalia. The muggy torpor of the summer evening made him achingly horny for her. What a sinful, cunning lady! Custer blinked as he pictured her making her way from bed to bed, or maybe from desk to desk, through the executive echelons of Schlammer Engineering. She probably knew everything and everybody at the place—including, perhaps, the woman in the van.

Maybe she can get me inside, Custer thought, blinking his eyes open. Grinning, he pulled out the pink business card and read it again: SEXCLUSIVE LOVE. What a gal!

Just when Custer had made up his mind to pay Rosalia a visit, he noticed a boy leaning casually against the car parked next to the Lancia, one hand lazily drumming on its hood. Custer yawned, scratching his forehead. Next thing you know, he thought, those itchy little kid fingers will start poking around in the lock.

Instead, the teenager suddenly ducked behind the hood, apparently to escape attention from a patrol car that was nosing into the parking area. In no hurry, the cops drove on past, then bumped back onto the main street.

Custer relaxed and turned his attention back to the grimy-faced kid who wore his cap street-style, peak pointing backwards. Now would you take look at *that!* Effortlessly, the lout had opened the door of the car, got in, and started up the engine. Custer marveled at the smoothness and speed of the action. No way did that little bum have a driver's license, and yet he handled the car like an expert, backing just enough to get clearance, then smoothly pulling away.

Again, Custer's reflexes got the better of him. He fell in behind what had to be a car theft in progress. Chasing vehicles up the mountainside—it seemed to be turning into his favorite pastime!

As they drove higher up the mountain, the cavern entrance, framed by the brighter rock face that surrounded it, beckoned darkly in the failing light of dusk. The kid passed it at high speed, with Custer hard pressed to stay on his tail. Flooring the gas pedal, he swerved as the kid suddenly cut right, churning up dust on a narrow gravel road.

Custer bullied the Lancia back into the right lane. He knew this road; after topping a low rise, it cut into the forest a couple hundred meters farther along. At a level spot, he guided his car off the road, through a patch of trees, and parked it in the underbrush. Grabbing his binoculars, he jumped out.

From the edge of the forest, he commanded an excellent view of the gravel road that wound upward toward what looked like a delapidated old building. In the waning light, Custer made out the smudge of red that had to be the car he'd been tailing—an observation quickly verified as he peered through the binoculars. Uh-huh! he muttered to himself, so that's where the snotty-nosed little punk was gonna stash his loot!

Custer lowered the glasses. Stash the loot in plain view of anyone on this road? Weird! And *interesting*. Might as well go up and have a look-see before it gets totally dark, he decided.

The digital clock built into the ceiling upholstery of the Dodge van indicated twenty hunded hours and forty minutes. Claudia was about to turn on the news, when she heard voices outside.

"Just some kids," she said to von Alp, who peered out while remaining hidden.

Draped nonchalantly over the handlebars of a rugged-looking mountain bike was a dark-haired boy in a black-and-red baseball cap. The youth was calmly examining the gleaming luxury van with its huge, tinted side windows that reflected the castle's brightly illuminated silhouette.

"Five-liter V-8 engine," the kid announced. Von Alp figured him to be about fifteen.

"Guzzles at least twenty liters," the boy went on. "Wonder if they're using it as a camper. Must be awesome, spending the night in a crate like this!"

The girl with him pressed her nose against a side window. "There's somebody in there," she told the boy.

Her dark face tilted straight up towards von Alp. Maybe fourteen, he thought, electrified by her exotic black eyes and dazzling white teeth as she beamed at him through the tinted glass. His curiosity aroused, he pushed the back door open.

"Hey, how would you kids like to earn a few easy Francs?"

Their bright eyes gazed expectantly at him out of grimy, dust-streaked faces. Von Alp read the tale of mysterious youthful adventures from their mud-caked sneakers and clothing adorned with dirt spots and holes. A bloodied kneecap peeked through a slit in the boy's jeans; shreds of cobwebs streaked the girl's black curls.

Having looked them over thoroughly at a close range, von Alp kept a stern poker face. "So you're roaming the woods! You look as if you've been on a treasure hunt."

The kids maintained an embarrassed silence. The girl touched an index finger to a fresh scab on her palm. Sneaking a look into the marvelous van, the boy boldly asked the two adults confronting him if they were private eyes or secret service.

"Anything to do with that old cavern over there?" he inquired wistfully.

Von Alp and Claudia exchanged glances. These kids certainly were acting strangely; maybe they knew more than they let on. Von Alp glanced at the control panel in the van. Everything looked fine.

"What cavern?" he asked casually.

"The old nuclear plant over there. There's something fishy about it," the boy said, looking steadily at them as he spoke.

"Shush," said his companion, "keep that to yourself. How do we know they really *are* detectives?"

"You're absolutely right," Claudia laughed. "Don't ever trust a member of the opposite sex."

Von Alp gazed intently into the kids' bright, alert faces. Having learned long ago to take children seriously, he knew that—since time was not important to them—they looked at everything more patiently and thoroughly. Maybe these two could be helpful.

Abruptly he asked, "Where do you live?"

The girl looked at the ground; she seemed embarrassed. The boy awkwardly shifted his weight from one foot to the other.

"What does your dad do?" von Alp asked.

The boy consulted his colorful Swatch wristwatch. "He'll be home soon. He's the company pilot."

"Now look," said von Alp, "I want to let you in on something. Let's say something secret, okay? Can you keep a secret?"

"Sure we can," the girl exclaimed. "This is exciting!"

"Hold it," Claudia cut in sharply. "What are your names, anyway?"

The boy answered, "I'm Mark, and this is my sister, Jessie. We have a brother named Tony. He's busy right now, but he'll be here later."

"Okay," replied the woman, "I'm Claudia, and this is Theo."

They looked each other over in the uncertain dusk of the balmy summer night. Across the valley, a full moon swam above the mountain top. Beneath them, the glittering lights of Nucleanne vied boldly with the first faint sprinkling of stars.

Von Alp broke the spell. "All right, then. We *are* private investigators, and we want to know what's going on over there in that cavern. Maybe you've seen something that can be useful to us."

"Yesss!" the boy and girl answered as one.

"But first we'll have to talk to your dad. He has to agree, of course."

Their faces drooped. Von Alp patiently waited them out.

"Then we might as well forget about it," Jessie shrugged in resignation. "Daddy doesn't doesn't like us snooping around. He's afraid it'll get him in trouble."

"Fine, I can appreciate that," von Alp said calmly. "On the other hand, it wouldn't hurt to *ask*, would it? Unless you're *afraid*. Of the answer, I mean." He clapped his hands, a man with a busy schedule. "I'll tell you what, you go home, and when he gets back from work you ask him. Then we'll meet here later, say around eleven. How's that?"

"Deal," Mark agreed, "but no guarantees."

Having said this, the youngsters gave no indication of wanting to leave. There's more on their mind, von Alp thought. Using a voice that was father-confessor soft, he asked, "Anything else?"

"Well, yes, over there," Mark drawled, equally soft, "there's *weirdness* going on inside that place."

He glanced expectantly at Claudia, who asked, flabbergasted, "So you think there's something wrong at Schlammer?"

They nodded, but seemed to have trouble formulating an answer. Finally Jessie said, "Counterfeiting operation!"

Theo and Claudia exchanged eloquent looks.

"That's a fact," affirmed Mark. "They've got loads of space in there. And there's equipment that has nothing to do with the factory. Probably minting coins, they are!"

Von Alp gestured for them to come into the van and make themselves comfortable. Jessie climbed in first, sighing deeply as she sank into the luxurious upholstery.

"And what makes you think it's a minting operation?" von Alp asked.

"We've found scraps," Mark supplied eagerly. "Filings and metal discs the size of five-Franc pieces."

Jessie added, "They've got high-tech equipment in these. No one is allowed to see it, not even daddy." She winked at Mark, who pointedly avoided looking at her.

"Absolutely no one," she insisted.

Claudia had meanwhile trained the powerful nightscope on the cavern entrance, slowly scanning the viewer up along the wooded slope. "Nothing suspicious that I can see," she announced.

Jessie would not give up her high-tech angle. "I've read that there is technology so sophisticated it can duplicate a coin down to the subtlest detail."

"Spark-erosion process," Claudia said to von Alp. "The minting dies they produce using this technique will give any treasury man the goosebumps." Then she turned to the kids and told them that, somehow, she didn't think counterfeiting currency was what was going on inside the mountain. "But the only way to make sure is to get inside. Is there anyone else, besides your dad, who knows what's going on? How about you? Would you happen to know how one might get inside without being seen?"

"There's Haluk," answered Jessie, "the window washer at Schlammer. He's a Turk. He's the one who showed us the filings. And there's Marianne."

"Who's that?" asked von Alp.

"She works in the Schlammer highrise, in the office. She often comes to see us, because . . . because . . ."

"Because she's interested in our collection," Mark put in. "We have a large collection of rare snakes."

From the town below came a ringing as the church clock began to strike the three-quarter hour. As the beats boomed out dully over the valley, von Alp considered the situation. The kids' neglected, unkempt appearance bothered him. They should be at home, in bed, at this hour. He sensed something else, intangible indications that some unknown danger was in the air, threatening them.

"Okay," Mark said, sliding across to the nightscope. "If they aren't counterfeiting, what *are* they up to in the cavern? I mean, all this stuff you've got in here, that's for surveillance and spying, isn't it? What *are* you actually after?" He pressed his eyes to the viewfinder. "Wow, man, awesome! Everything's as clear as day!"

Slowly he swung the instrument sideways, moving the viewing field along the edge of the forest until it framed the old house, where Stephanie's red car stood parked beyond a picket fence. A splash of yellow light from the ground floor windows gave the scene a cozy feeling of peace and security.

"She's still there," the boy muttered, moving the frame along to a moonlit meadow where, he knew, deer often grazed at this hour. Just then another car came into view. Mark figured this was probably the man who was supposed to pick up Stephanie. "Not a sign of Tony," he concluded.

"You see anything?" von Alp asked, apprehensive.

"I don't think so. Everything seems fine." The nod he gave his sister was full of hidden meaning. The expression in her eyes told him that she understood.

"So what're you actually after?" Mark asked casually. Still, von Alp sensed a strange tension behind the words. He was beginning to think it imperative that he win these kids over as allies.

"Well, it's kind of dangerous, especially for kids," he intoned dramatically. "But seeing as how you seem to be exceptionally *bright* kids, we might as well put our cards on the table. We believe the cavern is being used as a clandestine depot for weapons and ammunition."

Jessie and Mark exchanged looks that amounted to asking: What else is new?

Mark said casually, "Maybe we can help. There may just be a . . . well, maybe there's a way of getting inside, but we have to discuss this among ourselves first, okay? That's because we have certain, uh, obligations." He rubbed his hands together, eager for the enterprise. "But we'll be back later. Deal?"

"Deal," Claudia and von Alp chimed in unison.

Waving casual good-byes, the kids stepped out into the moonlit night. Mark saluted snappily, touching an index finger to the edge of this cap. Then they were off on their bikes, their silhouettes melting into the darkness under the castle walls. Claudia got out of the van and gazed thoughtfully after them.

"Well, *Mr. Detective,* what do you make of those kids?" she asked her companion.

"Don't really know, *ma'am,*" Theo smiled. "Except, what they didn't tell us would fill volumes. There's something important that they're holding back, probably something their father has told them not to talk about. Certainly we should make friends with them. They know the area like the backs of their hands, so you never know when they might come in handy. Besides, I like kids."

"I've heard that tune before," Claudia teased. "And children and dogs like you, isn't that right?"

"For you, lassie, I'll gladly give up man's best friend. I certainly wouldn't want you to hurt yourself throwing a jealous fit if I happen to scratch some other mutt. *Ma'am!*"

They shared an easy laugh on that one. Claudia leaned in the frame of the side door, with Theo's hand resting lightly on her back.

"But seriously," he said, "kids still believe in an open-ended world with unlimited potential. The turn of the millenium—that is something that holds tremendous fascination for them. It exerts a sort of magical pull; even I can feel it! Maybe I'm just a kid at heart! But, I mean, look at what's been happening in the world, how everything has started moving, as if pulled by some great magnet. All the changes, all the systems that have stood unmoving like the Rock of Gibraltar, defying change, have suddenly come crashing down. The Berlin Wall fell, the Soviet Union collapsed. South Africa gives up Apartheid and elects Nelson Mandela. Israel makes peace with the PLO. There's a truce in Bosnia. Even Britain and the IRA want to join the peacemakers. Who would have thought it possible, only a few short years ago! There are moments when I think all that old negativity will be flushed down the river before the year 2000. Maybe that big magnet can do it. Yes, maybe that mysterious power, that strange Force 2000, can rid us of all our nuclear weapons before this millenium is over!"

Claudia turned her head and looked up at him. He leaned forward and touched a tender kiss to her forehead. She put her bare arms around his shoulders, tilting one thigh against his legs. Their lips gently touched. Von Alp's palms cupped the rounded firmness of her buttocks, sensing her naked flesh beneath the rough fabric of her jeans. They climbed back into the van's welcoming wine-red upholstery. The woman pulled the rear door shut, pushing aside the architectural drawings she had obtained that morning from the Records Office at Nucleanne Town Hall.

"Come . . ." Theo touched Claudia. Did *he* pull *her*, or did *she* sink down to *him?* Who could say, who could care? Tenderly, she kissed the fearless hero of her life. Her hands moved to his neck, followed along his shoulders, pulled at his shirt, until his back lay bare to her caress.

Using the treeline for cover, Custer moved cautiously upward in the steepening terrain, taking almost half an hour to reach the vicinity of the old schoolhouse. Custer recognized the red car parked there. The building stood downhill from the road, at the edge of an open field crowded with masses of noisily cawing crows. Only the far-distant sky to the west still held a pale reflection of the dying day, no competition for the moon's illumination. The front door of the house was closed. From an adjoining shed, a row of bushes ran parallel to the road. Faint light fell through the windowpanes in the front door.

Not much happening, Custer thought. He moved on. In two seconds, he had bounded across the street and slipped noiselessly through a half-open door into the shed. Now he commanded a direct view of the building's front windows and door. Just as he was about to vault the low wooden parapet between him and the house, the sound of an engine stopped him—at first faint, then louder, closer. Custer pivoted, a predatory leap taking him back into the shed's protective shadows. His back flat against the wall, he pulled his Walther PPK from its shoulder holster and routinely worked the action a couple of times.

The crows, blacker than the luminous summer night, had risen from the field and were circling above the schoolhouse, filling the air with their ominous cawing. A car pulled up. The headlights were cut; footsteps approached the house. The silhouette of a tall man, his left hand in the pocket of his jacket, crept up to the front door. He stealthily looked around to make sure he was unobserved, then repeatedly thumped the wooden door with his right fist. Firmly gripping the Walther, Custer silently moved forward.

Distant reverberations penetrated through Stephanie's oblivion. The booming, knocking sounds, aggressively insistent, tore her from slumber. She stared, momentarily disoriented, then jumped up and ran to the door. Ralph, at last! Ecstatic with joy and relief, she pushed back the heavy bolt and pulled the door open—then recoiled, horror-stricken.

His features twisted into diabolical grin, long strands of greasy hair curtaining his face, the killer Matak stood pointing his big Beretta directly at her forehead.

Custer watched increduously, unable to take in what he saw. Seconds passed as slowly as minutes. The scene had the impact of a heavy, slow-motion blow to the head, a picture he would never forget. One moment an exuberant face smiled radiantly at the long-awaited visitor; the next an ashen mask of deathly pallor stared transfixed before the killer. The woman gazed, aghast, at the black barrel of the automatic, its muzzle less than two inches from her face. Glints of moonlight mingled with the unspeakable terror in those wide open eyes above lips that were drained of blood.

Custer's professional reflexes took over. In one single, seamless move, he raised and aimed his weapon. Matak, too, held his gun in a professional, double-handed grip, aiming at point-blank range. No way he can miss, Custer computed coolly; unless I blow out his cerebrum, snuff out all the connections, even the death twitch can move his trigger finger.

The woman screeched.

Custer fired.

The killer's skull jerked forward, his body flopping dead before it hit the floor. Two leaps, and Custer was bending over the woman, who lay motionless on her back. Her blouse was spattered with blood and brainstuff. Her features had gone rigid; even the eyelids over the large irises seemed frozen. He tried to find a pulse, detect a breath however faint—nothing. He called out to her, intimate words he would never remember.

There was no reaction from the woman; she was in shock. Custer, the man, felt desperate; Custer, the trained survival machine, put his hands under her head and cupped her lips with his mouth, pumping long, slow breaths of air into her lungs. Nothing! Again he bent to that beautiful pale face, forced air into her lungs.

Dark rivulets of blood from the gory mess that was the killer's shattered skull meandered along the floor toward where Custer bent over the unconscious woman. This mouth is not one millimeter too wide, Custer told himself, redoubling his efforts when at last he felt a response. A tint of life began to color the woman's waxen face. He sighed with relief and reached for his cellular phone.

Snaking one arm out from under Claudia's soft embrace, von Alp's hand found the phone. "Yup," he answered, then listened. "Consider me there."

Gently heaving his lover aside, von Alp let out a controlled shout of joy. "That's Ken. Action! Let's *go!*"

At that very moment, deep within the Schlammer compound, Rosalia sat astride Schoenhof's naked buttocks, using the heels of her hands to massage his back with slow, powerful strokes.

"I saw it. Distinctly!" she insisted.

"An optical illusion," Schoenhof moaned.

"No! Through that windowpane, I saw a face. A woman, or a youth, or a young man, but definitely a *face.*"

"There you are," he groaned in bliss, "you had . . . an . . . orgasmic . . . hallucination. Ouch, not so hard! After that hysterical outburst of yours—*I said not so hard!*—the guards searched the entire place and found nothing. Not a trace of anything! Not even a door left open. Embarrassing! I tell you, nobody unauthorized gets into the domed hall, let alone wanders up to the catwalk along the windows. It just doesn't happen."

And that appeared to be the end of that.

Hunched over the physicist's back, kneading his flesh carefully so as not to arouse him too much, Rosalia smiled as she recalled how he'd flown into a jealous rage when she showed him the cut on her chin and told him of the encounter with Hannibal. When he finally calmed down, he'd vowed to protect her. But only on one condition: that he, and he alone, would be her lover.

"No problem, darling," she had assured him. "Why would I want to make love to anyone else when you're the best?"

It was a rhetorical question, full of faulty logic and tricky implications. But Schoenhof merely snorted like a stag in rutting season, and greedily rubbed his body against hers.

"Easy, easy, you're all right now, you're perfectly safe." A calming voice, as if from a great distance. Voice and features merged; a face swam into focus. Stephanie found herself gazing into eyes deep as glacial lakes. Happily abandoning herself to the dream vision, she let herself fall into blissful oblivion, drifting weightless through infinite space. Again she saw herself from far far above, a tiny speck resting on some inhospitable patch of ground down there. Clearly, her soul had departed and clearly, again, she heard that strong, sonorous voice calling to her.

Now there were two shiny mountain lakes, sparkling in—the tanned face of a man. Lips that felt ample, wide and soft, brushed over her mouth. A warm surge of feelings rose in her chest, radiating sweetness throughout her body. This kind of thing happens only in a dream, she told herself, even as she put one arm around the man's neck. She felt her lips responding to his. The tip of her tongue, probing those dream lips, tasted sweet flesh.

The face was real, not that of some ethereal saint testing her credentials for admission to paradise! This time she drank blissfully, and deeply, from the sweet cup of delicious reality so unexpectedly offered by the gentle stranger.

Custer gazed forlornly at the woman's face. Fiery, long-dormant feelings stirred in the innermost recesses of his being. Reluctantly and very, very gently, he shrugged out of her embrace, then lifted her to her feet. She touched the medallion on a gold chain that dangled in her face as he pulled her up. She whispered, "What is this?"

"That?" he smiled. "That's Saint Christopher, my patron saint. He symbolizes what I do, which is helping people across obstacles and protecting them from dangers that lurk in their path. In other words, I pull chestnuts out of the fire for other people."

"I like that," she said, half to herself. "I wish Saint Christopher belonged to me—forever."

"I'll give him to the woman in my life," he teased, whispering in her ear. "Saint Christopher can be hard to get, though." He winked at her. "Now let's get out of here. And pronto!" He pulled her toward the door.

Von Alp turned on the parking lights and shifted into low. Restrained only by its transmission, the Dodge moved steeply downhill. With a crash and a shudder, it seemed to plunge into a deep, dark hole, but then it bumped and lurched down a dirt road deeply gouged by runoff and crisscrossed by thick strands of roots. When the van rocked sideways into a narrow fire road, Custer was thrown head first against the roof. Groaning and moaning, he massaged the top of his head. Finally von Alp switched on the headlights.

"I discovered this shortcut when I was up here earlier today, scouting the neighborhood," he announced casually.

Custer leaned eagerly across the backrest to check up on the woman, and was relieved to see that Claudia had managed to keep her securely in her seat. Within a few minutes, they were on a back road, heading north toward the freeway. Thanks to von Alp's breakneck maneuver, they were now separated from the Schlammer compound by the steep, forested flanks of the elongated massif whose eastern face was cut deeply by a plunging ravine. Anyone trying to follow had been shaken off long ago.

The heady state Stephanie was in had cushioned her through the worst of von Alp's rough cross-country descent. During the long ride, she could not take her eyes off Custer. Time and time again she glanced at his bushy hair and powerful neck, absorbing the few words he spoke in his calm, confident voice. Now and then, when he turned for a searching look at her, she caught a glimpse of his striking profile. Saint Christopher . . .

Later, at Chalet Lindenegg, she lay naked in a bed, sheet drawn up to her chin. Custer came in and sat down beside her. She felt the warmth of his body against her right thigh. He caressed her temples, gently running his fingers over the thick, dark-dyed hair with the blonde roots. He bent down to her and touched a cheek to her face. She turned her mouth to him, and his lips brushed briefly against hers.

Stephanie's warm gaze released in Custer a profound, long-dormant longing for true happiness. A happiness without the burden of responsibility, free from the crushing stress of the past days and hours, free from a tomorrow full of tricky challenges and hidden dangers.

All of her longed for the warmth of this man. She wanted only to snuggle up against him, feel the strength of his body. Strange, she thought, I hardly know him, not even his full name—and here I am, wanting him as I've never wanted a man before!

Every cell of her body ached for fulfillment. She trembled in a rush of sensations she had never experienced before, as if that great wave she had dreamed about was sweeping through her, filling her with a million shimmering droplets of euphoric bliss. In an instant, all around her, everything she saw and sensed became more beautiful. Colors deepened, sounds became more melodious, and a luminous intensity suffused the world.

As if in affirmation, she heard music from downstairs: "I will always love you," or was it "Saving all my love for you"? Outside, crickets chirped in the summer night, their music mingling with the sugar-sweet melody that finally lulled her into contented, blissful slumber.

Custer sat for a long while, watching over her. At last he rose and tiptoed out.

The following morning, when Stephanie Kramer entered the dining room at Lindenegg, the two men at the breakfast table rose to greet her.

"I'm Ken Custer. This is Theo von Alp, our host," Custer said, shooting her a concerned look. Inviting her to join them, von Alp pulled back a chair. Custer suggested they call each other by their first names, expressing the hope that she would stay with them for a while.

Stephanie agreed with a barely perceptible nod, gratefully accepting a cup of hot coffee from von Alp. The strong, hot brew enlivened her spirits. She had slept well, and now she felt refreshed and energetic, but also strangely restless. All of her craved action. There was no time to lose; she had to get to the bottom of the conspiracy in the nuclear cavern. So, regretfully, she would not be able to spend any length of time in this wonderful chalet. Custer seemed to have read her mind.

"Lindenegg Chalet is a perfectly safe place," he assured her. "Let's take a little time to talk things over."

Stephanie first looked around, then shot a questioning glance at the host. Anticipating her question, Custer said, "Theo is the Lone Eagle of this region."

"I'm not sure I follow. . . ."

"Well," von Alp drawled, "what he means is that Claudia and I live in blissful seclusion. We have telephone and fax, and a modem link with the Internet for worldwide coverage. That's all I need to do business."

"Global communications?" Stephanie tried, lifting her chin in the direction of the adjoining room which was stuffed with electronic equipment.

"Aviation is my passion, just like Ken's. I buy and sell aircraft, as well as aircraft products and equipment."

Stephanie sipped some more coffee, then casually inquired what that might include.

"Well, to put it simply, I'm what's called a systems optimizer," he announced grandly. Noticing the puzzled look on the face of his charming guest, he added, "I specialize in aircraft modification. I might transform a passenger craft into a cargo or reconnaissance plane, or . . ."

"A bomber?"

"Could be. Take, for example, Third-World nations that can't afford factory-new aircraft and the equipment that goes with them. They look for used planes. That's the market I'm in. You might say I have a corner on it. From right here in Lindenegg, round the clock, through my global marketing network."

His eyes sparkled mischievously; she had struck the adventurous vein in him, which happened to be a very large one. Von Alp loved chess moves involving a lot of heavy hardware. For the Angolans, he had built up an air cargo fleet to shuttle supplies to government troops fighting in the contested areas. For this job, he had used a nonmilitary version of the Lockheed Hercules transport equipped with an air-drop system he'd acquired through a French source. Night after night, packs containing medical supplies, food and ammunition were dropped with perfect precision over the advance positions.

Custer was calm and composed, obviously deep in thought. Von Alp brought in some newspapers, while Claudia unfolded the architectural drawings of the former nuclear cavern on another table. By the time Stephanie got around to asking the two men where they had met, it was nine o'clock. Custer and von Alp exchanged looks.

"That's a long story," Custer said mysteriously.

"In Angola, during the civil war?" she suggested.

They shook their heads.

"In the pokey," von Alp ruefully confessed.

Skepticism mingled with amusement on Stephanie's face.

"Absolutely," Custer confirmed. "We were lying on a beach in Sicily. We didn't know each other. I was looking at the dark-blue sea and Theo was looking at the girls."

"Or vice versa," von Alp protested.

Stephanie laughed. "And then?"

"Well, then along came those two Moroccans with those watches," von Alp continued.

"Right, fake Rolexes, remember?" Custer added, his eyes twinkling. "They spread them out on a blanket and tried to pawn their stuff off on us. Suddenly they looked up toward the road, started jabbering excitedly, and took to their heels."

"Why? What happened?"

"That's precisely what we wondered," von Alp said. "Until we saw some carabinieris coming toward us. To arrest us. Off we went to the slammer."

"Those Rolex knockoffs were still spread out on our beach towels," Custer explained. "The police thought we were some smugglers they'd been looking for."

Stephanie shook her head in disbelief. "But weren't you able to prove your innocence?"

"They just wouldn't listen to us. Besides, they didn't speak a word of English. Theo, with his fluent Italian, was the one who got us out of that jam. Got them to release us on bail."

"Only because the judge was a woman and immediately fell for Ken," von Alp grinned. "She was a matron, ugly as sin, but Ken with his irresistible charm had her wrapped around his little finger in no time."

Custer gestured with both hands, denying the allegation. "Totally exaggerated. However, maybe she did find me a wee bit attractive. But then Theo messed up everything."

Von Alp responded to Stephanie's puzzled look with a guilty face and a resigned shrug. Custer continued mercilessly.

"The day before, Theo had made a conquest, a very attractive Sicilian lady, pretty as a picture and sexy, too. Serenella was her name. Theo got a message to her and she showed up with the bail money. But when the judge saw this raving beauty come in she got so mad she immediately doubled bail." Custer nodded significantly several times. "So we were stuck again."

"The judge was jealous, of course," von Alp said. "She thought Serenella was Ken's girlfriend." He allowed his words to sink in, then continued, "That was precisely the right moment for us to get out of there."

"You escaped?" Stephanie marveled.

Von Alp raised his eyebrows questioningly. "Sure, what else was there to do? It was easy as pie. With a neat uppercut Ken knocked down one of the bailiffs who got in the way. There was a commotion and we were outside."

"But then we made a mistake," Custer allowed. "We sprinted straight into a dead-end street. Embarrassing. When we saw the carabinieris' cruiser slowly rounding the corner into the street we thought we'd had it."

Stephanie's question dripped with irony: "But you didn't?"

"No, a freight elevator saved us," confirmed von Alp. "Without thinking twice we jumped from a small platform straight into the open elevator. Ken was so excited he hit all five buttons at once."

"Which turned out to be a good thing," Custer fought back, "because our pursuers couldn't tell which floor we'd gone to."

"And then?" Stephanie pressed, caught up in the story.

"Well, on the top floor we crossed an empty room," von Alp obliged. "I tripped over a loose floorboard and we lifted it up. Which was how we discovered the cache."

"Where a gang of Moroccans or maybe Libyans had stashed their cocaine," Custer explained. "We found it when we tore up more boards."

"Row upon row of neat little plastic bags full of the white stuff," von Alp recalled proudly.

"But that's awful!" Stephanie exclaimed. "And the carabinieri?"

"Well, I assume they were pleased when they found it," Custer grinned. "Naturally we didn't stick around long enough to watch but beat a hasty retreat across the roof. We got to Calabria on a motorcycle, a town called Cantanzaro. Not far from it was a radio monitoring station run by the Americans. That's where Ken ran into an old buddy from 'Nam."

"Right. My friend, a major, flew us north in a chopper. Compliments of the U.S. Navy, you know? So, that's how we met."

Custer excused himself and left the room. Gazing pensively after him, Stephanie said, "Tell me, Theo, is Ken also a . . . uh . . . systems optimizer? One who scrounges up modern weaponry at reasonable prices to help disenfranchised Africans?"

"More or less. But that's a legitimate business, you know."

Stephanie nodded and tried again. "And Ken is also in this business?"

"No, Ken isn't involved at this level. He operates a few pegs above that."

"Now what's that supposed to mean?"

"Maybe he'd better tell you himself. Let's just say he and I have worked together successfully on quite a number of projects," von Alp smiled. "I believe Ken is involved with certain organizations that are, shall we say, less than transparent?"

Stephanie was still pondering this hint when von Alp, unprompted, told her that Custer had known all about the weapons shipments into Iraq.

"After the Gulf War?"

"No, before. I myself flew dismantled helicopters from California to Baghdad. We picked the chopper parts up at an airbase, with a lot of nervous CIA people watching. For starters, we whisked them outside the country, up to Newfoundland. From there we flew shuttle back and forth to Baghdad in a B-707, each time with four helicopters in the hold. Custer was not involved in this but he told me recently that he knew about it. It was a secret government operation. Ken has connections in Washington. He's way up in the highest echelons."

It was 3:15 A.M. in Washington, D.C., on the day before the Fourth of July when the president was roused from sleep. He asked himself for the umpteenth time what, if anything, the vice president was actually good for. One thing was certain, whenever something really unpleasant came up, he himself had to deal with it. Which included being yanked out of bed because of some damn crisis in some place or other. He took a quick, cold shower in the spacious bathroom adjoining his bedroom on the first floor. Then something far more sobering confronted him in a conference room on one of the sublevels.

The director of the CIA—his face grim, his voice uttering solemn, chopped-off sentences—reported that the Iraqis were planning a bomb attack on the historical section of Philadelphia.

"In the cradle of the nation, sir. The Liberty Bell. The Hall of Independence—the very birthplace of the Constitution! The plan is to destroy it all. On the Fourth of July. Tomorrow, Mr. President! I know it's inconceivable, sir, but according to the information we have, they may be planning to detonate a portable nuclear charge."

"All right," the president mumbled grumpily, "how'd you get this message of doom? You sure this is not just some clever bit of disinformation, or a secret-service fantasy?"

"The situation is truly serious, sir," the CIA director insisted, handing his Supreme Commander a bright yellow dossier marked SCUDO. "Our information comes from a reliable source. We've checked and double-checked everything."

So, at 3:44 A.M. on July 3, the president of the United States signed the order for an emergency defense alert that instantly initiated a series of measures to protect U.S. territory against actions of nuclear terrorism. Within half an hour, precoded signals were electronically conveyed to the appropriate command centers of the U.S. Army, Navy, and Air Force, and to the border control sections of the Department of Immigration, as well as to the FBI, to NSA headquarters, and to numerous others entrusted with the SCUDO emergency package.

The SCUDO alert also reached the U.S. embassy in Bern and was placed on the desk of the CIA's agent-in-residence, Ben Atlee. Early on Tuesday morning, Atlee decided to discuss the matter with Bill Conklin from the National Security Agency, who was expected to arrive from New York later that day. Of Iraqi descent, Atlee felt extremely uncomfortable with the idea that Iraq was the suspected perpetrator of such an act.

Stephanie and Ken sat across from each other in comfortable recliners on the shady terrace. Thrown about pell-mell on a white, wooden table were the blueprints for the nuclear cavern.

"Strange," Stephanie exclaimed, "I can't find that ventilation shaft anywhere on these drawings. As if it didn't exist!"

She sucked on a lemon drink through a straw. A tiny ladybug with three black spots alighted on the back of her left hand and immediately started scuttling up toward the tip of the middle finger.

Custer leaned across the table to examine the blueprints. For the fraction of a hearbeat their hair touched. Static crackled. Amused, they looked into each other's eyes. Stephanie held the gaze, but Ken, embarrassed, turned back to the drawings.

"So much the better," he said. "When they can't find anything, their security personnel will think the black-haired woman was seeing things. No signs of a break-in, no burglars, no escape route. And since the air shaft isn't on any of these drawings, they won't look for it either. Logical."

Stephanie nodded. She was thinking intently: If the secret shaft remained undiscovered, she might be able to use it again! The little ladybug, a harbinger of good fortune, was walking circles on her fingertip, part of its takeoff routine.

Custer found himself with time on his hands; his meeting with Schlammer wasn't scheduled until the afternoon. Before that he would communicate with Don Cali via satellite. Von Alp was inside the house, plumbing his computers for the latest information. Claudia had climbed up on the garage roof. She was watching the light traffic on the nearby road through a pair of binoculars.

Stephanie felt anxious and jittery. Earlier that morning she had listened incredulously when they gently told her about the brutal murder of Ralph Christen. Pain churned relentlessly deep inside of her.

Abruptly, she said, "You know, Ken, Ralph Christen was trying to help me. He and his people were about to pounce on Schlammer Engineering. Someone must have got wind of it." She raised her hand to encourage the ladybug to fly.

"That military court judge of yours had become a deadly threat," Custer said, indifferently turning a glass of orange-colored Frutopia drink with his fingertips. "The people who murdered Kern had to eliminate him before he could cause more mischief. And the way they did it is meant as a warning to other snoopers. You'd better watch yourself, Stephanie."

"How so?"

"Anyone who gets in their way, they'll smash their skulls. Isn't that their gruesome message?"

Suddenly she knew she had to get back to Nucleanne. Determined to get to the bottom of this, she also knew she needed an ally. Ken Custer? She brought the fingertip with the ladybug on it close to her sensuous mouth and started blowing gentle puffs of warm breath over it. The lucky-lady bug got the hint and buzzed off, to land a short distance away among the blueprints, precisely on the spot where Stephanie had used a luminescent marker to draw a bright-red circle around the second door to the lab.

She asked herself who the devil this Custer was, anyway. And heard herself saying, "So, Ken Custer, who the deuces are you, anyway?"

Stephanie's sudden foray brought a smile to Custer's face. He wasn't sure exactly how much he wanted to confide in her.

Maybe he should back up a little, go back to Panama, December 1989.

"Well, I'll tell you," he said, "since you insist. . . ."

. . . Custer pulled desperately on the stick, "C'mon, baby, lift off . . . come on!" Ahead, at the edge of the clearing, he saw the two Vietcong. The 12.7-millimeter machine gun mounted on the chopper was yakking away. The detachment of Vietcong disappeared. Hit? There, a flash of lightning, a rocket shell missing by the fraction of an inch! Now the machine gun rattled again.

He tore and wrenched at the stick, pushed the pedal all the way down. Nothing happened; the old crate simply didn't respond. And everywhere bursts of gunfire, artillery, explosions banged in his ears. His arms seemed to be moving in slow motion. Nothing was working. Just when he at last lifted off with infinite slowness, a lance of white-hot iron tore into his belly.

Custer screamed. The bastards got him! Flaming pain nearly drove him out of his mind. Don't give up, hang in there, a voice hammered—Custer's own! Then he noticed that his muscles still obeyed. They were not crashing; the craft steadily gained height. His arms and feet moved automatically; the years of drilling now paid off, saving him.

Then came another booming explosion. Custer let go of the steering gear and bolted upright, drenched in sweat.

It was that damn nightmare again! Custer lay in his own bed, panting with exhaustion. Slowly, he began to realize where he was: in the visitors' quarters of the Comandancia of General Manuel Noriega in Panama City. And the hacking noise was real—and close!

In two bounds he was at the window, listening to the sound of chopper engines hacking, getting closer. Maybe a whole squadron making its approach. Explosions reverberated. Flares turned night into day. Custer saw the silhouettes of two AC-130-Talon attack helicopters, some three hundred meters away, going down to land behind the buildings across from him.

"Shit, an invasion! The Americans are here!"

Custer jumped into combat fatigues, tearing his jacket off the coat stand. "Holy cow, it's a commando raid," he screamed into the night. "They're trying to hijack the general—but they haven't figured on us!"

He sprinted across to the bungalow on the opposite side of a hermetically sealed-off area the size of two football fields. The bungalow was the residence of General Noriega, and to the right of it Custer's trusty Blackhawk helicopter stood parked. He figured the Americans would probably mistake it for one of their own.

Custer headed directly toward where the general slept. Everywhere lights went on, people were yelling orders. Then he saw Colonel Asvat, Noriega's chief-of-staff and confidant.

"Colonel!" Custer shouted. "To the chopper!"

The colonel nodded and screamed something toward the back. He had one arm clamped like a vise over a black briefcase, as if he were carrying a set of crown jewels. Custer's watch indicated 0:35 A.M. Amid the nasty explosions all around, he grimly prepared for takeoff.

Colonel Asvat hunched low as he moved toward the chopper. Dried-up leaves danced in the dust whipped up by the booming rotors. With his free hand, Noriega's chief-of-staff held on to his cap.

"¡Adelante, rápido! We've got to get out of here, dammit! Let's go!" Custer screamed, squinting anxiously toward the west. The way things looked, the Americans at any moment might land an assault force inside the general's compound. As if to prove him right, there was a series of blinding flashes. Three shells exploded with thunderous crashes nearby, making the earth tremble. Asvat fell to the ground and just lay there.

"Up with you, Colonel, get on board!" Custer screamed uselessly. He noticed two helicopters hovering above the building where he'd been sleeping.

"Colonel!" Custer leaped from the cockpit and aimed a hefty kick at the side of the motionless Asvat. "Come on now, Colonel, those were only stun shells!" Glancing nervously at the hovering choppers, Custer yanked the colonel up by his shoulders. "We're being visited by the Special Forces, Colonel," he shouted into his ear. "Where the hell is Noriega?"

It seemed to take forever to reach the craft. Custer jumped into the cockpit and reached down to help the staggering Asvat.

"General Noriega isn't coming," Asvat shouted. "He's escaped by a different route. We're going alone."

The colonel threw his briefcase on the bench behind the pilot's seat and clambered aboard. A bullet smashed directly into the back of his head. Blood and brain matter splashed across the passenger seats. Horrified, Custer turned to see the colonel spread-eagled a couple of meters to the right of the skids, stone dead and gone without a doubt. Half his face was missing, blown away.

Custer looked up. Approaching from the west and northwest, six helicopters descended in a semircle, to land in Noriega's residential compound. Clusters of men jumped to the ground and ran forward, moving lightly, purposefully, toward Noriega's building. They were special units, wearing black berets, clearly bent on capturing the Panamanian dictator. Assault rifle fire crackled, barrels flashing all around. It was like being back in 'Nam. The roar from the straining rotors drowned out the noise of small-arms fire. Custer pulled up.

Thank God, the old crate finally lifted! His nightmare vision of being shot down faded; he knew he'd got away by the skin of his teeth. Nobody fired at the Blackhawk; they actually must have thought it was one of their choppers. So Custer waved a friendly bye-bye, took his baby up to twelve hundred feet and headed for the mountains. . . .

Stephanie went into the house to get some notepaper. When she returned, she asked Custer to tell her everything: about the hunt for the Panamanian dictator, about the American invasion, about the drug business. Yawning and glancing at his watch, Custer excused himself and walked back into the house. His body was still suffering from jet lag, and he was worried about the scheduled call to his boss. What time was it right now in South America? Four A.M., he figured.

Antonio Gabriel Cali de Cali's freeze-framed face stared sullenly from the screen, as if he were sitting for a mug shot in a police station. All that's missing is the number and the name on the ID plate, Custer was thinking.

A message von Alp had glued on a piece of cardboard and propped up against the monitor cautioned: NO CONFIDENTIAL INFORMATION! Custer gestured and von Alp switched to Broadcast. The flickering image of Cali's face somewhere in the Colombian highlands brightened and became animated. The drug lord came straight to the point:

"Operation Quepos, Custer, you remember. Ninety percent of the Costa Rica shipment was returned!"

Custer sealed his lips with the right index finger and, with the other hand, held the NO-CONFIDENTIAL-INFORMATION sign up to the camera. In vain.

Cali continued blithely, "The fellow with the Stetson kicked the bucket, huhuh! Working for the gringos, for the DEA, the bum. Ended up in the same pit as the other one. Minus his heart."

Custer swallowed, hard. Cali wet his lips with his tongue, then said, "Now, Custer, will I have the merchandise on the Fourth of July? That's tomorrow! Up here in the Tierra Sagrada? Come on, Custer, let's have it, what's the situation?"

In short sentences, Custer reported that the money was ready and on stand-by. The digit code had been confirmed. The bank was taking care of its end. Negotiations with the supplier might be more difficult. He expected to be able to fly the packages out tomorrow, July 4, at the latest. As agreed. He finished by telling Cali that, so far, everything was going according to plan.

The mighty cartel boss's face flickered. He lifted an index finger, as if in warning. The connection was cut, and the screen faded to blackness.

Deep in thought, Custer strolled into the adjoining salon. He sat down at a white piano that stood unencumbered in a corner and started tinkering with the keys. A melancholy melody emerged, blended into another, and another. His musings revolved around whether he'd get out of all of this alive. Surely one day even he would fall from grace and end up in Cali's killing pit, with his heart torn out. The big boss was unpredictable, moody—and cruel.

Stephanie came in. She walked over to the piano and leaned on it with both arms. She was trying to sense what made him tick, this mysterious man who was so reluctant to talk about himself.

As he continued playing, looking up now and then to meet the woman's probing gaze, Custer sensed, to his own amazement, some sort of thawing deep inside. For years he'd been in the habit of listening rather than chatting, of watching rather than sharing, keeping a tight lid on his feelings. What had happened to cause this gentle rebellion inside of him? Was it this attractive stranger, or these tunes from times gone by?

He went on with his story, telling it dramatically, with precision, and sticking to the facts. As he captivated his audience of one, his hands moved lightly over the keys. Lighthearted, lively tunes suddenly gave way to serious, martial strains. Between musical interludes, he rested his hands in his lap, calmly talking. Then, quite unexpectedly, he'd pound out weighty, majestic rhythms, or abruptly toss off a steely staccato passage as he continued painting an evocative musical canvas of those dramatic events on that December 20, 1989, when the Americans went into Panama.

In nearby Bern, Bill Conklin had just received news from the National Security Agency that a coded message had been beamed into Switzerland via several satellites. The scrambled signals transmitted to a location in Switzerland originated from a private station located in the highlands of Colombia. Computation of the coordinates had pinpointed a receiver site southwest of Bern, approximately where Switzerland's public shortwave transmitter was located. Since Conklin could think of no plausible reason why Switzerland's public broadcasting station would be receiving secret transmissions from faraway Colombia, he decided to personally get to the bottom of the mystery. And he'd start by taking a closer look at the area around that station!

As a result, two hours later, Conklin stood on a rise of land, looking down on the Lindenegg Chalet. He whispered to his skinny companion from the CIA's Bern office a single word,

">Keycop<."

The two repaired to a shady spot by some hazel bushes on the side of the mountain road to discuss their options.

His fists thrust deep into the pockets of his trousers, Ken Custer paced the Lindenegg terrace, surveying the countryside that lay before him in all its distance and depth. To the south, the jagged peaks of the alpine foothills shimmered through the bluish haze of the hot summer's day, fronted by olive-green meadows streaked with dark bands of forest land. In the far distance shone a gleaming intimation of the Alps' snowfields. Billowing clouds, which Custer at first mistook for rocky peaks, created the illusion of a great ocean above the summits. To the west lay lakes, like shiny shields below the bluish hump of the Jura mountains.

The shortwave station's antenna masts rising from the plain beyond the village shattered Custer's contemplation of nature, reminding him of his mission. He sighed and turned to the journalist, gazing at her for long moments. He was finding it easy to tell her these stories, sensing that she entered into and was thrilled by them. He sat down next to her and picked up where he'd left off.

"It might not have occurred to me immediately, maybe never, if that black briefcase hadn't been trailed by a pack of agents a mile long."

Stephanie connected instantly. Custer was referring to the documents Colonel Asvat had carried.

"They tailed me all the way to Cerro Punta, up in the mountains near the Costa Rican border," Custer said. "I think the people from the Cali cartel were first, then came the CIA. Both broke into Asvat's cabin and came out with the black briefcase."

"Excuse me," the attentive Stephanie protested, "I thought there was only one black briefcase and that was in the helicopter. So who got what?"

Custer seemed not to be listening. Absently gazing right through her he suddenly realized that he had gone too far; he shouldn't be talking about this at all. What's got into me, he wondered, to be telling all this classified stuff to a woman I don't even know, and a media person at that! Still, deep inside, something told him that it was all right to open up a little for this woman. She appeared to be waiting for him to do just that. Somehow, much had changed in his life during the past few hours. Maybe the time had come for him to confide in someone!

"What?" he said, startled, returning from his ruminations. "Yes, of course, the facts." Smiling to himself, he told her about Colonel Asvat's granddaughter, who was alone in the cabin when all those people started showing up.

Actually, he told her, his plan had been to get a few days of solid rest in the colonel's cozy mountain retreat, but that was not to be. Monicita, that bright, cute kid, roused him with the news that a posse of people was on its way up, looking for some documents. She had received an anonymous phone call. That seemed ridiculous to Custer, and he did his best to calm the girl down. But just to be sure, he looked through the briefcase that Asvat had thrown into the helicopter before he got hit.

"When I saw what I'd been lugging around all that time," Custer told Stephanie, "I realized that the situation was serious indeed.

"I told Monicita we had to keep our cool and asked her if she'd be willing to help me. Those big brown eyes of hers literally sparkled with mischief. We sat down in her grandfather's study, surrounded by the trophies and awards he had won in athletic competitions. The son of a simple campesino, Colonel Asvat had come up from the ranks, thanks to his boxing talent. Panama has produced fourteen world champions in boxing. If you knew how to box, your military career was all cut out for you. Asvat won the Panamanian championship in Panama City's legendary Marañón ring. So he owed his military career to his achievements in the national sport of Panama.

"Strangely enough," Custer continued, "the plan Monicita and I came up with seemed like shadowboxing to us, which was just what it turned out to be. As we had expected, the Cali mob arrived first. Monicita invited them into the colonel's study, where they threatened to blow up the safe unless she produced the keys. Protesting very convincingly, she fetched the keys for them. They were already excited as they pulled the door open, but when those hoodlums saw the briefcase they'd been chasing, it must have felt like a shot of prime-time heroin to them. Anyway, they triumphantly grabbed the briefcase and hightailed it out of there.

"A couple of hours later Monicita gave another award-winning performance. This time, there were two gentlemen at the door. They flashed a shiny badge in a leather frame, claiming to be employed by the CIA. Looking like some Latinate Carol Baker in a remake of *Baby Doll*, she pretended to be intimidated, Hollywood-fashion, as she led them into the study. She pouted bashfully as she handed them the keys. The two CIA stiffs opened the safe, reached in and went for the bait—hook, line and sinker. Unlike the Cali hoods, they gave her a receipt. Then they burned rubber. All this time I was flying totally relaxed across the border into Costa Rica."

"With all those secret documents nice and neat in the real briefcase in your helicopter?" Stephanie laughed.

"We'd found a whole pile of identical briefcases in Asvat's office, army issue, probably. We stuffed two of those full with copied military documents and sealed envelopes, and dumped the others in a garbage can. The original portfolio with the documents they were after went along with me, of course."

"You lead a pretty crazy life, don't you! So what was it in those documents that was so terribly important?"

"Well, Colonel Asvat's briefcase contained a few bits of information which the DEA and the FBI had been after for years," Custer played down her question. When he noticed genuine surprise darkening her eyes, he continued casually, "The briefcase contained the codes for the financial transactions of the cartels. There was accounting information, electronic access codes, satellite links, lists of various functions for certain computer systems, broadcasting relays for radio transmissions—all sorts of vital info. Since I'd been working on building up a worldwide communications system for Noriega, much of it looked familiar to me, but some items puzzled me at the time.

"When I got to Costa Rica, I ran a spot check. I used the international SWIFT circuit at a First Manhattan Bank branch and fed it the opening code. On the screen, the Swiss Banking Union politely welcomed me. Then the message ENTER PASS CODE ONE appeared. I entered the code as instructed. The screen seemed to melt like an ice-cream bar on a hotplate at the equator. Another message then asked for PASS CODE TWO, which I supplied. The ice-cream soup coalesced and the luminescent frame of a bank account in Zurich appeared on the screen. Great, I thought, except the commas and the period are all jumbled up! Because the plus balance shown was 1,125,000,000.00 Swiss Francs. So I activated DISPLAY, and the current activities figures for the past two months appeared. That's when I did a double take and nearly swallowed my tongue. There was nothing wrong with the punctuation, no, ma'am! There really was one billion one hundred and twenty-five million Francs in the account.

"Then I learned the disposition limit. The codes I had lucked into apparently authorized me to play with 500,000 Francs per month. Amounts above that required an additional authorization. The documents also included the names of people authorized to make withdrawals and transfers, which is really beside the point. The main thing was that I got to try out the system."

When Stephanie gave him an amused look out of wide-open eyes, he continued, "Well, of course! What do you think? After all, General Noriega still owed me, and the way things looked, it might be some time before he got around to paying me. So I transferred a hundred grand, I mean one hundred thousand dollars, to an account in New York."

"And it worked?"

"Like a charm. What it said on the screen was *Transfer Completed—Thank you for favoring the Swiss Banking Union.* I was so flattered, I decided to go for broke. Tried to transfer a cool million."

"Into your account, you greedy little thing!"

"Of course not," Custer said patiently, "to the Red Cross in Geneva this time, and it didn't happen. I was politely informed that the sum I'd asked for required an additional authorization. Well, I let it go for the time being. I couldn't reach anybody anyway, what with the general cooped up in the nunciature in Panama City and probably unable to get his paws into the electronic banking facilities of the Vatican, and Colonel Asvat lying dead in the

Comandancia compound. So, the only person accessible to me, and authorized to move such sums, was Don Cali, who happened to be a close friend of Colonel Asvat."

After a long silence, Stephanie asked, "And how did the secret services react? They shouldn't have had any trouble at all tracking you down to get hold of all that highly explosive material, am I right?" Her bluish green eyes held an alarmingly calculating expression. Custer thought he'd caught a hint of skepticism flickering through them.

"Well, let's just say I took precautions," he replied evasively. "As you can see they haven't caught up with me yet."

Scowling across at her, he thought he caught a superior, patronizing look from her. He turned huffily away and felt a sudden thrill as he watched Claudia coming up to them. She was wearing floral-patterned shorts and a skimpy top held up at the neck by white straps that contrasted excitingly with her lightly tanned skin. Smiling sweetly, she handed him a sheet of paper. For an instant, a whiff of her pleasantly earthy odor made his nostrils billow.

"A fax for you," she whispered. Then, with a meaningful glance at Stephanie, she added loudly, "From Susan, in New York."

Ken snatched the paper from her hand, to stare incredulously at the message. "Oh no," he moaned, "no no no, that freaky bastard abomination of a whoremongering sonofabitch!" He pivoted, bent over the dense currant bushes bordering the terrace, and threw up.

Stunned, the women watched him anxiously, with big eyes. Claudia immediately went to him and put an arm around his shoulder. Stephanie jumped up, then hesitated.

Gesturing reassuringly, Custer gently put his arm around Claudia's waist. "It's all right," he gasped, "everything's fine."

What he needed now was understanding, and warmth. Sensing his inner turmoil, Claudia embraced him firmly, with both arms, then stepped aside. Together, they walked past Stephanie, across the terrace and into the house.

Susan's fax message was marked CONFIDENTIAL/K. W. CUSTER/EYES ONLY, in big letters. The text portion was brief and to the point:

Operatives in Colombia reliably report that New York Times stringer John Rutherford, who for several days has been presumed missing in the Colombian highlands area, was brutally murdered at a cultist temple site controlled by Colombian drug lord Don Cali de

Cali. John Rutherford is the son of renowned Hollywood film director William Rutherford. According to an eyewitness, Cali's only son Filiberto, acting the part of executioner during an idol-worshiping ceremony, cut the heart from the living flesh of the young reporter.

Beneath the main text, a handwritten message stated, *We're sorry, Ken. We feel for you. Susan and C.*

Stephanie fumed inside while she watched the little scene between Claudia and Ken, realizing that Custer had slipped away from her. During the early hours of the morning she had come up with a plan, which she hoped to be able to carry through with Custer's help. She'd been trying to get closer to him, but he had turned away from her abruptly, remarking that, being a foreigner, the Kern assassination didn't interest him, that it was an internal Swiss affair.

"Really, I don't give a shit about your prime minister," he had stated crudely. "And I don't want to waste my time on your scandal story. As far as I'm concerned you're lucky to even have survived your little adventure. As for this fellow Schlammer, it seems to me nuclear waste management is absolutely the right thing for him to be into. Didn't you yourself tell me that in Switzerland major projects can no longer be carried out, simply because there're too many fingers in the pie, everybody is part of the decision-making process, and every project is talked to death? What this country needs is a firm hand, plus the courage to take action over the heads of bureaucrats. Now, I understand these are two departments in which Schlammer is not without talent."

Stephanie loved this man, and she hated him. She desired him, regardless of what he was involved in, but she knew he was totally unromantic: an adventurer in the rough company of other men like himself, free, and used to going his own way—alone! A confession of love was probably an odious thing to him. First he enticed her with seductive looks, then he punished her with harsh rejection. Now tender, then tyrannical, what a monster he was! So, let him have his fun with Claudia, who just now was making some wonderfully appetizing sandwiches for him.

Stephanie got up and strutted defiantly into the house. Right this moment, she couldn't have cared less about Ken Custer. She had no desire to hole up at Lindenegg while Mr. Custer looked after his million-dollar deals with Schlammer. She had to get away from here, try to dig up material on her own, come up with the decisive information that would expose Schlammer as the kingpin behind the killings.

Of course she had hoped to gain Custer as an ally. But when she was about to ask him for help, he turned a hardened, unsympathetic mask of a face at her, weakening her resolve. There was nothing else to do but go through with her plan on her own. And, anyway, Custer at this moment seemed totally occupied with the bad news from America. Unapproachable! All that remained of his affection from the night before was a brief moment illusively remembered. Yes, once again the intrepid reporter was left to her own devices!

True, Custer was busy with his own life. The deal with Schlammer required all of his attention, and that damn jet lag was still sapping his strength! Only moments ago, numbed by anger and pain, he had made a solemn vow to himself to avenge John Rutherford. This was the last straw—the one thing he would not let that snake pit of filthy Cali vermin get away with. Not this time.

A little while later, he made a long call to his mother in Philadelphia. He spoke insistently in a low, calm voice, as the minutes ticked by. Scarlett assured him she would do exactly as he'd told her.

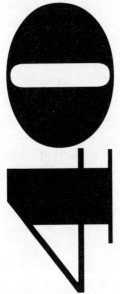

In a house not far from the historical center of Philadelphia, Scarlett sat at the small desk in her living room. She picked up the telephone, started tapping out a number, then hesitated. She depressed the cradle, gazing pensively up at the paneled wall that held her framed Olympic gold medal from Tokyo, 1964. Again she recalled the instructions Ken had drilled into her. Brushing a strand of gray-blonde hair from her smooth forehead, she released the cradle and connected to the number.

"Detective Byrne, please," she said calmly, then waited until a sonorous voice said, "Hello."

"Mr. Byrne?"

"Yes."

"I have a message for Robert Donner of the DEA. The code name is Jellyfish," she said, her voice trembling slightly. "Please don't ask any questions or I'll hang up."

"Agreed, ma'am, go ahead."

"Filiberto Cali de Cali, the man who murdered John Rutherford." Scarlett intoned. "He lives at 220 East 70th Street, between Third Avenue and Lexington, in Manhattan. The apartment number is PH 34." She hung up, breathing deeply. The entire thing had lasted no more than 35 seconds. Ken would be proud of her!

At NYPD headquarters, Detective Byrne stood frozen, his head cocked sideways, staring at the receiver in his hand. Then he slammed it down and pensively massaged his chin. Jellyfish, huh? The hands on the big old wall clock indicated 9:15 A.M. Twenty minutes later the commanders of the special units of the Metropolitan Police were facing Lieutenant Byrne.

Flattening a ball of chewing gum against the inside of his front teeth with his tongue, Byrne said, "Grab time, gentlemen!" He swiveled in his chair, turning his back to them. Pointing the antenna of his transceiver at one of the wanted posters on the wall, he said, "There's your suspect," then jumped up. He tore the poster off the wall and tossed it on the table. The three commanders didn't bother to examine the mug shot more closely. They knew exactly who Filiberto Cali de Cali was and what he looked like—one of the biggest fish on the most-wanted roster of big-time drug pushers.

Anticipating questions, Byrne said, "As of right now he's the prime suspect in the Rutherford murder." Then he proceeded to give his instructions. The building on East Seventieth Street was to be placed on round-the-clock surveillance. The moment the subject's presence in the apartment was confirmed, they'd go in. Byrne asked that he be given detailed information on Cali's cadre of bodyguards, as well as a precise floor plan of PH 34, and as many photos as possible of the penthouse and terrace. Also, he expected to be provided with progress reports every hour.

While the task force commanders stepped up to the huge wall map of Manhattan to start planning for the big grab, Byrne placed two urgent calls through the operator: one to Bob Donner, head of the DEA, the other to the director of the FBI.

As Byrne swung into action in New York, Stephanie Kramer in Switzerland crossed the terrace at Chalet Lindenegg and went into the house to look for von Alp. She found him in front of his computers in the communications room. Wasting no time with preliminaries, she said, "Tell me, Theo, how would you go about smuggling hot merchandise out of Switzerland, say a shipment of plutonium or, well, a hostage?"

Sensing a fresh challenge in the making, von Alp blinked, his eyes sparkling mischievously. "Aboard a private plane, of course. A VIP flight. No problem. If there're any checks at all, they're perfunctory."

"But airports like Zurich-Kloten have tight security, even for private traffic," Stephanie insisted.

"I wouldn't go through Zurich. Basel-Mühlhausen is much better suited for a covert operation. Security there is full of loopholes. Take my word for it, I wouldn't have any trouble getting your plutonium and your hostage aboard a plane without anybody noticing. But why're you asking?"

Hesitating, Stephanie gave the big, sharp-featured man with the blond hair that glinted gray at the temples a searching look. She liked his determined, carefree, fearless manner, apparent in every one of his gestures.

"Just a question," she murmured absently, as she looked around in the studio, noticing a video camera on a tripod in a corner. Smoothing out her hair with both hands, she flopped onto a couch. An idea came to her.

"Theo, would you turn on that camera and sit here with me? I want to get some things off my chest, and on tape."

"Sure," von Alp said, "my pleasure." He took a cassette from a shelf, went to the camera and inserted it.

Gesturing at his casual attire, he said, "If you don't mind, I'll put on something a little more . . ."

"You look fine, Theo," she laughed, patting the couch, "come here and sit down." The sound of an engine starting up outside made her look out through the window. It was Custer, driving off. She noted that Theo had seen her look out and was checking his watch: He'd shortly follow Ken to Nucleanne. But not before he helped her get her mental notes on tape!

"The assassination of Peter Kern in some fashion is connected with mysterious goings-on inside the Schlammer Engineering company," she began, her voice calm, matter-of-fact, professional—the way she was used to speaking in front of a camera.

"As a journalist and reporter, for many years now, I've been investigating nuclear energy, nuclear plants, radioactive waste management, and the risks and hazards that abound in the nuclear sector. I met Peter Kern while I was conducting research in these areas. The prime minister and I shared the view that, in the energy field, it's high time we start setting out for new horizons. Among the greatest obstacles to progress is the rigidifying of the existing power structures. As I see it, the current situation has three important components."

Von Alp stepped away from the camera and, nodding encouragingly at Stephanie, sat down beside her.

"The first involves a rigidified nuclear technology. The energy business is slavishly stuck in totally outdated thinking patterns. Any fresh impetus is met by blind faith in the current reactor systems. This results in systems that are complex and hazardous—systems designed with built-in instabilities, generating far too much radioactive waste. Moreover, radioactive waste disposal today is still far from safe, and if anyone claimed it were, no one would trust such assurances. The public has been deceived far too often."

"I totally agree," von Alp interjected, trying to justify his presence in the picture.

"Rather than investing in new technology," Stephanie continued, "what the owners of nuclear plants are interested in is cashing in on the boom. All they care about is how to increase energy production. No one wants to know where all this megalomaniacal greed is leading us."

A smiling von Alp handed the reporter a glass of water. She took a few sips, then continued:

"The antiquated approach used by the old technocracy is highlighted even more sharply by the second component of the current situation. The call for giant multibillion dollar projects to expand our hydro and nuclear energy capacity is totally absurd, running counter to current economic realities. What we need today aren't more and costly new megaplants, but efforts to ease the energy burden on existing facilities. What we should be doing is saving energy where it is being wasted in order to divert it to where it is urgently needed."

"You mean lights out a couple of hours earlier every night?" Alp cut in. "And no more street lights?"

"Of course not! Those are the slogans the nuclear energy lobby uses to subvert the energy-saving idea. Saving energy is a strategic measure. I'll give you an example.

"Approximately twenty percent of our current electricity production is wasted. How? Well, it's wasted in unprofitable production processes, or to run inefficient machinery, and in many other wasteful applications. In other words, if all consumers used energy more efficiently, we could get along on twenty percent less than our current electricity production. To achieve this goal, we need improved distribution systems, optimal equipment, rationalization of work routines, energy-efficient industrial facilities. But, of course, someone has to show us how to maximize energy savings, someone has to develop such improved, energy-efficient systems, then introduce them in the marketplace. Clearly, a lot of money is needed for this type of research and development. To implement a strategy of energy saving we're talking megabucks."

Stephanie paused, broke into laughter. "That's an arena where a systems optimizer like Theo von Alp could do a world of good!"

As the Lone Eagle gestured violently in protest, Stephanie continued, "However, there appears to be little interest in saving energy, due mainly to the bureaucratization of the energy sector, where politicians with long service records crowd the boards of directors, and managers spend their days in nostalgic daydreams of the visions of the sixties. Peter Kern was an innovative thinker who battled the sclerotic mindsets inside the established power structure. This put him on a collision course with people like Adam Schlammer. Kern simply happened to get in the line of fire. Now that the shots have found their mark, you won't find anyone in the energy arena shedding tears over him."

They sat quietly for a while, the faint humming of the camera dramatizing their silence. Then von Alp inquired as to why this improved technology wasn't being put into service.

Stephanie sighed. "The people who run the nuclear industry in Europe, in the United States, and here in Switzerland, want to get as much as they can out of the existing facilities, not invest in a brand-new technology. Raking in the dough is still the name of the game. No wonder the nuclear industry is losing credibility with every day that passes. And the people who ought to be making decisions are hidebound, or ill-informed, or both. Anyone with novel ideas and suggestions is labeled an opponent of nuclear energy, a nutcase, an environmentalist. They risk being condemned and executed, like Peter Kern."

Von Alp abruptly inquired how Schlammer Engineering might be involved in the Kern assassination.

"I believe that Prime Minister Kern was on to a conspiracy," Stephanie said slowly. "That is why he had to die. I have seen the man who killed him. First at the assassination site, then later on the premises of the Schlammer Group. He tried to kill me, too. It probably has to do with the nuclear waste disposal situation."

Talking straight to the camera, the reporter then proceeded to relate what she had experienced since Monday morning. Captivated by Stephanie's report, von Alp did not interrupt her. When she had finished, he made a copy of the tape, then handed Stephanie the original cassette, keeping the backup copy for himself.

Stephanie stretched luxuriously, then rose from the couch and went upstairs to get her things. Not much later, she wrote a note and placed it on the driver's seat of the van, for von Alp to find. Then she got into Claudia's small car, gunned the engine and was off, kicking up a rooster tail of gravel and dust.

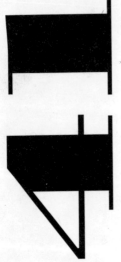

Tuesday, July 3, in the showroom at Schlammer
Engineering

"And now, the showpiece of our recent
production, the very cutting edge of technology!" Adam Schlammer intoned dra-
matically. He flung out one hand, five fingers spread wide, as if
invoking some specter of ultimate perfection on the bare wall to
the left. As all eyes automatically focused on the imaginary spot
indicated by Schlammer, a portion of the wall moved soundlessly
aside, opening up a black space. Like a conductor heaving his baton
to signal the beginning of the overture, Schlammer's right hand
spiraled upward, his eyes sparkling fiercely above that eagle's beak
of a nose. Instantly, a figure emerged dramatically from the black
void: Schoenhof, the physicist.

Clad in a white lab coat, a pained smile imparting an air of
lunacy to his craggy features, the physicist shouldered through a
curtain of black velvet slats and limped forward, using both hands
to lug a voluminous brown suitcase with a hard shell and shiny
aluminum edges toward a display table. It might have been a scene
from a Marx Brothers movie, and Custer fought down an attack of
laughter: the situation was entirely too serious for that! He knew,

as did everyone in the room, that this beautiful piece of travel equipment did not contain a pile of clothing, much less a collection of fine whiskeys and cigars to tide Groucho through the Fourth-of-July celebrations.

"On the table!" Schlammer commanded.

Custer and Hannibal were up out of their armchairs, moving to help Schoenhof lift the suitcase, but the physicist managed it on his own. Wasting no time, Schoenhof began lecturing the assembly, punctuating his delivery with a sporadic drumbeat of knuckles on the suitcase's hard surface.

"This is a standard, commercially available suitcase. It contains a nuclear device with an explosive power of fifteen kilotons," he announced.

Custer recoiled, involuntarily thrusting out his hands in a defensive reflex.

"Have no fear," Schoenhof smiled. "A series of specially designed baffles reduces its inherent radiation to a negligible minimum. You could sleep for two hours using this suitcase for a pillow and absorb no more radioactivity than you'd get from spending a day sunbathing on a beach."

Unimpressed, Custer inquired how much fissionable material the suitcase contained.

"In order to achieve an explosive power of ten kilotons, sir," Schoenhof lectured, "the quantity of uranium-235 required is precisely 21,800 grams."

"Fine," Custer nodded. "And on what operating principle does this bomb work?"

Well prepared for such a question, Schlammer switched on a projector, pointed at a screen.

"What you see here," he said, "is the slightly cone-shaped tube inside the device. And here, this is where we cause the two subcritical masses of uranium-235 to collide." He pointed to a spot at the left-hand edge of the cylinder shown on the screen. "One of the two masses must be accelerated to critical velocity in order to trigger a chain reaction when it collides with the other mass. Thus, the subcritical particles of the explosive are fused to form one supercritical mass. At that moment—bingo—we have a nuclear explosion. Greatly simplified, of course."

Clearing his throat, Schoenhof pompously added, "The challenge is to calibrate the acceleration ratio with perfect precision.

The two masses must collide inside the extremely narrow time slot of one-twelfth of a nanosecond—that is the twelfth part of one billionth of one second, Mr. Custer."

"And how do you generate such phenomenal acceleration?" Custer asked.

"With conventional explosives, as you see here," Schlammer replied, clicking a new picture onto the screen. "This is a schematic diagram of the process. Looks simple, doesn't it? The trick is hair-trigger precision in computation."

"Hold it," Custer exclaimed, pointing at the image on the screen. "What's that tiny black box next to the cylinder?"

"That contains the trigger mechanism and the lock codes."

His brows raised, Custer calmly outwaited his hosts.

"This particular trigger system constitutes a benchmark first for Schlammer Engineering," Schoenhof stated proudly. "You can trigger our device from any push-button telephone." He paused briefly to allow these portentous words to sink in, then added, winking obscenely at Custer, "Like they say on TV, sir—'Why not give us a call?'"

Schlammer beamed happily at Custer. "You can make your call from any Jacuzzi, Mr. Custer, and halfway around the world this little baby will do exactly what you expect it to do—through the miracle of satellite telephony, if you catch my drift."

"And our sophisticated counter-coding system, which accepts only authentic code calls, makes triggering the device due to someone else accidentally dialing the code sequence impossible," Hannibal announced.

Schlammer reached into a pocket and pulled out a small red unit, which he held out on his palm to Custer. "We've built our own microtelephone units into the system, like this one. Just a bit larger than a matchbox," he added redundantly.

Examining the device, Custer said, "If this gismo remains in the standby mode over a period of days or weeks, where will you get your power?"

"Excellent question, Mr. Custer," Schlammer nodded appreciatively. "Dr. Schoenhof, please explain!"

The physicist, who had just lit a cigarette, adjusted his horn rims. "We use solar cells." He nodded at the shiny brown suitcase. "The receiver is in there, of course. It is equipped with a set of especially powerful storage batteries, backed up by a generator which in turn is fed by the solar cells. The cells are built into the aluminum frame, along the edges."

Custer ran a hand across the shiny metal. "And the antenna for the telephone is also inside the frame?"

"Yes," Hannibal acknowledged. "The coding, the ignition approach, and the detonating mode, all function on the dialog principle. Allow us to demonstrate."

He connected his cellular phone with an amplifier and tapped in a number of digits. A mechanical voice could be heard: *If you wish to prime the fission pack for ignition, press 1. For alternate functions, press 2."*

"I'm pressing 2," Hannibal announced as he pressed the 2 key.

If you wish to alter the ignition time, press 1, droned the voice. *For alternate functions, press 2.*

"We will choose 2 again," Schlammer told Custer. Hannibal nodded.

The amplified computer voice continued, *If you wish to ignite the charge now, press 1. For alternate functions, press 2.*

Handing Custer the phone, Hannibal said, "You can alter practically the entire program from a distance. You can change the standby mode, the ignition time, the—"

"What exactly does 'standby mode' mean?" Custer broke in.

"Well, you can switch the device to a timer and program ignition for a certain month, day, hour and minute. Or you can use an override to circumvent the timer and trigger it directly. There are other options as well, such as a reduced energy standby mode, altering the access clearance requirements, as well as a number of other functions—they're all in the manual."

What Hannibal carefully refrained from mentioning was the secret master code, a four-digit sequence that enabled Schlammer Engineering to access the system at any time. The active ignition code could then be monitored, or the entire system shut down—a convenient function in the event Schlammer decided the bomb should not be allowed to go off.

"Great," Custer said, taking a step toward the suitcase, "let's have a look inside."

"Stop!" Schoenhof's voice rang out, trembling with alarm. "The lab is the only place where we open this thing. When the top is up, U-235 radiation increases to fifteen roentgens, which makes it slightly hazardous. No need to expose yourself unnecessarily."

The men passed through the black aperture in the wall and walked down a short, narrow stretch of corridor that led to a larger hall. Pausing by a personnel lock on the right, Schoenhof put his mouth to the grate of a wall microphone.

Damn, a voice lock, Custer noted. He was disappointed: the four-digit code he had swiped from the old man yesterday would be useless here!

Sure enough, in response to a password enunciated by Schoenhof, a stainless-steel grid rolled back. As they were being issued protective coats inside the lab, a female voice paged Schlammer over the intercom. The tycoon pulled out his cellular phone and answered, "Yes."

What he heard clearly upset him. He rudely shoved Custer aside, stepped up to Hannibal, and whispered something to the security man.

Taking advantage of the commotion, Custer darted a quick look at the map spread out on a table. Pennsylvania, New Jersey, New York and Maryland were marked with equidistant concentric circles whose common center lay somewhere in Philadelphia. Custer's impression at first was of radio broadcasting perimeters . . . until he realized they looked more like nuclear radiation perimeters!

Squinting more closely at the map, he recognized a fan-shaped configuration with lines opening conically from the center in Philadelphia in a northeasterly direction, toward New York City. All that was missing was the division of the fan-shaped design into contamination zones: the closer to the blast zone, Ground Zero, the greater the damage from heat, blast, and radiation.

"Stop that!" Schoenhof sharply ordered Custer. He slid the nuclear suitcase over the map where it came to rest almost precisely on Ground Zero, in Philadelphia. "You understand, Mr. Custer, these are our technical impact perimeters. Top secret, of course."

When Custer failed to comment, the physicist explained that their cellular miniphones naturally had to be adjusted for application inside the operational radius of a given target area. "These units only work in areas with an operational cellular telephone infrastructure. . . ."

Disturbed by a thought that was tugging at the back of his mind, Custer only half-listened to Schoenhof. What was a map of the eastern seaboard doing on this table anyway? As far as he could see, Cali had nothing to do with this. So, was somebody trying to double-cross him? He made a mental note to talk to Susan or Cosmo about this.

"... and a broadcasting license is mandatory," Schoenhof finished.

Even though he didn't believe a word of what the physicist had said, Custer nodded. Technically, Schoenhof's explanation was correct, of course, but it had nothing to do with the map on the table. Custer could have sworn that Schoenhof himself had drawn these lines to simulate a nuclear blast somewhere above the eastern seaboard of the United States. His ominous ruminations were abruptly cut short by Schlammer and Hannibal marching out of the room, leaving a dumbfounded Schoenhof in their wake.

"May I?" asked Custer, reaching for the red phone that lay next to the suitcase.

"Here, use mine," Schoenhof offered. "The red one is already programmed, and it's a little clumsy to use it for regular traffic."

He connected the set to an antenna cable from the console, then handed it to Custer who, without a word, punched in the number of von Alp's phone in the Dodge van parked across the valley. Never taking his eyes off Schoenhof's acne-scarred face, he spoke just one word—his own name. And then he listened intently.

After Custer disconnected, Schoenhof handed over the user's manual, making him sign a receipt. Then they agreed to meet again the following day—Wednesday, July 4. Independence Day in the United States. Custer was playing for time: he needed to call Cosmo. So he pretended to have to check back with his principals on some of the details of the deal. Also (he lied), it would not be possible to arrange for cash payment of the entire purchase amount before tomorrow.

When Custer climbed into the black Lincoln Town Car waiting for him by the rear entrance to the firm's headquarters building, neither Schlammer nor Hannibal were anywhere to be seen. As it moved toward the road, the limousine rolled past the ancient draw well. The sun hung as a fiery ball low in the west. Custer noticed nothing unusual, even though von Alp had just warned him of two strange men lurking about the premises: a Laurel-and-Hardy duo, Theo had chuckled. Yet Custer saw neither the blubbery big one, nor the tall figure with the pitch-black hair his pal had mentioned.

Indeed, he was more concerned with something else von Alp had told him: Stephanie Kramer had taken off, borrowing Claudia's little Citroën. She had left a note to the effect that she would be back tomorrow.

Custer doubted Stephanie would make good on her promise. He now admitted to himself that she had probably misinterpreted his brusque, absent manner that morning. Just as long as she doesn't do anything foolish, he thought hopefully as he got out at the train station in Nucleanne. A few minutes later, with a deep sigh, he settled into an aisle seat aboard the express train to Bern.

At about this same time Schlammer and Hannibal burst into the rectangular command center with the sea-green walls where "General" Breckerlin sat ramrod straight and motionless at the oval table. With a tired gesture, Breckerlin indicated the speaker phone in the center of the black granite tabletop.

Just then, the angry voice of Viktor Gisling rasped from the speaker, "This situation stinks. In Bern the shit is hitting the fan. Borli wants to turn Schlammer Engineering inside out, and this time he won't have any trouble securing a search warrant. Matak getting blown away right on our doorstep is a dead giveaway that Schlammer Engineering is involved in this mess."

Gisling's nervous, amplified panting filled the room. Chewing violently on his lower lip, Schlammer sharply ordered Gisling to stop panicking. "Listen, Gisling, I want to know precisely what is going on. Meanwhile, all operations continue as planned. Your job is to delay police action until tomorrow night. Do you understand?"

Gisling's voice, now calmer, affirmed, "Yes, sir! Hold them off until tomorrow night—Wednesday, July 4."

"By that time all of our merchandise will be out of here," the president of the Schlammer Group continued, "including the clock housings and the new suitcases. All the hot components as well. But I need at least twenty-four hours. Summermatter is flying the SADAM and all its parts and accessories up to the cave today. So, Gisling, twenty-four hours, you hear!"

"And what happens with the fission pack in the clock housing, the unit that's earmarked for the Iraqi?" Breckerlin piped up, a bit too eagerly.

Schlammer made a dismissive gesture. "The deal is off. That piece goes up into the mountains along with all the rest. There's nothing more to discuss, Breckerlin, do you get that?" Schlammer's eyes flashed dangerously.

Breckerlin's monocle dropped and he started trembling. Then he banged his fist on the table, shouting, "So let's hit the bastards, let's launch that rocket! Attack is our best defense! In the chaos we can take care of business. Yes, folks like us will be needed!"

"The old boy's gone off his rocker!" Gisling's voice rasped from the tap-proof speaker phone.

Schlammer signaled to Hannibal with a nod of his head. The security chief took Breckerlin by the elbow and gently steered him toward the exit. His face flushed a deep red, Breckerlin allowed himself to be led from the room. When the two men had left, Schlammer lowered his voice, speaking directly into the phone.

"Now listen, Gisling, we can't afford any slip-ups now, so we're implementing FUGA. Repeat the details of FUGA to me now, so we have it perfectly straight."

"Yes, sir."

From Bern, Gisling proceeded to describe the planned maneuver. They would begin by turning the nukes over to the negotiator from the drug cartel, against cash payment of course. As soon as the money was transferred, Custer would be eliminated, his body stuffed into a hazardous-waste container and stored in one of the subterranean vaults. Schlammer would then pick up Gisling at a prearranged spot, carrying the nukes in the trunk of the Mercedes. If need be, they would use the bombs to obtain safe passage.

"I'll be standing by for further instructions from you, sir," Gisling finished.

Schlammer nodded, satisfied. Promising himself to take care of that crazy Breckerlin later, he left the command center.

Outside, Dr. Adolf Breckerlin shook off Hannibal's hand and said, "Come to my bunker tonight—for a strategy session." His right eye produced a wink of eloquent ambiguity as he turned on one heel and marched off, muttering to himself, "Hazmoudi must be warned! The hour is nigh! Philadelphia! Baghdad! The Fourth Reich!"

His forehead burning hot, eyes blazing feverishly, Breckerlin chanted ecstatically as he descended to his bunker, the former observatory, located on one of the sublevels.

In the valley below, the train accelerated, leaving Nucleanne station behind. Custer surveyed the countryside, gazing up at the proud castle, where in olden times bishops and feudal lords had reigned, wreaking havoc in the neighborhood and torturing anyone they didn't like. Custer saw the dark-green top of the Dodge flash in the setting sun. The van was moving down the castle road.

Out of the corner of his eye, von Alp at the wheel saw a big helicopter lift off the pad at Schlammer Engineering. The heavy craft crossed the valley, heading straight for the Dodge. It thundered low overhead, skimming across the castle roofs. The daredevil pilot up there had to be those kids' father, Urs Summermatter!

Von Alp ducked reflexively. Coming out of a curve, he picked up speed, then turned into the main street at the bottom of the hill. Within a quarter of an hour he would rendezvous with Ken at the site they had agreed on.

Deep inside the cavern, old Breckerlin's wrinkled, liver-spotted hand picked up the phone. His gravelly voice informed the person at the other end that the helicopter was on its way. The merchandise was on board, the raid could be launched as planned. He disconnected.

Earlier, Bill Conklin and Special Agent Ben Atlee had watched the Lincoln leave the Schlammer Engineering compound. They had parked among the buildings near the top of the hill, where the road started to turn downward. They allowed the limousine to pass them, then swung in behind it, tailing it at a safe distance. With Conklin and Atlee in cautious pursuit, the big Lincoln headed for the train station. When they got there, they parked their Fiat in the shadow of a freight shed. Using the building for cover, they hurried over to the tracks.

Custer looked around a few times, then proceeded to the front of the platform, where the train would come in.

Conklin and Atlee parted company. Seeing Custer climb aboard in the center portion of the train, they exchanged rapid hand signals: Conklin jumped into the coach behind Custer's, while Atlee entered the one in front of it. As the train pulled out of the station, they began to close in on their prey. Conklin felt for the Smith & Wesson under his coat. Atlee pretended to be hitching up his pants as he touched the automatic he carried in the waistband, fitted snugly into the small of his back.

Steadily moving in on their man, they almost simultaneously pulled the opposing doors to the center car open. Every seat in every partitioned section was taken.

>Keycop< sat in the middle, near the aisle, his back toward Conklin, his head turned sideways toward the window and its view

of the castle. Then he shifted his gaze to the gangly kid who sat across from him, long legs casually stretched all the way over to Custer's bench. The boy wore tinted glasses and held a rucksack in his lap. As Custer tried to make out the eyes behind the kid's cool-looking shades, he glimpsed the reflection of a massive figure entering the coach—the blubbery dude von Alp had mentioned! Every fiber in Custer's body tensed. He shot a quick glance at the facing door, where the skinny guy with the black hair stood. Their eyes met. Custer knew he was trapped!

Moving slowly along the aisle, the two agents approached from opposite directions. Custer drew his Walther PPK and fired a shot into the ceiling, causing instant pandemonium. Women screeched; some men hit the floor while others jumped up, wild-eyed. Most of the passengers stampeded toward the exits. The gangly kid sat petrified, his mouth wide open.

Custer jumped up and grabbed the boy's rucksack. He swung it high, yelling, "There's a bomb in here! Everybody out! Now!"

Even those who had been rooted to the spot now panicked, joining the wild rush to the doors. Trying to get to Custer, Conklin and Atlee grimly fought the tide of desperate passengers, in vain. They were swept away and shoved back out through the doors.

Custer pulled down the window, pushing himself through it and climbing up. Fumbling blindly to get a hold on the aluminum roof, his fingers caught a curl of metal. He pulled himself up, braced his legs and lay flat on the roof, clutching at a tiny protrusion from the ventilation system. Facing forward, he sternly instructed himself not to try to stand up unless he enjoyed getting fried to a crisp by the train's electricity conduits.

Custer belly-crawled toward the end of the roof. Its aluminum surface was caked with a reddish layer of dirt; the train's airstream pelted his face with metallic dust. He flattened himself on the swaying roof, squinting around for something to hold on to. The train boomed on, seeming to pick up speed.

Cowed by the high-tension conduits above him, Custer feared raising his head even an inch. He decided to climb back down between the coaches farther ahead. Clinging so tightly to the roof that he could feel the warmth of his own breath on his face, Custer continued bellying forward.

At first he paid no attention to the insistent honking somewhere behind him. When it continued—stubborn, aggressive, moving closer and closer—Custer risked a backward glance. There, to his amazement, was the Dodge, barreling down the road alongside the train.

Custer reached the accordion connection between two cars and managed to lower himself onto a small platform halfway down. The train was shaking and rocking. The Dodge had now caught up with it, and Custer stared blindly across to von Alp, who gesticulated wildly at the wheel, dipping the high beam on and off. Custer measured the distance with his eyes; the road was too far away, the ground rocky, no way he could make that jump! When a strip of white gravel suddenly appeared, zipping along next to the train, Custer finally understood what was going to happen.

Von Alp bulled the skidding Dodge to the right, swung onto the gravel path, and again caught up with the train. A thick plume of dust trailed the wildly bouncing van, which was now no more than two meters away from the side of the thundering express train.

"You crazy bastard!" Custer shouted, as von Alp inched the Dodge closer and closer to the train. Now abreast of Custer, the van's right-hand wheels slid off the gravel onto grassy ground. Bouncing precariously, the Dodge was chewing up earth, pummeling the train with gravel, dirt and chunks of soil, its topside only a meter or two below where Custer clung to his hazardous perch. Then the van fell back slightly. A final blast of the horn and Custer jumped, the train's slipstream yanking him backwards.

Von Alp had calculated his position perfectly. Custer landed flat on top of the van, flailing and clawing to stay on. As Custer's body hit the roof, von Alp stepped on the brakes—just enough to reverse Custer's backward slide. The would-be stuntman managed to grab onto the roof's edge in front and hang on.

Ahead of them the tail lights of the train faded in the late-afternoon haze, with a red-faced Conklin gaping through a window in the hindmost car. He'd watched Custer's death-defying leap. It reminded him that his family's medical history had a preponderance of ulcers.

A huge harvester now rose up in front of the Dodge, blocking the narrow gravel strip. Staring aghast at the monster, von Alp hit the brakes—thirty, twenty, now ten meters to impact! Then the towering machine cut from the path into an open field, with only inches between them as the Dodge finally skidded to a halt.

Custer slid down across the windshield, his knees trembling. Shaking himself like a dog out of water, he started wiping the dirt from his face and beating clouds of dust from his suit. Incredulous, with a broad, admiring grin, he shook his head at von Alp.

The harvester operator came running toward them. He wore a cap whose legend proclaimed, *Need a Charmer, take a Farmer!*

"You people rehearsing for a movie? That's some stunt you pulled back there!"

Custer had already climbed into the van. Von Alp, one elbow sticking out the front window, winked conspiratorially at the farmer charmer. "Next time, we'll try it with that monster of yours," he laughed and stepped on the accelerator.

The van's wheels spun wildly in place, then caught. They watched the Harvester Kid shrink in the mirrors. He had taken off his cap and was punishing the air with long, happy swipes.

Bern, Tuesday, July 3

Stephanie threw a bundle of laundry into the washing machine, closed the porthole, and inserted a coin in the slot. Water started rushing in; she watched the drum go through a couple of tentative spins prior to starting the first cycle, then left the launderette to look for the shop Ralph Christen had mentioned. She had no trouble locating the establishment on the street level of a nearby shopping center. Looking up at the sign, she recalled how Ralph had sung the praises of the manager.

Crack Shoppe, she read with a puzzled frown. How cynical! But the message beneath—*Ye Olde Computer Foole*—did much to put the cheeky label in perspective. The manager, a handsome woman who was probably one of Ralph's former heartthrobs, immediately understood what Stephanie needed. After guiding the reporter through the pop-style interior to the back of the sales area, she plunked her down in front of a monitor with a jumbo-size screen. While showering her customer with instructions and explanations, Melanie Borli subjected Stephanie to a silent, critical scrutiny.

"Every few minutes, the word-processing program will automatically remind you to save the text," Melanie explained.

Adjusting her tinted glasses, Stephanie nodded as she inserted a diskette, clicked open a file, and began to write. An expert touch typist, she wrote smoothly, with a light hand, caught up in the flow and swirl of the narrative as she had lived it. She became oblivious to the world around her.

Earlier that day, after lunch at Lindenegg, she had touched up her hair with dark dye and borrowed a magenta-colored shirt, a white pant skirt, and sneakers. The outfit's effect now made her feel safely anonymous. After writing for about an hour and a half, she saved everything on the hard disk, closed the file, and instructed the computer to eject the diskette, which she slipped into an envelope.

When a hand touched her shoulder from behind, she flinched. It was only the manager, asking her with a smile if she would like some coffee. Relieved, she accepted enthusiastically. While Melanie Borli went to fetch the coffee, Stephanie penned a few lines on a sheet of paper, folded it up and placed it in the envelope with the diskette. After drinking half of her coffee and chatting for a couple of minutes, she left the Crack Shoppe and returned to the launderette. It took her only a few minutes to transfer her laundry to a dryer, feed the machine some coins, and buy a piece of pizza and two ham sandwiches. She extracted two cola drinks from a vending machine, then purchased a blanket and a Walkman at a corner supermarket. A large folding knife in the display window of a hardware store attracted her attention. She walked in and bought the long, sharp murder tool.

Later, she went to the Archives section of the Swiss National Library and sat down to search for newspaper items on the death, some twenty years ago, of a young man named François Clissot. She soon found the microfilm files for that year, including copies of *24 Heures* and *Le Matin*, Swiss dailies that gave a comprehensive coverage of the tragedy. A reporter from *24 Heures* had interviewed friends of Clissot, as well as the village constable, the dentist, and members of the local rifle club.

She copied what she needed, then drove out to the city stadium, parking the Citroën at the periphery of the enormous sporting complex. Securely hidden from view behind a group of multi-axle trailers, she devoured her snack and washed it down with one of the cola drinks. In the dim glow from the Citroën's ceiling light, she took her time studying the news clippings. A passage from *24 Heures* told how, from a perch high above the valley, a bird-watcher had seen the young man's plunge into the ravine, then notified the police. Apparently, the details of the accident were shrouded in mystery at the time, although, at a press conference, the examining magistrate ruled out foul play.

Since the bird fancier claimed to have seen another man with Clissot on the rocky ledge, the 24 *Heures* reporter had filed an additional report with the authorities. According to the old newspaper report, the police did nothing to follow up on this lead. Stephanie made a note of the bird-watcher's name. The man had lived in the same town as François Clissot.

Leaving the microfilm copies aside for a moment, she again bent over the Schlammer cavern drawings which Claudia had copied in miniature. She found a longitudinal cross section and compared it with the corresponding altitude on a topographical map of the cavern area. She concluded that it might be possible to reach the laboratory, which housed all that mysterious equipment and all the maps, through the ventilation shaft the Summermatter kids had discovered. Grimly determined, she decided to penetrate the nuclear cavern again tomorrow, in order to secure as much material evidence as she could. She could only hope that the kids would be willing to help her in this enterprise.

By the time Stephanie stretched out on the narrow back seat of the Citroën, it was way past midnight. She adjusted the Walkman headset and pulled the spanking new blanket up over her ears, letting the soft, melancholy strains of Vladimir Ashkenazy's interpretation of Chopin's Mazurka in D-flat major, Opus 30, carry her off to dreamland.

About this time, Hannibal was busying himself at a workbench in a windowless niche of the control room, carefully sealing the underside of a book-size parcel with brown adhesive tape. Turning the package with his fingertips, a feeling of pride and satisfaction spread through him as he contemplated his little masterpiece. The address, the Colombian postage stamps, the postal seal, the customs sticker, all looked perfectly authentic. The parcel's content, however, originated not in South America but in the Czech Republic. Three hundred grams of Semtex explosive, equipped with a draw-trigger, made an ideal parcel bomb.

"Real macho mail," he mumbled as he carefully put the parcel back into a drawer, from which he then took a number of color photos and lined them up against a computer screen.

One of the telephoto shots taken by Rosalia showed Custer landing a heavy right hand on the bald-headed thug's chin. Custer, the mail carrier! Hannibal tapped a key to summon to the screen the data on one Kenneth W. Custer. Massaging his chin as he studied the fact sheet, he had to admit that the fellow was good! Ex-CIA agent and bearer of the prized DCCLW classification, which certified him to be an expert in demolition, close combat, and lethal weapons.

"So I was right all along!" Hannibal cursed softly to himself. "That bitch Rosalia is playing footsies with the ex-spook! But nobody double-crosses Hannibal and gets away with it! High time for some very-special-delivery mail from South America."

He switched off the monitor, put the photos back in with the parcel, then carefully locked the drawer. He picked up his nine-mm automatic and took the elevator down to the Combat Center. High time, too, for some live-ammo target practice.

In the Swiss Alps, Tuesday, July 3

Urs Summermatter flew straight on course, into the gathering night. The steady beat of the huge rotor wings helped dissolve his inner tension and loosen up his thinking. Pictures flashed through his mind; the brutal murder of Peter Kern had shaken him up. For a moment, the two men had looked into each other's eyes; now, the prime minister appeared before Summermatter's inner vision as if alive, with a friendly gaze and some encouraging words.

Never would the pilot be able to forget that scene! And now— gone. Over. Finished. Blown away!

Summermatter tried hard to imagine Kern's final seconds. Had the man actually felt the bullets smashing into his head? The pilot's thoughts wandered from Kern's picture on the magazine cover, to his children—his sons, Mark and Tony, and Jessica, his adopted daughter from Sri Lanka. Sunday night, they'd had this lively conversation. . . .

. . . Summermatter and the kids were just finishing dinner at the round breakfast table in the spacious kitchen. Karma, everybody's favorite collie bitch, had just eaten her fill and was lying, fat and listless, under the table, inviting loving abuse from the heels of the youngsters.

Mark, the eldest, announced that he'd seen the prime minister in town. Summermatter looked up, shocked.

"Nonsense," the father irritably told the son, "you don't even know who he is."

"Oh yes I do," Mark insisted. "For starters, he looked at me from inside the car, through the side window. That was by the traffic light at the main intersection. Then he gave this big, beaming smile, exactly like on this picture—"

He jumped up and grabbed a magazine from the top of the TV set in the corner. "Exactly like this."

Mark displayed the cover, which showed a beaming Kern petting his Saint Bernard.

"You said 'for starters.' So, what else?" Tony challenged his brother.

"Well, I also memorized the car's license number—a very short one, strictly VIP. But I must say, for a prime minister he drives a real junk pile of a car!"

"Maybe it belongs to one of his slaves," Jessica suggested.

"Nada, baby! The car is registered to one Peter Kern, Chairman of the Council of Ministers."

"And how did you find *that* out?" asked Summermatter senior.

" 'Twas easy," Mark proclaimed imperiously. "The people at the Shell station keep a big binder that includes the car license register."

"Now listen, all of you," Summermatter interjected, "I don't want you to talk about this anymore, okay?"

"State secret!" Tony whooped, his eyes sparkling. "Wow! Probably in town to see his mistress, eh?"

"Stop this nonsense! What I mean is I want nobody besides us to know that Kern visited the Company today. You wouldn't want me to get into trouble, would you?"

"Of course not!" Jessie exclaimed. "But, Dad, why *did* he visit the Hole? And how would that get you into trouble?"

"Not another word about it! Am I making myself clear?" Using both hands, Summermatter eloquently drew what had to be a bottom line in the air. Then he waited for their reply.

"Okay, Dad," Mark grumbled at last, disappointed. Then he stood up. "I've still got some snakes to feed."

The boy administered a comradely pat to his canine buddy, then ambled through the open door onto the terrace. As Karma watched him go, her pleading eyes were filled with the soft flow of unconditional loyalty. In a corner of the terrace, Mark propped up the lid of a large crate. The enclosure was crawling with white mice, all peeping, darting this way and that, probably multiplying at approximately the same rate they were being gobbled by the snakes.

Mark gathered a handful of the prey into an old hat. He carried them over to the terrarium cases, where he fed two to a gray-brown Aspis viper.

"Will you be flying tomorrow, Dad?" he called to the kitchen.

"Guess so."

"Any idea where to?"

The boy let a mouse drop in a corner of the case, right in front of a lazily uncoiling Gabon viper.

"Yeah, sure, up to the quarry. Why're you asking?"

"Dad?" said Tony, absently contemplating a small convocation of arrow-poison frogs in a separate terrarium. "Why does the Company need all that stuff you're flying all over the place, like those granite slabs, and all the crates?"

Summermatter answered carefully, "Granite provides the perfect insulation against electric currents and electromagnetic waves."

"Also against *radioactivity*," Mark added pointedly. He petted the collie when she tried to snap at the hat with the white mice in it. "Fifty centimeters of granite will reduce radioactive radiation by ninety-five percent."

"Very impressive," Summermatter grinned. "You really know your stuff, don't you! And you're right, we need this type of insulation in the Hole because there's a lot of radioactive material still lying around. Used-up fuel rods and so on, from when it was a nuclear plant."

Still staring into the glass case, Tony asked, "How dangerous are they, really?"

His father smiled indulgently, "Let's just say a nuclear plant is at least as safe as a police station. The risks—"

"No, Dad, I mean these *frogs*."

"Oh, those!" Summermatter sounded relieved. "Well, Tony, the arrow-poison frog, I believe its Latin designation is *Phyllobates terribilis*, is a deadly little thing. Its poison will kill a human being instantly. Cardiac arrest. You haven't got a chance. Even a minuscule trace of it in your system will kill you. The natives scrape it off the back of these frogs and put it on the tips of their arrows, hence the name. A deadly weapon. Just like some snakes have poisonous fangs, these frogs have poisonous backs."

"Yeah, and some *people* are poison, through and through," Jessica put in. "Like that skinhead fatso at the Company. Looks like a poison *pig*, that one. Short arms, fat paws, a leather jacket, and always bad-mouthing Haluk. Twirling that switchblade and telling people the only good Turk is a dead Turk. He even painted a swastika on Haluk's back, with a spray can! I wouldn't want to meet *him* in a dark alley." She slapped her left hand into the hollow of her right elbow, a stiff middle finger jutting up from her right fist.

Summermatter was sensitive to the subject because he despised Hannibal's gang of skinhead hooligans. He asked his daughter if she knew fatso's real name.

"I call them as I see them, Dad, so I call him Fatso, or Scumbag, or Scuzzball," she replied archly. "No, I don't know the name his unfortunate parents saw fit to bestow on the wretch. By the way, tomorrow we're going up the mountain to catch lizards. I hope we don't run into Fatso up there. For *his* sake!"

"Fine, but make sure you don't stray into the security zone. I don't want any trouble with security personnel up there, okay?" Sensing that further admonitions might be counterproductive, Summermatter decided to drop the subject.

After a moment of silence, Jessica nodded pensively. "Yeah, Haluk knows the scene up there. He talks to the skins and to the Italos. Knows the security routine, too. I'm sure he carries a knife."

As the kids ambled off to their rooms, fragments of conversation drifted back to Summermatter in the kitchen. He heard Tony say, "We'll take one of them along . . . dogs kick the bucket . . . I know which way to go. . . ."

That night, Summermatter kept tossing and turning in his bed. Not on account of his children; they were great kids with a lot of crazy ideas in their heads, just the way they were supposed to be at that age. Nor was he the least concerned about the accumulation of potent animal poisons in those glass cases on the terrace. What bothered him was that, unwittingly, he'd been a witness to something he'd rather not have had anything to do with.

In the future, he'd have to be more cautious; keep his eyes and ears open. He'd better be on guard at all times! He had a hunch something was rotten in the Schlammer Group.

Before he at last drifted into a deep, dreamless sleep, Urs Summermatter tried to imagine, over and over again, why the safety door to the personnel had failed that afternoon. Why had it opened to admit Prime Minister Peter Kern?

At the controls of his chopper, Urs Summermatter's practiced eye zoomed in on the vague, smudgy streaks that translated as high tension wires, practically invisible in the gathering dusk. He eased the collector up a bit, climbing to clear the five thick steel cables with their lethal loads of electricity. High tension wires and ski-lift cables were among the most dreaded components of any military or civilian helicopter pilot's nightmare. Even though such obstacles were indicated with the utmost precision on the army's special flight charts, time and time again they turned into deadly traps for pilots distracted by inclement weather, gusts of wind, or blinding sunlight.

"What on earth . . . !"

First, a wave of air pressure, then, fractions of a second later, the deafening roar of an F/A-18 thundering low across the Super-Puma's rotors, abruptly forced the craft down onto the wires. Summermatter never knew how he managed to duck down in the cockpit in reflex to the sudden threat from above while simultaneously pulling up on the collector to clear the wires.

"Come on, baby, do it for me, start climbing—for Pete's sake, climb!" Summermatter pleaded. And the great turbo rotors answered his prayer. The infernal wail of its mighty engine was music to his ears as the Super-Puma rose majestically above the obstacle.

Summermatter wiped the sweat off his brow. He had just begun scanning the darkling skies for the air force jet, when the delayed reflex hit him. "Goddamn son-of-a-bitchin' bat out of hell!" he screamed, as he checked his position and made a minor course correction to west-by-southwest.

The puffy features of the man who accompanied Summermatter had shifted from an already unhealthy pink to an even more sickening hue of green during the sudden evasive maneuver. With a pitiful groan, the bald-headed goon from Breckerlin's gang of thugs clutched his fat stomach beneath the folded-up AR-90 assault rifle. Summermatter's disdainful grin reflected the intense dislike he felt for every one of the nasties on the Company's security staff. If it had been up to him, he would have taken that porker through a controlled roll down some ravine and made him puke his guts out, but then he himself would've had to clean up the mess, which would be worse. The two hadn't exchanged a single word since liftoff, as the vicious curl of Summermatter's upper lip gave a clear signal to the heavily-armed tough to keep his distance.

Lieutenant Colonel Henri Carrard had a queasy feeling in the pit of his stomach as he pulled his F/A-18 jet out of the narrow valley, up into the wild blue yonder above the Alps. "Damn idiot!" he muttered into his oxygen mask, reaching for the flight chart. What he saw was precisely what he thought he'd see. On the chart, the entire valley was clearly hatched with red lines, designating it a military zone. Which meant that dummy of a chopper pilot had absolutely no business being there! He radioed details of the incident back to the base, only to be informed, drily, that the matter would be taken care of.

"Okay," Carrard said into the mike, "I'm aborting this run. And make sure you catch that bum. I'll personally wring his neck. *Ritorno in venti.* Over and out." As he headed for his home base in the mountains, the horror show he had just lived through reeled off on the screen of his mind. . . .

. . . he'd been trying out a new laser-targeting device designed to improve the F/A-18's ground raid performance, which was currently being tested by the air force. Personally, Carrard didn't have very high hopes for the project; as far as he was concerned, the F/A-18 was and would always remain a classic interceptor. Still, he didn't mind the simulated raids on ground targets that were a part of the test program. They demanded perfect concentration from him. On this particular evening, he had dived into a screaming run at the western flank of the Dents-du-Midi, then banked sharply into the side valley where the power station was located. The plane's target sight quickly and accurately locked on to the small transformer station below, the camera started filming, the air-to-ground rockets would be launched in a few moments—all in simulation, of course.

The valley lay in shadow, Carrard's craft thundering across the valley floor at less than one hundred meters altitude. The high tension wires he had memorized now came into view directly ahead. When Summermatter's helicopter suddenly rose in front of him as it tried to clear the power lines, Carrard barely had time to react.

Skimming treetops in a narrow mountain valley at Mach 0.9 during an attack run on a hidden target requires top-notch piloting skills. Which, as the lieutenant colonel was wont to assure his colleagues in the U.S. Air Force, were the only kinds of skills Swiss Air Force pilots had. To date, not one of the Top-Gun aces visiting from the United States had ever succeeded in keeping up with Carrard during simulated dogfights on his own alpine turf.

Due to momentum and inertia, a lateral evasive maneuver was out of the question; the F/A-18 would have smashed into the mountainside. At this rapidly diminishing distance, his only chance was a carefully executed pull-up. Hundreds of hours of flying time now helped him do his stuff: inches before contact, the heavy, hurtling missile of a jet lifted its nose. Lucky the damn chopper's red, Carrard thought, as he powered into the skies above the valley. A collision would have been just the thing to round off my career, he cursed, then blinked as he did a double take on the instrument panel.

"What the hell's this!" Had he, or had he not, seen the needle on the dosimeter move? He snapped his right middle finger against the instrument that measured radiation dosages in milliroentgens.

"Probably just the hiccups," he muttered, "or else, who knows, maybe one of those supposedly airtight infinity dumps for nuclear garbage is leaking?" Carrard chuckled at the thought as his stress faded.

The red craft, which looked like a Super-Puma to the lieutenant colonel, had banked west toward the French border. Backlighting from the evening sun created a silky mist that enveloped the majestic mountain heights. The chopper slipped into this natural cover, and vanished. It was over. There was nothing for Carrard to do but bank steeply and head home.

"Ritorno in venti"—the message had come clearly through Summermatter's headphones as he flew low over the mountain pass. After the scary encounter, he had immediately switched to the F/A-18's radio frequency, relieved to note that traffic on that band had not increased, which probably meant he had gotten away unnoticed.

Had Summermatter thought of doubling back, he might have noticed another helicopter tailing him at a safe distance. Instead, his attention remained focused ahead, on the valley basin where the quarry was located. As he continued his descent towards coordinate 1794, the sun sank beneath the alpine summits, painting a streak of grayish red across the sky above the horizon. At this hour, the quarry lay deserted, the day's last shift normally ending at six. The men then crowded into an ancient VW camper and drove back to the village, which, seen from above, seemed a mere stone's throw away. In fact, the fifteen-kilometer gravel road meandered downhill through an endless series of serpentine turns; even though they drove at breakneck speed, it took the work crew at least half an hour to get home.

As Summermatter cautiously set the Puma down on the distinctly marked landing area, allowing the rotors to wind down, the pursuing helicopter, a black Cobra, shot up over the basin's western rim, then dove down into the shadow-filled valley. Banking, its nose angled downward, it headed straight for the landing area where Summermatter's craft stood out like a red flare against the bright green sheen of the granite rock walls.

Aboard the Cobra, two men prepared to jump. They wore tight black combat coveralls and grim expressions. As they stared fixedly ahead, past the pilot, three Uzis, their magazines in place, lay ready for action.

Urs Summermatter, this summer evening, was carrying not contraband but a magnificent clock housing made of green granite. Had he been aware of his cargo's true nature, he would probably have preferred smuggling cigarettes and booze, maybe even sampled a bottle or two of the latter. However, he happened to be blissfully oblivious of the fact that the elegant Rock'O'Clock unit in the rear of his Super-Puma housed a nuclear package of the SADAM type, Schlammer's very own Special Atomic Demolition Ammunition.

In fact, the pilot's thoughts were eons away. His wife, Brigit. He still loved her, even though she'd abandoned him and the children over a year ago. There'd been a note on the kitchen table one morning: *Can't stand it anymore. Be good to the kids. Adieu.* Since then, not a word. Rumor had it she'd gone into the river, but her body was never found. The truth was, she had suffered—because of his job, because of Schlammer's ban on talking about it, because of her husband's devastating silences.

One day Brigit had flown up to the quarry with him. They climbed to the summit, thrilled by the view of the glacier to the west, with the last rays of the setting sun spreading a rosy glow over the magnificent panorama. Up there, he had finally told her everything. He spilled the beans on his flying missions, the radio-active materials, the strictly off-limits facilities he was not allowed to enter. He told her about the mysterious visitors, people like the Iraqi today (whose car license number he'd routinely jotted down).

Brigit had wept. She told him she couldn't go on living with him. She felt totally isolated, she said; nowadays he seemed to live only for this Schlammer fellow and his shady dealings. She had pleaded with him to report his observations to someone—a journalist, an attorney—so there could finally be an investigation into Schlammer's doings. She begged him to leave, take the whole family and start a new life; wherever they went, pilots were sure to be in demand.

He knew she was right, of course. But still, he'd been irritated by her pleading. He was making good money, had a lot of freedom in his job. He would have hated a change right then, but most of all he was afraid something might happen to him if he tried to turn his back on Schlammer Engineering. What about that young, ascetic physicist, the one who loved to fly hang gliders? Didn't he simply disappear one day? His glider had crashed on the shores of a mountain lake, but his body had never been found. Apparently he'd been considered a security risk. . . .

As he guided the Puma up to the quarry, Summermatter had at last made up his mind to talk to Chief Borli, who'd been on TV appealing to the citizens for help. Tomorrow he'd take the time to drive to Bern and spill the beans on the Company. Meeting the prime minister shortly before he was assassinated had strengthened Summermatter's resolve. Yes, there had to be a connection!

When the rotor blades stopped moving, Summermatter climbed out to shake hands with the two men in blue coveralls who'd been waiting outside the marked area and now came running up to the chopper. Ponderously, the bald-headed goon also climbed down from the cabin. Firmly planting his feet on the ground, he took a deep breath of fresh air, then unfolded his AR-90 assault rifle with a practiced slap of his right hand. The two security guards gave Summermatter questioning looks. The younger of the two touched his belt just above the holster.

Summermatter smiled, "Come on, fellas, don't you know the general, that old battle charger? He wouldn't do anything without his bloodhounds. Now let's get a move on, lads, untie that load!"

He walked over to the shed that housed the small forklift. He kicked the engine alive and backed it out. The cube-shaped clock with the CLISSOT imprint had been intended as a gift for an Arabian prince, or so he'd been told, but the order had been canceled. "Hmmh," Summermatter shook his head as he recalled this curious explanation. Then he heard the chopper.

He stopped the forklift. Bent low over the steering wheel, he watched the Cobra come in. Those men in black coveralls on board looked dangerous! Summermatter barely had time to tell himself that he didn't like the looks of this, didn't like it one bit, when something entirely unexpected happened.

The two security men heard the engine noise and jumped down from the cargo hold of the Super-Puma. As they stared up at the approaching craft, shielding their eyes against the still-bright sky, Breckerlin's skinhead henchman stepped up behind them. He smashed the butt of his assault rifle against the backs of their heads, one after the other, in rapid succession. They crumpled to the ground.

Summermatter slipped down from the forklift and ran into the shed. Quickly scanning the interior for a weapon, he yanked a blue sports bag down from a rusty nail in the wooden wall, then busied himself at a cagelike enclosure in the rear, where he kept a dozen reptiles from his growing collection which was threatening to expand beyond the limited space available in their crammed apartment down in Nucleanne.

He felt the hopelessness of his situation as if he'd been stabbed right through the heart. Pain, anger, bitter regrets and disappointment first numbed him, then gave way to ice-cold planning. With something approaching a sleepwalker's confidence, he tore a shotgun off the wall, found a round of shot in the pocket of a worn-out leather jacket that hung nearby, and loaded the gun.

The entire raid lasted no more than four minutes; the black-coveralled terrorists knew their business. As the first one, a stocky fellow with blond hair, leapt from the chopper, he started raking the shed with bursts from his Uzi. Meanwhile his buddy sprinted toward a pile of granite boulders that lay on the other side of the shed.

Breckerlin's skinhead had dropped his assault rifle. His arms spread wide, a broad grin on his face, he came out from behind the Super-Puma and walked toward the blond raider. One of the security men on the ground began to stir. The black-coveralled terrorist executed a half turn, bouncing a disdainful glance off the skinhead. Fire flashed from the muzzle of his Uzi. Hit in the chest by two short bursts, Breckerlin's goon whirled around and fell. His head hit the rocky ground with a sickening thud, obliterating a terminal expression of dumb incomprehension.

From an awkward position, lying on his side, one security guard aimed at the terrorist, who hadn't missed the move. His legs spread wide, the raider lifted the Uzi to his shoulder, aimed, and fired several rapid bursts that hit the guard in the head, his colleague in the neck and back. Both died instantly. No prisoners, no witnesses—that appeared to satisfy the order of the day.

When the first bursts of Uzi fire ripped through the boards with a hellish clatter, Summermatter was already flat on the floor. A ricocheting bullet tore open his left calf. He squeezed off a load of buckshot at a figure diving for cover behind the granite boulders, and he must have drawn blood because the fellow cried out and fell. Then, suddenly, there was the blond raider, no more than three meters away, his chunky frame planted squarely on spread legs. Summermatter didn't bother to look up. He closed his eyes and saw his kids, saw them as clearly as if they stood where his executioner was taking careful aim. They were smiling at him, waving cheerfully, ready as ever for a joke or a prank.

A hail of bullets tore the pilot's head to shreds, killing him instantly. The killer moved closer, picking up the blue sports bag from which the top of a first-aid kit protruded. He jogged back to his wounded buddy who lay groaning behind a granite boulder. Kneeling down, he opened the metal box with the red cross.

Released from its confinement, a hissing Gabon Viper streaked at the man's neck. There was an infinitesimal moment of mutual recognition during which the roles of executioner and victim were established, then the deadly poisonous fangs found their mark. The man let out a terrible yell that reverberated through the valley basin. One hand flew to his neck where Summermatter's viper had struck the jugular. He leapt up, darting aimlessly this way and that. Overwhelmed by the powerful, fast-acting toxin, the man collapsed on ground that was covered with granite shards. In a matter of moments—shaking and whimpering pathetically, his staring eyes wide open—he stiffened grotesquely.

The man they called "The Avenger" was smoking a cigarette, calmly watching the action from behind the Cobra he had piloted. Totally indifferent to the fate that had befallen his accomplice, he now strolled over to the forklift and got on. Cigarette dangling from a corner of his mouth, he set about transferring the Rock'O'Clock unit from the Super-Puma to the Cobra.

"Hey, you, get busy!"

The Avenger's shouted order spurred into action the wounded terrorist who'd been cowering despondently behind the granite boulder. He pulled himself up and limped slowly toward his dead companion, glancing nervously about for the viper. He grabbed the body by the ankles, lifted up the stiff, heavy legs, and dragged it carelessly across the stony ground toward the black helicopter. Three quarters of an hour after they had arrived, with the granite clock securely lashed down in the cargo hold, the Avenger lifted off, taking his Cobra across the west rim of the mountain valley. Only minutes later, they had crossed the border and were flying over French territory.

After twenty minutes of low-level flight hugging the contours of the terrain, the Avenger and what remained of his team set down on an asphalted parking lot near a ski lift that operated only in the winter. A cool wind drove rain clouds up the valley slopes as darkness fell quickly upon the surrounding mountain meadows, green and lush. A truck with dimmed headlights, trailed by a black Peugeot, turned into the parking area and stopped beside the helicopter. The Avenger ambled over to the Peugeot and bent down to the open side window, where the Iraqi with the pencil-thin mustache sat, squinting up at him. They exchanged a few words. Some men jumped down from the truck and jogged over to the helicopter. In accordance with instructions, they cautiously transferred the green granite cube from the Cobra to the loading ramp of the truck, paying no attention whatever to the other object aboard, a Clissot cube clock from the Schlammer Group.

Hazmoudi had every reason to be pleased with the success of the operation. The intelligence he'd received from inside Schlammer Engineering had proved accurate. It had been explained to him that Schlammer feared a police raid on his premises, which was why the Rock'O'Clock, complete with nuclear charge, had been flown into the mountains. These explanations left Hazmoudi cold. The main thing was that he was in possession of the merchandise, and that he hadn't fallen into a trap.

With a sigh of contentment, the Iraqi tapped out a number on his cellular phone, leaned back in his seat, and waited. In Tehran, not far from Prime Minister Rafsanjani's office, Colonel Reza Fahimi picked up the phone and breathed a skeptical "Hello" into the receiver.

"Hazmoudi speaking. Operation 'Holy Lightning' is under way as planned. The bolt has departed from the zenith. We're ready to hurl it into the heart of the enemy on the day of the big fireworks. Everything went perfectly. We have the user manual for the ammunition, as well as photos of Custer. We'll be leaving the snowy mountain area early tomorrow morning. The Avenger has successfully completed his mission. One man down."

Fahimi answered, "Excellent. Now listen carefully, there is a change of plans. The Avenger will accompany you west tonight. Over."

"I understand," Hazmoudi confirmed, "the Avenger will go with me. End of transmission."

He looked across to the truck. The Avenger was leaning casually against the tarp, smoking. A professional killer and demolition expert, one of the most-wanted of the Hamas terrorists! That this man was to accompany him to the United States had not been planned. So what was Fahimi up to? As his gaze swept the bleak parking area, then returned to the Avenger, a chill of apprehension crept up Hazmoudi's spine.

In Tehran, Colonel Fahimi opened a hidden drawer in his desk, extracted a bottle of Chivas and took a stiff, down-the-hatch swig from it. Watching the most ingenious plot of all time take shape step by step gave him a great deal of pleasure and satisfaction. Killing several birds with one stone! He happily rubbed his hands together.

The United States, stung to the quick, would be the victim, he told himself. The Iraqis, who hatched the plot, were the scapegoats; drug lord Cali de Cali, who paid the piper and benefited in his own ways, was the villain. Finally, they, the Iranians, were the strategists. When the dust had settled, they would emerge as the superpower in the Middle East. First they would take Kuwait, Saudi Arabia, Iraq, and Israel. Then, as they locked a scissor-hold on Europe, from North Africa to the Balkans, they would move in for the kill!

The thick-bellied bottle in one hand, he stepped up to the small mirror on the wall and stared himself in the face. Visions of glory, of recreating—no, exceeding—the ancient Persian empire of Darius the Great were spinning in his head. Overcome, he shouted to his reflection, "You're the greatest, Genius!"

As if to affirm his own heroism, he raised the bottle to his lips and, with a sudden tilt, tossed back another guzzling swig. As he drank, he squinted at the mirror, watching his Adam's apple move and a trickle of whiskey meander down one unshaven cheek. A warm feeling of bliss spread through his body. He felt strong, successful, powerful. This one stroke of genius would carry him to the very pinnacles of power!

Those pictures of Kenneth W. Custer in action, he would pass on to the CIA branch in Bern, exposing the most-wanted weapons smuggler as an Iraqi agent. All that was missing to make Fahimi's happiness complete was Rosalia, his talented, fiery, raven-haired, state-of-the-art undercover agent. The poor woman would simply have to do without him a little while longer over there, amid the bleak wastes of those faraway snowy mountains. That she missed him, and badly, seemed a matter of course to the macho colonel of the Iranian secret service.

Fahimi staggered back to his desk and threw himself into the desk chair. He opened one of the top drawers, pulled out a color photo, and studied it with a lopsided grin. What a shiny picture, and what a magnificent Rock'O'Clock! Just like the one those naive, stupid, unsuspecting Americans would soon set up in Philadelphia . . .

Fahimi pushed himself up out of the chair. Again, he lifted the bottle, greedily guzzled more, and lowered it. He started slapping one knee, each slap a noisy counterpoint to his roaring laughter. "I'm the greatest," he shouted. "I'm a genius!"

As the truck moved out of the parking lot, Hazmoudi was certain that nothing could go wrong at this stage. The fast little rig would be in Basel-Mühlhausen in less than three hours, and runway access was no problem at that early hour. With painstaking thoroughness, Hazmoudi had scouted security on the airport that was run jointly by France, Germany and Switzerland. His people had discovered at least four ingress points where a vehicle might enter the runway area to rendezvous with the private jet that stood ready to receive its cargo. The pilot of the sleek-looking Falcon 900 had been issued a special permit for takeoff Wednesday morning at 0300 hours.

The three-engine jet would reach the East Coast of the United

States at approximately six A.M. local time on Independence Day, Wednesday, July 4—with plenty of time to deliver the sensational, four-faced Rock'O'Clock to Philadelphia, where it would be installed not far from Independence Hall. And on that evening, as the great fireworks show lit up the skies above Philadelphia, a terrible luminescence would suddenly blot out the exploding Roman candles and star showers. A holy bolt of lightning would blind the millions of watching eyes shiny with excitement and patriotic fervor. Within fractions of a second a nuclear inferno, emanating from within the harmless-looking green granite cube, would engulf Philadelphia.

Hazmoudi was beside himself with excitement. Nothing like this had ever been planned and executed. It was great, it was brilliant, it was un—unprecedented. Ecstasy overwhelmed the passionate Iraqi. A sopping warm wetness spread through his Armani trousers.

"Holy . . . piss!" he shouted, cursing and roaring with laughter.

The black Cadillac rolled slowly through the residential neighborhood of mansions and villas. It turned onto Springfield Road, where Scarlett's house was located. Cosmo sat in the back seat, thrusting out his chin as he scanned the neighborhood. The impending meeting with her made him nervous. She had not been eager to see him when he'd called.

"We separated. Remember, Jack?" she'd told him on the phone. "So leave me alone. Besides, I don't have time right now, I'm meeting the Swiss ambassador."

Cosmo had been in no mood to give up. "We still have Kenny," he told her. "Our boy's in trouble."

This remark had hit her where it hurt. Ken was the apple of her eye. That she had rescued him from the icy river waters back then in Switzerland, right after Franky Boy's terrible death, had always seemed like destiny's great gift to her. Now she reasoned, superstitiously, that turning Cosmo away might be bad luck. Besides, what if he was planning something that could harm Kenny? So, finally, reluctantly, she had relented.

"Franky, oh Franky . . ." Cosmo sighed as the Cadillac turned into Scarlett's driveway. Right here, over there, on the sidewalk, they had found his son that morning in May. Dead. A bloody, ragged, mutilated bundle of flesh, tossed out of a car. The eighteen-year-old had been pumped full of dope, raped and tortured, in some big-shot's mansion. Apparently it was dealers squaring accounts, or so the story went. No arrests were ever made. Even now, after all these years, Cosmo fairly trembled with hatred and disgust.

Only a handful of insiders in Washington's political establishment were certain that a man named Cosmo actually existed. And all they knew was that he ran an organization so secret, with operations so covert, it bordered on the mythical. Having suspected this for many years, Scarlett finally could no longer put up with the devious secretiveness of the man with whom she shared her life—and especially not with the kind of man Jack had turned into after Franky's death.

Surrounded by a well-kept lawn framed with rhododendron bushes, Scarlett's modestly-sized bungalow adjoined a golf course near Media, a suburb of Philadelphia. A Japanese gardener was busy weeding along the edges of the immaculate expanse of grass.

She greeted him with frosty politeness. He threw himself on a couch and came straight to the point.

"I want to come back to you. I'm lonely."

"If that's what you came here to tell me, Jack, you could have saved yourself a trip. Forget it. You're a perverse sort of loner, which I suppose you'd have to be to function in that obscure business of yours, whatever it may be."

Cosmo raised his hands, begging indulgence. "My work is of great import to the nation," he pleaded. "I mean, look, the CIA subverts foreign dictators it doesn't like; the FBI engages in heavy breathing exercises on your telephone, and the NSA is one of the major decryptor hackers worldwide. Me, I operate above all of those bureaucrats."

"And what is it you actually do do, Jack?"

Cosmo theatrically sealed his lips with one finger. "Those three agencies do the groundwork for me. They stick out their necks to do what I tell them to. Granted, I use their vast informational resources, but—"

"You plan wars, Jack, you break people's necks, and you get others to do your dirty work for you, am I right?" Her question hung in the air like so much cigar smoke above a gambling table.

Cosmo answered by telling her that ninety percent of the CIA's and NSA's work was everyday routine. "They gather intelligence, analyze, classify, study developments, hire agents. All that spectacular stuff you see in the movies? Well, that's only in the movies. The CIA is much too big to be able to conduct genuinely covert operations. They simply can't plug up all the leaks, the enemies infiltrate them—ah, but you know all that. The thing is, they need people like me. They need a Cosmo."

"All right, so what about these clandestine operations our government engages in?" Scarlett felt uncomfortable with all this. It occurred to her what a perfect cover Cosmo had; no one could possibly imagine a super secret service behind Jack's high position in Washington.

As Cosmo absently massaged the bulge in his crotch, Scarlett noted with a nauseous heave of her stomach that his old habit of constantly fondling himself had lasted even beyond their ostensibly painful separation.

"Okay, let's just say we allow Saddam Hussein to stay in power," he grinned, "or we smash some country's nuclear potential, or we take down the head honcho of some other government somewhere else, or we wipe out the drug lords . . . just for the sake of argument, as an example. How about a drink? And tell me, what is it you're talking to the Swiss ambassador about?"

"I can't see where that would be any of your business." She paused for a moment to think, then said, "Don't tell me you've got Kenny involved in those obscure affairs of yours."

The man known to a select few as Cosmo raised his hands defensively, energetically shaking his head. "And you, what sort of business do you have with Switzerland?" he shot back.

"The ambassador is making a donation to our organization," she said, "one of those big granite Rock'O'Clock street clocks. Genuine Swiss quality, haven't you read about it? We're installing it in front of the City Tavern, with special permission from the mayor. He was also kind enough to approve the logo of our organization: *Time to Change*. We're having it posted on a plaque next to the clock, something for thousands of visitors to look at and ponder. Oh, the dedication ceremony is tonight."

Her voice carried an unmistakable ring of pride.

"Liberalization and legalization of drugs is a dangerous madness, Scarlett," he told her coldly. "You're on the wrong road. Trying to legalize coke and crack is simply insane."

Scarlett remained perfectly calm. "What *Time to Change* is trying to do is take a first step by legalizing soft drugs like marijuana and hashish. We want to start by decriminalizing sale and posses-sion of small quantities of those substances."

Cosmo leaned forward, keen as a pit bull. "Scarlett, will you listen? Drugs are a bigger threat to us than all the terrorists put together. Where do you and your people get the nerve to prose-lytize for the right to get high?"

Shaking her head, Scarlett hurried into the kitchen to put the electric kettle on for some tea water. When she returned, she sat down in an armchair opposite his, crossing her legs. "Sorry, Jack, but you can't get rid of drugs in America, that's a fact of life. Just as you can't outlaw alcohol or tobacco. The only ones who benefit are the Mafia and the other organized crime groups. And remem-ber, booze and tobacco are still being consumed in much larger quantities than grass and hash."

"Bullshit, baby, legalizing narcotics would be the beginning of the end—"

Scarlett jumped up and started pacing the room, her eyes flash-ing.

"Wrong, Jack. How wrong can you get! Americans swallow, in-ject, smoke or otherwise imbibe dope, that's the way it is. Is it my fault that so many of them are so dumb? When you're fighting narcotics, humane aid and therapy are far more effective than re-pressive legislation and imprisonment, and you know it. But all you and those geriatric buddies of yours can think of is more punitive legislation. You know that crime and recidivism go hand in hand, and that both are steadily on the rise. It's time for a change, Jack!"

"Oh yeah? Hash for cash, and coke and crack for Jill and Jack, right? You're off your rocker, all of you. And if I were you I'd listen to good advice, Scarlett, and keep my pretty little mitts out of this. Remember Franky Boy."

"*You* don't have to remind me," she fought back from the brink of tears. "You want to punish and incarcerate millions, just to get even for what happened to him, and in your rush to justice you forget that he was the victim of a drug policy that failed. Or have you forgotten about Prohibition?"

"Look," he said, "if every convicted drug dealer were sentenced to a spot of caning, the way he might be in, say, Singapore, the drug trade would be reduced along with the rate of recidivism, believe you me. People are really getting tired of the deteriorating crime situation."

"Baloney," Scarlett cut in. "You sound like Ed Koch, that right-wing pruneface. If that's how you feel, why not whole-hog it, introduce the death penalty for drug dealing and have offenders summarily executed, preferably by firing squad? You know very well that capital punishment doesn't work."

"Crime's out of control," Cosmo insisted, "we need new and tougher forms of punishment. Join me in a drink?"

"I'm making some tea," she called back over her shoulder as she hurried into the kitchen. "Whiskey is in the bar, help yourself. Good thing you can't outlaw booze, isn't it? What a disaster Prohibition turned out to be. The only business sectors to profit from that self-righteous little interlude were moonshining and bootlegging operations run by organized crime."

As Cosmo mumbled an unintelligible protest, Scarlett called from the kitchen, "And now we're making the same mistake again, this time with drugs. As long as amphetamines, heroin, coke and crack are illegal, all we're doing is increasing crime. To say nothing of grass. What we're doing is producing new Al Capones, nasty drug lords like Escobar, a whole army of dangerous drug mobsters." She returned to the living room, carrying a cup of tea on a saucer.

"So what's *Time to Change* really after?" Cosmo asked. "Making narcotics available to kids, like booze and smokes?"

"Sure, why not? Are you aware of any insurmountable problems relating to booze and tobacco in this country, Jack? Legalizing soft drugs like hashish and marijuana would split the drug market in two, which is our initial goal. In the future, if you want to smoke a little grass, you won't have to contact your not-so-friendly neighborhood hood who carries his stash of hash in one pocket and a supply of hard drugs and a six-shooter in the other. *Time to Change* wants to start reducing consumer crime through a step-by-step decriminalization process. Which, incidentally, happens to be what the Dutch, the Germans, the British and the Spanish are doing. As for the Swiss, they've gone as far as introducing the controlled administration of heroin to addicts. However, Jack, I really do have to run. Think about it. No, don't think, *do* something for us."

She placed her cup on the low glass table where Jack had parked his whiskey. Cosmo's face succumbed to an expression of clumsy cunning. "And if I do, *then* will you take me back?"

Scarlett eyed him with cautious repugnance. "Jack, I'm seeing Philip de Steck. You remember him, don't you? He was with UNICEF, in Geneva in the old days. Well, he was appointed Swiss ambassador to the United States a few months ago and is now based in Washington. We get along famously and he does everything he can to help me. In plain English, Jack, my passion for you is as cold as a witch's tit in a tin cup on Christmas Eve. However, there is something you can do for me."

"If it's in my power, consider it done. Shoot."

"Get lost and stay lost!" she shouted.

Cosmo's eyelids contracted until only two narrow strips of orbs glared at her. Then he rose and shuffled off to the bathroom. Shaking her head in disgust, Scarlett hurried out of the house.

"Seriously and from the bottom of my heart, darling," he called down the hall as he returned from the bathroom, "I really do want to come back to you, come back home. I can help you, and your organization. You know that. And I have a plan . . . Scarlett? Darling . . . ?"

Outside, her car started up and she drove off.

That Tuesday, as a somewhat dispirited Cosmo was being chauffeured down Springfield Road back to Philadelphia to catch a flight back to Washington, it was not quite 8:30 P.M. in Nucleanne, Switzerland. At Schlammer Engineering, Marianne Chaudet was about to leave the Legal Department on the fourth floor of the main building, when the discreet bleeping of a fax machine stopped her agitated rush for the door. Momentarily disoriented, she veered off into the secretarial section, where the machine had just disgorged a single sheet. The attorney snatched it up without bothering to read it and put it in her briefcase. Then she hurried down the corridor and ran down the stairs.

She felt a great urgency to see the Summermatter children. Shaken and chilled to the bone by news of the murder of Urs Summermatter, of which she had just received word from Chief Borli, she felt rage and sadness. Tears welled up whenever she thought of the gruesome deed.

"Bastards!" she hissed, slamming the personnel entrance door shut with such force that the walls shook. Her rage was directed at Hannibal and the other bosses, like that caricature of a general, Breckerlin, and His Holiness Adam Schlammer himself, that slicked-back greaseball! What nerve to announce earlier that evening that Summermatter had defrauded the Company by engaging in smuggling activities! His death, Schlammer employees had been informed, was the result of an internal feud between rivaling gangs of smugglers, a dispute involving cocaine, or weapons, or both. The

Schlammer Group's executive management expressed its regrets over losing such a valuable employee, assuring everybody that Summermatter's children would be well taken care of, of course.

As she hurried toward her dark-blue Alfa Romeo, her growled exclamations came in disjointed bursts, "Filthy—gang—of killers!"

The time had come to get even with Schlammer. Tomorrow, she'd hand her entire dossier over to that dashing chief of police.

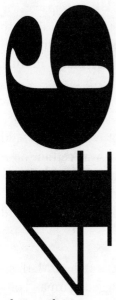

Thick strands of roots covered the small cave in which the kids had established their secret base camp. The densely woven branchwork of a majestically weathered, stubborn old fir tree shielded their hideout from view. The only way in was from above, along a steep, overgrown path, well camouflaged by nature.

Staring up into the luminous night sky, Mark, Tony, and Jessie Summermatter lay in silence on their sleeping bags. Mark tightly clutched the sobbing Jessie's hand, while Tony chewed mechanically on a twig he had broken off the tree. It seemed as if the bright, full moon was the only friend left to them.

The police chief, in person, had brought them the terrible news as they sat at the kitchen table around seven o'clock, waiting for dad to come home. Everything was prepared. Jessie had placed a dish of ready-made pasta and spring rolls from the neighborhood deli in the microwave oven. The moment the unmistakable wheeze of the old Volvo announced his arrival, she'd start up the oven, which she had set at eighty seconds. Tony was slicing tomatoes. Mark gently lifted two tiny frogs out of the terrarium and placed them in a small tin box dotted with air holes.

A giant of a man, the chief of police did his utmost to dampen the shock, squatting to embrace the boys with his powerful wrestler's arms. Then, in a low, gentle voice, speaking slowly and carefully, he told them that their father had suffered a fatal accident up in the mountains. All help had come too late, he told them, and broke off to wipe the tears from his eyes. Urs Summermatter's children stared at him with wide-open eyes: speechless, incredulous, in shock.

Jessie's movements were stiff, like a sleepwalker's. She sat down on the couch as if in a trance. Outside, a bell tolled the hour; a faucet's hollow drip reverberated through the kitchen space; the police chief slapped his notebook on the table. Forever after, to the end of his life, Mark would remember these sounds, live with them and with every movement, every gesture, made in that kitchen during that eternity of death.

He himself had ended the silence by asking, pragmatically, how this thing had happened and where his father was now. The police chief evaded the questions by telling them that everything would be sorted out in the morning, though one thing was certain now: their dad, an outstanding pilot, had not crashed with the helicopter.

"He was . . . there were weapons involved. Gangsters. Your dad was . . ." the police chief broke off.

"Murdered," Tony finished for him.

The chief sheepishly kneaded his neck as he watched Mark silently feed white mice to the snakes. Jessie hugged Karma. Tony sat at the table, stunned, gazing dully at the sharp blade of his folding knife. The chief forced himself to give them some information as to what would happen next. Then he took his leave, with a clumsy admonition to Mark to be strong, the way his father would have wanted him to be.

Marianne Chaudet, who was next to be informed by the police chief, rang the doorbell at nine o'clock. Marianne frequently visited the Summermatter home; she gave piano lessons to Tony and got along well with Urs. The children trusted her, but their decision to run away had already been firmly made. All they wanted was to get out of there, away, not to have to face people anymore, to be alone with their grief.

When Marianne left again to quickly drive home and get her things, she laid the fax sheet from her bag on the kitchen table. Mark glanced at it while Tony silently rolled up their sleeping bags and packed the rucksack. Moving like robots, they picked out their favorite things: Mark—the box with the frogs; Jessie—her mouth organ; Tony—his firecrackers and fuses. They wheeled silently through the deserted streets of Nucleanne on their mountain bikes, with Karma trotting along beside Jessie. Unnoticed by anyone, they reached the footpath through the meadows. Only the crunching of the bike wheels on the bright gravel path disturbed the nocturnal silence.

Their mountain cave hideout lay approximately three meters above the broad rocky promontory that jutted like a pulpit out over the ravine. Mark and Tony had tied a bright yellow nylon rope, thirty meters long, to the mighty trunk of the sheltering fir. Intended as a means of escape in case their hiding place was attacked from above, the rope allowed them to descend to the other ledges and footholds below.

Far down in the ravine, turbulent whitewater rushed through a bed of glacial rock, as it had since the dawn of history. Time seemed to stand still, but the kids' minds were moving at a frantic pace, torturing them with questions. Familiar pictures reeled off; they heard their father's voice. Crushed by the horror, they wept and moaned softly to themselves, inwardly calling terrible vengeance down upon the heads of the killers.

At last a merciful sleep enveloped them. Only faithful Karma stayed alert and watchful, now and then casting a sad look at her beloved charges.

As the morning sun rose above a grayish-blue ocean of billowing clouds, a soft pink glow spread over the sleek, white body of the Falcon 900. Its three tail engines quickly boosted the elegant craft to its cruising altitude of 33,000 feet, keeping it firmly on a north-westerly course. The projected flight route led across the English Channel and the southern tip of Ireland, out into the black Atlantic night, then on toward Newfoundland and the eastern coast of North America.

Inside, amid the luxurious appointments of the walnut-paneled interior, Hazmoudi dozed in a black leather seat. Up front, in the cockpit, the pilot chanted his ID mantra as he tried to establish radio contact with air traffic control in Shannon: "Hotel Romeo Lima Tango Bravo to Shannon Air Traffic Control, come in Shannon!"

At this hour, just before five A.M., it took some time before the Shannon traffic control responded to the routine communication. The pilot reported position, course and designated flight route. In return, he was given the weather report, radar frequencies, routing information, and instructions to climb to 42,000 feet, the customary cruising altitude for privately owned aircraft.

Satisfied, the captain checked his watch. The unusually weak head winds reported by Shannon allowed him to calculate that they would arrive one hour earlier than expected.

The Avenger was seated in the tail section, eyes half closed, his face a pale, impenetrable mask. For the umpteenth time he went over the details of the carefully worked-out plan in his mind. The bomb was operational. Before taking it aboard, Krauthammer had subjected all its functions to a fastidious point-by-point check, adhering meticulously to the user manual that had been played into his hands. This task completed, the eccentric old bird had assured him that the detonator would function as smoothly and reliably as a Swiss watch. They had then given the ignition dialogue a dry run, finally setting ignition time at 2100 hours EDT on July 4.

Everything humanly possible having been done at this stage, not much could be expected to go wrong. Still, the seasoned terrorist remained skeptical, continuing to wrack his brains for weaknesses that might foul up the operation. Like this Hazmoudi, the Iraqi, that arrogant bastard, who couldn't be trusted. Who, as far as the Avenger was concerned, would look much better with a big hole in his head.

At dawn, the sleek craft landed at the small local airport at Reading near Philadelphia. Three men quickly transferred the Rock'O'Clock granite housing and its content from the plane to a waiting Toyota Landcruiser for the short ride to the outskirts of the city.

Hazmoudi rode up front with the driver. Sensing the Avenger's gaze on the back of his neck, he turned his head. The Hamas terrorist's hard, gray eyes rested indifferently on him; the man's thin lips twisted into a disdainful grin. Hazmoudi turned away, uneasy. The Avenger's presence was a bad omen! Again the Iraqi reminded himself to be careful.

Shortly before six o'clock that morning, on a deserted street off Lancaster Avenue, the driver of the Landcruiser got out and opened a side entrance to the Schlammer North America warehouse. Bushes and dense shrubbery spreading out from an adjoining patch of forest shielded the gate from casual observation. Quickly and silently, the men went to the intricately locked partition where the real Rock'O'Clock was kept. Having been employed as a watchman in the warehouse for several months, the driver knew what he was doing as he applied the entry code. With a furtive glance at the man, Hazmoudi wondered how much Fahimi was paying him for this job: twenty thousand dollars, or twenty-five?

It took the inside man only moments to open the steel grid door. Hazmoudi noted the moldy air and wrinkled his nose. A small, lean shadow scurrying away made him blink. Rats, he observed. Disgusting! A narrow gutter ran along the side to a barred opening in the wall. Hazmoudi gave it a cursory glance. Was the wire mesh damaged? Possibly. So what!

While the driver brought up a forklift, Hazmoudi jogged back to the Landcruiser. Three of them pushed the green chunk of granite from the Toyota's loading gate onto the forklift. The driver cautiously drove his load to the clock cage, where he slowly lowered it to the concrete floor. Then he lifted the identical-looking Rock'O'Clock unit from its wooden pallet and maneuvered it along the storage racks out the door.

He drove the forklift past the Landcruiser, to a gaping hole in a tree-lined corner of the warehouse yard. The driver lowered the Rock'O'Clock unit to the rim of the open sewage pit. Hazmoudi and the Avenger strained to tilt the heavy object, until gravity took over and the masterpiece of Swiss watchmaking splashed down and was gone.

After the forklift had pushed the heavy cover sections back in place over the pit, the two men returned silently to the warehouse. They placed Hazmoudi's granite clock bomb on the empty pallet inside the partition where, only moments before, the original Rock'O'Clock had stood. Hazmoudi stepped around the pallet to read a computer printout tacked to a shelf:

CLISSOT >Rock'O'Clock<, Schlammer North America. Delivery: July 4, no later than 3 p.m. On order from: Swiss Embassy, Washington, D.C. Deliver to site: City Tavern, Philadelphia. SCHL/NA-694793-BBA.

He nodded, pleased. The granite housing was sealed in a skin of thick, hard plastic. Hazmoudi stepped onto the edge of the pallet and leaned over the clock's cover section. He carefully sliced the plastic open with a knife, baring a hinged flap the size of a large notepad. He twisted a key out from under some heavy-duty carpet tape that held it in place on the granite surface. Next, he unlocked the flap and flipped it open, then jogged back to the car to get a flashlight.

The commotion in the storage area alerted a young weasel, which had wandered in from the surrounding woodland to feast on the warehouse's rat population. The predator was a dark blur as it leaped from the shelves to the top of the Rock'O'Clock package. Its shiny eyes bright with cunning and curiosity, it pawed and sniffed at the strange material, pricking up its ears when it heard the man returning. Flanks palpitating with nervous energy, poised on the brink of flight, the weasel pivoted suddenly and slipped through the open hatch into the clock's interior.

The Iraqi bent once more over the housing. Frowning, he compared the diagram on his checklist with the electronic gadgetry he saw inside the clock. Outside, the Landcruiser's engine started up, combining with the whine of the forklift to form a high-decibel sound curtain. Hazmoudi located the master switch for the power supply inside the housing, some four, five inches to the side of the hatch. He pushed it to ON, closed and locked the flap, then refastened the key with the carpet tape.

The watchman-cum-burglar locked the entrance. A scant thirty minutes after the Falcon 900 had landed, the Landcruiser left the warehouse area, with only the watchman staying behind. Hazmoudi and the grimly taciturn Avenger headed south towards the Pennsylvania Turnpike. In a couple of hours, a local trucking company would pick up the false granite clock with the nuclear charge and take it into Philadelphia. As a special transport on official business for the Swiss Embassy, the truck would be accompanied by a police escort. Quite inconspicuous, no problem! Hazmoudi congratulated himself on a job well done.

After half an hour of monotonous driving, Hazmoudi suddenly pulled off the road into the parking lot of a roadside diner and truck stop. The Avenger stirred from a professional half-slumber and reached for his gun. Shrugging, the Iraqi calmly told him to keep his shirt on. "Stopping to take a leak, that's all."

He rolled down the front windows and took a deep breath of cool morning air, wondering how to get rid of that nasty fellow sitting next to him. Well, he told himself, you'll come up with something. You always do!

They moved slowly past an enormous eighteen-wheeler whose

driver was just climbing up into the cabin. Hazmoudi rolled to a stop hard in front of the tracks leading into a carwash. NEXT CAR, NEXT CAR, NEXT CAR, flashed a sign above the entry port. Hazmoudi had an inspiration.

"Get you anything?" he casually asked the Avenger, pushing the gear stick into neutral.

"Yes. Coffee. With cream, and plenty of sugar. And let's not waste any time here!"

The Avenger impatiently checked in the mirrors. The parking area was relatively deserted. With a roar of power that shook their vehicle, the big rig next to them came alive. Hazmoudi switched off the ignition and got out. He walked casually around the rear of the Landcruiser, stopped, put one shoulder down, and pushed with all his might. The Landcruiser's front wheels moved slowly onto the descending track. Hazmoudi kept pushing until all four wheels had engaged.

As the vehicle rolled forward and broke the light beam, the wash cycle started up with a jolt and a rattle. Hazmoudi jumped on the footboard of the moving truck and stuck a handful of hundred-dollar bills through the open window. The Landcruiser had disappeared into a deluge of steaming water and foam.

Seasoned though he might be, the Avenger was caught off guard by the sudden action. He reacted swiftly, but not swiftly enough, frantically punching the window controls to close the windows. But the power was off. As he fumbled to get to the ignition key, hot, pressurized water splashed into his eyes. He pushed the door open, managed to get a leg out. Heavy rotating brushes mercilessly jammed his foot between door and frame. His scream got lost in the roar and splash of the water and the whirring hiss of the brushes. Encountering no obstruction until they connected with the man's head, the two sets of brushes knocked him half-unconscious, and their violent soaping, rubbing, and hosing did the rest. As the brushes retreated, they tore open the front doors.

The Avenger ended up out of the car with his head on one of the tracks, directly in front of the heavy rollers. The axle section of a fiercely spinning brush sliced into his skull. An alarm began to hoot as the entire system ground to a halt. Foam frothed pink on water dyed crimson by the Avenger's blood.

Without bothering to check in the rearview mirror, the truck driver casually pocketed the five hundred dollars Hazmoudi had thrust at him.

It wasn't until the Iraqi got to New York a few hours later that SCUDO finally received an urgent report on the Falcon 900 that had landed at Reading airport. Flight control detailed the flight route of the suspicious aircraft with the Honduran registration HR-LTB. Inquiries at Reading elicited the information that, half an hour later, after refueling, the plane had taken off for Durham, North Carolina. In Durham, the Falcon's captain had requested rerouting to Miami, where the procedure was repeated. This time, the craft received permission to proceed to San José, Costa Rica. By the time all of this was established, the Falcon had been flying outside U.S. airspace for over an hour.

Bern, Wednesday, July 4

Heavy rain drummed on the low tile roof as Stephanie Kramer gently pushed against the door and cautiously peered into the twilight that contoured the room's furniture with the pale light of dawn. The loud drumming of the torrential rain almost drowned out the bell of the nearby cathedral as it tolled the hour: five A.M. Her heart beat high in her throat as she stood again under the ancient roof beams of Ralph Christen's bachelor pad—for the second time in forty-eight hours.

But something was wrong. The antique couch where she'd dozed off only the day before lay overturned in front of the panoramic window. As her eyes adjusted to the dim light, she beheld a terrible chaos. Stunned, she made herself move forward. With the third step she stumbled over something soft on the floor. Screaming, she fell, then bounced back up, propelled by the sight of a man's horribly twisted features. The body lay stretched out on the dark floorboards, the head angled grotesquely against a paneled wall. The bulging dead eyes in a ghostly, distorted visage stared blankly at the mess.

As she began to recover from her shock, she noted mechanically that the cacophony of water sounds had given way to silence. The rain had stopped; what a relief! She began to look more calmly at the situation. This was clearly an officer, posted to guard the apartment. Somebody came in and killed him, then searched the place. She advanced cautiously into the bedroom. In there, the closet doors stood open, drawers were yanked out of chests, and articles of clothing were strewn around the room, covering the beige carpet.

She groped her way into the kitchen and switched on the light. What she needed was a stiff drink to give her courage. Surveying the counter by the sink, she noticed some leftovers: bits of prosciutto, bread crumbs, an opened box of Amaretti candy standing next to a neatly sliced half tomato. Sorrow flooded her heart. It was as if Ralph had just walked out to answer the door. Sighing deeply, she was about to open the refrigerator, when she heard footsteps outside the apartment.

Her blood ran cold as ice. It had to be the police, a new guard! Her mind spun; she feared being caught red-handed. She looked frantically about for an escape route. That little window over there, yes! No, impossible! She'd never be able to squeeze through it. She heard the door to the hall open, voices whispering. There was light. Please, please, don't come into the kitchen, she prayed.

A tiger-striped kitten prowled the ledge outside. It pushed a window sash open with its nose and silently leapt down to the counter. Velvet paws, Stephanie noted admiringly, as the kitten poked and sniffed at the leftover bits of ham. The reporter cautiously moved closer, but the cute little animal recoiled shyly, brushing against the candy box as it retreated. Stephanie watched helplessly as the box wobbled over the edge and hit the stone tiles of the kitchen floor with a shattering crash.

There was a shouted exclamation from the living room, followed by quick, approaching footsteps. Only now did she notice a diskette amid the spilled candy on the floor. She stooped quickly, picked it up and slipped it under her jeans, inside her panties. Maybe this floppy disk contained the evidence which the intruder or intruders had been looking for!

"You'll be safe here, Ralph," she whispered, patting her jeans where the diskette lay snug against her sleekly curving belly.

A big man burst into the kitchen. He held a huge revolver, raised high in a two-fisted grip, its muzzle aimed straight at the space between her eyes. Crouching in the firing position, his back to the wall, he quickly scanned the room. Satisfied that there was no one else, he straightened up and shouted at her, "What the hell are you doing here?"

Stephanie stared at the huffing, puffing, fat-bellied man with the weather-beaten face who looked to be around fifty. His grayish blond hair was cut short, barely covering strategic portions of his bullet-shaped head. As he chewed nervously on his thick lips, his small, mischievous eyes studied her intently. Again, he darted quick, practiced glances around the room. His bulbous nose and carelessly shaved chin gave him a mercenary look.

"I'm the new shift," she said coolly. "As you can see, my partner is down and I've called for backup. Who're you suppose'ta be? And stop waving that revolver in my face!"

Inwardly, she was shaking. This could never work! The chunky guy certainly looked like a cop. His partner came in, took one look at her and told her, "We're FBI and you're under arrest. Let's go!"

This other man was skinny as a scarecrow, with a pale face and worried expression that contrasted sharply with his jet-black hair, meticulous haircut, heavy eyebrows, coal-black, deep-set eyes and bushy mustache. The one with the gun moved his shoulders in mock pity. Smiling cutely, he said, "We have your picture and description. A pretty face is easy to remember. You're Stephanie Kramer, aren't you?"

Stephanie responded with a very slow, minimal nod of her head. The game was up. Still . . .

"Where's the police? I mean our police?" she blurted out. The two men exchanged quick glances.

"I'm chief investigator, FBI office, American Embassy," lied the scarecrow. "Bill here's based in Washington. We're working hand in hand with the Swiss police on the Kern assassination. Sorry, Ms. Kramer, but you're a prime suspect. This here," he tilted his head back in the direction of the living room, "doesn't do anything to brighten the picture. Right now, you happen to be the most wanted person in this country. You've taken your police on quite a merry chase, haven't you?" He forced a smile. "So, please, cut out the Virgin Mary act. You're coming along for a little chat."

Her arms combatively akimbo, the reporter dug in.

"I'm not going with anyone, least of all you," she said. "You have no authority over me. I'll run out and scream. The tenants in this house will back me up, and I have nothing to hide from the police. So you know what you can do. Don't make me spell it out for you."

Summoning the last bit of courage in her reservoir of fading strength, she marched out of the kitchen, past the corpse in the living room, toward the front door. But the scarecrow caught up with her, locking her upper arm in a viselike grip that belied his scrawny stature.

"Don't be a fool, Ms. Kramer," he said in excellent German. "If the police find you here, you're done for." Stepping up to the body, he pointed at the bloody head. "This man's skull was bashed in with a heavy object, probably that ashtray there, which is made of stone. What do you think will happen if the police find your fingerprints on it?"

With a start, she remembered that she had indeed touched the ashtray, thoughtlessly, to push it aside. For a few moments she stood motionless, her mind racing. Should she start screaming and try to make a run for it, then get von Alp to rescue her? What if the police were already downstairs, in the street? She'd run right into their arms! What she really needed was time.

"So, what's the difference," she said, stalling. "You'll hand me over to the cops anyway."

"No we won't," Bill said emphatically. "If you cooperate with us, we'll protect you. We'll put you in a safe house. Here, let me show you what we're after." He reached into the breast pocket of his coat and pulled out a crumpled photograph. "This is the man we want to talk to you about."

She felt a stab in her heart that continued all the way into the pit of her stomach. In the photo, Ken Custer beamed his most charming smile at the world.

"Why? What do you want with him?" she stammered. The two men exchanged eloquent glances. Instead of replying to her question, they started pushing her toward the door. Enraged, she pushed back, swung around and angrily faced them.

"I asked you what you want with this man!"

She threw a stunning if-looks-could-kill glance at the scarecrow.

Instead of dropping dead, he gestured placatingly, saying, "All right, ma'am, if you really want to know, the man's a criminal, a mercenary employed by the drug cartels. He's a killer and a traitor, right at the top of every respectable wanted list in the world."

Waving a hand at the body on the floor, beer-bellied Bill added, "We're sure this . . . uh . . . police officer here is just one more of his victims. Custer tried to set you up, pin this kill on you. The police should be here any moment. You'll be arrested and—"

As if on cue, the wailing of police sirens could be heard from the street outside.

"All right, that's it. We're out of here," Bill shouted.

This time she obeyed meekly. Shocked and demoralized, all she wanted was to give up, throw in the towel, and tell all. Downstairs, on the wet sidewalk, they shoved her unceremoniously into a dark-green Detroit marvel with golden-spoked wheels. With a savage roar, the engine came to life, and the big Pontiac leaped like a tiger out of its parking slot, nearly sideswiping the first of the three squad cars that came tearing down the street.

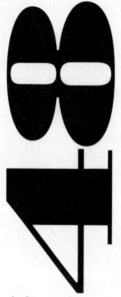

They parked at the train station near a low building with phone booths, elevators and escalators. On the square, people were hurrying to and fro to catch their trains. Buses arrived and departed, and the sun broke through the clouds and warmed the wet asphalt, sending up pale wraiths of steam. Stephanie stared entranced at the escalator. Heads appeared out of the murky depth of the stairwell, followed by bodies, supported by legs, stepping off and carrying them away from the stair segments which were being swallowed up again by the floor.

Only yesterday I was a perky bundle of energy, she mused darkly. And now look at me—broken down, depressed and abandoned!

Turning, Bill Conklin glanced at her from the passenger seat in front. "You know, Kramer, what with the police suspecting you of killing Peter Kern, I'd say you're in a hell of a fix."

If her neck hadn't felt as if someone was strangling her, Stephanie might have tried to object.

Speaking matter-of-factly, like a home-appliance salesman telling a housewife how to operate a toaster, Conklin continued, "Kern's housekeeper saw your car parked in front of the prime minister's mansion. The police secured evidence pointing to you in the vicinity of the bodies—threads of clothing caught in the underbrush, footprints, that kind of thing. A farmer saw a woman running along a roadside ditch. He picked your picture out of dozens of photos. Also, you've got a motive."

"What? You must be crazy!" She started pummeling Conklin's broad shoulders with her fists, a courageous but ineffectual effort. He shrugged her off, unimpressed.

"Fact is, you do have excellent contacts in circles where terrorist operations against nuclear plants are planned."

"That is absurd," she said, trying to sound calm and collected.

"So you say, but we happen to know that Custer is in Switzerland to buy nuclear weapons. For the Iraqis. We have photographic evidence placing him on the premises of the Schlammer Group— where they threw him out. While covertly trying to get back in, he got into a brawl with Schlammer security personnel. After that, the real slaughtering starts. First, a security officer of the Schlammer Group, shot in the head execution-style. A Custer trademark! Then the brutal killing of the chief magistrate, arranged by Custer because the clever Christen got in his way. I'm only citing facts, Ms. Kramer."

Although she appeared apathetic as she listened to the man's tirade of nonsense, Stephanie in fact was wide awake. Thinking ahead to her appointment with the Summermatter kids that afternoon, she glanced up at the large clock above the entrance to the station: a quarter past eight! The commuter action had picked up further, with people swarming all over the square. Nothing in the world could make her run out on "her" kids! The very thought of Mark, Tony and Jessie gave her fresh courage, rekindling her fighting spirit.

"Custer is the kind of guy who befouls his own nest," she heard Conklin drone on. "He used to be one of us; the secret service taught him all he knows. Now he does his killing for others, blowing away our own best people. Nor would I be surprised to learn that our old friend >Keycop< is behind the killing of that pilot. The president of the Schlammer Group has told the police that the pilot had stolen electronic components from the company and would have made a profitable business out of it if it hadn't backfired. Custer appears to have been a receiver for this stolen merchandise—"

"A pilot? What pilot are you talking about?" Stephanie cut in. Even though she dreaded the answer, she leaned forward to hear it.

"His name is Sommerman or some such," said the supposed FBI man, shrugging indifferently.

Stephanie could not suppress a groan. "Where is Summermatter now?"

"Dead."

Shutting her eyes, she sank back into the Pontiac's leather upholstery. Her heart ached as if ready to burst. She breathed deeply in and out, a single thought—flight!—pounding in her head. Her elbow was only a few inches away from the door latch. I'll push open the door and plunge into the crowd. Yes, why not, what have I got to lose, she thought feverishly.

In that very instant, she saw a bald-headed motorcyclist get off his heavy bike and stride toward the restrooms inside the windowless building. Her plan matured in seconds.

"If you don't mind, gentlemen, I have to go . . . uh . . . pee-pee?" she exclaimed, pushing open the door. She had caught Conklin napping.

"Fuck!" he shouted as he stumbled out of the car and ran after her. Just inside the entrance, the restroom area was divided into two sections: Ladies, and Gentlemen. Conklin saw instantly that there was no other exit. Easy does it, he told himself, you've got her up a tree, there's no way she's gonna get away from you! He slowly walked back out and positioned himself on the sidewalk, taking advantage of the opportunity to light a cigarette.

Stephanie had taken a few steps into the brightly-lit restroom section, then turned abruptly toward Gentlemen and boldly walked into the pissoir. Apart from the bald-headed biker, to her immense relief, there was not a soul in sight. The leather-armored road warrior was going through a series of contortions in front of the urinal. When he managed at last to free his member, Stephanie stepped up and aggressively started ogling the exposed flesh. The man looked up with a puzzled frown.

Before he could say anything, she shoved a 100-Franc bill under his pug nose. An inane grin spread over his face. She explained hastily what it was she expected him to do for the money. Her grim expression gave ample evidence of a desperate determination, her fierce tone and flashing eyes tolerated no argument. Never had the burly tough met a woman like her, least of all with his dick hanging over a piss bowl! Totally flustered, he missed the bowl with an anguished spurt of urine. It trickled down his right leg onto a knife sheath that protruded from his leather boots.

Never leaving her eyes off him as he stuffed his Willie Wednesday back in his pants, she ordered him to repeat her instructions. He managed with some difficulty, garbling everything in his excitement. With admiring and encouraging glances, she urged him to go ahead and do his thing, all the while making sure the now quite plainly aroused fellow was walking ahead of her as they left the pissoir. A few moments later, when she heard the throaty growl of the bike starting up, she sprinted out onto the square.

Outside in the Pontiac, Special Agent Atlee was gazing dully across to Conklin, who stood in front of the restroom entrance—now impatiently rocking up and down on his heels, now ponderously pacing the sidewalk. Atlee was thinking that maybe his newfound partner needed to go in and relieve himself as well, when a big bus drove up and stopped closely in front of the Pontiac, distracting him for an instant. When he looked again, he saw the Kramer woman come bursting out of the restroom building.

"Action!" he shouted through the windshield at Conklin, who of course couldn't hear him and moreover was looking in the wrong direction. Stephanie's sudden sortie totally discombobulated Conklin. By the time he regrouped and managed to get his reluctant bulk into gear, she was already straddling the motorcycle's passenger saddle, her arms wrapped firmly around the massive torso of the bare-headed biker. Judging from the fellow's blissed-out expression, she was positively making his day.

The biker retracted his head turtlelike into the leather folds of his shoulder padding and ecstatically turned up the throttle, jump-clutching his hog. The bike reared up and sprang forward with an earshattering roar, doing wheelies along the curb and all across the square, scattering pedestrians left and right. Before Atlee lost sight of the pair, the biker's orgasmically transfigured grin was imprinted forever on his memory.

A snorting Conklin rushed back to the car. He squeezed in behind the wheel, cursing as he fumbled with the ignition. From the back seat, Atlee saw what would happen: the bus slowly started moving just as Conklin gunned the Pontiac out of the parking slot. They slammed into the right front fender of the bus, which was crowded with commuters. His face lobster-red, the enraged Conklin belabored the steering wheel with both fists. Accident, cops, insurance reports, that was all he needed right now! Cursing his luck, he twisted head and shoulders to look backwards, then shifted into reverse. Just then he caught a glimpse of the big motorcycle disappearing into the multilevel parking complex across the square. Gnashing his teeth, he floored the gas pedal.

"What's your name?" Stephanie shouted into the rushing wind as the bike leaned precariously into the spiral driveway leading to the exit two levels up. The monster road warrior turned his head, his face a gargoyle grimace. "Bison," he shouted back.

Her laughter froze as she saw the Pontiac, sliding through a turn behind them, its headlights on high beam.

"Faster!" she shouted as they hurtled out into the blinding daylight and heavy traffic on a steeply declining street. Up the hill came a Landrover with a flashing yellow light, pulling something that looked like an aluminum horse trailer. A sign above the windshield read *Caution Animal Transport*. Bison saw the blinking light out of the corner of his eyes. With a couple of breakneck swivels he just barely scraped by a descending streetcar which had got halfway through the intersection in front of the parking complex. Accompanied by angrily shrilling streetcar bells, Bison gained the opposite side of the street, thundering past the Superior Court Building.

Just as Conklin and Atlee came barreling through the exit, the Landrover and streetcar passed each other and blocked the intersection. Brakes squealing, Conklin tried to bull the Pontiac around the obstacle that loomed ahead. Atlee barely had time to read the second inscription on the trailer: *BÄRENGRABEN—BEAR PIT— FOSSE AUX OURSES*. Then they slammed into the rear of the Landrover. Locked in a death grip, the two cars collided with the streetcar. The force of the impact threw the rear portion of the green streetcar off the tracks. Then the entire streetcar slowly keeled over, accompanied by showers of sparks, a cacophony of screeching metal and shattering glass, and the screaming of the passengers aboard the tram.

The animal trailer had been torn from its hitch and upended. Twisted off the hinges, its heavily barred door hung open. Inside the Pontiac, Conklin wrestled the inflated airbag aside. Moaning and groaning, he laboriously inched out of the vehicle. Atlee, too, managed to crawl out onto the sun-blasted asphalt, bouncing up amid terrified shrieks from the gathering crowd. Conklin was bracing himself to face an enraged lynch mob when he saw that the screams were caused by two bears that had scrambled out of the trailer.

At least as scared as the crowd, the animals were now ambling up and down alongside the upended streetcar, looking for an escape route. People screamed and scattered. The bears suddenly rushed the crowd, disappearing up the street in the direction of the university. In the confusion, Conklin and Atlee discreetly strolled back to the parking complex. When they got close enough, they reached the sheltering darkness with two extravagant leaps.

That Wednesday morning, Melanie Borli viewed with great interest the list of contents for Central Archives, a function linked with all the terminals and computers in her Crack Shoppe. This arrangement allowed her to store texts from all her computers in a database, freeing the hard-disk space in all of her desktops. However, Central Archives was a demand function, activated only upon request. Even though last night's client had not requested this service, her report was now listed in Central Archives! Melanie Borli was staring right at it, so there could be no doubt. How this was possible was a mystery to her—one she'd have to get to the bottom of!

To guard against possible loss of the document by the client, Melanie copied it onto a diskette. As she did this, the sensational title aroused her curiosity. SLIMY, SLIMIER, SCHLAMMER, she read. Since there appeared to be a lull in the store, she clicked the text onto the screen. What she read almost took her breath away:

Kern Assassination Facts

I, Stephanie Kramer, had no part in the assassination of Prime Minister Kern, but I was an eyewitness to it. I believe that I, too, was meant to be killed. The fact that I was late for an appointment to accompany the prime minister on a jog saved my life, at least for

*now. I saw the assassin, who has since made two attempts to kill me.
I managed to get away. I then penetrated the nuclear cavern at Nucleanne. Schlammer uses these underground facilities for the clandestine storage of weapons, probably nuclear, and to store hazardous
radioactive materials. I am certain that Prime Minister Kern had to
die because he found out about this. My own life was saved by an
American, Kenneth W. Custer. >Keycop< works for a drug cartel
and is probably buying weapons from Schlammer. This is a matter
of life and death. The following facts serve to indicate who engineered
the assassination of Prime Minister Kern and the murder of Ralph
Christen. I am about to obtain the final bits of conclusive evidence.
Should I lose my life in this endeavor, this report is to be published
in the* International Herald Tribune. . . .

Melanie Borli could read no further. Impulsively clicking the
document shut, she inhaled and exhaled deeply a few times. Call
Thomas, now! she told herself, reaching for the phone. Then she
drew back and took time out to think. One line in Kramer's report
stood out in her memory—a matter of life and death!

Like Christen, Thomas stood in the frontline of this sordid business. She must not endanger him. Then she had a crazy idea. She
stuffed the diskette into her handbag and resolutely dialed the
direct-access number.

The killing of the chief magistrate, one of their own, had whipped Borli's grim-faced staff into frantic activity. Forensic specialists from the criminal investigation department, just arrived from Zurich, were busy evaluating microevidence secured at the site. International cooperation via Interpol was functioning smoothly: >Keycop< had left a trail.

Day and night Borli's people were called upon to process a mountain of data and information. He himself had picked up where Christen's trail of evidence left off. Watching Schlammer with eagle's eyes from a safe distance, the chief of police patiently drew his circles, tightening the noose with each turn. At the same time, Borli was careful not to repeat the mistakes Christen had made. The chief magistrate had attacked, threatened to break taboos, causing the powers that be to close ranks.

Along with all the other information was a strange report concerning an F/A-18 pilot who had just barely avoided a collision with a helicopter in the mountains. Borli decided to call the Emmen air base. The pilot in question was still on duty, and again related the details of the incident, adding that civilian air traffic in that particular restricted zone was considered highly unusual. Either air safety had erroneously approved the routing, or some joker of a chopper pilot had violated it in order to take a short cut. Either way, this was unheard of!

Borli asked the pilot if he'd been able to identify the helicopter, or noticed anything else that might be relevant.

Lieutenant Colonel Carrard told Borli that identification had been impossible at the speed at which he'd been traveling. All he'd seen was a red Super-Puma, a type of rotorcraft also used in the Swiss Army. However . . . Carrard hesitated, then mentioned the dosimeter with which the F/A-18 was experimentally equipped. He told Borli that its warning light had flashed briefly. Back on base, a check had indicated that a small dosage of radioactivity had indeed been measured. In the pilot's opinion, only the red Super-Puma could have been the source of the radiation.

The minister of justice, who had dropped in unexpectedly, knew nothing of all this. In the police chief's considered opinion, the joker who sat across from him didn't know his ass from his elbow when it came to police work. Borli was still hemming and hawing in response to the man's accusations of sloppy police work, when the telephone rang. On the other side of the glass partition Max nodded and grimaced, pointing importantly at the phone. Borli picked it up, making regretful gestures at the minister.

"Hi, it's me," said his wife. "Listen to this—your phone is bugged."

"I'm in a meeting, Sweet, can I . . ."

"I've got to see you. Right now!"

Borli sheepishly scratched the back of his head. "Not now, Dindin, please!"

The stuffy-looking minister of justice shot a suggestive glance at the secretary he had brought along.

"For god's sake listen, Thomas. You remember that spot where we made love the other day? And you told me . . . there's nothing like getting laid out in the wild? I'll meet you there."

"Getting what . . . out in the wild? Lai . . . d? Sorry!" Involuntarily, his hand went to his mouth. "Laid," he whispered to the minister, "Laid back. Just a figure of speech," then into the phone: "You mean now? Do you have any idea what you're asking, Dindin? Dindin! Hello?"

But Dindin had already hung up. Borli jumped up, gesturing apologetically at the minister, who suddenly looked constipated.

"Sorry, sir, it's, uh, Dindin, my wife, I mean," he stammered, hastily backing out of the office, "it won't take long." He sprinted through the office area, toward the exit.

Frowning at his secretary, the minister of justice tapped impatiently on the edge of the desk. "Tell me, Mrs. Schneeberger, do you know this, uh, Dindin? Chief Borli's wife? Sounds like a real hot tomato, what? Well, Schnee, perhaps you should take a closer look at Borli's personal file. If the wife of the chief of police is a sex maniac, why, I believe that would be of concern to all of us!"

Stephanie Kramer was in high spirits as she rested her cheek against the road warrior's shoulder, enjoying the wind ruffling her hair. The cool, fresh breeze did wonders for her. Squinting upward, she watched the contours of roofs and trees rushing by. The sensation of speed and the low, even purr of the engine were intoxicating.

As they hit the freeway, she shouted into his ear, "Bison, you're great!" Bison responded by wrenching the accelerator as far as it would go.

As they barreled through the morning on the big Honda, her mind took wing. Abruptly, she thought of Old Man Arik. His country hideaway was very close to here—why on earth hadn't she thought of this before? Better late than never, she told herself, slapping Bison's shoulder and gesturing in the direction of an upcoming exit.

He nodded, grinning suggestively, and turned into a narrow path toward a field of wheat swaying invitingly in the summer wind. Stephanie figured it was time to straighten out a potential misunderstanding.

Without fuss she pulled the knife from the biker's boot holster and pushed it through his leather pants until she felt the sharp tip of the blade nicking his butt. He let out a savage roar.

Stephanie screamed in his ear, "If you don't get back on the road, I'll cut your balls off, Bison. What we have is a business deal, hombre, not a roll in the hay!"

"Shit," moaned the monstrous biker, pressing a palm to his throbbing buttock. As he pulled his hand back, it brushed over Stephanie's supple thighs, brushed over them again, then came to rest on one. She did nothing to stop it.

Ten minutes later they trundled noisily into the large gravel yard in front of the old winery mansion. Hillside vineyards enfolded the estate, which bordered on a lake some distance from town. A tall, broad roof with weathered brown tiles sheltered the spread's whitewashed residential portion as well as the adjoining stables. A field-green Range Rover was parked near one of the buildings.

A great linden tree cast its shadow over the low terrace that jutted out from the residential section. Next to a tarp on the tile floor knelt a lean, dark-skinned man in a khaki shirt. He put down the center portion of the assault rifle he had been disassembling, then stood up and strolled over to Stephanie.

Bison watched as Stephanie negotiated with the lean dude, whom she called Joseph. He pointed towards the road warrior and his bike now and then, shaking his head every time. Finally, the woman simply shoved the fellow aside and marched toward the building.

"The bitch has balls," Bison muttered to his bike. He heard her call out a name he didn't catch, saw another man appear in the door. Nodding, satisfied, the road warrior kicked his hog alive and roared off, churning up a rooster tail of gravel and dust. Wow, he told himself, guffawing, a yard in cash for a ride in the country, a poke in the ass and a hard-on. Not bad for a morning's work!

The Old Man's silhouette filled the doorway as Stephanie approached. He wore elegant, dark-blue slacks and a subtly striped powder-blue silk shirt open at the neck. He brushed a strand of hair from his forehead. His sharply-cut features defied age; stout and of medium height, he might have been forty. Or sixty.

His gaze rested with benevolent interest on the young woman before him. There was a slightly testy note in his voice.

"What can I do for you? Do we have an appointment?"

"Arik, it's me!" said the woman, taking off her sunglasses.

"Stephanie!"

The Old Man stepped closer, looking her up and down. An expression of pure bliss swept away all doubt on his face, as his skeptical gaze yielded to a dazzle of beaming charm.

"That's what I call a surprise!" he exclaimed, embracing her tenderly, gently kissing her on both cheeks. "I hear the cops are after you. So what is your role in this Kern thing?"

Gallantly putting one arm around her waist, he walked her across the lawn to the terrace, where they seated themselves amid a constellation of comfortable-looking deck furniture.

"The suspense is killing me," he smiled, "I want to hear everything. What kind of craziness is this anyway? Is everything okay? Come, sit by me, over here!"

"Everything's just hunky-dory, Arik," she sighed, sinking into the green-and-blue striped upholstery. The lake lay broad and calm before them, not a breeze stirring its gray-blue waters this fine summer morning. Arik's estate sloped gradually down to the lakeshore; above their heads, leafy trees framed a brilliant July sky.

She began briefing the Old Man on what had happened since she last saw him a few days ago. Joseph brought iced tea and assorted cookies, then returned to cleaning his rifle. The Old Man listened attentively, munching on salt sticks, occasionally interrupting with a question. He was silent for a long while after Stephanie had finished. Lost in thought, he gazed across the water, at the darkly verdant, wooded hillside that lay above the far shore like a huge, broad back.

"That reminds me," he said at last, "a few years back we had a bit of a hand in the game. At that time, Switzerland was in danger of becoming something of a shunting yard for American weapons technology. You know, all the stuff the Soviets were dying to get their hands on. Even government agencies were involved."

"Which ones?" she asked.

"Several, and they all had the same goal—to prevent the Soviets from getting their hands on highly sensitive weapons technology that might have been used against the West. We established a sort of local branch here, for COCOM in Paris and OTT in Langley, Virginia."

"OTT? What does that stand for?"

"It's an agency for supervision of technological information, the Office of Technology Transfer. It's still in business today, in Washington, D.C."

"As part of the CIA?"

"Whatever!" Arik shrugged, getting up. A new thought struck. He excused himself to Stephanie and strolled off into the house.

New York City, Wednesday, July 4

On Independence Day morning, at precisely 8:59 A.M., a task force comprising
personnel from the special antiterrorism
unit of the NYPD and specialists from the
FBI was deposited by two helicopters on the rooftop above Penthouse Apartment No. 34 on East 70th Street in Manhattan. Forty-
five seconds later they were inside the apartment belonging to
Filiberto Cali, junior drug lord and son of the infamous Don Cali
de Cali.

Greeting them in the bedroom was a scene from a horror movie.
Even these officers and agents, hardened through daily contact
with the seedier aspects of the human spectrum, had never experienced anything like it. On the enormous oval bed that dominated
the ostentatiously gilded chamber, slumped against the headboard,
lay the naked, bloody body of a woman. Her forehead had been
grotesquely disfigured by the entry wound of a large-caliber bullet.

Between the obscenely spread thighs of the corpse, deeply embedded in its lap, was the head, and only the head, of a man. The
dead woman's hands clutched at its temples, as the wide-open,
broken eyes of Filiberto Cali stared blankly through a jungle of
matted pubic hair. Don Cali Junior had been decapitated.

The young man's headless torso lay in a messy pool of blood on the wall-to-wall carpet. Gathered in silence, law enforcement officers stared, their gaze flitting from the head to the body and back to the head. A chunk of raw meat—some body part—had been jammed into the head's gaping jaws. Aghast, they stared at the gaping hole in the torso's chest, then back at the stuffed head that had once been the crown of a living, breathing, talking human being named Filiberto Cali de Cali.

The perpetrators of the deed had torn the heart from that human being, severed the head, and stuffed the heart into the head's mouth—not necessarily in that order. There was really no way of telling exactly what sequence of events had transpired.

A message, scrawled in blood across one wall, screamed, *Vengeance! An eye for an eye, a heart for a heart!* On the bedroom floor lay the discarded casing of a Polaroid cassette.

Intelligence information obtained later would show that the Medellín cartel, one of Don Cali's major rivals in the drug business, had learned the whereabouts of Cali Junior just hours ahead of the special unit. They had broken into the apartment, eliminated two bodyguards in the front room, shot Filiberto's mistress, then executed the drug boss in a manner inadequately described as "grisly." Exactly how the Medellínos found out the location of Filiberto's flat was anybody's guess.

The most likely scenario postulated an informer inside police headquarters, who intercepted the relevant messages to Bob Donner and the director of the FBI, then sold his info to a contact, certainly for no less than a five-digit figure. The Medellínos, who blamed the elder Cali for the murder of their boss Pablo Escóbar, had been in no mood to fool around; thus their hit team easily beat the cops to the punch. The empty Polaroid cassette on the bedroom floor indicated that, for whatever reason, the Medellíno butchers had gone to the trouble of recording the slaughter.

As to the lead phoned in to the NYPD—it, too, continued to mystify the police, who had not been able to trace Scarlett's call. And Scarlett went around arguing with herself, wondering whether Ken had foreseen the gruesome deed in all its gory details—details soon spread all over the front pages of the tabloids, some in hideous, living color.

 Late that afternoon, Claude Hubert, Sr., received Stephanie Kramer in his study. The old room with its tall ceiling drew the gaze upward to a stuffed buzzard with spread wings and sharp claws that seemed about to dive down on some unsuspecting prey.

When Stephanie entered the room, Monsieur Hubert sat in a tall-backed armchair, gesturing at her to please come in. She'd learned from an enameled sign by the entrance downstairs that her host had, for years, been a lawyer before handing the business over to his son. Now retired, he devoted himself more than ever to his life's passion, ornithology. His study was packed with books, professional journals, and stuffed birds. A pair of binoculars lay on the windowsill.

Stephanie introduced herself as a journalist researching the history of the old Clissot family enterprise, which had turned into such a booming international concern. When she brought up the tragedy in the mountains, Hubert's expression changed visibly. His spirits seemed to revive; he gestured eagerly. After all these years he was still angry at the police for suppressing the information he had passed on to them. Without any prompting, he started rummaging about in the secret recesses of his charmingly chaotic environment, finally producing a carton filled with old photographs.

"You see, here, this is where I sat, high up there, my camera ready, finger on the trigger." He pointed up at the bird of prey under the ceiling. "Prepared to catch a buzzard as it dove. That's when I heard the scream on the opposite side of the ravine, where a ledge like a huge buffalo head juts out over the abyss. I must have pressed the shutter release intuitively. Later I discovered that, thanks to the telescopic lens, I'd taken a greatly magnified picture of François plunging to his death."

He held the fading snapshot out to her. "Here, take a look, I've never shown this to anyone—too traumatic, you know. Look!"

Frozen in perfect focus by the superquick exposure, a slender young body twisting horizontally hung in midair, as François tried in vain to grab hold of something. The extended fingers of the right hand pointed upward, at the ledge. Stephanie shut her eyes, unable to look at the falling young man.

When at last she tried to comment, she only produced a dry, croaking sound. Not one intelligible word came out. Embarrassed, she pulled some more photographs out of the carton and absently shuffled through them. Hubert watched, bent and gnarled, leaning on the back of her chair.

Suddenly she stopped short. She held up a black-and-white photo.

"Do you know this spot?" she asked.

"Do I ever! That's the Buffalo Head. That's where the poor boy fell to his death."

"There's someone standing there," Stephanie exclaimed.

Monsieur Hubert pulled a magnifying glass from a drawer. "Right you are. Incredible! *Parbleu!* All these years all I ever looked at was that silly bird!"

Suspended proudly in midair in the center of the photograph was a mountain swallow, but in the far distance two figures were clearly visible on the rocky promontory. Stephanie excitedly compared the two pictures.

"The one on the right is François. Look at his clothes. Those black gym shorts with the white stripe along the seam, and the sleeveless gym shirt, exactly like the one where he's falling, here!"

"I knew it!" the old man shouted. "I've always known there was another man. Told them about it, too." He leaned heavily back into the soft upholstery of his armchair. "But the police didn't believe a word I said!"

"Of course not, Monsieur Hubert. You were the only witness, and the body of François was never found. So from their point of view there was no crime. But if you let me borrow these photographs, maybe we can get the case reopened."

"Let you borrow them?" The oldtimer chuckled at the thought of getting back at the cops after all those years. "You're welcome to them. You have my blessings!"

Later, Joseph drove her down to Nucleanne in a small Chevy pickup. Before them lay the broad vista of the valley, with its gently rising hillsides, the fields shimmering in the sun and, to the left, a glittering sliver of lake, set off against the rising terrain. The road turned abruptly, revealing a sudden view of the castle in the distance. Stephanie gestured for Joseph to pull over. She showed him the photographs and explained that she needed enlargements in several formats.

"I want to be able to identify the people on these pictures by their faces, so some of the copies have to be enlarged down to the grain. Here . . ."

She tore a page from her notebook, wrote an address on it and handed it to him. "You take care of the originals. Have a messenger deliver the enlargements to this address."

Joseph swung a mountain bike down from the pickup's tailgate. As Stephanie started to mount the bike, he insisted on checking her equipment one more time. The lens cap on the miniature camcorder Arik had provided was given an utterly superfluous twist. Then, shaking his head, he watched her pedaling fiercely along the narrow path that led through a field, across a gentle rise, and down into the craggy, fissured terrain along the river.

Thomas Borli walked discreetly into the jam-packed auditorium of the Congress Center in Bern. A tumultuous applause had just crested through the enormous hall. At the lectern on the stage, Adam Schlammer waited in triumphant silence until the thunderous ovation faded, then continued his oration in stentorian tones.

"We will not allow those green obstructionists to interfere with our projects. The ecology movement is bent on abusing democratic principles. They fight progress and, if we let them, will destroy the very foundations of prosperity in Switzerland. We demand expansion of our nuclear energy resources. We want more nuclear plants with more efficient reactors. We need more research and development, and we want to be able to manufacture our own reactors. Accordingly, we postulate construction of a fast-breeder type reactor for the production of plutonium." Schlammer paused briefly, then entreated his audience. "No energy without research! No progress without energy! No prosperity without progress!"

The members of the general meeting of the Swiss Nuclear Society rewarded him with another long round of enthusiastic applause. In the first row, a bald-headed, bespectacled, darkly attired man with an envelope in one hand now rose and made his way to the rostrum. Striking a somewhat affected pose of patient humility, he waited until the applause had died down. Then he cleared his throat, brought his pursed lips to a delicate point close to the microphone and said, "Honored members of the Nuclear Society, I'm delighted to be able to give you not one but several reasons why today we are honoring one of our most esteemed members, Adam Schlammer, by bestowing upon him the Society's Annual Award for Meritorious Service."

When the wave of excited whisperings and murmurings that swept through the auditorium had spent itself, the speaker continued. "In a true pioneering effort, Dr. Schlammer has provided an enterprising and altruistic solution to the complex challenge of radioactive waste management."

The bald-headed speaker in the dark suit was given another big round of applause. He raised his hands in a benedictory gesture, which he held until silence reigned again in the vast auditorium, punctuated only by perfunctory coughing and expectant rustlings of paper.

"However, Dr. Schlammer's prospering enterprise, Schlammer Engineering, has done much more. It has helped to substantially advance scientific research. As you may know, Dr. Schlammer is a generous patron of the nanotechnology sector. Without the vision and the admirable financial contributions of this, one of our most dynamic members and colleagues, this Society would never have been able to tap the SINQ neutron resource. We fully expect this investment in an exceptionally innovative area to result in a strong upturn that will usher in a prolonged period of prosperity for all of us."

Seated in the last row, Borli recalled that, a few weeks ago, Schlammer Engineering had announced its entry into this attractive new research area with a breathtaking contribution of 100 million Swiss Francs. While up on the stage the award ceremony continued its pompous eulogizing and backslapping, Borli took stock of the cards he would put into play. Then, as the bald-headed old member of the Swiss Council of Ministers closed the session with a final appeal to resist the ecology activists who were aiming to close down all nuclear plants, Borli rose and walked slowly down the aisle toward the stage.

Schlammer, who saw Borli coming but felt not the slightest urge to meet the man, detached himself from the bunch of well-wishers clustered around him like grapes, and made for the rear exit.

Borli cut him off at the pass. "Police business, Mr. Schlammer. You are under arrest. Please follow me as unobtrusively as possible. This way. Please!"

Borli pointed at a half-open door, where a Swiss Television team was packing up their gear. An alert young camera operator saw the two men coming and discreetly trained his SuperCamcorder on the well-known faces. At that moment, Schlammer blurted out, "If this is your idea of a joke, Borli, you're not tickling my funny bone. Nobody arrests me! If you want information, call my secretary and make an appointment. I have to go now."

He took a couple of steps, trying to get ahead of Borli, but the chief of police grabbed him by the collar and yanked him backwards. The camera caught all of the action.

"My men are waiting outside, Mr. Schlammer," Borli said sternly. "However, if you prefer an unpleasant scene in public, be my guest!"

Schlammer pivoted angrily, trying to twist out of Borli's grip. "Take your greasy paws off me," he shouted, "you're ruining a perfectly good suit!"

Then, more softly, "This is outrageous, Borli. You can kiss your job goodbye as certainly as God made little green apples. Nobody arrests Adam Schlammer, least of all an asshole like you, and on top of that without even the feeblest excuse for cause!"

Clearly unimpressed, Borli said, "No cause, Mr. Schlammer? How about incitement to murder? Aiding and abetting in the commission of a crime? Illegal export of strategic materiel? Violation of the Regulations Governing Nuclear Products and Resources? Infringement of the Radiation Regulations? Endangering a person's life? Conspiracy to endanger national security? Any of this ring a bell? Let's go!"

When Schlammer noticed heads turning to watch the scene, he forced a conciliatory smile. He made a show of buddying up to Borli, slapping him lightly on the back, then continued acting out the charade by pretending to be engrossed in conversation with the chief of police as they walked out together. By the time Borli noticed the two skinhead types Schlammer had called into action with a wink, it was too late.

As the door closed behind Borli and Schlammer, the goons

grabbed Borli from both sides and held him in a viselike grip. Set free, Schlammer hurried down the passage, unimpeded. Borli watched helplessly as Schlammer's henchmen tied his hands and feet, then yanked off his tie and used it as a gag. A moment later, the head of the Special Investigation Unit found himself tossed like a rag doll into a corner, landing among mops, pails and industrial-size bottles of floor polish. He was shut inside a lightless cleaning closet. In the deserted service area behind the stage, the incident had gone unnoticed.

If it hadn't been for the tie that cut brutally into his lips, Borli might have frothed at the mouth with rage at his own stupidity. How grossly he had underestimated Schlammer! How could he have imagined the man would allow himself to be arrested in the crowd without putting up a fight? And how amateurishly he had allowed himself to be outwitted by the tycoon! And all this time, a police detachment stood by outside the Congress Center, ready to back him up at any moment!

Producing impotent gargling sounds, straining and twisting among the cleaning paraphernalia, Borli finally shook his head and forced himself to relax. He even managed a wry grin as he recalled how promisingly the day had started. . . .

Early that morning, he had met his wife under the giant fir tree at the edge of the park, a spot that offered a magnificent view across the roofs of the city. Melanie sat with her back against the trunk, legs spread, laughing seductively, playfully fanning herself with the envelope she had brought along. They reveled like children in their conspiratorial rendezvous. When Thomas mentioned the dumbfounded minister of justice who had misunderstood and misinterpreted everything, their happy, carefree laughter rang out over the remote corner of the park. It made them feel like young lovers again.

Finally, gazing somberly at her husband, Melanie handed him the envelope containing Stephanie Kramer's fact sheet and the persuasive first-hand evidence it documented. Not only had Kramer been an eyewitness to the assassination, but she had encountered the killer again, in her apartment. Subsequently, she had identified him in Nucleanne, when she saw him enter the nuclear cavern on the Schlammer Engineering premises. Would this hold up in court? If the woman were mistaken, then Schlammer had been warned, and the killer was long gone!

Were Kramer's observations of the laboratory—the suitcase, the granite clock housing, the maps, the drawings of nuclear weapons components—merely fantasy props created by an eager reporter who believed herself hot on the trail of the scandal of the century? There wasn't much Borli could do with this. He'd have to search the Schlammer premises, precisely as Ralph Christen had intended to do before he was murdered.

The attempt on Kramer's life, on the other hand, might yield more. The gunman Matak had been employed in the security department of Schlammer Engineering; that much had been established by the inquiry into his death. But who had killed *him*, up there at the edge of the forest? Had he really been trying to murder Kramer, as she claimed?

Forensic inspection had confirmed that Matak actually did break into Kramer's apartment. That part of her story, at least, appeared to be true. However, on the whole, her dramatic account of these alleged events would not be sufficient grounds for arresting a personage like Schlammer.

Yet Borli had discovered such grounds, though indirectly, in Ralph Christen's notes. Shortly before being murdered, the chief magistrate had pinpointed a group of skinheads who formed a secret paramilitary cadre, with its base in the underground facilities of Schlammer Engineering. One of the cadre members was a man named Stucker, who had fought in Croatia with the HOS, a neo-Nazi phalange. Upon returning to Switzerland, Stucker was indicted and sentenced by a military court. It was Christen who had investigated the case and hauled Stucker into court.

Following a gut hunch, Borli had ordered a review of the Stucker files. Apparently, Stucker had gone underground after serving his sentence—until Christen flushed him out a few days ago. Borli then had the fingerprints from Stucker's file checked against those secured from a broken beer bottle found near Christen's body. The prints matched. Thus, it could be assumed that Christen's murderer was part of the Schlammer organization. The way Borli saw it, this was sufficient cause to arrest the president of the Schlammer Group.

In addition, there were leads provided by the American Embassy in Bern. U.S. intelligence agencies had received information generated inside the PKK, the Workers Party of Kurdistan, to the effect that Schlammer Engineering was negotiating arms deals with Iraqi buyers. Since the Kurdish sources were anonymous, this information in and of itself constituted no evidence, but a search of the Schlammer premises would probably yield clues as to whether Schlammer was illegally exporting sensitive armament technology to Iraq.

Straining at his fetters in the makeshift dungeon, the police chief was certain that he would have had sufficient grounds for an arrest. But he had badly messed up, and had missed the opportunity. Schlammer would use his head start to cover up incriminating evidence and eliminate witnesses. By the time the police caught up with him, they'd find nothing.

Angrily redoubling his efforts to free himself, Borli rolled this way and that in the narrow closet. First he bumped against the wall, then into a shelf, which tilted. A container crashed to the floor and broke open, creating a puddle of dark fluid from which thin acidulous tributaries slowly meandered through the crack under the door and out into the hall, where they made a stinking mess on the floor.

As Borli struggled in the closet, Hannibal, in the command center at Schlammer Engineering, opened a workbench drawer and gingerly extracted the parcel with brown adhesive tape on the back. He wrapped a newspaper around it and left the building. A few minutes later, as he rolled out of the parking lot, he called Rosalia at work, telling her that a package had arrived for her, from Colombia.

"It's addressed to you, care of Schlammer Engineering. In future use your private address. No more private mail addressed to the company, okay? This time it's all right, though. I'll send somebody over to deliver it. Anyway, I'll be over to see you later tonight. I have the key."

He parked the Cherokee in front of Rosalia's building and walked up to her door, which he opened with his key. Lovingly he arranged the parcel from South America on the kitchen table. Ten minutes later he was back in front of his monitors in the command center, thinking pleasant thoughts about Custer. Only a few more hours, then it was time to take that boy apart.

Where the river bent, the narrow path Stephanie had been pedaling along petered out in dense underbrush. No use trying to continue on this side! Close by, a huge rock bellied deep into the swiftly flowing waters; above it towered tiers of sandstone thousands of years old. The cliffs were dominated high up by a rocky promontory, jutting out into the blue sky. Frothing wildly, the river's turbulent waters dashed against the underbelly of the huge rock and were thrown back to whirl on through the deep, dark-green pool which the powerful current had gouged into glacial slate.

Stephanie turned away from the elemental spectacle to look at the sketch Mark Summermatter had drawn for her. It showed a serpentine footpath higher up, invisible from below, winding its way upwards among the rocks. Ditching the bike, she put on her backpack and pulled the waist strap tight. Placing each step cautiously, pulling herself up by small tree trunks and roots, she started climbing.

Not much later she stood huffing and puffing on the rocky ledge, helplessly scrutinizing a thicket of shrubs and young firs. No sign of the hidden path the kids had told her about! They had also told her under no circumstances to take the path to the left that led uphill, since it would expose her to view farther up the mountain. Again, she parted the impenetrable thicket with her hands, looking in vain for a trace of the secret path. All she saw was a woodpecker with a red crown and yellow tail feathers, perched elegantly atop a fir sapling.

The bird seemed as surprised at seeing her as she was at seeing it. For a moment she stood stock-still, allowing the splendor of its plumage to open her eyes to the subtleties of the scenery around her. That was how she noticed some broken twigs near where the gently rocking woodpecker was perched. As she stepped closer, the bird took wing. She parted the branches and saw the path. Greatly relieved, she blew an enthusiastic kiss at the woodpecker, which alighted close by to watch her curiously out of bright, black eyes. Then she slipped into the thicket.

A few minutes later the hidden path led her to the spot where they had agreed to meet. As she looked around she discovered a sign: small stones on the ground, shaping an arrow that pointed at the open ventilation shaft. The opening looked exactly as it had the day before; the same sweetly pungent scent of sage and pine resin still suffused the air. She clutched the safety rope firmly, cautiously swung her legs over the edge, and began the descent, thinking that those Summermatter kids better be waiting for her down there.

And indeed, when she slid through the open hatch in the shaft wall, into the niche, there they were, all three, huddled together. Relieved, she hugged them, one after the other, trying to offer some solace. Then, businesslike, she produced the drawings, which they began to examine under the feeble beam from a flashlight.

"We'll follow this narrow supply channel, here, to this point, here," she told them. "From there we take this passage, which leads to the laboratory."

The kids, who had painted their faces a ghostly black, nodded and followed their leader. As they felt their way past the stacked-up, gray burlap sacks, Tony asked in a whisper why anyone would need fertilizer this far down in the mountain.

Stephanie herself had puzzled over this. Earlier, von Alp had ventured that the bags probably contained cement to serve as binder for nuclear waste. But she had insisted to him that the label she saw as she cowered behind the sacks said "Fertilizer." Then Theo had come up with what seemed like a plausible explanation: nitrate-enriched chemical fertilizer could be used to make bombs.

"If you mix this type of fertilizer with diesel oil, you get an explosive," she whispered into Tony's ear. "We're up against a dangerous bunch!"

They ambled along in single file, their already faint source of light seeming to grow feebler as they moved deeper down the long passage. On either side of the tunneled walkway they noted niches containing electrical apparatus, as well as service bays with maintenance equipment. The passage to the lab was located precisely where Stephanie had said it would be.

"We're coming back this way, so remember our escape route!" she cautioned the kids.

However, when she tried the door, it wouldn't budge. Pushing and shoving didn't help either. Upon closer examination, they found that the entrance to the lab passage, which had been indicated as unobstructed on the drawings, was walled shut. Ten minutes had passed. Stephanie thought of Ken, whose appointment with Schlammer was scheduled for fifteen minutes from now, at six-thirty. Whatever that meeting might be intended to accomplish, she figured that any sensitive material would be removed from the lab. If von Alp was right, the laboratory contained components for the manufacture of nuclear weapons, and Stephanie was determined to return from the cavern with as much incriminating evidence as possible. Now she feared that Schlammer's people, or even Custer, might beat her to it.

Only fourteen minutes left! Three pairs of eyes watched her every move, and she didn't have the slightest idea what to do next! On top of everything else, there were metallic sounds in the direction from where they'd come. It sounded as if people were moving toward them from the distant domed hall.

At that moment Jessie gestured excitedly upward at a metal grate above the walled-up door. Bracing themselves against the wall, Mark and Tony heaved her up. With one desperate twist, she yanked the grille from its hold, exposing the opening of a ventilation duct wide enough to admit a man. Moments later they were inside, crawling along, with Stephanie in the lead. She was desperately looking for an end to the pitch-dark tube. Then one of the ceiling cover plates, spaced at one-meter intervals on the bottom of the duct, moved under her hands. She pushed it the rest of the way, squeezed through the opening, and dropped down onto something soft that turned out to be a broad, old-fashioned bedstead on the floor of the gallery loft inside the laboratory. The bed's hot-pink satin sheets were covered with lace panties, brassieres, and mail-order catalogs advertising seductive lingerie, all strewn about in wild disorder.

The kids dropped down from the scary confinement of the duct as if hopping off a hot plate. Seconds later they stood marveling at the bizarre, sultry decor of this love nest right above the gleaming high-tech lab.

Mark visibly flinched. "Looks like some kind of bordello!"

Stephanie waved him down the stairs into the lab itself, where stickers on two large, brown suitcases with massively reenforced aluminum edges proclaimed: DANGER, RADIATION! DO NOT OPEN WITHOUT WEARING PROTECTIVE GEAR! The suitcases stood ready for pickup next to a large centrifuge. On a nearby rack, Stephanie recognized a cube-shaped housing consisting of six-finger-thick granite plates with an internal metal casing probably designed to hold a clockwork box. The map of the East Coast of the United States, including those mysterious overlapping circles, was still spread out on the table. What sort of impact-radius lines were these? And what about those vectors, cutting like section lines across the circles?

She was about to fold up the map and put it in her backpack, when Jessie pulled at her sleeve, pointing at the warning panel above the door, now lit up with the message: CAUTION—LAB LOCK ACTIVE!

"They're coming," Stephanie rasped, hastily folding and pocketing the map. She rushed over to the drawing board, tore a drawing marked CARRY-ON MODEL, SCHLAMMER off the wall. She pointed at the wheeled rack.

"Come on, give me a hand! We're taking the suitcases!"

It was a hopeless enterprise. They'd never be able to lug everything upstairs to the gallery in time, then hoist the heavy travel cases up into the ventilation duct and push them all the way back across to the other side of the cavern.

Mark seemed to have read Stephanie's thoughts in her frown. He pointed at the shiny aluminum of an elevator door, partially concealed from direct view by a minitower of measuring instruments.

"Hurry, Jessie, get the elevator. Mark and Tony, bring those suitcases over here."

Outside, there was a hissing as electronic bolts unlocked. A turnstile squeeked; muffled voices and footfalls drew closer. Any moment now, the lab door would open. Stephanie bit her lips, trembling inside. In the nick of time, Mark and Tony pushed the suitcases into the narrow elevator space. As Stephanie gently pulled the door shut, she caught a glimpse of the scientist in a white lab coat pulling the black-haired woman into the laboratory, heading for the staircase that led up to the gallery space. His eyes were glazed over with animal lust.

"He's got better things to do than to start looking for these suitcases," she whispered, greatly relieved. Now at last she had time to fold up the drawing and properly tuck it away. Smoothly and silently, the elevator moved downward.

They got off at Sublevel Four, stood rooted to the spot. A sign on a concrete wall of the gigantic hall said: ELEVATION 499.00 METERS. Stephanie estimated the far end of the enormous underground vault to be at least three hundred meters away. She peered helplessly out into the gloomy space.

"Yesss!" Mark called out, breaking her spell. He had discovered the tracks of an electric trolley, and Jessie, the whites of her eyes incandescent against her dusky skin, had no trouble figuring out how the vehicle worked. They heaved the suitcases aboard and soon were slowly gliding along past enormous stacks of metal cylinders on iron racks painted red.

"Must be bombs," Mark said.

"No, those are nuclear waste containers," Stephanie informed him, recalling von Alp's dissertation. "But over there," she pointed, "those dark-green containers, now those look a lot more like some type of weapon."

In the direction she'd pointed, the kids noticed a stack of army-green metal boxes labeled SADAM, in white lettering beneath the radiation-hazard symbol.

"I have no idea what SADAM stands for," Stephanie answered the palpably unspoken question, then slapped her forehead and shook her head, as she pulled a miniature video camera from her backpack. With practiced professional moves, she filmed the SADAM boxes and the stacks of cylinders from a variety of angles, keeping up a running commentary on each segment as she worked. Date and time indicators winked in the lower left-hand corner of the viewfinder.

The electric conveyor slowed and automatically came to a stop where the tracks ended against a towering gray wall. As the four passengers disembarked hesitantly and began to lift the heavy suitcases off the train, a portion of the cavern wall rumbled aside, exposing an elevator door of dully gleaming steel much like the one up in the laboratory. It opened.

"Oh no, it's Fatso!" Jessie moaned softly.

They faced the fat skinhead who stood grinning in the door, his fists thrust triumphantly into the bulging mass of lard around his nonexistent waist. A voice thundered at them through concealed intercom speakers: "All right, playtime's over! Follow the man you call Fatso to the elevator. I'll be waiting for you on the command bridge!"

When the Conference Center's security personnel finally happened upon a foul-smelling liquid leaking from the broom closet in which Borli was imprisoned, and set him free, much precious time had been lost. Oppressive heat lay over the city as the DRS-TV cameraman argued with the assistant director of the evening news, who refused to broadcast the footage that purportedly showed the arrest of Adam Schlammer without first checking with Police Chief Borli. And when the chief ruefully walked back into the command center, he had more important things to do than think about TV reporters. He issued an official order to seal off the Schlammer Group headquarters and premises, then had an All Points Bulletin put out on Adam Schlammer, Dr. Adolf Breckerlin, Manfred Schoenhof, and Martin Deubermann, also known as Hannibal.

Next, Borli took a call from the director of the Federal Police, a formidable lady, who expressed concern over what she termed "his condition," in particular, as well as over the status of the Kern assassination inquiry, in general. She pointed out that even the most charitable interpretation of the way Chief Borli had bolted from an important conference with the minister of justice to keep a rendezvous with his wife would raise serious questions as to his manners, to say the least. And, frankly, Borli's attempt to arrest Adam Schlammer left her downright puzzled. While she empathized with him and the high-stress situation in which he found himself as head of the special investigation unit, she felt that a serious discussion of these matters was now in order. And, by the way, the minister of justice had just called to tell her that he had spent the better part of fifteen minutes on the phone trying to calm down an irate Mr. Schlammer.

Grinning, Borli hung up.

"We're out of here—to Nucleanne," he told the stunned Steiner, grabbing the man's arm and marching him out the door, to the cars that stood waiting for them in the yard.

Though Custer had noted the telltale signs of an impending police action as he drove through Nucleanne on his way up to the Schlammer compound in the late afternoon—von Alp pointing out to him the drab-looking Volvo limousines which indeed were idling casually at strategic intersections—his drive to Schlammer Engineering went unobstructed. From his old observation post on the castle hill, Theo also reported that armored military vehicles had moved into position in the woods behind the cavern facilities. All those military types in camouflage outfits sneaking about with transceivers, Theo added, tended to confirm his impression that something was brewing across the valley.

During the afternoon, the temperature had climbed to a sweltering twenty-eight degrees centigrade in the shade. Clouds of fine dust, stirred up by harvesters busy on the wheat fields around the town, wafted like pale veils up the steel-and-glass facade of the Schlammer Building as Custer strolled to the entrance.

Indeed, he noticed a rust-red Volvo near the compound, with a short antenna sticking up in the rear—a dead giveaway for an unmarked cop car. The youthful-looking gent wearing a short-sleeved green leisure shirt sat behind the wheel, staring dully ahead and pretending not to pay the slightest attention to the much-wanted former CIA operative in his light summer suit. Moments later, a grim-faced Hannibal received the visitor in the hall of the main building and immediately herded him toward the elevators.

After Custer had disappeared from view inside the Schlammer Building, Borli in the rust-red Volvo activated his transceiver, gave the established code word, and ordered his team to close the pincer encirclement. Yes, now the suspects were in the bag, and the noose was tightening inexorably! Happily rubbing his hands together, the police chief started the engine and drove to the nearby farm where he had previously established his operational base.

As Custer entered the subterranean command center of Schlammer Engineering, feeling a wave of hostility from the assembled men wash over him, the engines of the armored vehicles stationed only five kilometers away came to life. Their turbos whining hellishly, the units advanced into the assault positions that had been reconnoitered for them around the cavern.

Custer had barely set foot in the room when Schlammer rushed to him, lips savagely compressed, eyes flashing, waving a single sheet of paper. "Can you explain this," he shouted in a rage, spitting out the words in staccato delivery, his face flushing a deep crimson that reached all the way down to the prominent cheekbones.

Without a word, Custer took the paper and read it with studied calm, while his mind raced in high gear.

"Where did you get this?" he countered icily.

"We found it in the chief magistrate's flat," Hannibal burst out, pushing his face threateningly close to Custer's. "This morning! Too bad for the cop on duty. We make short shrift of cops, Custer."

He pulled a color print from his jacket and stuck it into Custer's face. Perfectly focused, the picture showed the ex-CIA man in the act of landing a heavy right hand on the skinhead's chin. A moment of silence ensued.

"We know a double cross when we see one, Custer."

The American slowly moved a hand to his breast pocket. Suddenly, Hannibal aimed a heavy revolver at him.

"One false move and you're dead, Custer!"

"Now, can we get down to business?" Custer said casually, removing a slim, leather-bound notebook from his breast pocket and piercing Schlammer with an icy gaze. Schlammer nodded, motioning at the chief of security who slowly, reluctantly, returned his gun to the shoulder holster.

"The money is ready for transfer. I arranged everything this morning," Custer said, consulting his notebook. "A phone call from me to the bank suffices to have the agreed-upon sum transferred to your account." He smiled indulgently.

The thought of the big money he was about to receive relaxed Schlammer and at the same time excited him. Under the slick Armani exterior, he felt his male ardor stirring. Less easily distracted, Schoenhof insisted Custer explain the letter they had found in Christen's flat.

"Slander, gentlemen, disinformation," Custer said, appearing calm as a cucumber. "Somebody is obviously trying to mess up our deal."

The statement was allowed to stand for a moment, then Hannibal snorted heatedly, "The nuclear device your people hijacked up in the mountains yesterday is programmed for the East Coast of the United States. Without the proper codes, which we're holding, it'll be useless to you. By the way, what did you do with that unit?"

Shrugging, Custer said, "Whatever the dickens it is you're talking about, I had nothing to do with it. Really, gentlemen, I haven't got the foggiest! But lemme see, are you telling me you can defuse a bomb that's been hijacked?"

"You bet we can," Schoenhof replied eagerly. "Provided we know approximately where the device is located, we can use a four-digit override code to shut down the detonator."

He cupped his hands over the back of his head, stretching voluptuously: Rosalia made him feel good. Much in demand as a lover, he felt strong, calm and superior to others. Except that his tryst with Rosalia had almost made him miss the meeting!

"Which four digits?" Custer asked matter-of-factly, watching Schoenhof's face light up.

"It's simple and brilliant. The twin reflection of a number."

"Twin reflection, hmmmh!" Custer went. "Like how?"

"Mathematically quite specific. For example . . ."

Cutting the scientist off with an aggressive gesture, Schlammer turned to Custer.

"I don't give a damn if you're involved in the raid on Summer-matter up there. The main thing is you pay. I mean right now, and for both carry-ons, as well as for the hijacked SADAM fission pack. Frankly, Mr. Custer, we're in no mood to waste any more time on this." He exchanged glances with Hannibal, who nodded in agreement.

"And what if I don't? Pay, I mean. What happens then?" Custer said, playing for time.

"In that case you won't leave this place alive."

Since he knew that, either way, he was a dead man the moment the enormous sum of money was transferred, Custer took his time considering the threat. Early that afternoon he had discussed all the details of payment with the bank, receiving assurance that the transfer could be effected by telephone. Watch your timing, kid, he told himself; if you let go of the money a moment too soon, these boys will take you down. In cold blood!

"How about cash on delivery?" Custer suggested in a sober tone of voice. "You hand over the suitcases. I check them out. You give me a car and a chauffeur to transport the merchandise. We will leave the cavern by the large gate on the main court. As the cavern entrance opens, I transfer the entire sum by telephone. We're talking money for merchandise, plus safe passage!"

The three men exchanged eloquent glances. Schlammer and Hannibal stepped to the side and started whispering. Schoenhof nervously fingered his collar, which bore fresh, smudged imprints of lipstick. Impatiently checking his watch, he depressed an indentation next to one of the monitors. The wall slid to one side, revealing a corridor that led deeper into the mountain, toward the laboratory.

"All right, Custer," Schlammer drawled reluctantly, "your solution is acceptable." At these words, Hannibal angrily clenched a fist behind his back.

They agreed to meet later, in the lab, to hand the suitcases over to Custer. Schlammer would, as the tycoon put it, "look up" Breckerlin in his command center, then rejoin them with the old general, so the transfer would take place under strictly controlled conditions.

At about the time Custer walked down the corridor with Hannibal and the scientist, Borli in his base on the nearby farm was reading a letter by the director of the FBI, which Max had just handed him. Its content was identical to that of the letter found by Schlammer's henchmen in the apartment of the murdered Christen. Borli read the same text Custer had seen on the sheet Schlammer waved in his face:

Copy of encrypted fax, sent July 1, to Ralph Christen, Chief Magistrate, Military Court of Inquiry, Bern, Switzerland.
My dear Ralph,
In regard to your inquiry on Custer alias >Keycop< and in

consideration of operations currently underway, I urge you to look upon the fugitive subject as if he were one of my most valuable operatives, and to ignore all information or evidence to the contrary. >Keycop< is under orders from the highest governmental authorities. It is of the greatest importance to them, and to me, that he succeed with his mission.

Most cordially,

Director, FBI

The police chief dropped the fax sheet on the tabletop and stared absently out the window, asking himself if he hadn't just committed the greatest blunder of his career. Through the fading light of dusk, he looked out at the low-slung factory buildings of Schlammer Engineering in the distance, where the man known to some as >Keycop< was probably up to his neck in trouble. Sighing as he got up, Borli told Max to call the entire team together for a briefing in half an hour.

"One more thing, Max," he called after his investigator. "Get that jurist over here, that Chaudet woman, I mean Marianne Chaudet, the pilot Summermatter's girlfriend. Tell her to report here without fail, immediately—if not sooner!"

Washington, D.C., July 4, afternoon

While Thomas Borli in Switzerland was staring at the Schlammer Group headquarters, some three thousand miles across the Atlantic as the crow flew, a black Cadillac pulled up in front of Union Station. The driver got out, discreetly letting the door rest in its frame instead of letting it close fully. The passenger in the rear seat, safe behind the tinted, bullet-proof windows, tapped the FBI director's access number into a cellular phone.

Cosmo always felt a flutter of uneasiness when he was about to talk to the boss of the FBI. This time was no different. An executive of impeccable credentials and a legend in law enforcement circles, the FBI's head honcho had, in a few short years, succeeded in restoring the Bureau's image. It shone anew, like a brightly-polished silver dollar rescued from the muck of scandal. Cosmo envied the director's reputation as a Mafia buster feared even by the dons of Sicily.

At the sound of the director's familiar voice, Cosmo came straight to the point.

">Keycop< must be allowed to leave Switzerland with the merchandise *tonight*, do you understand? Can I rely on you keeping your bloodhounds off of him?"

After a brief silence, the director calmly answered, "My authority does not extend to the Swiss police, and certainly not to Swiss secret service agencies. >Keycop< will have to fend for himself. The man is on his own."

"Listen," Cosmo pleaded, "there must be something you can do."

"I understand he's in trouble. What is the nature of the merchandise he's transporting?"

"Gold," Cosmo gave his prepared lie. "And eyes-only documents."

"Well, no matter." The director sounded apprehensive. "We have given clear instructions that >Keycop< is not to be interfered with. In our experience, the Swiss are exceedingly reliable."

"Let's hope so," Cosmo muttered grudgingly and broke the connection. Thoughtfully pursing his lips, he dialed a new number. It was answered immediately by his contact inside the Cali cartel. Cosmo decisively instructed the man to proceed with all necessary preparations. Then he added, even more emphatically, "The operation is to be carried out *tonight*, the night of the Fourth of July. Over and out."

Soon thereafter, the black Cadillac stopped at the curb of a front street of Washington, D.C.'s Georgetown district. The man some knew as Cosmo, others as Jack Weisborn, and a tiny handful as both, got out and walked briskly down a street abustle with midday holiday crowds. Two blocks later, he turned left into a quieter side street and stopped in front of a house. After looking around to make sure he wasn't being followed, he quickly marched up a short walkway through the front yard to the entrance.

A fat man with a greasy mustache and an unhealthy complexion opened the door and admitted the customer. Without as much as a word of greeting, the greaseball waddled ahead to the elevator, where he halted, gruffly intoning, "Third floor, Room Three." Cosmo nodded and handed him an envelope.

The greaseball checked the contents and growled his approval. The face of the distinguished-looking caller seemed familiar, but name and station were of no concern to the fat man, as long as a customer paid well, in cash and in advance. Even if he knew that this particular high-class john was Cosmo, head of the most secret of all the nation's secret agencies, he wouldn't give a damn.

The almond-eyed girl with the jet-black hair was sitting on the edge of the bed. When an old man she had never seen before stepped into the room, she got up. The only garment she wore, a short mauve shirt, reached barely to her belly button. She stood with spread legs, waiting for him to smile. The man's eyes flicked indifferently across hers, then dove to focus greedily on the silky black down that covered her small, delicately shaped mound.

He threw his jacket on the bed and marched into the bathroom. She heard the toilet flush. When he came back out, he motioned to her to undress him: first tie and shirt, then trousers and shorts. His member hung pale, soft and listless between his legs.

"Well, do something, make it grow!" he growled at her. Hadn't that greaseball sung her praises: Thirteen and chaste as the driven snow? "Start dancing! And keep looking at my dick!"

Awkward at first, the girl began to traipse around the room, soon strutting and prancing almost gracefully, unabashedly proffering her youthful charms. She playfully brushed against him, fleetingly touched his thighs. But her naturally innocent game of seduction left Cosmo cold; his penis stayed slack as it had been ever since she pulled off his shorts.

Grumbling, he bellied down on the bed and drew up his knees, thrusting his ass up into the air.

"Ride me!" he ordered, grabbing her crotch. A grimace of pain flitted across the child's exotic features. Forcing a smile, she climbed on his back. She clamped down on his neck with her butt and began pounding his buttocks with her fists.

"Harder, faster!" he huffed, squinting between his legs to see if anything was moving—but nothing was. He bellowed at her, "Scratch it, you fuckin' bitch, scratch!"

Now, at last, as she started to scratch and slap his testes, the penis nodded a little, but just a little. Snarling viciously, he threw her off him. He jumped off the bed and positioned himself in front of her.

"Jerk me off!" he commanded, inwardly ranting at the little China bitch who just wasn't doin' it for him. Next time, he thought, I want that hunk of a black boy, the one with the rock-hard ass!

As he visualized the romp with the boy he'd had previously, he ejaculated, squirting a couple of thin spurts of sperm on the girl's face. After wiping his wienie on her silky skin, he grabbed his shorts and started to get dressed.

"My God!" Stephanie exclaimed, as they stared aghast into the enormous, domed hall.

Keeping the small video camera clamped under one arm, she squeezed Jessie's hand as they were herded toward their destiny by the bald-headed fatso. Mark and Tony lugged the brown suitcases. Finally they reached the console with its gauges, switches, and monitor displays. There, the old general stood, rocking back and forth on the heels of his spit-polished boots: pompous, arrogant, a disdainful grin on his face, one hand clutching the belt of his silly uniform. An ID tag above the flap of the left shirt pocket read: BRECKERLIN.

They stood on a platform designed as a monitoring station. Suspended some ten meters above the dome-hall floor, it offered a wraparound view of the entire installation, which was dominated by a huge, black missile. Stephanie and the kids were entranced, their gazes traveling up the dully gleaming missile body that towered more than halfway to the ceiling. Its tip pointed at the seam of the old observatory's retractable dome.

The rocket's three power plants hung above an enormous blast well below the docking platform. Vertical supports held the great, sleek body in place at an angle of fifteen degrees. The unmistakable odor of kerosene hung in the air. Stephanie estimated the missile's length to be about twenty meters, and it was shaped like a rifle round, tapering toward the tip where the bulky warhead capped the slimmer, second-stage section.

Grinning insolently, Fatso suddenly stepped up to Tony from behind and roughly grabbed his butt. The angry boy whirled around, landing a crushing kick against the fat one's shin. The grin vanished from Fatso's ugly mug and he doubled over, howling with pain. Swift as lightning, a knife flashed in the goon's hand, his howl escalating into a demented roar of fury as he went after Tony.

Everything happened within seconds. Breckerlin took two steps forward and fired. The report from the big 9-mm automatic reverberated through the enormous dome. Jessie screamed, Stephanie cringed. When she looked up, Fatso lay on his back, his head smothered in blood. Recoiling in slow motion, the four clutched the railing and hung on for dear life.

"Get rid of that!" Breckerlin barked, gesturing at Fatso's body. The order was carried out by a big bald-headed fellow in a black leather jacket who had silently taken up position by his side. "Down into the vault. Now!"

The big man stooped, grabbed his deceased buddy under the arms, and started dragging him to the open elevator. As he maneuvered to twist the body into the elevator cage, Breckerlin again fired, hitting the leader of the goon squad execution-style, in the back of the head. The impact of the large-caliber bullet made the man pitch forward into the cage, which responded by trying to close. Time and time again the automatic door came up against the victim's protruding legs and his black combat boots—pushing and retracting, pushing and retracting, pushing...

Dumbstruck and horrified, Stephanie watched the three kids staring apathetically at the senseless mechanical jerking of the elevator door. She noticed Mark starting to move slowly, discreetly, to one side. She erupted, shouting at Breckerlin from the very depth of her being, "You...you...creep!"

She would have started to pummel him if the light pressure exerted on her upper arm by the video camera hadn't given her a better idea. Coolly activating the camera, she stealthily aligned the lens with the general, who was nervously blowing away gunsmoke from the muzzle of his automatic, regretfully shrugging his shoulders.

"My apologies for the rough introduction," he snorted disdainfully, "but I really have no more use for these schmucks. We're about to start the countdown for this baby—an SS-20 from the Soviet arsenal. She may be an old lady, but she's still in optimum condition."

He took a couple of steps backward, reaching. Pointing his gun steadily at Stephanie, he nonchalantly tapped out a sequence of keys. Instantly, the large color monitor displayed a cartoon view of an enormous brick wall. The wall started to crumble along its top edge. In an electronic hourglass in the upper right-hand corner of the screen, a thin stream of virtual sand grains began to trickle into the bottom portion of the simulated clock.

"Yesss, we have a countdown!" Breckerlin enthused. "And the moment that wall is down, we'll have ignition. That'll be in exactly ninety minutes. We're now initiating the pre-launch routine."

As if to confirm this, a loud hissing noise could be heard, and steam gushed from the lower portion of the rocket. On the opposite wall, an orange warning light started to blink. Somewhere in the distance an alarm horn boomed at regular intervals. The ceiling of the domed cavern remained shut.

"And exactly sixty minutes after the launch, it'll be liftoff time for this entire cavern," the general grinned. "We've got about a ton of powerful explosives ready for triggering, stored in special detonating chambers. That's approximately as much explosive material as you'll find in one of the army's underground ammunition dumps. Remember the Susten Pass disaster? The blast will tear this entire mountain apart and bury everything inside forever. Any fool caught down here at that time will be killed outright—or buried alive!"

Breckerlin's voice trembled with excitement. He lifted his monocle to his left eye, clamped a heavy brow over it as he checked his watch, then barked: "Sit down!"

Stephanie and Jessie reluctantly sat down on swivel contour chairs at the command console, while Tony hunkered down on the floor by the railing. Mark squatted on a metal box that stood against the wall, between the switchboard and the elevator. His eyes followed Breckerlin's every move. The general sat down in his own swivel chair.

"So now you're my hostages," he told them. "In about half an hour we'll leave the launching area through the underground escape."

He pivoted ninety degrees and pointed the snout of his automatic at a narrow footpath that led to the opposite side of the cavern.

"A car will take us to a small airfield nearby. From there we take a helicopter."

Jessie focused intensely on the monitor screens. Next to the crumbling wall, white windows flickered on a background of dark blue. She could see that a touch of the finger would activate the desired function. The console was equipped with a joystick just like the one used for playing Nintendo computer games. The longer she studied the equipment, the more certain she became that the missile program worked very much like a computer game. Fascinating! Her mind eagerly accepted the challenge of figuring out the guidance control menu on the dark-blue screen.

Meanwhile, Mark, his hands now behind his back, was leaning casually against the wall. A hydraulic valve began to hiss, an electric motor started up with a throaty hum. A rushing sound, as if from a far-off waterfall, began to fill the vast domed hall.

"This is a Soviet-made, fourth-generation SS-20 intercontinental missile," Breckerlin intoned. "It's known to NATO as SABER, an exceedingly fitting label I'd say. Yes, indeed, with this *saber* we'll cut down our enemies!"

He clearly delighted in observing his hostages' big eyes and open mouths as they stared incredulously upward to where the nuclear warhead sat ticking atop the sleek black rocket.

"In 1976," Breckerlin continued enthusiastically, "the Soviets deployed approximately 600 of these fine old rockets. And they kept 245 in reserve. This one here comes from that backup batch. She's in fine fettle and raring to go!"

Stephanie was dumbfounded; the spectacle she was witnessing literally left her speechless. She rubbed her eyes, blinking repeatedly, as if to wink away some fantastic mirage. Yet, somehow, all this madness interfaced with her own expertise: nuclear energy, the problems of nuclear weapons proliferation, bomb makers. Someone had smuggled that terrible weapon into this place! That incredible fact brought her back down to earth, and cool reason returned. Surprised at the firmness of her own voice, she heard herself asking, "And where does this baby come from?"

Flattered by her interest in his diabolical scheme, the fake general happily plunged into another elaborate lecture. "This particular Saber was manufactured at the Barrikady Works in Volgograd. Some of its components come from the Votkinsk Machine Works somewhere in Azerbaijan. This is a so-called mobile missile which can easily be transported. It comes in a container that resembles a giant thermos. It's shipped on top of a six-axle rig which also serves as the launching pad."

Breckerlin kept rattling on—how through the years, under Schlammer's leadership, they'd built up a clandestine organization right here in this cavern. As for Schlammer himself, he was a powerful mover, rank of colonel in the Swiss Army, knew all ministers of state, and had numerous contacts inside the Council of Ministers. A generous donor of funds, for his party as well as for research. A man with a fist of iron: you got in his way and you were through!

Schlammer had financed his empire through technology transfers and weapons sales, Breckerlin told them. And right now, if he sold the bomb, he'd again make hundreds of millions. There were really only four reasons Schlammer wanted a nuclear bomb, Breckerlin grinned: money and power, and power and money.

"Schlammer used to be a sort of missionary," he went on, "trying to rid humanity of the scourge of Islam. In those days, he enthusiastically advocated a limited nuclear war to wipe out the Muslims, the blacks and the Chinese. Which was why he agreed to install this SS-20 here in the mountain. But now he's gone soft. Money is all he still cares about—addicted to it, I'd say. As for myself, I'm sticking to the original plan. I will use the bomb!"

"On what target?" Tony asked, abruptly, in a choked voice.

Breckerlin pivoted in his contour chair. He pressed a button and tapped out a sequence on sensor fields. The large monitor instantly displayed a map with a city at its center.

"That's where—Baghdad. This SS-20 has a 5,000-kilometer range, even though the CIA insists the range is only 4,400 kilometers. Not that it matters, since Baghdad is only 4,290 kilometers from Nucleanne. We do have a slight accuracy problem—the old lady has a target error margin of about one kilometer. However, with a little luck, we can compensate for that. Not that that'll make any difference, considering what this baby will do when it hits."

Aghast, the hostages stared at the slim, elongated shape before them. Inevitably, their gaze traveled to the tip, which was painted red.

"Is it . . . uh . . . armed?" Tony managed.

Guffawing as he rocked back and forth in his chair, Breckerlin delightedly slapped one knee.

"Armed? I'll say she is! The old dame is fitted with a nuclear warhead that'll blow Baghdad off the map. And who'll be blamed for the disaster? The United States, of course! And that suits me perfectly fine!"

"But why Baghdad, that doesn't make any sense at all," Stephanie exclaimed angrily, unabled to contain herself.

"On the contrary, Madam, that's brilliant," Breckerlin fired back. "It'll look as if the United States did it. In retaliation for *Philadelphia*." He glanced at his watch, then nodded triumphantly. "Tonight, good old Philly goes into orbit! And tomorrow the Yanks will turn Baghdad into a pile of rubble—with this old lady showing them the way. Brilliant, isn't it?"

Stealthily training her video camera on the monitor screens, she scowled. "You're crazy! I don't believe a word you're saying. You must be out of your mind! Philadelphia, you say? That simply isn't possible!"

"You don't think so? Well, it is! Because I, the brilliant Breckerlin, have made sure that a SADAM explodes in Philly tonight. Nine o'clock their time . . ."

"You're bluffing!"

"Madam, I regret you won't have to live long enough to see it. A SADAM nuclear device developed by Schlammer. At nine o'clock sharp. Swiss precision timing . . ." Breckerlin's maniacal laughter echoed eerily through the cavern: "Huh huh huh huh huh . . ."

Gasping as he recovered from his bout of mirth, he told them that, once Iraq had been wiped out, the Iranians would mount an offensive, thrusting deep into the southern reaches of Saudi Arabia.

"And what do you suppose the United States will do, my sweet? Guess! They'll drop a few little nukies on Tehran and other Iranian targets. Wiping out that entire worthless tribe of Muslim camel drivers. About time, I'd say, high time somebody does it . . . huh huh huh huh huh . . . !"

Tony tapped his right middle finger against his forehead and whispered, "Missing a few megabytes up here, I'd say!" Stephanie felt clammy, staring in morbid fascination at the lethal load atop the SS-20. Breckerlin was all business again as he worked the keyboard at the console. The monitor screen now displayed a map of Germany, marked with circles and triangles.

"Our operational bases," the general explained. "I'm the head of Action Group East, known as *Brandenburg*, the seminal core of the neo-Nazi movement in Germany. Up until today, the command center for Brandenburg operations in the Federal Republic was right here in this cavern. All the operations aimed at inferior foreigners, all the countless successful incendiary actions, all elimination of undesirable individuals—all that has been coordinated and financed by *me*. And we've been running a comprehensive training program, including individual instruction on how to make bombs."

"Right, with fertilizer and diesel fuel," Stephanie injected sarcastically.

Momentarily baffled, Breckerlin shook his head, then laughingly told her that he meant receiver bombs, letter bombs.

"Do you remember that series of receiver-bomb incidents? That was I. Quality work, I'd say."

The loony old soldier glanced irritably across at Mark, then turned his attention back to Stephanie.

"Schlammer knew well what we were up to, and he gave us plenty of support, but then he started messing up. You want to know how? Well, the first major fuckup was when the prime minister barged in on us. Next, Schlammer decided Kern had to be eliminated. That was decisive error number two. Even the measures taken against Christen did more harm than good," Breckerlin lectured with cynical fervor, "because now Police Chief Borli is siccing his bloodhounds on us! On top of everything, against my advice, Schlammer refused to sell the bomb to the Iraqis, no matter how much money they offered. That's when I decided to take things into my own hands. I was the one who informed Hazmoudi that the SADAM would be flown up to the quarry. Too bad Summermatter had to bite the dust. Good pilot! Well, what was I to do? Leave him alive so he could talk?"

The hissing from the missile's thrust aggregates abruptly ceased. For a moment, a graveyard silence enveloped the little band of intruders. Then that monotonous, nervewracking alarm horn tore their hopes to shreds. As Breckerlin nonchalantly swiveled to face the screen, Mark's arms slowly moved forward. The length of small-gauge pipe he held in his right hand was only slightly longer than an ordinary ruler. Stephanie had noticed his movement in the corner of one eye and slightly dropped her left shoulder. With eerie composure, Mark removed the cap from the makeshift blowgun and raised it to his lips, his cold, penetrating stare never straying from Breckerlin's skull. Their eyes met: the hunter and his prey. The assignment of roles was instantaneous—and clear to both.

"What the hell?" Breckerlin exclaimed as he tried to buck fate, going for his gun.

At that moment, Mark blew forcefully into the pipe. The tiny, plumed arrow of steel coated with poison from the kids' pet frogs thunked into the general's cheek just below his left eye. Breckerlin's left hand jerked reflexively up toward the eye, but got only as far as his heart. Clutching his chest, trembling spasmodically, his terrified eyes protruding and glazing over, the old soldier silently pitched forward. He hit the unyielding concrete floor.

For an interminable half-minute or two, Jessie, Tony and Stephanie stood frozen in their poses. Gradually, one after the other, they looked across the platform at Mark. He sat slumped in his chair, the blowgun resting on his knees. His face was buried in his hands, his body wracked by big sobs.

As she squinted at the corpse on the floor, Stephanie became aware that the countdown was continuing. Clouds of vapor rose to the domed ceiling. A mechanical voice announced: "Thirty-nine minutes and forty-five seconds to ignition. Thirty-nine minutes and thirty seconds to ignition. Thirty-nine minutes and fifteen seconds to ignition. . . ."

The SS-20 was vibrating noticably. At its tip, the red, protective hood over the nuclear warhead slowly began to detach. The insistent honking of the alarm broke the spell, yanking Stephanie back to reality. She pushed herself up out the chair and aimed her video camera at the launch pad. Mark, too, was back on his feet, urging everybody to get out of there.

"If we're still here when this thing lifts off, we'll be fried to a crisp, just like your Sunday morning toast. So let's burn some rubber!"

"Wait!" Jessie pleaded. She stood at the console, trying desperately to locate the program that shut off the countdown. Savagely pounding the keyboard, she kept up a running, sotto-voce dialogue with the monitor on whose screen a tiny, comical-looking fellow was wrecking the brick wall with his head. The icon then advanced to a higher level to fight a gooey ball of a monster.

A spellbound Tony stared at the one-on-one combat: if the little fellow lost, he'd plunge into the abyss. He would then have to work his way to the top again to get back into the fight, which would cost precious time. Luckily, Jessie succeeded in outmaneuvering the bulging meanie, so that the little fellow ended up above a cloud bank, in front of the entrance to the sanctuary that contained the control panel.

Meanwhile, reconnoitering along the metal walkway, Stephanie and Mark had groped their way to the hidden exit. Far below them the SS-20's power plant fumed in an advanced phase of the countdown. The hissing hydraulic noises had become more insistent, while the alarm horn bellowed at briefer intervals, threatening them ever more intensely. Other than the lift that was blocked by the bodies of the men Breckerlin had dispatched, there appeared to be no way out of the missile silo. They had no choice but to duck into the corridor through which the crazy general had intended to abduct them.

The door opened to the inside, leading into a dark, low tunnel hewn into the rock. On either side, jagged boulders protruded from the rough damp walls that arched into a low ceiling to form a wet, dripping vault. Small lamps inside grid cages, spaced far apart, cast faint patches of yellowish light on the graveled footpath.

A stench of lime, urine, earth, and gunpowder residue from empty cartridges on the floor filled the passage, which appeared to lead straight into a pitch-black hole. Stephanie cautiously advanced a probing foot into the cold aperture, her free left arm reaching out to Mark for support. His unshakable composure, regained after his sobs following the blowgun incident, had given her confidence. She sensed how their nightmarish predicament, the threatening disaster, all the terrible dangers they had faced and were facing, including his victorious encounter with the fiendish Breckerlin, combined to imbue the young man with astonishing, Herculean strength.

She cried out, "Mark, what can we do? That missile will trigger a nuclear war! That cannot—must not—happen! We've got to tell the police, bring in the army. Fighter planes could be used to destroy the cavern. . . ." She broke off, helpless, her strength at a final low ebb.

A telephone rang. Mark glanced up to the warhead atop the SS-20, then back at Jessie in the control room. She was squinting feverishly at the screen, oblivious to her environment as she fought the clock. Behind her stood Tony, as if rooted to the spot, fixing the monitor in a wide open stare. But wasn't any attempt to fight the inevitable hopeless? The army, the police, what could they do? Looking into each other's eyes, Stephanie and Mark shared the same thought: Even if we ever get out, who'll believe us?

Time was running out on them. They'd have to try singlehand-
edly to interrupt the countdown, and Jessie was their only hope!
Fate alone was not enough. . . .

The phone rang again.

Stephanie remembered that Ken, who was probably somewhere
inside the cavern, suspecting nothing, had to be warned at any cost.
Her head was spinning in fatigued confusion. Leaning apathetically
against the rock face by the tunnel entrance, she wished with all
her heart that Ken were by her side.

The cacophonous din in the domed cavern was rising to a fever
pitch. Hazy fumes enveloped the command platform where Jessie
and Tony stubbornly continued their fight, glued to the control
monitors as if hypnotized. A new, grating sound from above made
them look up to the apex of the domed ceiling, which slowly
cleaved open as the silo cover retracted. For an instant, stars
winked from unattainable heights down into Breckerlin's inferno,
and Stephanie screamed.

Her cry of desperation drowned out even the raucous horn. Jessie
and Tony at the control console flinched. Mark laid a protective
arm around Stephanie's waist. He felt her knees starting to buckle
and signaled to the others to hurry up. As he shifted his weight to
better support his weakening friend, he saw the dog—a huge
shaggy beast that must have come through the tunnel behind
them. It stood, fixing Stephanie in the vacant stare of its bright
eyes.

Stephanie had no time to take in any details. All she saw was
an awesome canine monster, baring its teeth in a vicious snarl.
Then it jumped her.

Trying to get away, she slipped and crashed backwards to the
floor, uttering not a sound, resigned to the inevitable—the slobbering jaws of the beast only inches away, gaping death as it went
for her throat. A dream, it flashed through her mind, a nightmare!
A horror vision from hell!

As Stephanie and Mark battled the hell-hound in Breckerlin's silo, Conklin and Atlee were cautiously advancing through a big field of corn, using their hands at eye level to part the tall stalks and leaves. Muddy soil stuck to their shoes. The thunderstorm that had cleansed the air and swept the sky clean had passed, and the moon, just beginning to wane, cast a faint, pale twilight over the terrain. The two men now emerged from the cover of the cornfield and reached a high wall that led to a gate whose rusty, cast iron posts overtopped the wall. The wings of the gate were secured with a big chain, and weeds covered the ground. Clearly, the entrance had not been used in ages.

Conklin looked between the bars of the gate at the house with its faintly illuminated terrace. He played the beam from his flashlight in brief bursts along the inside of the wall, looking for movement sensors. At a sign from him, Atlee also advanced to the wall, and both men climbed over. Once across, they crouched low in the orchard, trying to orient themselves. To their right, they sensed the garage building on whose roof they had seen the parabolic antennas the day before.

Conklin's orders in this situation were to shoot to kill. Taking

Custer alive was out of the question. They'd eliminate him—on the spot!

Further, Conklin hoped to grab, or rather regrab, the Kramer woman. He'd put a bit of pressure on her, just a wee bit of torture maybe, until she talked, like a nice gal, yes, if only to get even for the morning's fiasco!

Conklin ducked low and began to move toward the building. Atlee followed close behind, carrying his gun at the hip, ready for action. Slowly, they crept forward, using trees for cover. Then a penetrating animal odor hit them, and they stopped dead in their tracks as a series of fearful grunts rent the night asunder. Before they knew it, the ferocious grunters were upon them.

Something massive plowed into Conklin, who was hit from the front and tossed lengthwise up into the air, to come down with a thump on bone-hard roots. He blacked out. Atlee tried to sidestep his beast, but the snorting, grunting wild boar was nimbler than the hapless agent. Using her snout to scoop him up from behind, she tossed him onto a dung heap next to the rusty gate. At that moment, light flooded the site of the sneak attack and a bright voice called out to the trained wild boars. A couple more yells, and the enraged beasts finally desisted from inflicting further humiliation upon the two intruders.

With a Kalashnikov from von Alp's collection slung under one shoulder, Claudia ran out into the orchard. She caught up with the gaunt, dark figure that was limping hurriedly toward the barred gate, and pressed the muzzle of the gun into his back. Atlee, who was supporting a broken arm with one hand, surrendered meekly to the young woman as she frowned grimly at him down the barrel of her weapon.

Conklin was less fortunate; he wheezed and clutched his chest, having broken several ribs. Blood from a head wound trickled down along the side of his face, which twisted with fear and pain. Embarrassed and demoralized, both agents accepted the defeat—once again humiliatingly inflicted upon them by a woman.

"Are all women in this country this rough?" Conklin growled with some difficulty, as he flashed his badge across the barrel of the Kalashnikov.

"You haven't seen anything yet," she replied coolly. "I'll string you up by the balls!"

Even though Conklin thought her fully capable of such an act, she mercifully called the police, who took quite a while to get there but finally arrived. The squad of six, all zipped up in bullet-proof vests, had nothing to do but shuffle their feet in mute embarrassment after staring in amazement at the spunky lady of the house who had singledhandedly rendered not one, but two, U.S. agents hors-de-combat!

Counting that the two mud-caked victims wouldn't mention the real heroes of the encounter, Claudia allowed herself to bask in the glorious reflection of victory. After congratulating her with an unmistakable undertone of envy in his voice, the squad commander informed her that the two intruders would be booked for attempted armed robbery of a defenseless woman. He also told her that he had confiscated their firearms, and that, in addition, a variety of charges, illegal entry and disturbing the peace among them, might be filed. After Claudia thanked the gendarmes and politely turned down their offer of posting a couple of men on the premises for the remainder of the night, they finally departed, taking the two injured—and tarnished—spooks with them.

Claudia had barely heard the doors of their squad cars slam and the engines start up when she rushed back into the house to get on the transceiver. She radioed von Alp, who was nervously waiting in the Dodge Ram parked by the Nucleanne castle, suspiciously scanning the Schlammer Engineering compound through his nightscope. The Swiss soldier-of-fortune was on standby, backing up Custer's second visit that evening for the purpose of picking up the carry-on nukes. Actually, it felt more like pins-and-needles than standby to von Alp, since any sign of life from Custer was long overdue. Things apparently were not going entirely according to plan.

Moving his infrared scope slowly over the premises as he searched for any sort of suspicious movement, von Alp detected nothing but a peaceful nocturnal still-life. Beneath the bulk of the fir and pine-covered mountain, meadows lay shimmering in the moonlight. The buildings on the Schlammer premises looked deserted, with only a few solitary patches of light breaking up the dark facades. Not a soul was stirring inside the lighted rooms. All seemed quiet.

The calm before the storm, von Alp thought, frowning uncomfortably as he picked up a barbecued chicken leg and started munching on it. He drank a long swig of beer, set down the can, and again swept the nightscope slowly over the wooded mountainside. This time a bright spot near the top of the dark mountain shoulder attracted his attention. He took half a minute intensively studying a patch of firs, and decided that the smudge of light marked an access road from the west. Maybe a fire road, or a forestry access lane. Or just maybe the faint gleam of some sort of technology installation from the cavern reflected in a clearing. Whatever else this might be, von Alp told himself, it's certainly a good excuse to get moving, take a closer look at it, instead of sitting idly in this parking lot!

At that moment the transceiver buzzed. It was Claudia. She told him what had happened at the chalet. Von Alp listened in astonishment, then lavished praise on her for so resolutely taking charge. He was about to hang up, telling her that he had to go take a look at a mysterious clearing he had discovered, when she sighed deeply, right into his ear.

"Theo, I'm totally bushed. This was just a little too much. I need you, you . . ."

"Pssst, darling, I'm on my way. I'll be with you within an hour. Where are you right now?"

"Lying on the bed. With the lights off." Her voice sounded hoarse, sensuous.

"Naked?"

"Yes. Completely."

"Legs spread?"

"Yes, if only you were here. My hand . . . uh . . . oh . . ."

"What?"

"My hand is . . . down there . . . in my crotch."

"Is it . . . uh . . . inside?"

"Yes, yes, inside! It's so . . . wonderful. I'm thinking of you. What are you doing?"

"I uh, well uh, I'm sitting here by the scope . . . I uh it's uh . . . out . . ."

"All the way out? Is it big?"

"Yes, very big. I mean huge. Say something . . ."

"I want your prick, that hard prick of yours. Hold on to it for me!"

"Yes, I'm holding it. Tight. Tell me everything now . . ."

"My finger is sliding gently up and down over my clit, and now . . . in, inside, uh ohuuuh, it's wonder . . . I'm horny, Theo."

"You're making me hard as a rock. I can feel your lips, see your tits . . ."

"My lips wrapped around your prick, I'm going crazy, wait, I'll turn over, on my belly . . . I . . ."

Von Alp heard a car drive up and turn into the parking space next to his.

"Come," she said, "come on . . . now . . . come . . . !"

"Darling, I can't . . . come," he replied, " 'cause I've got to . . . go . . ."

He disconnected, sat motionless in the dark, peering cautiously out at the parked car on whose front seat a couple were necking and kissing, applying loving suction all over each other's faces. Softly muttering unpleasantries to himself, von Alp slid behind the wheel of the Ram, kicked the engine to life, backed out and roared off with a mighty blast of frustration that tore the lovers apart. They sat bolt upright, distraught and pale in the flash from von Alp's headlights.

Lieutenant Colonel Henri Carrard switched on the afterburner. The silver-gray body of the Mirage-S bearing the insignia of the Swiss Air Force trembled as the craft rose, thundering at full throttle into the blackness of the sky. The experienced test pilot kept a practiced eye on altimeter and power-plant performance indicators as he reached an altitude of 9,500 meters. After ninety seconds of afterburner action, high above the glittering resort town of St. Moritz, Carrard pulled the jet into a tight rollover, then began a thunderous bottom-up descent toward the northwest.

The instrument panel showed that all indications were within the normal range. Carrard noted that the entire run since takeoff had been absolutely normal. He went into a roll above the faintly shimmering granite rockfaces of the Gotthard Pass, then thrust down into the broad, dark valley of the Rhone River, all the while automatically checking his coordinates on the map display and confirming his findings by optically scanning the area. Set off against the gleaming white peaks and forbidding black chasms of the mighty fourteen-thousand-foot massifs, the familiar lights of the small town which was his home base winked cozily up at him.

Carrard called into the radio, "Tivoli Uno, Missione Finito, Securo via Fendant, then Ritorno."

"Roger, receiving you loud and clear," acknowledged the control commander at the base, chuckling to himself. Fendant was Henri's favorite Rhone Valley white wine. Securo normally meant reconnaissance, but sometimes, like now, after a successful night run, it simply stood for a brief bonus sightseeing tour.

Carrard had throttled the engine and reduced speed, while keeping a constant altitude of 3,150 meters above sea level, or approximately 2,000 meters above the actual valley floor. He was approaching the area where yesterday he had nearly collided with the helicopter. In the distance the lofty peak of the Mont Blanc massif glittered in the moonlight. To the north, behind the Dents-du-Midi peaks, there was an intimation of the vast pale mirror of Lake Geneva.

It was quite in keeping with the thoughtful character of the experienced test pilot that he hadn't simply banished the near-collision with the Super-Puma from his mind. Now, in the light of the brutal murder of the pilot Summermatter, the incident developed a dramatic slant. The notion that there was a connection between the indication of radioactive radiation in the cockpit of the F/A-18 and the murder of the helicopter pilot wouldn't let go of him.

Pulling his craft upward at a slight angle, he headed for the Italian border.

Carrard cut away shortly before the mighty, black north face of the Matterhorn. The Mirage-S roared along above the glistening white snowfields, taking a northwesterly course into the clear, moonlit summer night. The lieutenant colonel had decided to take a short detour via Nucleanne before returning to the base. After all, you never knew. "Securo via Fendant . . ."

Under each wing, the Mirage carried a container that looked like an air-to-air missile but in fact housed a high-resolution camera capable of taking perfectly focused images from several hundred meters altitude, even in the dead of night. While the flash-photo equipment Carrard carried certainly could not be described as state-of-the-art technology, it was more than adequate for what he had in mind.

The moment Carrard had noted the reddish glow on a wooded mountainside, he'd gone into a long loop, thinking he might have happened upon a forest fire. The heavy craft again passed over the area at an altitude of 250 meters. For the fraction of a second, the electronic flash from his cameras turned night into day, and the thunderous blast from the jet's power plant shook the treetops even as the Mirage was shrinking to a tiny, glowing dot in the night sky.

A little over an hour later, in his office, the test pilot put down the receiver after having phoned in a detailed report to the chief of Air Force Intelligence.

"This doesn't look good at all, Henri," the chief's stentorian voice assaulted his ear. "Our people took a good look at those pictures of yours and immediately called for a red alert."

After Carrard returned to base, the base laboratory had digitalized his photos in record time, then electronically transmitted them to the appropriate department at General Staff Headquarters in Bern. Carrard blessed the day the computer scanners of the base's image transmission facilities were spared the axe during the recent cost-cutting binge. Sighing, he asked to be connected with Police Chief Thomas Borli.

On the desk before the pilot lay three black-and-white photo enlargements which all showed exactly the same thing: a small forest clearing high on the mountain. Its floor had cleverly been made to look like rock; its edges were lost among the sparse underbrush of the surrounding forest. In the center of the clearing, a broad, black steel frame clearly delineated a hexagonal area, which in turned encompassed a circular opening approximately two and a half meters in diameter.

A crackling noise in the receiver broke Carrard's concentration on the photographs. A voice asked him to please hold.

Squinting some more at the prints, he began to see that the whole thing looked like an enormous armored hatch. Two hydraulic arms appeared to have pushed open the heavy cover, allowing a partial view into the interior of the silo. Between the silo's edge and the hexagonal frame ran thick strands of cable, probably part of some hydraulic system. Again he noted the heavy lateral braces that anchored the big pipe into the mountain. Circular cover plates, bolted into sheer rock, indicated abutments.

Even as he studied the evidence before him, Carrard still believed he might be looking at one of the military's fortified mine-thrower entrenchments. Wedging the receiver between shoulder and ear, he used both hands to hold two of the pictures up to the light for closer examination.

An electric shock went through him like a bolt of lightning.

What he now saw was the outline of clamps that stabilized what looked like a warhead atop a missile, which reached almost to the edge of the half-open hatch. Below that, he made out a flat, white launch pad. In the depths of the pipe, the flash of light had sharply silhouetted the contours of the entire installation.

Carrard suddenly understood that he was looking down into an open silo containing one missile ready for launching. And, it so happened, Switzerland had neither short- nor medium-range rockets, or missiles, and certainly not any stationed at camouflaged underground launching sites.

"Sir? Are you still there? One moment, I'm putting you through," the female operator said.

In the half minute or so he'd been waiting on the phone, Lieutenant Colonel Carrard was jolted into realizing that he held the evidence of an extreme emergency—a major disaster about to happen.

Borli, who received Carrard's call at the operational base he'd improvised on the farm near the Schlammer Engineering compound, listened incredulously to the test pilot's report.

"Are you absolutely certain of this, Lieutenant Colonel?" he finally asked, his voice heavy with growing apprehension. "What can we do to abort this thing? How about wiping it out with laser-guided air-to-ground missiles?"

"Not possible, sir," Carrard retorted drily. "We don't have any. Our new crates are interceptors, pure and simple, not equipped for air-to-ground combat. Sorry, sir, but that's what they call our cutback strategy, or our disarmament policy, or . . . well, take your pick. Yes, we are testing laser targeting devices for air-to-ground combat, but they are far from operational. Sorry again, sir."

"Just one moment, Lieutenant Colonel. Are you telling me you're at the end of your tether here? I mean, surely the Air Force can think of something to do in this situation."

"The answer still is no, Chief. We've looked at all the options here, believe me. The best we can come up with is shooting it down with air-to-air missiles just after it's been launched."

"Well, there you are."

"But that's much too risky. If we shoot it down it could explode on the ground. On Swiss territory. It's safer to just let it go wherever it's going. Sorry, sir. Even if this particular missile in this particular silo is equipped with a fail-safe ignition function, we . . ."

"What's a fail-safe ignition function?"

"That's a detonator safety function which delays the weapon-head's ignition program until the missile has covered a certain distance. That way, you prevent an explosion in the event of a launch mishap. But we don't know if this rocket has such a function. In any case, it's nothing we can rely on. So we've decided to just sit tight, sir."

"Hmmmh," went Borli. "And what if we blow it up inside the silo?"

"It's an idea, but in my view it would take too much time to get a demolition team ready for the job. Besides, it wouldn't really solve our problem. Blowing up the missile might well set off its warhead. And judging by the pictures I'm looking at, that could easily be a *nuclear* warhead. That's why we don't want to interfere with the launch. Let her fly, Chief—as far away as possible! NATO will probably lock in on it very quickly and shoot it down somewhere else."

An extended silence ensued on the line. Carrard could well imagine Borli's furrowed brow; the athletic police chief was a casual acquaintance with whom he sometimes shared a workout slot at the MACH-2 Fitness Club.

"So, what's your verdict, Chief?"

"Well, I'd say right now air surveillance is our best bet. Especially since we can't be sure the missile will actually be launched. But let's assume the worst case, and put close round-the-clock air surveillance on the silo site. Also . . ." Borli hesitated.

"Yes?"

"I understand the chief of the General Staff and the defense minister have been trying to alert NATO headquarters."

"Trying, sir?"

"Right. Apparently Brussels didn't take them very seriously. They came back with a polite inquiry as to whether this might have to do with Swiss Army maneuvers. They also asked to see the aerial photographs. So, right now, Lieutenant Colonel, those pictures of yours are being studied by NATO specialists."

"Great, and thanks for the information, but what *else* are we doing?"

"I'm sending in a counterterrorism squad. As soon as my men have a ground fix on the silo, we'll know more. In the meantime . . . well, Lieutenant Colonel, let's just pray that rocket doesn't get launched."

In the nuclear cavern, July 4

Tony started running toward them just as Mark slammed a vicious kick into the neck of the dog that was attacking Stephanie, sending it flying to one side. Howling with pain and fury, the beast was back on its feet, baring its fangs, crouching low for another snarling leap. Stephanie was on her stomach, her face buried under her arms. Over the intercom, the mechanical voice intoned: "Twenty minutes, repeat, twenty minutes, to launch. Five minutes, repeat, five minutes to launch-lock time."

His keen reflexes working overtime, Mark grabbed Stephanie's black bag and jammed it into the jaws of the raging brute. The dog's teeth clamped shut and held fast. Still holding the bag, Mark tried to wrestle the monstrous hound over toward the railing. Suddenly, the beast let go and turned on Tony, who'd stepped in to shield his brother with his own body.

"I've got it!" they heard Jessie shout, and then the dog was on them again. Tony caught sight of the bright patch of hair on its chest, saw its fumbling paws, the gaping black hole of its stinking maw, the pointed canines flashing at him. Tumbling backwards, holding his hunting knife in a two-fisted grip, he thrust deeply into the neck of the shaggy bulk that descended upon him. As the dog collapsed without a sound, Tony shifted his weight, using his body as a lever to tilt the still-trembling carcass over the edge. It seemed to take forever before it bounced off the docking station and slid down beneath one of the power plants, where it hung slack, sending up clouds of stinking yellow smoke as it fried to a crisp.

"Man oh man that was close!" panted Mark.

"Listen! You hear that?" Tony said and they listened up into the domed ceiling. The rattling and booming noises from above had suddenly lost intensity, as if someone had cut off the steam.

"I did it, yesss! It works!" Jessie shouted as if to confirm their observation. She jumped up, performing a veritable dance of joy in front of the monitors. The siren had stopped its cacophonous wailing.

Stephanie risked a glance upward from under her sheltering arms and saw Mark and Tony rushing over to the elevators. They grabbed the brown suitcases and began to pull them toward the tunnel. She got up shakily, holding on to the banister.

"Once I figured out what to do, it wasn't hard at all," Jessie enthused, still caught up in her computer victory, as they trudged through the passage. "You had to wall the four compartments shut before the sand ran out of the upper portion of the hourglass!"

The others weren't really listening. Still seeing the snarling dogs in their mind's eye, they couldn't yet grasp that she had succeeded in aborting the launch at the very last moment.

"The point of no return was fifteen minutes before the actual launch time," Jessie panted. Her voice reverberated eerily from the rock walls of the narrow tunnel. "Another minute and we wouldn't have been able to stop it. But there's still the ignition of the detonating chambers." Her voice sounded pressed, her breath came in gasps. "I couldn't figure out how to get to that. If that crazy Breckerlin wasn't bluffing, we'll all be blown to smithereens in about seventy minutes!"

Tony automatically checked his watch, calculating that the hellish fireworks would begin at one o'clock in the morning. Then he noticed a patch of luminous night sky farther ahead, at the end of the subterranean passage.

They had no difficulty getting through the barred door. Cautiously, one after the other, they stepped out into the open. Rubbing their eyes and blinking up at the sky, they found themselves standing on a rocky slope in the forest. The bulks of two vehicles were indistinctily silhouetted on a narrow road ahead. Someone had already pushed open the heavy concrete door that was made to look like a part of the surrounding rockface. But now the four nearly panicked at the sight of a big, threatening figure that materialized out of the twilight.

"You're about as quiet as a rampaging herd of elephants!"

They heaved a collective sigh of relief when they heard von Alp's voice and saw his big, welcoming grin. He led them to the Dodge, which faced in the direction they were going.

"A welcoming committee for you got here before I did," he said, motioning toward the other car. "I took the liberty of neutralizing its two members," he continued casually as he lifted the two suitcases into the van. "Now let's get out of here. If what Jessie says is true, this will soon be a highly inappropriate spot for a picnic!"

But instead of getting into the van, the four put their heads together in a conspiratorial huddle. Then Stephanie spoke up to von Alp.

"I've got to go back into the cavern," she said in a voice that tolerated no objection. "Tony will guide me down through the air duct. Mark and Jessie will wait in the cave above the rocky ledge. We've no time to lose. We have less than an hour to the big bang!"

She felt a lot better now; her fighting spirit had returned and along with it the tracking instincts of the investigative reporter. She sensed strongly that somewhere down inside the mountain, Ken Custer was in serious trouble.

Watching the four jog off into the darkness, von Alp started up the engine. He left the clearing slowly, without switching on the lights. The two carry-on nukes, each packing fifteen kilotons of explosive power, rocked imperceptibly back and forth on the softly carpeted floor as the Ram negotiated the welts and bumps of the narrow forest road. The time was just before midnight, July 4.

July 4, Washington, D.C., 6 P.M.

Chin thrust forward, lips grimly compressed, the president of the United States hurried through a desolately gray corridor in the subterranean complex of the White House. Members of his staff floundered in his wake, trying to keep up with him.

Every time the supreme commander approached the Briefing Room on the lowest sublevel of the great subterranean installation, an oppressive feeling made him regret that he had never served in the Army—unlike his predecessors, who routinely used their wartime service records and combat experience to make an impression on the generals of the Joint Chiefs of Staff. He would have given a lot to make up for this handicap and be able to stand his ground when discussing military operations with the general staff.

Forging ahead, his torso at a bold forward angle, determined to impress with at least a posture of resolve, the president yanked open the door a second before the secretary to the White House Chief of Staff, who eagerly rushed forward to help him, managed to get there. Instantly, the hubbub of voices in the room ceased.

"All set, gentlemen?" the president called out—his voice a bit too loud, his tone a bit too cheery—as he moved to the large, round table whose top gave off a subtle sheen under the indirect lighting. The uniformed men rose from their chairs and greeted their supreme commander with a curt lifting of their chins, some of them touching fingers to their foreheads in brisk salutes.

"Strategic Air Command is keeping the area of operations under constant surveillance, sir," said the chairman of the Joint Chiefs, handing the president a red dossier.

"AWACs?"

"No, sir, two EC-135s."

"Ah, our magnifying glasses," the president said, trying out some of his newly acquired, but still limited, flyboy lingo. He was staring at the legend on the dossier cover: TOP SECRET—EYES ONLY—FIREBIRD.

"The combat units involved in the operation were given their orders one hour ago, sir. It's all in there."

"Fine. And are we all clear on secondary and tertiary side effects?" The president's coldly calculated bluff achieved precisely what it was meant to. Consternation reigned among the generals assembled around the table.

Frowning and staring intensely at the operational map of the Persian Gulf projected on a screen, they wondered just what secondary and tertiary side effects the supreme commander might be referring to. As for the president, he noted with satisfaction that his play for time worked. At a gesture from the chairman, a brigadier general cleared his throat and went into a stammered improvisation concerning the direct radiation effects in the Euphrates and Tigris region following a nuclear blast over Baghdad.

Listening with his poker face, the president used the time to casually leaf through the red dossier, making mental notes on the main points of the proposed operational agenda. After two or three hectic minutes of listening to the embarassingly simpleminded strategic babble, he interrupted the speaker.

"Fine, and what are our backup options? What if something *does* go wrong?" His angry gaze impaled the generals as if on a trident. Damn if he hadn't caught them napping again!

"Well, uh, sir," the chairman began, "one of the Armed Services committees is currently at work ironing out the fine points of Operation Firebird. The deputy . . ."

"Fine, fine, General, good to know you're ironing things out. In the future, when I walk into this room, I want everything ready and spread out on the table, I mean ready and I mean everything, am I making myself clear? All right then, now I'll talk to whoever's in charge of Firebird."

In the tense silence that filled the room with subliminally crackling static, only the hum of the monitors could be heard. The uniformed women and men at the other tables in the room had all paused in their work to stare at the president. One could have heard the proverbial pin drop.

On the large screen the picture of the captain of the cruiser *U.S.S. Monterey*, on patrol off Qatar in the Persian Gulf, coalesced into focus.

"Good evening, Mr. President, I'm Commander Fitzgerald Clifton McClosky aboard the *Monterey*, Combat Unit Independence."

Somewhat redundantly, the president said, "Commander, do you recognize me?"

"Affirmative, sir, I do."

"Fine. Commander McClosky, do you have your orders for Operation Firebird in hand?"

The president held up the red folder for the tanned, square face on the screen to see.

"Affirmative, sir, I have."

"Then you know that this operation posits destruction of the city of Baghdad by nuclear means, using nuclear warheads on missiles."

"Yes, sir," McClosky retorted evenly, "I do know that."

"As well as, optionally, the destruction of the cities of Mosul and Erbil in northern Iraq, where experimental stations serving Iraq's nuclear effort are located."

"Affirmative, sir, I am aware of these options."

"Fine, Commander. Now, in the event we do not succeed before ten P.M. Eastern Daylight Time, tonight, in tracking down and disabling the nuclear device sequestered by terrorists somewhere in Philadelphia, I shall order you, Commander McClosky, to launch the Tomahawk missiles equipped with nuclear warheads that are now on standby aboard your ship and earmarked for this operation, at the designated targets, precisely as detailed in the order package for Operation Firebird which you have told me you have in hand. Is this clearly understood and are we in agreement, Commander McClosky?"

"Affirmative, Mr. President," McClosky said without hesitation. "I have understood you clearly and we are in complete agreement. Operation Firebird may be implemented at any time starting at ten P.M. Eastern Daylight Time tonight, yes, sir, Mr. President!" Commander McClosky's large, wide front teeth clamped down on the thin center portion of his lower lip.

"What we are looking at here is a retaliatory measure, avenging the destruction of the historical center of Philadelphia, which may occur tonight," said the president. "We're certain that Muslim fundamentalists are behind this scheme."

"Yes, sir, I know. My family is in Philadelphia." McClosky paused for the barest fraction of a second. "I know what needs to be done."

At a gesture of the president, the Navy chief of staff spoke directly to the image of McClosky. "Next briefing will be sixty minutes from now, Commander."

"Roger, sir, understood. Briefing at nineteen hundred hours and fifteen minutes Eastern Daylight Time."

The screen went blank. Again a din of voices rose in the White House Briefing Room, as the generals at the table put their heads together. The president went over to another table. Behind a battery of monitors and telecommunications equipment, hastily put up in the morning, sat the director of the CIA. Now he rose and took a few steps toward his superior.

"Hello, Mitch," said the president, "what's new on the SCUDO front?"

"Sir, I've put our Cray-X-2000 super mainframe on full priority for SCUDO. We're investigating all possible terrorist cell formations and we're processing and reprocessing all data from the past six months in that area. I hope that wonderful Cray of ours soon coughs up something solid, sir."

"Any suspicious movements? In the air, or on the roads, Mitch? Special transports, noteworthy events or incidents?"

The director shook his head.

"Well, let's not be bashful with this, Mitch, go for it! Put everything you have into Philly. Is there anything or anyone you can think of who could be useful to us?"

This question remained hanging in the air, ominous and unanswered.

The government of Iraq doggedly denied any involvement in the anticipated attempt on the city of Philadelphia, while at the same time accusing the United States of trying to manufacture an excuse for launching a retaliatory strike against Baghdad. Beyond offering their support, the allies of the United States appeared to be helpless. The burden of responsibility now rested on the shoulders of the National Security Agency, who were frantically sifting through the past seventy-two hours' worth of communications with other countries, searching for clues. The Cray-X-2000 super mainframe computer was analyzing telephone calls, fax messages, and other electronic transmissions, in an all-out effort to come up with some shred of information that could help unravel this insidious plot. Meanwhile, the FBI carried out an in-depth surveillance of all U.S. airports and· seaports. And the CIA was squeezing its foreign sources for all they were worth, trying to follow up on the initial clues these latter had yielded.

At SCUDO headquarters, specialists ran down every conceivable tip. And the police chief of Philadelphia stared pensively at the Magic Marker lines on the map before him, indicating factors such as deployment of security personnel, roadblocks installed, and helicopter surveillance of key areas.

Only 120 minutes remained until zero hour.

While the president and the chairman of the Joint Chiefs were absorbed in their discussion in front of the electronic wall map, Mitch Taylor went back to the table where he fell into his chair. For a moment, he sat there, frowning at the messages on the tabletop before him. It seemed to him that, somehow, the imminent, and cowardly, sneak attack on Philadelphia, which had been confirmed to a virtual certainty, bore the unmistakable imprint of >Keycop<. In fact, it had Custer written all over it. Now why the hell weren't they able to get to the bastard?

Audibly gnashing his teeth, the head of the CIA knocked his fists together. "Goddamn son-of-a-bitch," he cursed softly under his breath, "if I ever get my hands on him, I'll personally wring the bastard's neck!"

Just then a voice called out from a far corner of the Briefing Room, "Custer. On line five."

But Taylor's grinding teeth muffled the words, while the operator tried to get rid of the unidentified caller. An Air Force colonel strolled casually into the room, pretending professional interest in the situation by stooping a look over the shoulders of the computer operators at the long table for NSA specialists. This room, which functioned as a—they were hoping—temporary emergency center, was now the hub of all telecommunications with SCUDO branches, with the police, and with units of the National Guard, as well as with the regular troops deployed throughout Philadelphia. Any sort of communication with the outside could be switched to the intercom system, or be made to appear on one of the giant monitor screens.

The men and women in the White House Briefing Room who, on this Fourth of July, were locked in a desperate struggle with an invisible enemy, could certainly be counted among the nation's finest. But would that suffice to avert the impending disaster?

While the president of the United States was talking by satellite to the commander of the *Monterey*, Tony Summermatter and Stephanie Kramer were climbing quickly down the ventilation shaft. The two hurried through the passage to the lab entrance. There they stood, staring up at the grate that blocked the heating duct. Just to be sure, Tony climbed up on Stephanie's shoulders to take a close look at the heavy screws that now anchored the grate into the cement around the opening. Obviously, someone had taken care to plug up this particular hole. Now the situation seemed hopeless—and time was running out!

Grim-faced and deep in thought, Tony marched up and down in front of Stephanie. His hands thrust deep into his trouser pockets, he suddenly became aware of the fuse he had been fingering. His dark gaze brightening, he rushed back to the maintenance turnout for the forklifts, where he found what he had unconsciously registered when they passed by the niche on their way to the lab duct: tools and canisters with fuel!

He pulled up the cap of one of the gray fuel cans marked *Diesel* and tilted it forward. Stephanie, who'd followed close on his heels, watched intently as some of the liquid poured out. Before she could utter a sound, Tony addressed her in a commanding tone of voice: "Get the fertilizer!"

She automatically grabbed the pail he handed her and rushed back along the passage to the depot of sacks in front of the hatch to the ventilation shaft. Using her hunting knife, she cut a hole into one of the sacks. A thin stream of fine, gray granules trickled into the pail.

She was panting heavily when she returned to the spot where Tony had been busy with his folding knife, cutting the length of fuse and squeezing it into a small detonator cap made of copper. He silently poured the fertilizer through a funnel, which he had found in the tool box, into the half-full canister with diesel fuel.

When he was done with this, he wedged the funnel into the canister and carefully threaded the fuse through the flex-jointed funnel spout until the detonator cap dangled freely in the gas fumes under the canister neck. Then he fixed the fuse in place by stuffing some bunched-up rags into the funnel. All of this took no more than four minutes.

Together, he and Stephanie lugged their homemade canister bomb back to the massive, walled-up door beneath the bolted-down heating duct.

"Wow, Tony, where did you learn all this?" Stephanie marveled, exhaling forcefully.

"From Dad, up by the quarry. We did a lot of blasting up there. He and I." He swallowed hard. For a moment, moisture glistened in his eyes, and tears seemed about to well up. He clutched his forehead with both hands and stared at the angle of the canister, then exclaimed, "We need something to hold this in place!"

Tony ran off before Stephanie had time to figure out what he was talking about. Soon she heard the hum of an electric pickup Tony had discovered near the forklift. The youngster handled the cart elegantly, having been taught by Haluk, the window washer who often allowed one of the Summermatter kids to scoot about on the Schlammer yard, collecting and delivering window-cleaning equipment.

They wedged the canister in between the walled-up opening and the cart. Tony locked the cart's brakes and lit the fuse. Then they bolted down the passage, seeking cover behind the fertilizer bags. There they cowered, pressed against the rockside, chins on their chests, hands covering their ears. Tony prayed that the explosion, blocked as it was by the bulk of the cart, would tear a hole into the door rather than flashing freely out into the tunnel.

"I've cut the fuse down to fifty centimeters," Tony shouted at Stephanie. "It'll burn about thirty sec . . ."

A tremendous explosion made the rock shiver. The shockwave from the blast left them gasping for air behind the barrier of fertilizer sacks.

"Forward!" Tony screamed, his voice hoarse and high, like that of an officer in combat. They rushed up to the devastated doorway and leapt through billowing clouds of acrid fumes, across piles of brick and metal debris, through the jagged hole into an anteroom to the laboratory. Exactly eleven minutes had passed since the moment they had started climbing down the ventilation shaft.

The stiff punch thrown by Hannibal hit a totally unprepared Custer deep in the gut. Doubled up with pain and gasping for air, the man some called >Keycop< went down.

"Where've you got the carry-ons?" Hannibal raged, landing a heavy kick on the writhing figure before him.

Hannibal's brutal attack turned out to be Custer's salvation. As the far wall burst and Tony's improvised blast propelled a hail of debris like shrapnel into the lab, Custer was on the floor, shielded by his adversaries' bodies.

The shower of rock and brick fragments mercilessly struck Schoenhof and Hannibal from behind. As if punched in the small of their backs by an invisible fist, the two twisted bodies whirled past Custer, toward the centrifuge.

Wiping dirt and dust from his face, the dazed Custer pushed himself up. Miraculously, some of the neon tubes still flickered in the lighting wells, enabling Custer to see—with some alarm—two crouching figures emerging from the grayish-white blast cloud.

Custer exhaled with relief when the shape in the lead turned out to be a coughing young man, followed by Stephanie. They stumbled across the mound of debris that the blast had thrown into the room. The reporter stopped dead in her tracks as she came up against the two bodies on the floor. A sturdy piece of concrete protruded from a gaping wound in the back of Hannibal's head. Clearly, no life was left in the ugly hunk of flesh that had once been Schlammer's head of security.

And Schoenhof had been propelled across the drawing board, head forward, into the wall. Strictly speaking, he lay on his belly, his arms and legs grotesquely twisted, but the impact had wrung his neck, breaking it. His horribly disfigured face with its bulging dead eyes stared dully upward from the body's back.

Custer motioned Stephanie and Tony over to the large map table, which was outside the main path of the blast, while he stooped to remove the red transceiver phone from the white lab coat on Schoenhof's twisted body. When Stephanie blurted out that the mountain would be blown to smithereens inside thirty minutes, the adventurer made no reply, but instead gazed thoughtfully back at her.

He connected the red handset to the antenna cable, the way he had previously seen Schoenhof do it. And when Stephanie impatiently asked what was to be done about the nuclear plot on the city of Philadelphia, he simply told her that, considering how little time was left, only the secret code could abort the ignition process that had been initiated.

As Stephanie scanned the map and rifled through the drawers in the lab rack, searching for some useful clue, Custer told them what he had learned from Schoenhof. All ignition codes embedded in the weapons made by Schlammer Engineering could be broken by means of a certain sequence of digits.

Frowning, Custer continued, "The only thing Schoenhof said to me was that the codes were based on a four-figure sequence with a dual mirror image. Something like 8888, I believe."

"A dual reflection? It doesn't make sense to me. How many combinations could there be?" Stephanie said, dumbfounded, as she slipped off her backpack.

"We can't afford to experiment," Custer decided. "We've got to look for clues here in the lab. Take another look at those maps, while I try to get help."

Custer began to belabor the transceiver keyboard, peripherally aware of Tony, who had climbed up to the loft. The youth soon returned with a garish red bedspread, which he threw over the twisted, broken body of Schoenhof. Then Custer's efforts on the transceiver were answered by a female voice. He asked to speak with the director of the Central Intelligence Agency.

"Nationwide emergency," he rasped.

Eminently unimpressed, the voice said, "Hold on, please."

"*Ut desint vires tamen est laudanda voluntas*," Custer intoned, rolling his eyes heavenward. Stephanie shot a surprised glance at him, trying to remember her rusty Latin. She translated, *The strength may be flagging, but the will deserves praise*, then bent low, redoubling her efforts to find some clue to a four-digit code in the Pennsylvania area on the map.

"One moment, please. . . ." the voice told Custer. A brief static pause ensued.

An indignant male voice came on the line. "Who the hell are you, man? The director is busy. I'll connect you with Coordination, where you can . . ."

"Damn you, this is Custer. Kenneth W. Custer," Custer swore. "Now put me through!"

For a moment none of them spoke. As if heard from a conch shell, the distant roar of the Atlantic filled the transceiver. Then Custer sensed approaching voices. Someone on the other end cleared his throat.

"Mitch Taylor here, Custer, what do you want? Why don't you cut out the crap, we've got a national emergency on our hands here. If you're trying to mess with us, forget it. On the other hand, if you're serious, tell us where you are and we'll call you back."

"Keep your shirt on, Taylor," Custer shot back. "I know that what you've got is a nuclear charge ticking away somewhere in Philadelphia right this moment. Matter of fact, I've got—"

"We're well aware of that," Taylor cut in gruffly. Aping Custer, he continued, "Matter of fact, we believe what you've got is your grubby little fingers in this pie!"

A distant babble of excited voices ebbed and swelled in the transceiver. "Listen up, you damn fools," Custer shouted angrily, "I have vital information, are you listening? Information on how to defuse the fuckin' bomb you're fuckin' sitting on, understand? Now get with it, time's running out. And you can't rely on SCUDO!"

For a few heartbeats there was an eerie lack of response from the other end. Then Taylor's voice crackled into Custer's ear. "Okay, Mr. Custer, what've you got?"

Custer proceeded methodically, starting with the time setting on the detonator. Hoping Breckerlin's data were reliable, he then patiently explained the device's ignition program to the listeners, taking them step by step through the instructions he had gleaned from the manual. The only response was the silence of the grave from across the Atlantic; even the static ocean appeared to have been stilled by these devastating data. Custer suggested they check through all the licensing registers for recent transceiver service subscriptions in the Philadelphia area.

"Find the transceiver that initiates the ignition dialog with the bomb, and you can home in on the bomb," he told them. There was another, even more desperate, silence.

Then Taylor spoke, his voice drained of all affect. "And then what?"

"The name of the nuke is SADAM, tell them, Ken," Stephanie called to him. "The containers are black, we saw some stored in the cavern. Wait!"

She pulled out her video camera and activated Rewind.

"Taylor, listen, they're using a SADAM-type device," Custer said into the set. "What? No no no, it's got nothing to do with Saddam Hussein. S-A-D-A-M, that's the name of the bomb. Some dumb military acronym, you ought to know. Hold on!" He glanced intently at Stephanie.

"Ken, tell them, like the American weapon—this is really stupid—I can't remember the name." Her eyes pleaded with Tony for help.

"Listen," Custer bellowed into the transceiver, "we're talking demolition ammunition here. The Army's got it. It's called . . . uh . . . wait . . ."

"The great folk hero of the Alamo!" Stephanie shouted.

"Right," Custer roared, "Remember the Alamo! and I don't mean John Wayne. Damn you, Taylor, don't you take your kids to Disney movies? John . . . Bowie! No, wait . . . Davy, yeah, that's it . . . Davy Crockett! Ring a bell?!"

Stephanie nodded frantically, "Yes, that's the name."

"That's it, Taylor," Custer said, "my expert confirms—Davy Crockett ammunition, right! In heavy, black containers. Start looking for Davy Crockett, Mr. Taylor! What? Atomic demolition ammunition, yes, we're positive. Yes, a lot of it. Half a kiloton, maybe more. Where? Don't you think I'd fuckin' tell you if I knew? Somewhere, buddy. In Philadelphia. No, no idea. We haven't got any more than that. That's it!"

"So what do we do if and when we locate the bomb, Custer?"

"You enter the dialog mode, which you do by . . . hold on . . . uh . . . by entering STAR-ZERO-ZERO. Got that? That starts the dialog with the ignition program built into the fission pack." Custer darted a desperate glance at his wristwatch. "What? Yeah, right, it works like a multifunction answering machine. Electronic voice mail. A voice will ask you to enter digits for certain functions, get it?"

Custer mopped real sweat off his brow.

"Then, toward the end of the dialog, the computerized voice will ask you for the four-digit code that interrupts the ignition process . . . uh, no, not *fair*, you nerd, *four*. Four digits! Now, Taylor, that will be the moment of truth, do you understand? Now, with this four-digit figure you can defuse the bomb! Are you listening, dammit? Will you remember what I've just told you?"

He paused to fan away wisps of smoke with his hand.

"And just what are those four digits?" asked the breathless Taylor.

"Hold on, Taylor, that's what we're working on. . . ."

Stephanie stepped away from the map table, intent on once again ransacking the drawers for a notebook, loose sheets of notes, anything. Instead, she stumbled over a carton on the floor. Irritated and frustrated, she sent the obstacle flying with a vicious kick, then froze as she watched black lace panties and crimson garter belts whirl through the air. Her left hand came up automatically, to slap her forehead.

"Got it!" she called to Ken. "Of course! Four digits with a dual mirror image. Double reflection, yes, that's it! How could I have missed? That Schoenhof, what a pervert!"

"Bingo, we've got it!" Custer informed the team in the White House Briefing Room, where the call was being relayed through the intercom. He turned a puzzled frown toward Stephanie, wondering what she had come up with, hoping against hope, catching her eye, or rather, not quite catching it but following her gaze to the gaping hole in the wall.

There, legs spread wide, straddling debris, stood Schlammer, aiming a heavy, black handgun at them . . . firing.

Ducking reflexively, Custer heard the whiplash crack of the gun, felt a fiery burn like a bolt of lightning against the side of his head, then tumbled relentlessly down into an ocean of lethal red oblivion.

Stephanie screeched. Custer fell sideways against the wall and slumped to the floor, blood flowing down the side of his head. With a predatory leap, Schlammer reached Stephanie and twisted her left arm behind her back. Again she cried out, and felt the barrel of his gun pressing hard into her side. She tried to get out of the tycoon's grip, using her right hand to pull and scratch at her captor's wrist. All she managed to do was rip one of the cuff links from his sleeve, but she clutched it desperately in one fist, like so much booty, a sharp-edged hunting trophy.

It would have been silly to put up more of a fight. Sharply increasing the pressure on her arm so that she groaned with pain, Schlammer pushed her roughly forward, hissing at her to climb out through the hole in the wall. As the two stepped out into the cavern tunnel, Tony started crawling out from under the map table. With a pang of terror he realized that, without Custer, they were lost—all of them!

He began to crawl toward the motionless figure on the floor, taking a closer look. No sign of life! Beside himself with despair and fatigue, he stared at the steady trickle of blood from the wound in Custer's skull. He had no idea what to do next. Desperately surveying the chaotic mess in the debris-strewn lab, he noticed a first-aid box the blast had torn from its mount on the wall and smashed to the floor. Slowly, on all fours, he made his way toward it.

"Up until right now, Kramer," Schlammer panted as he pushed Stephanie along the tunnel toward a metal staircase, "anyone stupid enough to fight me has been destroyed. But in your case I'll make an exception. I'm giving you one last chance."

Stephanie shuddered as she looked down into the fuel-rod cooling basin whose deep, glinting waters reflected an ominous black in the lab windows. An impulse made her open her fist, stop. The tycoon's pistol jammed hard into her ribs, but she barely noticed the stinging pain. She was staring at the cuff link in her hand: a golden cross set in a dark blue opal. The base of the crucifix's vertical bar was shaped like an anchor, the figure on the cross flanked by two letters, S and F, with the combination of cross and anchor suggesting a connection with seafaring.

Countless times in the past, often through entire sleepless nights, she had stared at precisely such a cuff link as this, pondering its significance. It had been pried from the tightly shut, stiffened fist of her father after they pulled him out of the water. No one had ever had a plausible explanation for the stone the dead man was found clutching like a final piece of evidence. One interpretation of the letters S and F cited the popular Latin motto *Semper Fidelis, Loyal Forever*. Someone else had suggested that SF stood for the San Francisco naval base. Stephanie had finally opted for a personalized version of her own: STEPHANIE—STRONG AND FREE.

Schlammer understood immediately that the young woman had made the connection. His hollow voice gave him away as he told her that the cuff links were a gift from a friend in the U.S. Navy; then he beckoned her sardonically toward the basin below. Shielding her eyes with the open palm of one hand, a pale, proudly erect Stephanie slowly descended the stairs. She took each step as if she were moving to the measured cadences of a funeral march, cautiously making her way to the edge of the cooling basin. Schlammer was right behind her, his right arm loosely swinging the gun back and forth.

Stephanie turned abruptly, piercing Schlammer with a stare as pointed as a laser, as menacing as white-hot steel.

"You killed my father!"

Schlammer shrugged indifferently. "Yes," he said, "precisely in this spot, many years ago. Not that it matters at this remove. Right now, I'm helping you get out of here, and I'm protecting you from the cops who've surrounded the entire place. I want to propose a solution, out of respect for your father, who . . ."

"How did it happen?" The young woman's ice-cold voice belied her flashing eyes. She took a couple of steps away from the edge of the pool.

"There's no time for that."

"*Tell me!*" she bellowed, thrusting the blue-and-gold cuff link at him.

Schlammer recoiled as if she had shoved a gun in his face. At last he blurted, "All right. Your father, we called him Alpha. It happened over twenty-five years ago, right here in the experimental nuclear station in this cavern. . . ."

. . . Dr. Walter Kramer, the nuclear physicist, stepped at nine A.M. sharp that January morning in 1969 into the Swiss Government's underground nuclear facilities near Nucleanne. But first, he stopped to look back at the castle across the valley. Morning mists still enveloped the picturesque town while, up above, the morning sun's first rays touched the gold-on-red coat of arms with the black bear, mounted on the imposing face of the castle's valleyside wall. As he punched in the six-digit code that would open the entrance door, the man whom his colleagues respectfully called Alpha again reminded himself that a definitive decision was due within two hours. The heavy steel door slowly slid aside, opening the way into the cavern.

Alpha descended to the M-Level two stories below, where he stepped into the personnel lock. He carefully locked the door behind himself, took off his threadbare leather coat, and pulled on the yellow insulation coveralls. He put on a pair of gray safety boots, gloves, and a windowed hood, then exited the room marked PS 18 through the opposite door.

The M-Level, also known as Dome Hall, was situated directly above the reactor core. Normally, radioactive emissions inside the upper portion of the facility varied from 62 to 73 rem. This was considered within the critical range, but not an immediate health hazard. The moment Alpha routinely checked the dosimeter mounted on the wall near the entrance to Dome Hall, he knew something was wrong. The instrument indicated 234 rem. This constituted Hazard Level 2, meaning severe damage to any human organism after two hours of exposure, with death a virtual certainty after eight hours of exposure.

Now sharply alert to the situation, Dr. Kramer knew that he had to get to the control room as fast as he could. Slowed by the clumsy protective clothing, he hastened back to the staircase, halted, his heart beating high in his throat. Had he heard something? A door slamming shut? But all around him an eerie silence reigned. He clomped down two more stories, to the O-Level, at an underground elevation of 508.3 meters above sea level. Only two meters below, the reactor was boiling! In an instant of dazzling clarity, Alpha realized that something here was dreadfully wrong. He crossed the adjoining Room 19, pushed open the opposite door and stood at the edge of the fuel rod basin.

The heat! he exclaimed to himself. Recoiling from the temperatures that brutally assaulted him, he saw clouds of vapor gushing up near the entrance to the control room at the far end of the forty-meter-long basin. Alpha ran flat out now, panting inside the face mask, trying to impose some semblance of order on his runaway mind, shamelessly babbling to himself inside the windowed hood, "Some minor disturbance maybe . . . no . . . worse . . . a breakdown . . . the feared . . . no, not that . . . not a meltdown . . . it could . . . couldn't be true . . . not that, not now . . . !"

Today was to have been the day of decision—perhaps, for him, the crowning glory of all those years of research and experimentation. And today, of all days, an accident?! Perhaps that which the Germans called a GAC—the Greatest Assumable Catastrophe.

He stopped. There it was again, that heavy, metallic sound. There could be no tarrying now—on to the control room! Yet as he clunked along, hobbled by the bulky protective gear, bathed in a sweat of fear and agitation, the events of the past few weeks reeling off with frantic speed in his mind, he perceived every detail with the utmost clarity. . . .

. . . Two days earlier, on the eve of the decisive meeting in that auspicious year of 1969, a young Adam Schlammer had gone to see Dr. Kramer in his study at Nucleanne castle. Their plan had been to go through all the details—one more time, the two of them together. Once again, Schlammer had focused on the sheet with Dr. Kramer's formulae and equations, been profoundly stirred, and exclaimed, "Brilliant, Alpha, quite simply phenomenal . . . !"

"Nobody will believe me," Alpha replied in a tone of resignation. His tired gaze traveled through the window, to the reactor's cavern entrance on the far side of the valley. Yes, he had been tired and exhausted then, almost as tired and exhausted as he was now in his clumsy dash toward the control room. . . .

. . . but then . . . then, young Schlammer had made a remarkable comment, telling Kramer that, viewed against the backdrop of current international developments, he was twenty years ahead of his time.

"You see, Walter," Schlammer had said, "what we're facing are very tangible, very practical economic and military interests. You know better than most the harsh realities, the bitter truth that war furthers research, generates money, lavishes fame on individuals. In times of peace, research is financed by the arms industry. However . . ."

"However what? What are you talking about?"

"Well, without arms contracts, without the pressures of vital necessity, without pressures from the outside—you know what I mean—without these things nothing happens. No priorities, no deadlines, no moolah . . . which could, well . . ." He allowed his words to peter out into a calculated silence.

"Come on, Adam, out with it. Don't hold back."

"What I mean, is that all this research, everything you're working for, might be shelved, put on ice. If there's no strategic purpose, I mean. In fact, the process you've developed is diametrically opposed to the currently expedient nuclear technology. By the way, who besides the committee has a copy of your research brief?"

"No one, of course," Alpha had replied, trying to suppress an uneasy feeling. Schlammer's sometimes blunt manner was beginning to get on his nerves. The two had met at CERN: he, Dr. Kramer, the seasoned researcher with a brilliant career, having started as a novice assistant with Professor Hahn at the Kaiser-Wilhelm Institute in Berlin, later to continue in the United States. And Schlammer, still a blank page in an unwritten book, straight from the university: thirsty for knowledge, ambitious, power-hungry, and of remarkable impatience.

"Well, actually," Alpha told Schlammer, "strictly speaking, even the committee doesn't have my documentation."

"What?" Schlammer took an involuntary step forward, moving closer to Alpha. "You mean . . . ?"

"I mean, my findings, after all, are rather explosive, and they're strictly confidential. So I've taken the liberty to put all my formulae and drawings under seal, in a safe place."

"Under your pillow, I suppose. . . ."

"Not bad, Adam, not bad at all," Alpha laughed. "They're over there, in the closet, behind the picture, next to the bed. . . ."

. . . that had been then. And now, the control room lay deserted. Alpha stood stock still, as if rooted to the spot, hastily scanning the indicators on the control panel. This simple, visual check of the gauges and displays confirmed that a catastrophe was in the making.

All the position indicators were in the Red Alert zone. The ventilation status monitors all reported radioactive emissions. The cold gas line gauges displayed excessive pressure readings.

Speechless, as if hypnotized, Alpha stared at the dosimeter. The monitor needle stood trembling at—damn—300 rem per hour! The professor stumbled backwards: 300 rem was a lethal dosage! Where in hell was the personnel? Who the dickens was minding the store? Was such a thing possible? Dammit, this was an emergency! For the love of God, this whole plant was about to blow up!

Kramer lunged at the control panel. Years of experience with nuclear reactors channeled his intuitive reflexes in the right direction. He knew that the reactor was overheating, the cooling system was malfunctioning, and this would result in a meltdown. Damn and damn again! If his own innovative technology had been adopted, this could not have happened! With a couple of practiced movements, he activated the backup cooling system with its three rotary blowers.

"Come on, dammit, come on. . . ."

Seconds of waiting seemed like hours. At last the gauges indicated movement, their rpm rising steadily. Just when Alpha saw that, thank God, the blowers were working, the roar of a tremendous explosion shattered his eardrums. The blast propelled him headlong into the fuel-rod control board, shattering the glass partition. Blood streaming down his face, he fell backwards, crashing against the stairs he'd come down earlier, connecting so hard with the metal steps that he passed out.

Unconscious, he had a vision of a nuclear mushroom cloud: broad-based, round, evenly proportioned, its blast core high above him. On top of the dust cloud stood Adam Schlammer, dressed in insulation gear, grinning triumphantly, waving something in one hand. "The drawings, the drawings!" his disdainfully curled lips mocked Alpha.

When Alpha blinked his eyes open into waking reality, young Schlammer was indeed bending over him, clad in elegant evening attire. He wore a windowed hood, but no other protective clothing, not even gloves.

"Adam . . . ! Get help . . . we . . . we'll blow up! Listen!"

Then Alpha froze. On his face cold sweat mingled with blood. He was unable to move, had lost his sense of touch—there was no feeling anywhere in his body.

"Jesus, Adam, I'm paralyzed, help me! You must—"

"It's all over for you, my esteemed little buddy," Schlammer's voice boomed into his ear, cold, staccato sentences, muffled by the hood. "They'll find you right here. A tragic mishap. Their conclusion will be overheating due to faulty handling on your part. You're the man in charge, and you neglected certain duties and became the victim of a fatal accident."

Schlammer began to drag the helpless Kramer toward the banister.

"Ideologically speaking, you never did get the message, Walter. And, politically, you've always been a bungler."

Alpha sensed the closeness of the cooling pool. With a great effort of will he clawed at Schlammer's shirt sleeve, but Schlammer disdainfully shook him off.

"Poor old Alpha! You never understood that research is harnessed to the high and the mighty. Me? I'm getting even for all the humiliations I've had to suffer. I'll harvest a bounty of fame and admiration, yes! With the fruits of your labor. *I* will be the genius. So long, Walter!"

Panting with the effort, Schlammer thrust both arms under the helpless body and, with a powerful twist, heaved it over the basin's edge. There was a bright, noisy splash, then the dark waters enfolded the scientist. When his heart gave up halfway into its final, desperate palpitation, Alpha no longer felt anything. One fist remained tightly closed around the blue-and-gold cuff link he had torn from Schlammer's shirt sleeve, as the mortal shell of the great man slowly sank to the bottom of the pool. . . .

"Now, Ms. Kramer," Adam Schlammer said in a tone as neutral as if he were giving someone directions to the laundry room, "I've recently been asking myself where all that knowledge you have about the interface of nuclear physics and technology came from. Then, as my people put together a folder with your collected articles and publications, it all fell into place. You're an exceptionally talented and dynamic woman. A lady who commands admiration. Stephanie, you are . . . fantastic!" Almost imperceptibly, he began to sidle up to her.

Stephanie immediately went into an ostentatious crying jag. "I'm totally exhausted," she sobbed. "I just can't take any more. That awful thing with my father. Too much . . . too horrible!"

Her chest heaved, her breath came in labored gasps. And like any man enthralled by the pleading eyes of a beautiful woman in need of male strength and solace, Schlammer rose to the bait. A smile of pity and understanding on his face, he spread his arms. "You and I are made for each other, Stephanie, I know it! We can experience beautiful harmony together. Come with me and I'll make it all up to you beyond your wildest expectations!"

Her sudden knee jerk, executed with the crushing strength of the lethal contempt she felt for Schlammer, hit him in his undefended crotch. With a terrible groan, he plunged backwards into the deep, dark waters.

"I hope your balls sizzle!" she shouted, running toward the staircase. She staggered up the stairs, sprinted down the tunnel, dodging twisted metal and rock debris. Panting and wheezing and out of breath, she burst through the blast hole into the laboratory, desperately looking for Ken.

There he was—alive, thank God! Ken was all that mattered now. She mustn't lose him—ever again.

Custer was just propping himself up on the helpful shoulder and arm proffered by Tony. His head was wrapped in a white bandage, but he smiled at her, shrugging his shoulders. "Bullet just nicked me. Tony will be awarded the Bronze Star for saving a friend under fire. I'll personally commend him to the president of the United States."

This little speech having brought him back to earth, Custer found himself smack in the middle of a desperate situation.

"Holy cow, folks, where's that transceiver? We've gotta get that code! Stephanie, do I remember you telling me that you'd figured out that four-digit code?"

Stephanie gave him a blank look, then shouted, "Out, everybody, out! Don't you understand, Ken? All hell is about to break loose. Forget the code, forget the White House, let's just get out of here!"

Custer tore the red transceiver from the antenna cable. Once they got outside, the set's powerful, built-in antenna would be quite adequate for transmissions to the United States. They stumbled back along the tunnel to the niche where the fertilizer bags were stacked. It was only five minutes to detonation time when they climbed into the ventilation shaft.

Philadelphia, July 4, late afternoon

The convoy of cars had departed at the appointed time from the warehouse in Reading, taking the north-south freeway. After half an hour, the caravan had turned onto the Roosevelt Expressway and was now approaching Exit 39, which would take it into Market Street, then on into Philadelphia's historical quarter.

As he closed in on a slow-moving line of cars, the driver of the lead police vehicle activated siren and lights. Farther ahead, at the intersection of Market and 19th Streets, traffic had slowed to a crawl, as all vehicles were having to pass through a single-lane police inspection zone before being allowed to proceed toward the center of town. Since the early morning hours, highly sensitive gamma-ray detectors at numerous checkpoints such as this one were monitoring city-bound traffic for radioactive materials.

At 19th and Market, two officers carefully checked the response of their monitoring apparatus to each passing car, while other members of the team directed traffic at the ingress and egress points. One block farther down Market, at the 18th-Street intersection, another team conducted meticulous hands-on checks of all vehicles and persons that had aroused suspicion at the 19th and Market checkpoint.

Just then, police at the second checkpoint pulled a white delivery truck that had been identified via walkie-talkie over to the curb. The driver was told to get out; he now leaned casually against the truck, his shoulder blocking out the letters A and E in the logo *Aesculap Medical Supplies* on the side of the vehicle. While one of the officers checked the man's driver's license, another slowly ran a Geiger counter over the tops of the cardboard cartons inside the truck. After a few passes along the surfaces, he stuck his head out and called to the front, "Low positive, Chuck."

The truck driver poked his head back into the cabin and reached across to the passenger seat. He came up with a sheaf of papers which he held up to the policemen, who paid no attention to him as they busied themselves opening the boxes and examining their contents. At last, the elder of the two officers straightened up and said, "Radium for Frankford Hospital."

Moments later, Sergeant Charles "Chuck" Schultz dismissed the driver with a gesture. The man shuffled to the rear, pointedly slammed the doors shut and secured the latch, then slouched to the front and climbed back into his truck.

A few minutes later, the same procedure was repeated with another vehicle. Having observed a vigorous response on their monitors, officers at the 19th and Market checkpoint alerted their colleagues at the 18th-Street intersection: "Attention, high positive reading on Chevy van, red, license number . . ."

"Ten-Four from Chuck One," came the reply from 18th and Market. Moments later they waved the Chevrolet over to the curb.

The driver of the van, a black man, jumped out. Smiling and nodding goofily at the police, nervously chewing his lips, he pressed a small cellular phone to one ear while squinting anxiously past the officers toward the far end of the inspection zone. Seconds later all hell broke loose as the suspicious character took off with an olympic leap across the sidewalk, hightailing it around the corner, leaving a stunned gaggle of Philadelphia's finest in his wake.

Stirred into frantic action, they tore into the van and pounced on a massive, cube-shaped housing that made their Geiger counter click like a cloud of hungry locusts. The now ashen-faced sergeant in charge drew back, screaming, "It's the bomb!"

He brought his head so violently down on the Personal Instantaneous Communication unit attached to his left shoulder that he cut his face. With blood trickling down over one eye, he shouted: "Chuck . . . I mean Chuck One at 18th and Market. We've got it. . . . What? Right here, in the raid . . . I mean in the red Chevy . . . what? The bomb, of course. Yes. In a big container. Maxi reading on the Geiger! 18th and Market. Affirmative. Over. . . ."

The men at the advance checkpoint at 19th and Market who were listening in on the call stared incredulously down the street toward 18th. Within seconds, the screaming ululations from a dozen approaching patrol cars combined in an ear-shattering cacophony. All personnel at the sensors ran into the street and started pulling back the barriers so the patrol units could pass through. Shunting regular traffic aside, ignoring bewildered exclamations from civilian drivers, they energetically waved the approaching convoy through the wide-open passage they had just created.

Close behind the wailing cruisers with their ominously pulsing lights followed a dark blue van, which in turn was tailed by a black limousine with CD license plates and a red-and-white standard on the right front fender. The rear of the convoy was brought up by three police on motorcycles with electronic sirens and flashing lights. Watching from the barricades they had pushed to the side of the street, the checkpoint team was so mesmerized by the noisy spectacle that not one of them noticed the positive reading on the sensors as the blue van flashed by.

"Here come the bomb disposal boys," shouted Chuck at the 18th-Street intersection, where a helicopter was preparing to land, churning up dust and riveting all attention from passersby.

As the fast-moving convoy smoothly passed by the 18th and Market checkpoint, the driver in the blue van with the *Schlammer North America* logo waved casually to the policemen. Watching the limousine with the fender pennant glide by, Schultz sighed and exclaimed resignedly, "Now that's what I call the VIP treatment!"

While everybody's attention was focused on the red van with the suspected bomb, the convoy with the dark-blue van reached the historical quarter, drove past Independence Hall, and rolled to a stop in front of City Tavern. A tall, distinguished-looking gentleman with graying temples climbed out of the limousine. His gait measured, he strode up to a pedestal on the City Tavern lawn, nodding his head and pointing at the central portion of the smooth, empty surface. The van slowly backed up to the pedestal, and a team of men in blue coveralls began to transfer the Clissot Rock'O'Clock unit from the van to the pedestal.

"What was that convoy all about?" the younger officer at the 18th and Market checkpoint asked his older colleague. Schultz consulted his service notebook. "State Department, Washington . . . got it! Special transport for the Swiss Embassy." He looked up, grinning at his partner. "Swiss cheese, I guess."

"Right, Chuck, what else! Cheese, chocolate, cuckoo clocks or . . ."

"The Swiss Family Robinson."

"Yeah, with a numbered bank account . . . !"

Sharing a laugh on that one, they strolled off toward 19th Street.

With an amused expression on his face, the owner of City Tavern watched the activities on his lawn through the large front window. First, the coveralled men removed the plastic skin from the granite cube. Then they unsheathed the delicately crafted clockfaces. The one that faced the tavern indicated twelve o'clock; the proper time would still have to be set. With a shrug, the innkeeper retired to the kitchen, to continue discussing the fine points of the forthcoming banquet with his chef.

A little later, when he checked again, a lectern and benches had been put up in front of the pedestal. Two workers were just throwing a white sheet over the granite cube. Yes, indeed, this clock would make an attractive complement to the historical facade of his restaurant. But the dial on the big granite cube still indicated twelve o'clock.

Not working right, this Swiss clock! he mused, his curiosity aroused. As he stepped outside to take a closer look, the two workers crossed his path on their way into the tavern. They joined some members of the band that was to play at the unveiling ceremony, nursing beers at the bar. The innkeeper walked slowly around the cloaked clock, nosing at the sheet, then lifted a corner to see if the other three dials were working properly. If so, they should be indicating close to six P.M.

As he leaned forward to peek under the sheet, he heard a scratching noise. Turning his head this way and that, he saw only an expanse of grass around him. Had he imagined that sound?

There it was again! Puzzled by the strange noise, the innkeeper, an aficionado of state-of-the-art electronics, pressed one ear to the granite surface. Electronic clocks weren't supposed to make noise! Again, a scraping and scratching, then rapid ticking. He stepped back, nonplussed. A terrible premonition struck him like ball lightning. Police and soldiers all over the place! Something . . . something awful was in the air! And this ticking. This . . . this . . . clockwork was . . . a bomb!

The realization knocked him backwards. Reeling, he stumbled and fell. From the vantage point of an upended bug, he stared aghast at the gift-wrapped monster clock.

"I must be losing my mind—there's a bomb ticking away in there!" Mumbling and cursing to himself, he scrambled to his feet, giving the ominous installation a wide berth as he stumbled back to the restaurant.

Racing behind the bar, he picked up the phone and called 911.

"Police. Emergency," said a female voice.

"There's a fu . . . a bomb in front of my place, City Tavern. You've got to . . ."

"Stay on the line, sir."

For long moments, nothing happened. Finally, a male voice asked for the address. Again the innkeeper had to wait. Then a more sonorous voice came on, telling him to stay calm.

"There's no need to worry, sir, everything's under control. What you've got there is a clock, sir, a Swiss—"

"I know what I've got here is a clock, dammit, but it's an electronic clock and it's ticking, and I happen to know that . . ."

"Sir, don't clocks do that? But stay where you are, we'll dispatch a unit for you right away."

Morose, the innkeeper hung up. Maybe he'd been imagining things. Why would anybody want to plant a bomb inside a Swiss clock? And, come to think of it, electronic detonators weren't supposed to make ticking sounds either, were they?

Flares hissed and fizzled in the cloudless, star-studded night sky. Stephanie, panting and gasping for air, crawled out of the ventilation shaft. She crouched on the forest floor, straining to see in the shady twilight.

Far above the treetops, cascades of flares spread a strong white light through the night. The hollow sound of helicopter rotors throbbed up from the valley. She estimated that the missile silo lay near the hilltop, some three hundred meters above her.

Tony and Custer emerged from the shaft, both panting and full of questions. As they hunkered down next to her, she pointed silently at the rocky ledge. The narrow, footworn path lay distinctly before them, palely illuminated by the light from the fireworks. Stephanie motioned for Tony to take the lead. They would try to climb down to the river along the descending bands of bare rock face, in the hope that by choosing this difficult escape route they'd be able to elude the police and army encirclements.

Custer brought up the rear of the little column. Since leaving the lab, they had exchanged no more than a few grunted syllables. Silently, with firm grasp, they had climbed up the shaft, driven by fear and the single thought of getting out alive. All they wanted was once again to look up at the stars, breathe in the cherished scents of the forest, and experience that incomparably human sensation of boundless freedom.

A fresh batch of flares exploded above them, illuminating the sky. Then a huge helicopter thundered low across the treetops as the little troupe vanished undetected in the underbrush. Ducking reflexively, Custer watched the monstrous chopper, a Swiss Army Super-Puma, bank above the ravine, then head for the summit plateau. A manhunt was on, and he was the hunted!

When the trio emerged again from the bushes, the rocky ledge shone palely at them, snagging the black abyss like a giant tooth.

Enthralled by the magic vista before them, beguiled by the light of the moon mingling with that of the descending flares, Stephanie and Ken let their hands meet as they stepped out onto the great natural platform. Whispering, she indicated the kids' cave and showed him the entrance to the layered strata of rock that would lead them down to the river. He tenderly put an arm around her waist, kissed her forehead and looked across her tousled hair out into the nocturnal skies. Stephanie closed her eyes.

When she finally opened them and saw Schlammer approaching, it was too late. The tycoon stood behind Custer, on the ledge, drawing back to strike. With a strangled shout, she twisted out of Ken's embrace.

Custer whirled around—too late. He was still pivoting when Schlammer's pistol smashed against his head. Schlammer had aimed at the back of the skull, but instead the blow hit Custer directly on the bandaged gunshot wound above the ear. Losing his balance, he stumbled backwards toward the edge of the precipice. Torn off by the blow, the bandage sailed like a white flag of surrender out over the dark abyss. Stephanie cried out, her desperate shout punctuating this lightning-swift sequence of events.

His body teetered on the edge, but Custer managed to catch himself by twisting around. Falling, he tried to grab hold of the rock with both arms, but slipped. Clawing desperately at the rocky edge, his legs dangling above the abyss, he knew then he would fall.

A helicopter boomed beneath him, deep down in the gorge; a searchlight played along the mountainside. Police sirens yowled in the distance, and another chopper appeared as if from nowhere, thundering low overhead. From far off, muffled explosions could be heard, and somewhere Karma, the kids' dog, was barking furiously at everything.

Custer's fingers found no hold on the slippery rock face. He felt his strength fading. When he looked up, he beheld a terrible, hawk-nosed countenance grinning down at him.

At that moment something extraordinary happened inside him. His perception suddenly split and continued on two separate levels of time. He noted that Schlammer, above him, placed a shoe, the right one, heavily on the fingers of his left hand, steadily increasing the pressure, while using the gun to control Stephanie, who was so pale with rage her face looked as if cut from a block of glacial ice. Farther up above the ledge, he saw the bigger of the two boys holding a length of rope coiled in one hand, which he now began to twirl like a lasso. And at the same time as these external developments unfolded sharply before Custer's eyes, he entered an internal dimension where a film reeled off backwards, flickering out of time.

Nothing in this ethereal movie seemed tangible; all was feeling, sensations and emotions, coursing through him. Rising to the surface from the very depths of this torturous nightmare, Custer felt himself soaring above the waters, light as a feather, moving inexorably back through the years, toward his young manhood. Within moments, his true name came to him. He saw himself years, decades ago, as a young man, fighting to keep his balance on this very ledge—saw himself falling, precisely as he was about to fall now, plunging into the bottomless abyss—except this time there was no turning back to life. This time he would plunge to his true and final death!

With a sadistic grimace, Schlammer lifted his sharp-heeled shoe to bring it down and smash the fingers of his hapless victim. That instant, the very mountain began to tremble. A spectacular jet of a flame leapt up beyond the treetops, reaching high into the sky. Caught by surprise, Schlammer hesitated for a moment, drawing in his breath. When he realized what had happened, his sharply etched features turned into an insane grimace of evil. His eyes bulged from their sockets, his yellowish teeth chattered in a feverish staccato, the vulturous beak of a nose seemed to dig into the pointed chin. Then one heel descended on Custer's hand, which clawed into a rock fissure with his last remaining strength.

Custer saw the bright yellow rope uncoil and snake through the air towards him. He let go of the rock and reached for the rope before Schlammer could crush his fingers. Even though Custer felt himself clutching the rope with both hands, his free fall continued.

Schlammer let out a derisive shout as Custer plummeted into the deep. Responding to Custer's weight, the rope snapped into a taut, vertical line, tracing his fall.

Schlammer had no way to avoid his doom. Cracking like a bull-whip, the tightening rope cut his legs out from under him, catapulting him headlong into the ravine. Without uttering a sound, the man who had once controlled the mighty empire known as Schlammer Engineering vanished in the dismal gloom.

Custer's hands were on fire, and so was the mountain. Still, he managed to brake his fall. Then he swung back and forth along the rock face, as the rope sought the perpendicular beneath the cave where Mark had secured it. Dazed and dreamy, Custer floated above the abyss; he let go a second too early for a smooth landing on a narrow band of rock and came down hard. His head connected with a chunk of sandstone, and he lost consciousness.

Not that it mattered. Euphoric sensations coursed through him. Everything had softened. He drifted weightless through Elysian fields of joy and freedom such as he had never known before. At last, the nightmare that had haunted him for years lifted, and was gone.

Rosalia rushed breathless along the narrow sidewalk, anxiously glancing backward over her shoulder. Was the skinhead following her? The street lay deserted. Or was that a shadow she saw? The refuge of her apartment building beckoned ahead. The menacing pounding of helicopter blades made her glance up at the chopper that thundered low above the rooftops, heading for the Schlammer compound. Rosalia dragged herself along, out of breath. On the far side of the valley Nucleanne seethed with activity; army and police were pouring into the town. A fiery glow played along the mountain ridge as searchlights blossomed, red and yellow lights winked and circled. A great pincer movement to encircle the Schlammer cavern was in progress. It was lucky for her that she wasn't caught in it.

Still, she sensed the skinhead tailing her. She'd got away from him down by the train station by jumping out of the car and sprinting across the tracks. She'd managed to lose him—for now! Her lungs seemed ready to burst, her feet felt like lead. She was pushing herself forward by sheer force of will when a stupendous explosion threw her to the ground. Terrified, she got back on her feet to stare incredulously at the forest across the valley. Where she had seen the reddish glow on the ridge, the mountain now belched fire, like a volcano. Showers of sparks danced above the flames. Panic hit her, triggering an adrenaline rush that propelled her forward through the few remaining meters, to the building, up the stairs, and into her apartment.

She slumped down on the couch. The TV was on. Had she forgotten to turn it off? Still laboring to catch her breath, she stared dully at the screen, where a newsperson, positioned in front of a police car at a roadblock somewhere, was speaking directly into a microphone she held stiffly in front of her.

Fear made Rosalia jump up again to lock and bolt the front door, then hurry into the kitchen. What she needed was a strong cup of coffee! There she saw a package lying on the kitchen table—a parcel from her sister.

"... and the suspected bomb plot here in Philadelphia stirs all-too-fresh memories of the World Trade Center explosion in New York just a few years ago. According to our latest information, there is still no certainty as to whether or not a bomb has indeed been hidden somewhere in the city. According to police, no demands or other communication have been received as yet. As of right now, there appear to be no clues as to the identity or whereabouts of the perpetrators, if any, nor has any group come forward to take credit for the catastrophe that threatens Philadelphia and the nation. CIA director Mitchell Taylor appeals to the people of Philadelphia to remain calm. Police and National Guard units have been called in to ensure public safety, and massive precautionary measures have already been implemented. We'll go now to Carol Sanders, in the CNN helicopter above the Ben Franklin Bridge. Over to you, Carol . . ."

The dry, grinding noise of the espresso machine drowned out the voice of the reporter. Rosalia slid the cup out from under the spout and spooned sugar into it. Clamping the parcel under one arm, she walked back into the living room. Carefully balancing the cup, she sat down on the couch.

"... and that's Independence Hall down there, with the Liberty Bell pavilion right in front of it. The entire sector has been cordoned off since noon today, but as far as we can tell, Philadelphians are taking all this commotion in their stride. The Fourth of July spirit does not appear to have been dampened in the least, and the city seems confident that the police will locate the bomb, if indeed there is one. Ronald Peterson, former FBI agent and antiterrorism expert, who is up here with us, tells me that nine out of ten bomb threats turn out to be false alarms. Ron, what's your take on the rumor that

Iraq is behind the supposed plot on the historical section of beautiful old Philly?"

Rosalia briefly looked up from the job of undoing the string around the parcel. The camera zoomed in on a crowd of people that had gathered near an old building.

". . . the Iraqis may be crazy, Carol, but not that crazy—certainly not crazy enough to use a bomb to goad the United States into a retaliatory strike," the antiterrorism specialist shouted into the mike, "but since you brought it up, we've got a wide range of candidates for the role of terrorist bomber. For example, some misguided psychopath who styles himself as a patriot and thinks our own government is the enemy. Or a member of one of the militant Balkan factions, like the Serbian Liberation Front or the Bosnian Muslims, both of which make Abu Nidal look like Mother Teresa. Or the Palestinian Hamas, or the Iranian Revolutionary Guard, or—well, you name it, they've got it. . . ."

"Hold on, Ron," Sanders cut in, "something is happening down there. It looks like the police are in action. Blue-and-white armored vehicles are moving toward Market Street at high speed. Something is happening over there around Independence Hall. The time is just a few minutes over half past eight. A crowd of people has formed in front of the old City Tavern. People have gathered around something that looks like some sort of monument or something that's wrapped in a tarp. Anything new at Police Headquarters, Bob? Has the mysterious bomb been located? Bob, hello! Bob . . . ?"

Rosalia looked up at the picture. Ugly, squat-looking vehicles were speeding straight toward the crowd. She tore away the tape at the top of the package. A blinding flash was the last thing she saw. Of the devastation the parcel bomb wreaked on her body, she felt nothing.

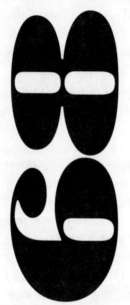

Switzerland, Thursday, July 5, shortly before
3 A.M.

Stephanie, Mark, Tony, and Jessie had
climbed down along the narrow path to the
uppermost layer of rock. Flares still burst in
the sky, and a helicopter skimmed thunderously along the edge of the
ravine, its powerful searchlights painting the terrain. Jessie was just
drawing in Karma's leash, when Stephanie stumbled upon Ken's lifeless body. Nearly frightened out of her wits, she fell on her knees and
immediately started giving him mouth-to-mouth resuscitation.

She was still desperately forcing air down Ken's pulmonary pas-
sages when she felt him playfully responding to the touch of her
lips. In astonishment, she broke off her rescue attempts, and found
herself gazing into a pair of beautiful, mischievously sparkling blue
eyes. She kissed him—first tenderly, then more firmly, and at last
passionately.

She teased him with the tip of her tongue, tickled his skin with
her eyelashes and would gladly have continued playing like this
forever, if a cone of light from one of the helicopters hadn't brutally
cut into her amorous trance. Shading her eyes with both arms
against the numbing brightness, she vaguely recognized a silhouette outlined in the loading dock of the craft.

Then Jessie shouted something about catching a rope with which to lower themselves. Custer fumbled reflexively for a gun in one of his jacket pockets, and unexpectedly came up with the red handset. He hesitated, astonished, then asked what time it was.

"Close to three in the morning," Mark told him.

"That's nine P.M. in Philadelphia!" Custer groaned. In a few minutes, the bomb would go off! Time had gotten away from them! Tony frowned at him. "Nine P.M.? So they're six hours behind . . . which means the ceremony is about to begin . . ."

"What ceremony is that?" Custer was suddenly wide awake.

"The unveiling ceremony for the Clissot clock! At least, that's what it said on the fax sheet Marianne left on the kitchen table."

She got no further than that.

"Yesss! The Rock'O'Clock!" Custer screamed into the night. "Kid, you're worth your weight in gold!"

On that rocky ledge, thousands of miles from Washington, D.C., the kids watched in amazement as Custer pulled out the transceiver and clicked it. A small digital display lit up in the active standby mode. Custer hastily tapped out a sequence of numbers for the White House.

A bright, robotic voice informed him:

"The number you are trying to reach is not in service at this time. The number you have . . ."

At that very moment a funereal silence reigned in the White House Operations Center. The digital wall clock correctly and indifferently indicated date and time: *July 4. 20:40.07.* The NSA communications specialist had just received the decisive number to be entered into the dialog mode of the bomb's multiservice answering function. He started tapping out the digits on his deskset. Mitch Taylor remembered what Custer had told him: *You enter the dialog mode, which you do by entering STAR-ZERO-ZERO. That starts the dialog with the ignition program built into the fission pack.*

If this damn Custer was right, the connection with the elusive ignition system of the nuclear charge that was ticking away somewhere in Philadelphia should be made in a matter of seconds. >Keycop<, hot damn! *Now, Taylor, that will be the moment of truth, do you understand? Now, with this four-digit figure you can defuse the bomb.*

Thoughtfully, Mitchell Taylor put down the receiver. *The computerized voice will ask you for the four-digit code that interrupts the ignition process.*

"Any news on that car bomb in Philly, Mitch?"

"There was no bomb in the van we searched at the 18th and Market checkpoint, sir. Just a pile of cesium. A diversionary maneuver, it seems, or else a very very stupid prank."

The president of the United States acknowledged the input with a slight nod and continued staring straight ahead. He was thinking what a good thing it was that they hadn't allowed themselves to be sidetracked so easily—that they'd kept on looking. Only minutes ago, after hours of hectic interaction with the nation's telecommunications companies and after running a nationwide total of 28,756 new subscriptions for cellular telephone services through their computers, NSA specialists had finally succeeded in tracking down the receiver—a voice mail function within the bomb's dialog program.

The president was gratefully amazed by the efficiency of the nation's security agencies. In this country, any terrorist will sooner or later get caught in an FBI, CIA or NSA dragnet operation, he proudly told himself. Then he gulped and ruefully added, except maybe this one crucial time! They had only minutes left before . . .

After more than four thousand tries, NSA trackers had finally come up with 696-6969, a sequence that had aroused their suspicion not because of the unusual pattern, but because the number's voice mail had reacted to the STAR-ZERO-ZERO code Custer had supplied. They quickly traced the telephone number to the head of a Muslim sect, a sheik. When police swiftly descended on the location that went with the number, the pigeon, or pigeons, had already flown the coop—leaving behind a cavernously empty warehouse.

Suddenly, one of the trackers in the room lifted an arm to attract attention. The president rose and walked over to him just as the dialog with the ignition program was being initiated. Through the speaker phone, an eerily neutral computer voice intoned:

"IF YOU WISH TO ALTER THE IGNITION TIME, PRESS 1. FOR ANOTHER FUNCTION, PRESS 2."

While the NSA man pressed 2, the president's eyes never strayed from the clock. It was fifteen minutes to H-hour, as the military soberly chose to label the blast time.

In Philadelphia, at venerable Fort Mill on the banks of the Delaware River, a team of electronic tracking specialists was frantically working to pinpoint the location of the telephone receiving function with which they were conversing. A huge monitor linked to sophisticated tracking equipment gave them a close-up of the area around Independence Hall.

"A message from the Police Department, sir," a young woman in uniform informed her superior. "The owner of City Tavern claims a bomb is ticking in front of his establishment. He probably means that weird clock they're putting up there. . . ."

She was about to turn away when the major's voice stopped her short.

"Hold it! Did you say City Tavern? That big clock, the ceremony?" He stared aghast at the city map. "For God's sake, Jane, that there is our baby!" He dealt his forehead a couple of resounding slaps, exclaiming, "How could I have been so dumb! City Tavern, of course! Let's roll!"

While the team at Operations continued tracking, the first squad cars went roaring in the direction of City Tavern, sirens blasting and red lights flashing. Helicopters lifted off, one by one, and emergency units of the National Guard moved into position as planned, effectively cordoning off Philadelphia's historical quarter. Still the nuclear fission pack inside the Rock'O'Clock on the lawn in front of City Tavern kept on ticking.

At operational headquarters in the White House a young female operator called out, "Custer on One!"

The director of the CIA tore the receiver from her hand. "Damn you, Custer, have you got the four digits? Where the hell've you been?"

"Hiking in the mountains, sir. Yes, we've got the secret number."

Above the ledge, a figure detached itself from the hatch of the hovering chopper. Dangling on a winch line, it began a slow descent. Something the CIA director said was drowned out in all the noise, and Custer shouted into the transceiver, "I can't hear you, sir, all hell's broken loose up here. Now listen. Can you hear me? Okay! Now, before I give you the number, I want some guarantees, do you read me?"

"What sort of guarantees?" came the lame, frayed response.

In a sharp tone of voice, Custer succinctly listed his demands: Total rehabilitation of Kenneth W. Custer alias >Keycop<. All warrants, APBs, etc. for his arrest to be unconditionally recalled and canceled. Safe passage by U.S. Air Force transport to a location of his choice. Merit citation by the president. He concluded with a few other, and minor, perks.

"Easy does it, Custer," Taylor stalled, "what you need is a rest. Come to Washington, relax, take a few days off. We'll work it out together. You have my word we'll take a close and kindly, I repeat kindly, look at all your concerns. How's that grab ya?"

"Negative. *Nada.* No friggin' dice!" Custer screamed into the handset. "I want those guarantees, I want them ironclad, and I want them now, you hear? I want everything signed and sealed at the blue-chip level, in front of witnesses, are you listening to me, Taylor? If not, you can all just kiss each other goodbye. How does that grab you, sir?"

A sudden warm updraft pushed the helicopter precariously close to the ravine wall, interrupting the winching operation.

In the White House Operations Center the electronic clockface mercilessly counted off the seconds. Now Custer heard another voice on the line. This one was calm and confident.

"Colonel Custer, this is the president. We accept your conditions. I am personally guaranteeing your safety. Now, get a move on, man!"

Custer cupped his hand over the transceiver grate, shouting at Stephanie through the infernal whine of the rotors. "They accept. The president himself says so!"

It was 20:54 in Philadelphia.

She gave him a puzzled shake of the head and he shouted, "The four-digit number, Stephanie! The mirror-image sequence, come on!"

"Oh, that!" Her expression brightened. "It fit Schoenhof perfectly, that old sex maniac. That's what made me think of it in the first place. And it's not a mirror-image number, Ken, it's centrosymmetric, a simple inversion in reverse...." Her arms performed laborious gyrations, while Custer signaled desperately at her to come out with it.

"SIXTY-NINE and NINETY-SIX," she chanted, smiling mischievously, her arms drawing sixes and nines into the night.

Custer grinned and clicked his tongue suggestively. Then he spoke calmly into the transceiver, "Mr. Taylor, the four digits you're looking for are 6-9-9-6, sixty-nine and ninety-six, I repeat, 6996. And you want to look for a clock. Right. A clock with a housing of green granite that's being installed somewhere in Philadelphia. Probably some sort of ceremony..."

The slim figure of the man who was rappeling down from the helicopter finally touched down on the rocky ledge. He unhitched the winch harness and moved toward Custer, hands raised to indicate peaceful intentions. Custer managed to put the transceiver away just as the tall, youthful figure smiled and stuck out one hand.

Philadelphia, July 4

From the passenger seat of the armored vehicle, Sergeant Watts cast a cursory glance
at Liberty Bell pavilion to the left as his
SCUDO unit moved down Chestnut Ave-
nue past Independence Hall. At 3rd Street, the tracking sensors
again reacted strongly.

Next to the small lectern that had been set up in front of the
old tavern, three men in starched, white shirts and black vests with
red piping were tuning their instruments. The man in the middle
puckered his lips to wet the mouthpiece of a ten-feet-long alpenhorn that extended all the way to the feet of the people in the
front row. His buddy to the right tentatively plucked at the strings
of his acoustic bass, while the third musician busied himself adjusting the angle of the accordion that rested against his chest. At
a signal from the bass player the trio swung into the opening chorus
of a popular country tune, while a tall, distinguished-looking elderly
gentleman with a sheaf of papers in one hand stepped up to the
lectern. With a flourish from the alpenhorn the music stopped and
someone introduced His Excellency the Swiss Ambassador.

Sergeant Watts, who'd been focusing on the gauges of his tracking equipment, was just pointing to the right, down 2nd Street, when a call from Fort Meade was received. An urgent voice instructed them to proceed to City Tavern. Immediately! Urgent priority!

The sergeant glanced at his watch: only a few minutes to 2100 hours. In the direction of the Ben Franklin Bridge a veritable bombardment of fireworks erupted in the sky. The strains of marching music could be heard in the distance.

The driver floored the accelerator and the heavy vehicle lunged forward. Beads of perspiration glistening on his forehead, Watts pointed forcefully ahead, shouting, "That way, let's go!" His hand was on the door latch.

The rig hurtled toward a cluster of people crowding around a shrouded sculpture or monument in front of the historical City Tavern. Behind the dais, side by side with the Stars and Stripes, hung the Swiss flag, its white cross glistening in a field of red. Watts sneered; some sort of highly inappropriate Red Cross meeting no doubt!

The hysterical shrilling of the sensor cut off his ruminations. Over its grating bleep, an authoritative voice boomed at Watts from a bullhorn:

"Get going, Sarge! The bomb is inside a clock and the damn clock's under that sheet. For chrissake, hurry up!" The voice caught its breath. "Break up this gathering right now, Sergeant. Its a dedication ceremony for a clock—a gift from Switzerland. But never mind that. Just break it up!"

All hell had broken loose. Helicopters, their rotors thrashing, descended on the lawn behind City Tavern; police vehicles hurtled and skidded across sidewalks; a tow truck tore through a pedestrian mall, scattering people. Plainclothes operatives waving guns were rushing this way and that, and marksmen from the National Guard took cover behind trees. Horrified, the Swiss ambassador broke off the speech he had just begun. He watched in a state of shock as Sergeant Watts broke up the panicky crowd and rushed up to the dais. The terrified musicians had dropped their instruments and made a beeline for the tavern. The ambassador, his eyes vacant, desperately looked for some higher authority to turn to.

"We've located the device," Watts panted, his voice booming out over the sound system—into patrol cars, through the cordless handsets of plainclothes operatives, all the way to operational headquarters at Fort Meade.

* * *

Thus, the good news also came to echo through the intercom in the White House Operations Center, causing monitoring specialists to look up from their equipment for an instant or two before turning back to the job at hand, redoubling their efforts. The dialog-in-progress with the bomb had entered the critical phase.

The mechanical voice that came to them from a black box inside the nuclear device somewhere in the center of Philadelphia made everybody's blood run cold. Its slow, monotonous, fractured drone was enough to test the sanity even of these seasoned pros. Second after second peeled off the big digital clock on the wall, dissolving layer upon layer of time as it moved swiftly toward the millimoment of ignition contact.

"IF YOU WISH TO ACTIVATE THE SOLAR CELL ENERGY-SAVING FUNCTION, PRESS 1; FOR ALTERNATE FUNCTIONS, PRESS 9."

"What're you waiting for, press 9!" urged a broad-shouldered colonel, beads of sweat glistening on his forehead.

"YOU ARE NOW IN THE INTERCEPT MODE," droned the voice. "YOU MAY ENTER THE FOUR-DIGIT OVERRIDE CODE."

With sweat pouring down his face in tiny rivulets, the communications specialist entered 6-9-9-6.

"IF YOU WISH TO ALTER THE IGNITION TIME, PRESS 1; FOR ALTERNATE FUNCTIONS, PRESS 2."

The man hesitated—only two minutes to the big bang! Fear immobilized his fingers. It took all of the colonel's will power to unfreeze them.

"Press 2!" he rasped, trembling with anxiety.

"IF YOU WISH TO HALT THE IGNITION COUNTDOWN, ENTER 6-9-9-6," the computerized voice intoned impassively.

The colonel grabbed the cordless handset from the specialist and tapped out the numbers himself: 6-9-9-6.

"IGNITION HAS BEEN ABORTED. THE DETONATOR CANNOT BE REACTIVATED," droned the ominously neutral voice on the intercom, delivering them at last from the nightmare. "REPEAT—THE DETONATOR CANNOT BE REACTIVATED. . . ."

At that very moment, with an equal amount of indifference, the digital wall clock peeled to 21:00.00.

The president of the United States slowly drew a heavy sleeve across his forehead, emitting a sigh of relief that was half a tortured groan. It seemed as if all of Washington followed suit, started breathing easier. A hubbub of excited voices escalated throughout the vast room. In an unusual burst of camaraderie, the colonel patted the specialist's shoulder. Others embraced enthusiastically, while again others hopped up and down, whooping, hollering and jumping for joy.

Sergeant Watts tore the white sheet from the shrouded object, and his men began to break open the four dials of the enormous clock made of green granite. A shout went up from the crowd. It had taken only moments to smash a black hole into the housing of the elegantly fashioned Rock'O'Clock from Switzerland.

Now the outline of the nuclear device inside the clock was clearly visible. Watts stared numbly at the black detonator box where a message in red letters blinked on a luminiscent yellow screen in the display panel: RELAX, THIS BABY HAS BEEN DEFUSED!

As Watts stared, some small, furry animal leaped out through the jagged hole in the housing. Its slim body arched gracefully as it touched down on the lawn and darted into a clump of bushes, slender furred tail trailing behind it.

The sergeant's eyes bulged. He muttered, "I'm losing it, I'm seeing things!" As he tried to shake off the hallucination with a couple of quick, determined jerks of the head, he did a double take again, focusing on the blinking display. Right next to the screen dangled a severed wire. Watts reached out and pulled up the frayed end. It had clearly been *chewed*. Running two fingers along the wire's length, he traced it back to a red switchboard marked IG-NITION.

Straightening, Watts stared pensively at the clump of bushes where the critter had disappeared. Then it hit him and he shouted, "Bit it clean through, the little bugger! Scratched and chomped and gnawed right through that darn power line!" He shook his head incredulously. "That naughty little devil saved us all, can you believe it?!"

He doubled over in an uncontrollable fit of laughter, slapping his thighs, tears streaming down his face. The fate of Philadelphia—the United States—the world!—decided by a weasel!

Later, however, no one would believe him. Nor would his ranger buddies be able to recall having seen a small animal come leaping out of the granite cube. To remember such a thing would have exceeded the bounds of official credulity. Only the joint efforts of a number of specialized agencies using the most advanced high-tech equipment in the world had succeeded in averting the nuclear disaster at the very last minute—that would be the approved version. As for Sergeant Watts . . . well, the man had been under tremendous stress, blown off some steam, hallucinated a little, nothing terribly unusual with that, was there? In the end, Watts himself would come to believe he must have been the victim of an optical illusion.

Right now, right here, Philadelphia was celebrating its Fourth of July. A curtain of fireworks rose into the sky along the banks of the Delaware, cascades of Roman candles bloomed, shiny rockets flung huge bouquets of brilliantly sparkling flowers at the stars. Sergeant Watts slumped exhausted against the granite cube. With a worried look, his driver held a can of Bud out to him. Slowly, ever so slowly, the sergeant's trembling hand came up to grasp it.

After the winch pulled them up, they sat belted into the contour seats of the big chopper, staring at the gigantic, glowing crater Breckerlin's explosives had torn into the mountain. Flames blazed in the forest and smoke belched up, billowing into the sky. The earth below offered up a picture of devastation.

The army had stopped firing off flares, but the entire Schlammer Engineering compound was illuminated by a ghostly glow. Blue emergency lights flashed, searchlights sprung to blazing life, yellow warning lights blinked. As the chopper banked steeply and thundered low over the factory buildings, heading for the valley exit, Police Chief Borli pointed down at the armored vehicles laying in wait like so many black toads, sealing off the area.

Mark petted Karma's back, soothing her. The collie bitch lay curled and trembling at his feet, looking up at him with frightened eyes. As soon as Jessie had figured out how to work the intercom, her voice came over the onboard radio, asking Borli why he had started looking for them in the ravine.

"Your friend Marianne Chaudet told me of a secret campsite on the rim of the gorge," Borli replied, pulling a brown envelope from his black sports bag. He shook his head in admiration, adding, "You're fantastic, all of you!"

A laid-back Custer lounged casually in his seat harness, his lips pursed in a cheerful, inner-directed smile. He squinted contentedly at Stephanie as his head lolled to the rhythmic vibrations from the giant airfoils. Yes, Colonel Custer felt as if he'd been reborn—reveling in these moments of total relaxation, relishing the sight of the intrepid Stephanie and the way she tenderly gazed at him, righteous determination transforming her face into a vision of timeless beauty. And he admired Mark, Tony, and Jessie who, so bravely and resourcefully, had put their young lives on the line in this dangerous enterprise.

For a few short moments Stephanie's gaze lovingly enveloped Ken. Then her secret ruminations about the man who had come to mean so terribly much to her were interrupted by the police chief, who handed her a number of large photo prints that he had pulled from his bag. Recognizing the pictures, she looked up at him in surprise.

Borli anticipated her question. "These enlargements were sent to me from the Soteria—you know, the Old Man's country retreat? Arik entrusted them to me, with his best compliments to you, of course. He wants you to know that the only reason he made Joseph hand them over was to make sure they didn't end up in the wrong hands."

Stephanie said, "Of course," but kept on shaking her head.

Borli hastened to fill her in. The Americans had been in fear of nuclear plots by terrorists for some time, but had lacked hard-and-fast evidence. For a long time there'd been only rumors, nor had the vague information concerning an Iraqi conspiracy, offered for sale by former secret service agents, led to anything. Then the leads had become more concrete. Apparently, an Iraqi group was trying to obtain a nuclear device. This had prompted U.S. secret service agencies to launch efforts to ferret out potential bomb makers who might serve as a point of departure for tracking down terrorists.

"The Old Man apparently had inside information," Borli said, "probably through friends in the Mossad." He went on to confess that at first he had considered this an American problem, paying no attention to it until he learned of Stephanie's observations in Schlammer's cavern. Her story, that Schlammer was tinkering with nuclear weapons in his underground facilities, had been passed on to him by Arik. It meshed seamlessly with Borli's own investigations.

With a rueful smile, the police chief told his passengers he had learned that an Iraqi named Hazmoudi had visited Schlammer Engineering. So Borli's investigators had asked themselves, why?

At the same time, the Americans had put on the pressure, believing a Kenneth W. Custer, alias >Keycop<, to be identical with a mysterious buyer who was acting on behalf of Arab terrorists. The Americans had been convinced that Custer had killed, or at least engineered the killing of, both Ralph Christen and Urs Summermatter.

Borli paused, glancing across at Mark and Jessie who had nodded off, lulled to sleep by the monotonous drone of the engines. Stephanie, however, was wide awake—and furious!

"And you actually bought that crock of bull from Conklin?"

"Not at all," Borli countered. "I'd been developing my own theories about the case from the start, even though I lacked tangible evidence. But probing into the Christen assassination led me straight to Schlammer Engineering. When we found those fingerprints on a beer bottle at the Christen assassination site, our investigation took a dramatic turn. But my superiors still considered Schlammer untouchable. Then suddenly I got lucky, or rather we, my wife and I, got lucky. As you know, Melanie runs the Crack Shoppe. She couldn't resist the title of the report you'd left in the computer: 'Slimy, Slimier, Schlammer.' Very catchy, Ms. Kramer."

Still fuming, Stephanie started to protest their snooping into her private business, but Borli gestured amicably, telling her they hadn't meant anything by it. Her text had been read inadvertently—a stroke of luck that ought to have resulted in Schlammer's arrest, but . . .

Slowly, Custer pulled his athletic frame together, leaned forward and squinted questioningly into Borli's embarrassed face. The chief quickly tried to change the subject, saying, "That's when we saw that all this related to Philadelphia. Well, to make a long story short . . ."

". . . but why would you think of Philadelphia, of all places?" Custer cut in, suddenly eager to join the conversation.

"Marianne Chaudet sent us a fax about this. But not until quite late, about midnight."

"And what was in that fax?" Stephanie insisted.

"Not much, actually," Borli told them. "It was a message from Schlammer North America to the effect that the unveiling of that confounded cubic clock had been rescheduled for nine P.M. But neither the location nor the occasion for the ceremony were mentioned. At Schlammer headquarters in Nucleanne, no one seemed to have heard of any sort of inauguration ceremony."

"So what about Schlammer North America?" Stephanie interjected. "Shouldn't they have known?"

"My thinking precisely," Borli agreed, "but they'd closed shop for the day. Fourth of July, national holiday, you know. By the time the FBI finally got hold of the night manager, it was way past nine. But tell me, Colonel, how did you find out about the plot on Philadelphia?"

"In the cavern," Custer said. "Schoenhof was explaining the function of their transceivers, and he started chatting about some extensive technical preparations he was engaged in on behalf of an Iraqi client, somewhere on the Eastern Seaboard. Later, in the lab, we came across maps with radio frequencies and broadcasting ranges, all emanating from the city of Philadelphia."

Stephanie looked down at the prints she still held in her hands. As the whirlybird headed for Geneva, she examined them one by one. We're probably crossing the Alpine foothills, she thought, and flipped to a picture of the young François Clissot, his body angled in midair, one hand flung upward. The powerful magnification clearly showed the right hand of the falling youngster pointing to the pale, rigid face of a man standing on the rocky ledge above. But something about this pointing hand wasn't right.

She squinted, focusing closely, then saw what it was. It struck her like a bolt of lightning: the right hand on this picture had only four fingers! She counted again, only four knuckles. The little finger was missing! A deformity, a glitch of nature, exactly as with . . .

"Ken!" she cried out. The picture trembled in her thrust-out hand.

Custer spread both hands and held them out, palms up, looking expectantly at Stephanie, who wouldn't take her eyes of his right, with its four fingers. Then he confessed that he knew.

"The moment I fell and reached for the rope, in those fractions of a second, it was like a veil was torn from my eyes. I saw myself as a boy. I understood who I was, and where I came from. My life was given back to me. I was, am, François Clissot. And all of that ended when 'Schladam'—that's what we called him as kids—pushed me over the edge. In cold blood! When I fought with Schlammer tonight, my second fall, in precisely the same spot, broke open all those locked-up memories and I saw everything with absolute clarity. It's almost—unbelievable. The curse has been lifted! I've been delivered from . . ."

". . . a living nightmare," she finished.

Her strong, clean mind powered by the tenderest empathy, she pondered how the deadly whirlpools of the river must have traumatized the young François. Only in the deepest recesses of his subconscious mind had this crushing experience been allowed to exist, rearing up periodically as a nightmare—always the same horrible nightmare—that tortured him but could never break through the self-protective bulwark his mind had built against the horrors of the past. It took another incident—the almost unbearably powerful experience of this night, Ken's struggle on the same rocky ledge—to smash through the traumatic barriers that shackled his mind.

Custer continued, glowing with the recollection. "I could see pictures from my youth, sharp as day. Everything I'd experienced reeled off like a movie, and this time it stuck in my memory—the nasty sneer on Schlammer's face, the clothes he wore, everything— all the way down to that devastating impact, when I hit those terrible, icy waters!"

He started to look through the photographs, nodding in confirmation here and there, shrugging his shoulders in other places. Yes, he did recognize "Schladam's" face in that shot. In these pictures his fateful plunge into the ravine looked just as he'd experienced it.

Suddenly, Custer looked up. "My friends, this calls for a party!" he shouted boisterously. "How 'bout we celebrate my new identity? Is there anything on board we can use to toast this rickety old warhorse?"

A female voice on the closed-circuit radio surprised him with a calm response to his challenge. "Why, of course, sir. The Swiss Air Force is prepared for any emergency."

Laughing, the lieutenant in the pilot's seat turned her head; a profusion of curly black hair stuck out from under her helmet. With a flourish, she passed a bottle of champagne to the nearest passenger, Stephanie, who immediately, and expertly, set about uncorking it. As she poured the frothing liquid into army-issue tin cups, the lieutenant's voice came on again.

"A call for you, Colonel Custer."

Custer took the field-green unit, listening to the static in the headset.

"Colonel Custer? Do you read me?"

"Loud and clear," Custer smiled.

"Colonel, this is the White House chief of staff speaking. Can you hear me?"

Custer twisted his face into a clown grin, motioning to the others to listen in on the conversation.

"Roger, sir," he said, "where's the fire now?"

Mark grinned broadly at this, while Stephanie looked down with hooded eyelids, listening intently.

"Colonel Custer, the president of the United States expects you for a briefing in the White House tomorrow. Transport is standing by for you at Geneva Airport."

Custer looked at his watch. Stephanie expectantly raised her brows and nodded encouragingly. The kids looked at each other with big eyes.

"Surely you mean today, sir," Custer said, grinning. "Here in Switzerland it's Thursday, the fifth of July."

"Yes, of course," the strong voice from across the Atlantic crushed through the white noise. "You're meeting the president on Thursday. You'll be flown to Andrews Air Force Base, where we'll pick you up. Good night, Colonel, or rather . . . good morning."

"Yes, sir, precisely, the time difference, God bless it! It may just have saved America."

"How do you mean, Custer?" the chief of staff asked.

"Well, sir, for us here, the Fourth of July is history, so to speak. I'll explain it all to you tomorrow . . . shoot, I mean, today."

Jessie chuckled. Stephanie exuberantly raised a tin cup. Custer laid the transceiver aside and swung his cup high, pouring champagne into his gaping mouth.

At Geneva-Cointrin International Airport, the chargé d'affaires of the American Embassy awaited them. There would be no Air Force transport, he apologized. However, the White House had chartered an Atlantic Airlines Boeing 737. He pointed at the great gray bird which, at this early hour, stood gleaming in solitary splendor on a feeder tarmac.

With a casually dismissive gesture, an apparently unconcerned

Custer strode toward the exit of the arrivals pavilion, leaving behind Stephanie, Tony, Mark and Jessie. Ever protective, Karma sat down in front of the group, her ears vigilantly pointed. She let out a single, admonitory bark.

Custer looked back over his shoulder and halted. Impatient, he motioned with his head for them to follow him. They stood still, gazing across to him with big eyes. Sensing their defiance and disappointment, he suddenly got the idea and started walking back toward them. He wanted to tell Stephanie that he loved her.

He saw love in her face, too, but instead of simply saying it, he stammered something about how they all belonged together now. "I mean, we'll never part again, all of us, we'll stay together, you're all coming with me to America. We're a family now. . . ."

He looked at her, his brows slightly raised, then his quizzical expression dissolved into an ocean of irresistible charm. That look!—a subliminal moan shook through Stephanie—one moment like tempered blue steel, the next, gentle as a summer meadow in the morning sun.

"Ken," she cried, flinging her arms around his neck. At last they kissed, oblivious to the world. The kids smiled, nudging and elbowing each other. Looking at the practical aspect of things, Jessie ordered the boys to pick up the hand baggage and carry it to the plane. Karma followed behind. Minutes later they had the huge craft all to themselves.

Ken tapped a number into the handset he had requested from a cabin attendant as soon as they came aboard. Stephanie watched this strange form of telephone conversation.

"So what are you up to now, pray tell," she teased him.

"Remember the story I told you about the time I lucked into some codes that gave me access to certain bank accounts? Well, that's what I'm doing now—redistributing money."

"To whom?" Her eyes were large and luminous.

"To the kids, natch. Among a lot of other things, they're entitled to a reward, don't you think? Fortunately I happen to be in a position to divert a little moolah in their direction."

With a throaty laugh that provoked a visceral response in Stephanie's groin, Ken entered more digits, listened, and tapped out another sequence.

"But Ken," she protested, "money is the last thing the kids want. You'll only embarrass them."

"You're absolutely right, madam," he grinned. "That's why I'm putting it into a family fund, something called the Urs Summer-matter Foundation, which I have just now established to ensure continuing livelihood and education for the Summermatter children."

There was a tender undertone of admiration in her voice when she asked him how much he was allocating to this worthy cause, all the while eyeing the touchboard with great curiosity—to no avail. The touchboard gave away nothing. While the plane's intercom disseminated a saccharine medley of romantic tunes, Ken gently took her head between his palms, fleetingly touched his mouth to her full lips, then whispered something into her ear.

"Oh . . . ," she whispered back, then gave him a searching look. "If there is anything special about me, something you really like, you might as well tell me. I mean right now, this minute!"

Smiling mischievously, Custer darted a probing look at her, as if he had to "check out the goods."

"Your eyes," he finally said. "they're warm, brilliant, kind, like a . . . a message embedded in crystal. It'll take me a lifetime to decipher it, too. Other than that . . . I love your mouth, most of all when it's at rest. . . ."

Before she could say anything, his lips sealed hers.

As the Boeing moved toward its designated runway for takeoff, Custer again entered the number he'd known by heart for ages. In Washington, Susan answered the phone and, noting the urgency in his voice, curtly told him that Cosmo wasn't available at the moment.

"But if you'll just hang on, sir, I'll try to find him for you."

The black limousine had left the U.S. Naval Surface Weapons Center facilities in Silver Springs, Maryland. It was now moving down New Hampshire Avenue into the heart of Washington, D.C., with the imposing, brightly-illuminated capitol standing out boldly against the nocturnal skies. Inside the car, a distinguished-looking gentleman in a custom-tailored suit of dark blue pensively ran a palm across his white hair. He was kneading his neck when the phone buzzed. He activated the tinted glass partition that separated him from the driver, then answered, his face lighting up when he recognized Custer's voice.

"The product has been delivered, as per agreement."

"Excellent work, Ken," Cosmo beamed. "Stay in touch!"

Earlier, Cosmo had been informed that the Gulfstream IV, with the carry-on nukes onboard, had taken off from Bern-Belp at 11:45 P.M. and was expected to reach the highlands region of Colombia at approximately 5:00 A.M. local time. Undercover agent Captain Jeremy Kline was under orders to supervise the transfer of the nukes to his helicopter, and thereafter fly them up to the headquarters of the Super Cartel. Sometime in the early morning hours of July 5, he would deliver his ominous cargo to Don Cali de Cali in person.

Everything was going like clockwork, Cosmo told himself. Custer was a man after his own heart, a fellow one could always rely on! Reassured, the man some thought of as smartass Jack Wisebrain allowed himself to sink back into the upholstery, to gaze out through a side window. In the distance, all along the banks of the Potomac, giant bouquets of iridescent fireworks flowers bloomed in the velvety Fourth-of-July sky.

At the Super Cartel headquarters in the megalithic ruins of the Tierra Segrada in the Colombian highlands, Don Cali de Cali happily kneaded his hands as he surveyed the stage that had been erected for the live video hookup with Washington, D.C. A video projector in the forward portion of the temple cast multi-colored splashes of light on a big screen above whose upper rim towered the hideously twisted form of a shaggy goat sculpted in black marble. And above the latter, in turn, rose the mysterious avenging deity hewn from gleaming white stone, its shiny sword raised high to dispatch the demonic goat creature with one terrible blow.

"Yes," Don Cali wailed up at the monumental angelic figure, "we will fill the gringos' hearts with terror and despair!"

Smacking his right fist into the palm of his left hand, he turned to survey the auditorium, where benches in long rows had been put up to seat the one hundred top bosses, lieutenants, and key personnel of the Super Cartel. Already, the drug lord could see the stunned expressions on their faces when the president of the United States himself appeared live right up there on the screen to negotiate with none other than Juan Antonio Gabriel Cali de Cali, the Don of Dons.

Early that morning a Boeing 737 had touched down on the airstrip along the stow-lake shore, discharging a cargo of drug bosses from Colombia, Costa Rica, Panama, California, and from as far away as New York, the Bahamas, Grand Cayman, and Florida. Busses took them to the barracks that would serve as their quarters. To pass the time while they waited to meet Don Cali in the temple, Jerry Kline divided the visitors into groups and took them on a guided tour of the base's communications center.

The men here, and some of the handful of women, were all key members of the Super Cartel. Many occupied prominent slots on the wanted rosters of the United States and other countries. Most of them had a price on their heads, the DEA having promised substantial cash rewards for information leading to their arrest and conviction. Ordered to come here by the big boss, these cadre people now stared impassively at all the state-of-the-art equipment before them: communications links via telephone, television, fax and computer networks, using optic fiber transmission, parabolic antennas, and satellites for worldwide coverage.

Not until Kline led them through the spacious munitions dump and weapons arsenal, located directly under the temple edifice, did they lighten up. Many a hand reached out, expertly fondling hand grenades and antitank rockets. Now and then someone would knock tentatively on one of the countless cases of ammunition, as if knocking on wood, exchanging a knowing grin with his partners in crime.

Above them, inside the temple, the old Don stood at center stage, supporting himself with both arms on the big, square table on which Kline had placed the two brown suitcases containing the bombs. Cali was putting himself through a dress rehearsal, stepping away from the table, mumbling sentences, gesticulating, then pausing, only to start over again. This show had to be just so! Around the table on the stage, six chairs stood waiting for the section heads, his most trusted associates, whom he called "commanders."

Regrettably, Custer would not be sitting at this table today, having missed his plane—or so the story went. A bit disturbed by this explanation, Cali decided to speak with Custer in person. As he walked over to the telephone that stood on a desk by the screen, he saw the ancient Padre hurrying through the temple nave toward the stage, his white mane flowing, one hand clutching a package which he thrust excitedly at old Cali.

"An urgent message," he exclaimed, "a videotape from Filiberto."

Instantly, Don Cali's irritation at this interruption evaporated.

"Put it in the tape deck," he ordered the anxious priest. "If I know my boy right, it's probably one of those special messages of his, you know, with lots of naked women."

But the lecherous grin froze on his face as his son's bloody, severed head came hugely into focus on the screen. Don Cali groaned as his vision took in the ghastly tableau of that brutally disfigured countenance which stared back at him from between the thighs of a dead woman, like some hideous, abortive miscarriage sprung from the cunt of hell.

The infernally obscene spectacle on the screen seemed to permeate the entire interior of the temple. Mumbling and reeling, the shocked Cali tried to steady himself against the table. His trembling arms rose heavily toward the image of the deity above the screen.

"Look, Padre, the archangel has beheaded my son, has mutilated him, choked him in some whore's cunt. Look, Padre, look!"

Both arms raised, he pointed at the deity's flashing sword, while the picture on the screen zoomed to a closeup of a big, bloody hole in the headless trunk of the thing that once had been Don Filiberto Cali de Cali. The heart that had inhabited that dark, empty cave now filled the gaping mouth of the severed head.

The priest had slumped on a chair, his eyes glazed, his mouth open, hands pressing against his stomach. Don Cali, his body wracked by vehement tremors, seemed to have shrunk to the size of a pathetic gnome. His palms slapped the deep-sunken cheeks of his ashen septuagenarian's face. He choked and shouted. He raised one fist and swore in strangled bursts of verbiage to exact the most terrible revenge. The Padre was the first to pull himself together and limp to the phone.

The gruesome video presentation ended with the words *Vengeance! An eye for an eye, a heart for a heart!* scrawled in blood across the screen, a final message that finished the drug lord off. Paying no attention to what the Padre shouted after him, he staggered toward the portals of the temple, wailing and lamenting like an old woman—straight into the arms of the medical orderly. The man steadied the drug lord, extracted a throwaway syringe with a sedative from his first aid kit, and plunged it straight into the distraught Don Cali's arm.

*   *   *

At about the same time, in a spacious apartment on Manhattan's East 69th Street, Stephanie Kramer snuggled up close to Ken Custer's naked body, allowing her gaze to travel across that broad, athletic chest, then down to the powerful, outstretched legs. Ken lay relaxed on his back, one hand exploring her right thigh which she moved slowly across his crotch, teasing him.

Sensations of sweet bliss, such as he had never experienced before, coursed through him. He felt like the hunter home from the hill: home at last from a long, long journey.

Since arriving in New York that morning, they hadn't slept a wink. While Mark, Tony and Jessie had fallen exhausted into beds in another room, the two lovers sought each other's passionate embrace, caressing and fondling to their hearts' content, with words and hands and looks and sighs. Each time Stephanie thought the wonderful male creature lying next to her would surely need a rest, Ken surprised her with a vigorous resurgence of his amorous powers, enveloping her in tender and imaginative lovemaking, transforming all her senses, breaking open in her a timeless dimension, transporting her to invisible, inaudible, intangible realms of bliss.

Stephanie reveled in the certainty of finally having found the hero of her heart. Yes, grandpa had been right in those dreams she'd had. There still were men, real and true!

Ken began to talk about someone named Cosmo. He told her that Scarlett, his adoptive mother, for many years had lived with that mysterious and powerful personage. Cosmo was the mystery man whose operations began where other U.S. secret service agencies came up against the limits of their authority.

"When the CIA put me on their hit list after the Libyan debacle, it was Cosmo who took me in," he explained. "Together, we planned the infiltration of the Colombian drug cartels—first in Panama, then in Colombia. I liked it in Panama, still do. I really lived it up during those years. I had a top job, with virtually unlimited resources for expansion. In a very short time I built up an efficient, comprehensive intelligence operation. I lived in a villa by the sea, with a luxury yacht at my disposal, and I flew my own helicopter. I got back into sports—jogging, karate, pistol and rifle practice, swimming, tennis, you name it. I felt healthy and strong, ready to move mountains. After Noriega's fall, joining the Cali organization seemed the natural thing for me to do."

Stephanie listened, fascinated. She had lost all sense of time. Police sirens and the whine of ambulances rose above the muffled hum of traffic down on Third Avenue. Lost in thought, she gazed across at the gray front of the building across the street, which tapered upward like a pyramid. But rather than ending in a slim, esthetically pleasing top, it culminated in an ugly, cube-shaped hump that housed elevator motors and air conditioning equipment.

"Cosmo gave me all possible support," Ken continued, his deep voice caressing, tickling her ear. "But my excellent cover as a trusted associate of Don Cali had one truly undesirable side effect—it landed me on the most-wanted lists for big-time drug offenders. You understand, we couldn't afford to tell anyone, not the CIA, not the FBI or any other agency, no one. If we had, sooner or later, my cover would have been blown."

He heaved a heartfelt sigh, then went on. "So, for better or for worse, I had to tussle with the fellows that came after me to take me down. Conklin, the NSA dude you outmaneuvered in Bern, well, he got too close for comfort on at least a couple of occasions. On top of everything else, at the very last moment, the CIA issued a directive to all agents instructing them to terminate me with extreme prejudice, meaning to blow my head off. But whenever I got into a real bind, Cosmo was there to help me. In return, I gave him important information about drug cartel operations. Remember all that communications equipment at Lindenegg Chalet?"

Stephanie nodded. Of course, how could she have forgotten!

"That's what we used to feed information into the U.S. intelligence network. Now, since Theo's broadcasting station was located near one of the Swiss' own short-wave stations, the NSA eventually came to believe that all this information was being fed to them by the Swiss themselves. So Washington issued a sharp protest, which for a time clouded their friendly relations with Bern."

Ken paused, smiling to himself in recollection of that little contretemps.

"Of course we kept on broadcasting. The targeted intelligence we provided probably helped save lives. It certainly helped the authorities gain much-needed ground in their struggle with the drug syndicates."

Stephanie traced Ken's lips with one finger, a tender gesture of admiration.

"And what happens now?"

"Uh . . . what? Oh! Yes, well, now we'll smash the entire organization. I know Cali's monetary transactions down to the smallest detail, including all of the secret access codes. Tomorrow, all their accounts will be frozen. Billions of dollars will be confiscated."

After a while she asked him how he had actually got to America, following his fall from the ledge those many years ago.

"Scarlett had come to Lausanne, on Lake Geneva, to write an article. I can hear her talking to me as if it happened yesterday, telling me everything . . ."

. . . she was staying at the old Grand Hotel down on the lakeshore. From the balcony of her suite, Scarlett had a panoramic view of the great lake all the way to the mountains at the western egress of the Rhone Valley. The city of Lausanne rose from the lake upward into the foothills of the mountains, its houses arranged in perfect rows, framed by hillside vineyards famous for their superb grapes.

She had arrived a fortnight before to write another article about prosperous little Switzerland. It wasn't the first time; National Geographic had commissioned a story five or six years earlier. Now she sat on a terrace down by the small harbor. Across the lake lay France, and beyond, in the distance, the gleaming silhouette of the Alps. The fair weather had attracted lots of people to the lakeside promenade: bicyclists in their club jerseys; stooped elderly ladies with canes and a determined cast to their jaws; lovers, arm in arm; old men in tight suits that held their fragile frames together; kids on skateboards. Out on the lake, white sails moved silently past Scarlett. Charmed by the tranquil scene, she decided to take a couple of days off and explore the hinterland.

"That was how she came to be sitting on a riverbank, picnicking, when my lifeless body drifted by," Custer said to Stephanie. "Scarlett was an outstanding swimmer, you know, a member of the U.S. team at the 1964 Tokyo Olympics, I believe. She simply dove into the ice-cold waters and pulled me out, saving my life. Lucky me!"

"Lucky us, darling. But how did she manage to smuggle you into the States?"

"Cosmo helped her, of course. He was stationed in Geneva, involved in some big project, as usual, and he arranged everything. In Switzerland I was listed as dead; in the United States I was resurrected. That's it in a nutshell. I was given a new identity. But if I hadn't met you . . ."

Snuggling up close to him, she asked what this mysterious Cosmo's real name was. He told her he'd have to take a rain check on that one. Still bound by a strict oath of secrecy, he couldn't divulge the identity of the "super brain" behind the Cosmo label— at least not right now.

"I'll tell you soon, darling," he smiled. "Since I'm quitting the service. After all, I'm Swiss now."

"And what a hunk of a Swiss," she breathed against his chest. "Come on, tell me more!"

There wasn't that much more to tell. Penetrating the cartel had been a long-term operation, undertaken in strictest secrecy. Apart from Cosmo and a handful of people from his innermost circle of confidantes, no one really knew anything about the mission. Probably not even the president.

"Eventually, Scarlett separated from Cosmo," Ken continued. "He was something of a ladies' man. There were stories involving women, young girls, actually, so . . .''

". . . so what about those carry-on nukes, who's got them now?" She changed the subject, being supremely uninterested in this Cosmo's amourous escapades.

"Well, my assignment ended the moment the bombs were delivered to Cosmo, which was yesterday. He tells me they'll be taken to the Government's nuclear weapons facility at Los Alamos, where they'll be dismantled and destroyed. I assume that those nukes have already arrived there."

Tenderly brushing her lips against his warm skin, she told him that she couldn't understand why that enormous flow of Cartel money through the banks hadn't attracted any attention. ". . . I mean, didn't those banks' internal auditors have any suspicions? Don't tell me that the entire internal security system designed to prevent money-laundering through Swiss banks is good for nothing!"

"Not for much, anyway," Ken chuckled. "Look, let's assume the Cartel delivers ten million in cash to the CTBP Commerce and Trade Bank of Panama in Geneva. The CTBP then transfers all that dough to its account with the Swiss Banking Union in Zurich. Okay? The Banking Union naturally credits this deposit to the CTBP. So, to all intents and purposes, one bank's money has been deposited in another bank. The real owner of these cash assets, which is the Cartel, remains anonymous. Only the CTBP in Geneva knows the true identity of the depositor, yet there isn't even an account for the Cartel on the CTBP books. It means the CTBP shields the Cartel with its good name, which is why government auditors can never find anything that's irregular."

She nudged him, amazed. "But, Ken, that's better than any numbered account! It guarantees total anonymity."

"Sure does," he smiled. "Who ever said Swiss banks weren't resourceful? Obviously, they grant this type of service only to a select handful of megabucks clients."

"Like the Cartel, right?" she insisted.

"Exactly. And naturally the CTBP in Geneva keeps a number of accounts with each major bank in Zurich, all in its own name," Custer went on. "This means that questions as to the account holder's identity and business record never arise. Like any other bank doing business with major Swiss banks, the CTBP enjoys most-favored client status."

"If that is so, then why all those self-imposed restrictions, why shut down such a smoothly functioning operation?"

"Phase down, is more like it, slow it up a little. The reason for the deescalation was that some nosy DA in Zurich smelled something and started snooping around. My man Grossenbacher, the attorney, found out that the state was actually gonna start shadowing our cash couriers."

"And what exactly does that mean?"

"Good question. At first, we ourselves didn't even know what it meant." He reached for his can of Citrus Obsession and took a couple of swigs, luxuriously smacking his lips. "Hmmm. 'Shadowing' sounds pretty harmless and old-fashioned. The fact was that the state attorney started taking an interest in the CTBP. Which we considered a sufficient incentive for lying low for a while. It wasn't until later that we learned the Swiss were using sophisticated monitoring equipment."

"Such as?"

"Directional microphones, video cameras, telephone and fax surveillance. Their primary goal was to crack the computers of the big banks, exactly as the NSA was trying to do. In other words, they started monitoring the banks' electronic communications."

Custer vividly recalled that crisis. For one thing, he'd suddenly become the target of a great deal of hostility from those who envied him. Seizing their opportunity, they accused him of gambling by putting all his eggs in one basket. They claimed that the lifeline had been cut, jeopardizing the entire operation, and held him responsible. They had wanted his head—preferably on a platter.

"Luckily, just then the Wall came down!" Ken exclaimed.

"The Berlin Wall?"

"Of course, was there any other?"

"Of course, of course," she mocked, "the Wall came tumbling down at your feet, by divine fiat, how else could it have happened!"

"By fiat or any other small Italian car, precisely," he joshed, unfazed. "As the East opened up, so did a whole range of new opportunities."

"Why, I simply can't begin to imagine what you're driving at," she cooed, giving him a pretend-nasty look.

"Well, if you lend me your ear," he whispered, nibbling softly on her left earlobe, "I'll try to enlighten you, darling. What happened was that our monetary transactions were being monitored ever more closely. The Swiss authorities worked in close cooperation with the FATF, a supranational task force put together for the purpose of stopping international money-laundering operations. The main weakness of the system I'd built up was the enormous quantities of dollars in cash which we were flying into Switzerland. Sooner or later, the CTBP in Geneva would have to explain where all those beautiful twenty- and one-hundred dollar bills came from. So I started looking for places where Uncle Sam's tens and twenties were not only not suspect but highly welcome."

"The eastern countries," Stephanie breathed.

"Right. First Budapest, then Moscow. Toward the end, we were funneling nearly eighty percent of all our cash into Hungary and Russia. The banks over there are crazy for dollars. They don't give a hoot about where the money comes from."

"Fine," she said, "but didn't this . . . this FATF care? Didn't they do something about it?"

"The FATF has absolutely no power over there. For the first time in decades huge quantities of cash are flowing into the former Soviet-dominated East—dollars, pounds, francs, D-marks, you name it. That's an enormously dynamic market. Do you think they'd allow outsiders to horn in on a multibillion-dollar business that's just starting to take off?"

"So, once the money has been nicely laundered in Budapest and Moscow banks, it goes right back to the CTBP in Geneva, am I right?"

"Bull's eye on first try," Ken grinned. "And these billions have now been confiscated in Geneva. Finally, our master plan worked. All's well that ends well. My hat's off to Cosmo, he's an absolute genius, even if . . ." he frowned.

"You're the genius," she protested softly. "You're the hero." Then, proudly, she added, "My hero."

He kissed her tenderly, got up and took a leaf-green envelope from a shelf by the corner window. He stood for a moment, looking out at 69th Street, with its rows of dignified old brownstones, most of which were protected as historical monuments. Tall trees lined both sides of the street, and trees abounded even on the wide thoroughfare of Third Avenue; the entire neighborhood exuded a tranquil, sylvan atmosphere.

"Scarlett used to read me this poem," he told her as he sat down on the edge of the bed, Stephanie putting her arms around him. "She used to tell me, 'Ken, one day you'll know what it is we're supposed to be doing on this earth.' She taught me that everything that happens has a profound, divine meaning."

He had spoken softly to her, and now he read the poem in the same tone of voice:

I circle round God
round that ancient high tower
not knowing my power
through millennia I glide
am I falcon or storm
or a great sacred song
to be sung far and wide?

For a while they lay quietly in each other's arms. Then Ken broke the silence.

"Last night, as I clung to that precipice above the abyss, I finally understood those lines. Now there's meaning in my life again."

She pulled him down on the bed, gently moved on top of him, covering him with her body, whispering in his ear, "You're my great song. You're my falcon and my storm."

In the south of Colombia, Thursday, July 5

Stephanie and Ken were still locked in that blissful, carefree embrace in Custer's apartment in New York, while, in the faraway highlands of Colombia, the key figures of the Super Cartel filed into the ancient temple. Their subdued voices echoed through the hall as they took their seats on the benches. On the stage, the bulky shapes of Cali's comandantes were silhouetted around the big table under the screen.

The others, the regional bosses, chiefs of operations, lieutenants and infamous hit men who had gathered here at Don Cali's behest, stared in dull expectancy at the flickering color patterns on the screen. Suddenly the random shapes condensed to form the sharply focused image of a grim-faced man who faced the camera in the manner of a newscaster. On a flagpole behind him the American flag drooped listlessly. The din of voices in the room instantly ceased.

At the same time, in the White House in Washington, D.C., an indignant chief of staff stared skeptically at his monitor. What he saw was a rogues' gallery of faces gathered around two open, brown suitcases in ominous display on top of a big table.

Old Don Cali had finally reached his goal, having forced a reluctant president of the United States to agree to this video conference. However, the president had sent his chief of staff to represent him on this occasion. The president himself would not respond to what amounted to an ultimatum.

Once Don Cali recovered from the shock of watching that gruesome tape of his decapitated son, his initial mindless rage had given way to a calmer assessment of the situation. His vast experience in matters of mayhem and murder reasserted itself. It seemed clear to him that the horrible death and mutilation of his son was the work of the U.S. drug agencies.

So Cali had regained his composure, and nothing, absolutely nothing, would prevent him from addressing his people on this historic occasion! On the contrary, now especially was the time for him to strike! The certainty of soon being able to avenge his son made Don Cali feel calm, infusing him with an evil elation, a malevolent ecstasy such as he had never felt before.

"Buenos dias, gringo," he grimly addressed the chief of staff through the video camera. As the camera segued to the open suitcases on the table, he came straight to the point.

"Take a good look, Mr. Bigshot Chief of Staff," Cali rasped. "The hour of reckoning is at hand, no? Each of these two suitcases contains a fifteen-kiloton nuke. Both bombs can and will be detonated in the United States. Plus we got more missiles ready to strike at targets in your country, unless your government agrees to our demands."

"What are your demands?" The chief of staff looked and sounded stressed.

Old Cali arrogantly tilted up his chin. "Not so fast," he said. "First, we want to show you we're not bluffing. The bomb in this suitcase really works. Both bombs are perfectly operational."

The camera zoomed to a closeup of the open suitcase. While a voice-over recited technical details, a hand holding a pointer indicated the clearly recognizable bomb sections under discussion.

"This portion, here, houses the ignition system, which is remote-controlled," the voice explained, as the pointer poked precariously at a small black box attached to the bulkier portion of the device in the suitcase. Standing proudly erect at the table, Don Cali triumphantly surveyed his commanders and the crowd in the temple.

In the White House, hastily-summoned experts confirmed that the drug lord was by no means bluffing. What confronted them on the screen were the unmistakable components of a small, artillery-type nuclear device.

As they watched, Don Cali stated the conditions for formal recognition of his drug empire—withdrawal of U.S. drug agency operatives, cessation of hostile interference with the Cartel's operations. These and other concessions would amount to a virtual legitimization of all Cartel business.

While Cali was engaged in this video dialogue with a distant power he hoped to hold hostage, a few miles from the temple, as the crow flies, a helicopter was hovering a couple of hundred feet above the vast coca fields.

Using a hilltop for cover, Captain Jerry Kline held his craft steady at low altitude. The elderly, distinguished-looking gentleman in the passenger seat beside him tapped out numbers on a pocket transceiver. The man held the handset to his ear, then repeated the procedure several times.

What Cosmo was doing was addressing the transceiver function in the carry-on device that stood on the table in front of Don Cali in the temple. And, indeed, Custer's code worked! The dialog had been initiated!

Now there's a fellow you can rely on, Cosmo thought, as he listened to a computerized voice instructing him to dial 9 if he wished to set off the bomb. Jack Weisborn hesitated, glancing appreciatively at the pilot who just in time had managed to inform him of Cali's forthcoming conference.

"Now, Captain Kline, those boys back there are sitting ducks," Weisborn told Kline. "The blast will wipe out the entire drug syndicate. Yes, indeed, this is the crowning glory of my life! There's no other way to rid ourselves of the scourge of narcotics that's driving America to perdition. What we're doing here is tearing out the evil by its roots!"

The pilot shot his passenger a look of surprise, then turned his attention back to the controls.

"Those bombs will have yet another, even more salient effect, Captain," Weisborn continued. "They'll rouse the world, alert people to the sinister threat of nuclear weapons proliferation, which is underestimated or repressed everywhere. This blast will open people's eyes to it. The world will ostracize such weapons and all the irresponsibles who have to do with them. Now that, Captain, is worth a sacrifice."

The helicopter yawed slightly. Kline said nothing, firmly clutching the control grip.

"You see, Captain, what we have here is what I like to call a Hamlet situation—to be or not to be, know what I mean? And it's a mental struggle. The Islamic fanatics in Iran think they're the smartest. What they were trying to do was wipe out Philadelphia and label the United States the victim. Iraq would then play the role of scapegoat, with the third party, Don Cali, as villain and smiling beneficiary. Cali was the one who financed the plot on Philadelphia. He would also be the one to profit from it. Philadelphia would have been the prelude to a devastating game of blackmail with the United States. The strategy for the entire scheme had been devised by one Colonel Fahimi in Tehran. And his game plan almost worked. Hazmoudi, the Iraqi who was on Fahimi's payroll, would serve to focus world suspicion on Baghdad. What the extremists in Tehran were trying to do was instigate a war between the United States and Iraq. In the ensuing chaos they would then topple the secular governments of the Arab nations and ascend to power throughout the Middle East."

The eyes of the man known as Cosmo to some, Weisborn to others, and as both Cosmo and Weisborn to a scant handful of people on earth, narrowed to dangerous-looking slits. "I'm afraid we'll have to cancel Colonel Fahimi's rather tall order, Captain. Mind if I call you Jerry? The fact is we're smarter than they are, Jerry. We know that fanaticism is an error of logic that must be eradicated. These bombs will not only wipe out Cali, but dispose of Fahimi and his gang of Islamic terrorists as well. So, Jerry, what does that make me? The real genius, that's what. I'm the genius here!"

The pilot glanced blankly at Weisborn.

"More important, though, we're saving thousands, no, hundreds of thousands of young American lives, Jerry. Two teensy-weensy nukes, and pow-ee, the Super Cartel is crushed dead and gone, a nice little nuclear barbecue to carbonize those arrogant hopheads. . . ."

Weisborn's laughter shrilled hysterically above the steady drone of the chopper's engine. Moving gently up and down, the rotorcraft rode the air above an ocean of undulating coca blades that stretched as far as the eye could see, endless rows of green plants melting into conjoining lines at the horizon.

Then at last, Jeremy Kline from Charleston, South Carolina, spoke up. "What about all the women and children down there?" He gestured to the plantation beneath them, where farmers' huts dotted the edges of the coca fields.

"What?" Weisborn looked puzzled. "Oh, them . . . well . . . I don't give a damn. They're all the same—all one big crazy coca-chewing family of hopheads. Now shut your eyes!!"

He rapped out the command as he punched the 9-key on the transceiver, expecting the awesome flash of the nuclear explosion some three miles away to penetrate his tightly shut eyes, burn painfully into his brain. A great, bright-red sea of flames would rise blindingly behind his eyelids. His fists pressed anxiously against the three-way buckle of his safety harness, he tensely braced himself against the stinging pain. Then—nothing.

After a few moments, Weisborn cautiously blinked his eyes open. "What the hell is going on!" Again, he pressed the 9-key. Again—nothing!

"I did hear an explosion," Kline muttered.

Weisborn gestured brusquely, dismissing the pilot's observation.

"Impossible! The blast wave would have reached us within seconds. We'd be bucking it right now, it'd be whistling around our ears, Jerry, snapping trees like matchsticks, churning up dust and dirt. That coca field down there would be whipped to shreds, and you'd have your hands full keeping this baby in the horizontal. No, Jerry, something's fishy here!"

He peered grimly ahead, then glanced down at the transceiver in his hand. "Let's get in a little closer, Captain, see if that'll improve radio contact."

The chopper put its nose down and headed for Don Cali's Tierra Sagrada. In a few moments they saw a thick column of black smoke ahead, spiraling into the dark-blue sky.

"Shit, Jerry, something's wrong! That's not a nuclear blast. Let's go in close, I have to . . . I want to . . . see what . . . Damn!" He broke off, his eyes widening in amazement, impatience, and rage.

As the helicopter, its rotors droning incessantly, churned closer to the complex of megalithic ruins, an apocalyptic picture of biblical proportions unfolded before the two men. The explosion had torn a vast, deep crater into the earth. The mighty red boulders of the temple compound were blown to pieces and blasted into the air, causing a hailstorm of rock fragments that pelted the area.

Where the temple had been, thick reddish-gray smoke shot through with whirling streaks of black rose from a sizzling fountain of flames. Kline stared speechless at the doomsday spectacle.

"Cali's people had stored at least five thousand tons of ammunition and explosives under that temple," he finally told Weisborn.

Nothing was left alive down there, not a living thing—only rubble and debris, dust, smoke, fire and . . .

Kline felt sick to his stomach as he looked down at a motley collection of bloody human limbs, shredded and charred. Squinting, focusing despite himself, taking in the contours of a woman's naked body, he screamed, "No!"

Then, with a sigh of relief, he recognized the shattered figure. Thank God, it was only the huge, broken marble image of Don Cali's abstruse deity, blown to pieces, sticking up pathetically from a smoking pile of ashes and debris.

Weisborn hissed dangerously through a gap in his teeth, impatiently pointing ahead, but Kline hadn't noticed the gesture. His attention was focused on the square between two buildings which had served as his personal landing pad. To one side of it, tossed chaotically about as if by some powerful earthquake, lay the boulders that only a scant fifteen minutes ago had formed Don Cali's residence. Across from that pile of rubble, flames blazed skyward from the ruined building that housed the radio transmitters, generators, computers, and all the rest of Cali's sophisticated communications equipment. All of it was furiously ablaze, topped by thick, yellow smoke fed by melting plastic components. From beneath the caved-in boulders and steel frames flowed a thin, glowing, gooey red substance, moving inexorably like lava toward the center of the square.

"There's a lot of fuel stored under that square in front of the temple," Kline cautioned again. "Everything is soaked through with gasoline. Let's get outta here."

The helicopter rose slowly. A 9-mm automatic gleamed dully in Weisborn's hand. "Go in closer, Captain! That's an order!"

As Kline bulled the chopper into a lateral slide, Weisborn screamed, "Those bastards fucked us, but good! Nukes my ass, those weren't nukes! There was something else in those suitcases, firecrackers maybe! You understand what happened here, Jerr? Those Swiss cuckoo birds put one over on us. Regular explosives, that's all there was in those suitcases. And Custer, jeez, that son-of-a-whorin'-bastard didn't notice, or else . . . ," Weisborn's falsetto rose to a screeching crescendo, ". . . or else he did this! I'm gonna—"

He got no further than that. An awesome wall of fire rose up in front of them. The tremendous force generated by the explosion of Cali's underground fuel dump picked the chopper up and flung it skyward like a toy. A barrage of rocks and boulder fragments pounded the craft's body, smashing the rotors. Weisborn's drawn-out wail of terror accompanied the chopper on its way down. The crippled craft plummeted to earth like a rock, impacting in a burst of flames right in the middle of the triangle that had been Captain Jeremy Kline's helipad. Both men were killed instantly.

In Washington, the men in the video conference room stared at the blank, flickering screen where only a few heartbeats earlier the self-confident drug lord had strutted and swaggered, arrogantly playing his trump cards. Then, in a sudden, poisonous, orange-yellow glare bursting from one of the suitcases, all contact was cut off.

The ghostly silence that reigned in the room was broken by the chief of staff's voice, whispering, "They've . . . blown themselves to pieces!"

Not much later, the U.S. Air Force Command reported a series of powerful explosions, their cause unknown, in the highlands along the Colombian-Peruvian border. With the consent of the government in Bogota, Panama-based reconnaissance planes were already on their way to photograph the blast site. The Colombian General Staff accused Peru of having launched an air raid on the megalithic ruins complex, and threatened with retaliatory action. Colombian fighter planes were reported to be straffing the supposedly-Peruvian border troops. Peru, in turn, accused Brazil and Colombia of collaborating on a project to develop a nuclear capacity, and of having violated international agreements by test-firing one of the weapons under development. On July 5, at 11:45 A.M., as a precautionary measure, the president of the United States issued emergency standby orders for portions of the U.S. Southern Command.

A few hours later, in the White House, Colonel Kenneth W. Custer took the envelope held out to him by Graham Rivers, the national security adviser, who mumbled awkward apologies: How the president had really looked forward to seeing Colonel Custer in person, but an urgent meeting with the Joint Chiefs of Staff prevented him. The events of the past few hours—well, the colonel probably knew more about it than Rivers himself—required the president as supreme commander of all the U.S. Forces to be on the command bridge, so to speak, as the colonel could well imagine. Rivers then told Custer that the president wondered if he might take a rain check on their meeting, to which Custer solemnly agreed, with a merry twinkle in his eye.

". . . better late than never," Rivers chatted as they made their way to the exit. Pausing in the doorway that opened on Pennsylvania Avenue, the national security adviser adjusted his glasses, touched Custer's sleeve.

"Quite a coincidence, that, Colonel," he said in a low voice. "Our plans for nuking the coca plantation areas of Colombia and Peru, planting a mushroom on top of those Cali gangsters, were all ready. Toward the end, most of us were in favor, with only the president holding out. I'm telling you we were this close, now isn't that curious? Colonel, I want you to know how much I admire the way you outwitted that fellow Cali and his gang of thugs, switching those suitcases—marvelous, simply marvelous!"

Shrugging, Custer pointed toward the street. On the sidewalk in front of the black speartip bars of the tall fence beyond the expanse of the well-tended lawn, demonstrators had gathered. Hand-lettered signs stuck up out of the crowd. "Mr. Rivers, people seem to think we did nuke 'em."

Rivers squinted across at the demonstrators, reading off some of the messages on the placards in that same low, confidential voice:

Nuke the Nukomaniacs!
Who's next in line—Mexico, Burma, Thailand, California?
Right on, Chief!
Nuke the Drug Lords to Kingdom Come!
Give us Hugs, not Drugs!

"Marvelous, simply marvelous," the national security adviser continued enthusiastically as Custer stooped to climb into the limousine waiting for him at the bottom of the broad stairs. "Just great, how it all worked out. What a coincidence! Now you stay in touch, Colonel. And don't forget that rain check . . ."

Custer nodded absently as the limousine rolled to the gate, then slowly moved through the crowd. A young woman pushed a sign against the window on Custer's side. It displayed a crudely drawn missile that was sheathed prophylactically. The massage read: *Condoms, not Atoms!*

Custer laughed, signaling both thumbs up to her. A fascinating idea: put electromagnetic condoms on all nukes, thus scrambling all the codes and rendering all missiles inoperative. When the limousine deposited him in front of the Lincoln Memorial, he noticed that he was still clutching the envelope Rivers had handed him.

Stephanie and Ken sat on the broad stairs, looking out across the still, oblong pond toward the capitol. A curved, enlongated line of ducks sailed high over the shiny dome. White pigeons were circling the Washington Monument. Earlier that morning, Stephanie had played tourist guide, first taking Tony, Jessie, and Mark on a quick tour of the Space Museum, then dropping in on the FBI, where Mark and Tony gaped in astonishment at the vast collection of confiscated firearms. Later, they drove past the Capitol and the Supreme Court, to stop for a few minutes of silent contemplation at the Vietnam Memorial Wall with its tens of thousands of names of soldiers killed in action. Finally, they bought hamburgers and settled down to wait for Ken on the steps of the Lincoln Memorial beneath the vigilant gaze of the great president.

Stephanie sat leaning against Ken's shoulder. Jessie, Mark, and Tony were spoiling Karma with bits of hamburger. Seagulls boldly snatched up the bread crumbs Tony scattered. Ken finally decided to open the envelope.

The single sheet inside bore an imprint that resembled the president's seal. Under the seal, in elegant lettering, was the name Jack Weisborn. Ken read the brief note:

Colonel Special Forces Kenneth W. Custer,
The struggle is over. We've exorcized the devil with some of his own medicine. The president has been informed that I alone am responsible for the nuclear blasts in Colombia. There are historical challenges that must be met by one man alone. This is one of them. The great nation of America demands to be led by strong individuals, be they women or men. The art of political and military leadership consists of doing what the people want but are not yet aware of wanting. What America needs is determination and vision. Take good care of Scarlett. She knows.
As ever,
Jack Weisborn

Custer slowly tore up the note. For a long time, neither he nor Stephanie said anything—not that anything needed to be said. Jack Weisborn, alias Cosmo, had made his last play—and blown it.

"You never told me that those suitcases only contained Semtex," Stephanie said, displaying, Ken thought, a rather seductive pout. "Did you have any idea that we almost died of fear when we were lugging those dreadful things out of the cavern? That wasn't fair, leaving us in the dark like that!"

"Really," Tony added, "not nice at all!"

"Please, my friends," Ken smiled disarmingly, "I myself didn't know. But, of course, I should have known. I should have known that crooks will cheat each other whenever they can. Schlammer never had any intention of delivering the nukes, and every intention of pocketing that nice piece of change he made off the deal."

"Whatever happened to the real nukes, or were there any?" Stephanie persisted.

"Oh, yes, there were. I saw one of them in the underground lab, and I assure you, that one was the genuine article. But when all hell broke loose, nobody bothered to check the suitcases. Would've been hard to tell the difference anyway, unless you were an expert."

"Ken, are you absolutely certain the real bombs exist?"

"Yes, I am. I got word this morning, when I phoned Police Chief Borli in Bern. They found them. Two carry-on type nuclear devices. State-of-the-art technology. Scary, I tell you. In external appearance, they're exactly like the ones Cali had."

"But the entire Schlammer cavern exploded," Jessie protested, "so wouldn't those bombs also . . . ?"

"You're absolutely right," Ken said, "most of the cavern blew up. But Schlammer was smart enough to hide the two suitcases with the real bombs in the trunk of his Mercedes, which was parked in the underground garage under the administration highrise. That's where they were found, hale and hearty. And not ticking."

Stephanie burst into laughter. "Imagine, Schlammer, the racketeer and weapons dealer, putting one over on Cali, the drug baron, to say nothing of your friend Cosmo. But thank heaven he did! Just think, Ken, Colombia under a mushroom cloud, all those beautiful, innocent people over there . . ."

Custer comically pounded his own chest. "Don't you know we Swiss are natural-born con artists? We're as cunning as they come. Remember your history lessons about the Battle of Morgarten? Always two steps ahead of the competition? But in the end, see, all's well that ends well."

It seemed to Stephanie she'd heard that little jingle before. The kids made funny faces, Mark projecting a V-sign with index and middle finger of his left hand. All seemed bliss and harmony until Stephanie abruptly asked if it was true that Ken had met Theo in jail. Inclining his forehead like a bull about to charge, his eyes glittering mischievously, Ken shot her a fierce look from under his brows.

"If the truth be told, I've never set foot on Sicily."

She guffawed recklessly. "All right then, where did you two scoundrels meet?"

Moving his head this way and that in a parody of rustic humility, Ken wet his upper lip with the tip of his tongue. "Shucks, ma'am," he drawled, "that's a mighty long story. It all started back in . . ."

She grabbed his head with both hands and kissed him squarely on the mouth. "Never mind, Colonel, it was in Africa, wasn't it? You and Theo had just been dumped into the cauldron by cannibals, the water was starting to heat up, when all of a sudden a tall, black native lady appears, stark naked, eyes blazing passionately, reaching out for you to just . . . uh . . . gobble you up? Isn't that how it was? Oh, Ken, I love your imagination!"

They fell laughing into each other's arms. After a while, he casually asked if she knew what the second most urgent priority in their lives might be. Smiling, she gave him a long, searching look and shook her head.

"We'll adopt the kids. Karma, too, of course," he replied.

"And the first most urgent priority?" she asked happily.

"Rent an island," Ken decided.

"An island?"

"Yes. A place where we can do anything we like without anybody disturbing us. Things like sailing, fishing, diving, sunbathing, eating and, well, whatever else you do when you're in love."

Stephanie gazed pensively out over the waters of the pond. Suddenly she pointed, "Look, Ken! See that white pigeon there, the one that's flying toward the flagpole? If it lands on it, I'll go to your island with you. And anywhere else you want to go."

The kids had heard those last, challenging words. Now all three sat spellbound, squinting up at the bird, which winged slowly past the tip of the monument. Jessie sighed. Stephanie shrugged her shoulders. She was about to tell them she'd only been joking, when the pigeon banked smoothly, gliding back toward the flagpole. After circling it a couple of times, it lightly touched down on the tip. The kids exploded into whooping and hollering.

"There, you see," Stephanie whispered at Ken's ear, "the falcon and the tower."

"A lucky omen," Ken replied in a low, soft voice. "It'll bring us good fortune."

He took her in his arms, held her close. Their foreheads touched as they gazed deeply into each other's eyes. He reached up to the back of his neck with both hands and deftly unclasped the delicately crafted gold chain. Holding it between thumbs and index fingers he lifted it slowly over his head and brought it down in front of his face until the medallion dangled, like a glittering lucky star, almost touching Stephanie's full lips.

"Take the St. Christopher," he said, his eyes a deep, brilliant blue, "it's yours." Tenderly, he slid his hands under her cascading dark-blonde hair and fastened the chain around her neck.

"Let's always strive for what is right, and it will happen," he told her, "that's what I believe. By the year 2000 there'll be no more nuclear weapons. That's what we're aiming for, anyway. I know we can do it."

"Amen," said Tony, unfolding his knife, as the others looked on, smiling knowingly. He made Ken turn up the heel of one hand, the right. Crimson dripped on white marble as they sealed their friendship in blood. It was the same ritual as a couple of days ago, up in the mountains above Nucleanne—with one important difference: this time, Abe Lincoln sat gazing down on them like a comrade-in-arms.

Epilogue

The old cavern at Nucleanne was taken over by the Swiss Government, which first decontaminated it, then poured it full of concrete.

Hazmoudi, the Iraqi, was arrested in Bern by Chief Borli's men. He confessed to having been a paid agent for Iranian principals. In Tehran, public fear of retaliatory action culminated in a series of uprisings, eventually leading to the fall of the militant Islamic regime which had never made any bones about its support of terrorist action against the United States.

The body of Adam Schlammer was found on the morning of July 5, on the riverbank not far from the SS-20 missile's nuclear warhead, which had been blasted into the ravine by the tremendous explosion.

Having tired of the brouhaha surrounding his person, Theo von Alp decided to leave Lindenegg Chalet. For a while, he had reveled in all the media exposure. Then, with the pressure from interviews and photo stories showing no signs of flagging, business began to suffer. When animal-rights proponents got hold of the story of his wild pigs and hauled him into court, the Lone Eagle had had enough. He and his fearless, red-headed Claudia simply packed up and moved to Angola.

Stephanie Kramer legally adopted Mark, Tony, and Jessie Summermatter.

Kenneth W. Custer, alias >Keycop<, né François Clissot, was recognized as the legitimate heir to the virtually defunct Schlammer Group. His identity as heir-apparent of the once-illustrious Clissot clan had been indisputably proven by the ornithologist's photographs, as well as by extensive archival documentation, including the young Clissot's dental records and medical reports on the birth defect of the missing digit on his right hand.

Ken and Stephanie changed the irreparably damaged name of Schlammer Engineering to Kramer-Clissot. Marianne Chaudet, whose dossier on Schlammer's activities had been turned over to the police as evidence in the case against the Schlammer organization, was appointed director of the revitalized enterprise.

Stephanie Kramer chose to continue her work as an investigative reporter. "Slimy, Slimier, Schlammer," her three-part article on the Schlammer affair, won that year's Pulitzer Prize for Best Foreign Reportage.

The erstwhile Ken Custer, now François Clissot, took over Old Man Arik's "Refuge for the Weary" on the shores of the beautiful lake, founding an association he named SNTO, The Safe Nuclear Technology Option. He devoted much of his dynamism and creativity to the bringing up and educating of the Summermatter children. Pronouncing the current school system beyond cure and hope, he took it upon himself to supplement the three gutsy kids' formal education by guiding them into languages, art and music. He stimulated their creative imagination, took them to movies, recommended books, and they went on long trips together.

He did, however, discourage them from further adventures, sternly voicing his conviction that they'd all had their fill of adventure for a while. Jessie, Tony, and Mark wholeheartedly agreed. At least for now.